SKUNK

A Love Story

SKUNK

A Love Story

JUSTIN COURTER

OMNIDAWN
RICHMOND, CALIFORNIA
2007

This is a work of fiction. All characters and events portrayed
in this book are either fictious or used fictiously.

Cover Design: Quemadura
Interior Design: Ken Keegan

Offset printed in the United States on archival, acid-free recycled paper
by Thomson-Shore, Inc., Dexter, Michigan

green
press
I N I T I A T I V E

Omnidawn Publishing is committed to preserving ancient
forests and natural resources. We elected to print *Skunk: A
Love Story* on 50% post consumer recycled paper, processed
chlorine free. As a result, for this printing, we have saved:

21 Trees (40' tall and 6-8" diameter)
8,859 Gallons of Wastewater
3,563 Kilowatt Hours of Electricity
977 Pounds of Solid Waste
1,918 Pounds of Greenhouse Gases

Omnidawn Publishing made this paper choice because our
printer, Thomson-Shore, Inc., is a member of Green Press
Initiative, a nonprofit program dedicated to supporting
authors, publishers, and suppliers in their efforts to reduce
their use of fiber obtained from endangered forests.

For more information, visit www.greenpressinitiative.org

Library of Congress Catalog-in-Publication Data

Courter, Justin, 1968-
   Skunk: a love story / Justin Courter.
      p. cm.
   ISBN 978-1-890650-20-9 (pbk. : acid-free paper)
   1. Skunks--Fiction. 2. Fetishism--Fiction. 3. Social isolation--Fiction.
   I. Title
   PS3603.O8866S56 2007
   813'.6--dc22

                                              2007007074

Published by
Omnidawn Publishing
Richmond, California
www.omnidawn.com (800) 792-4957

10 9 8 7 6 5 4 3 2 1

ISBN: 978-1-890650-20-9

Acknowledgements

The first three chaptes of this novel first appeared as the story "Skunk" in the anthology *ParaSpheres: Extending Beyond the Spheres of Literary and Genre Fiction — Fabulist and New Wave Fabulist Stories,* published by Omnidawn Publishing in 2006.

The author would like to thank Ken Keegan for his guidance and suggestions, which dramatically improved this novel.

For my cobbler

1

Only three years ago did I finally decide to get a skunk of my own. This was after a long, tentative courtship of the skunk scent. If I were driving on a country road and smelled skunk, I immediately pulled over and sat, sometimes for hours, with all the windows rolled down, breathing deeply and letting my thoughts drift among whatever day-dreams the scent inspired. I often packed a lunch and devoted my Sunday to one of these drives. But I longed for the pleasure of enjoying the scent of the skunk entirely at my leisure.

By the time I was thirty years old, the notion that I was complete-ly self-sufficient and could do, more or less, what I pleased, began to take shape somewhere in my mind. I had a job as a copywriter for Grund & Greene, a publisher of law books, and I had my own small house in New Essex, a relatively tranquil suburb. I was proud of my house—sad, gray shoe box that it was—with its knee-high hedge, which I kept squarely trimmed, running across the front like a fender. Having scrimped and saved, having lived in tiny, roach-ridden apart-ments for years, I was at last the owner of something more substan-tial than the old, smoke-colored Eldorado in which I got around on weekends.

As I am one who has learned to prepare for all of life's inevitabili-ties, I built a six-foot fence along the perimeter of my tiny back yard and constructed a hutch about the size of a dog house. Thereafter, several weekends were devoted to tramping around some woods out-side town until the day I came across Homer.

It was a crisp autumn afternoon. The sky was a gray sheet of legal bond resume paper upon which were scribbled the leafless branches of maples and birches, and I strode through woods carrying a large burlap sack. When I first spotted Homer, he was rooting around in a pile of dead leaves. Though I tried to approach him stealthily, my feet crunched leaves and snapped twigs. The skunk stopped what he was doing, turned to face me, and sprung suddenly to attention like a pup-pet on a string. I froze. He arched his back and seemed to grow taller. I took a slow step forward. The little beast hissed, I took a second step, and he began to thump the ground with his forepaws. He became in-creasingly agitated, gradually raising his plume of a tail until it stood straight up. Then, when I was still about six feet from him, he spun around, quicker than a gunslinger, and sprayed in my direction. He wasn't a bad shot. The yellow juice he emitted splattered my trousers, and any other predator he could have considered thwarted. Poor fellow. He couldn't possibly have known that what he was doing was tantamount to slipping an aphrodisiac to a nymphomaniac.

The scent of skunk musk is the richest of all olfactory pleasures. It is a bitter-sweet combination of lilac, tilled earth, McDougal's beer, dogwood blossoms, apple pie, fresh snow and Moschus—the miniature Himalayan musk deer. And the effect on the mind is astonishing. Skunk musk brings the innocence of childhood, the lasciviousness of adolescence and the wisdom of old age to the surface of one's consciousness all at once. I sucked Homer's perfume deep into my lungs. My vision blurred, eyes teared, the burlap sack fell from my hands and I became slightly dizzy. Homer began to mosey off through the forest. I returned to my senses and snatched the bag up from the ground. I simply had to have him. I chased him as he scurried about—under bushes, through piles of leaves—and was able to get the sack over him just as he was about to scoot down a hole at the base of a tree. He writhed around and sprayed more of his delicious scent as I tied a knot at the top of the sack and carried him out of the woods. I placed him beside me on the seat of the car and he continued to wriggle for the first quarter hour of the ride home, at which point he got tired and lay still. I opened the sack in front of the hutch I'd built in the back yard and he moseyed right into his new apartment as if he'd never lived anywhere else. It was then that I decided upon his name. "Welcome home, Homer," I said. But he ignored the hutch after the first night and dug a hole beneath it the next, so that he only used the floor of the structure I'd built as a roof for his subterranean abode.

There was very nearly what one might call a spring in my step on Monday morning when I left the house to walk to the commuter train. Spending the weekend with Homer had given my life an exciting new dimension. I actually waved at Mrs. Endicott, the annoying old widow who lived next door and who owned a high-strung Chihuahua called Tesa. Mrs. Endicott was retrieving the newspaper from her front yard and Tesa stood at her side yapping at me like a battery-operated toy. Mrs. Endicott liked to talk to me practically whenever I stepped outside, providing me with updates on her children, her grandchildren, her rheumatism and other dull topics. She also badgered me with questions. She asked me who my girlfriend was, when I intended to get married, and so forth.

"Hey, Damien," she said that morning, waving me over to her. I was embarrassed for her because she was standing there in the middle of her yard in a flower-print housecoat, with pink curlers decorating her head. I walked over to her. "What's going on in your yard, there?" she asked. Her face was wrinkled like a used paper bag, and her sagging cheeks quivered when she spoke. Tesa continued her yapping throughout our conversation.

"Nothing's 'going on,' Mrs. Endicott," I said. Of the long list of unpleasant qualities this woman exhibited, her prying nature was the most abhorrent.

"You've got a dog now don't you, a little puppy? That's good, companionship is good. I'm always saying to Noah, my nephew, you oughta get a nice dog, I says, you need a friend. Living all alone like that makes you crazy. But *you*," here Mrs. Endicott jabbed me in the chest with a bony finger and smiled, "you got a good head on your shoulders. I always said you did. Now all you need is a good woman to take care of you."

I began turning away. I detest being poked and prodded physically or psychologically. Crazy indeed. Mrs. Endicott had told me that she herself had lived alone for the past ten years. "Thank you Mrs. Endicott. I think I'll be on my way."

She grabbed my arm and held me there. "The only thing is, Damien, you gotta clean up after a dog. I can smell it over in my yard. Wait." She pulled me a little closer and sniffed deeply. This caused a most disagreeable racket—snot burbled in her nose and phlegm rattled in her throat. I doubted she'd be able to smell the smoke if she were sitting on a burning sofa. "I'm a little stuffed up," she said, "but I can even smell it on you now. It's not good. You take him on walks or train him to go in the far corner of the yard, you hear?" She smiled, peering with her cataract-clouded eyes into my bespectacled ones for a moment, then released my arm. "Run along now, you'll be late for work," she said.

As I turned and began to walk away, I noticed that Tesa had stopped yapping. Then I felt her attack from behind. Her tiny teeth slipping from around my ankle, she contented herself by yanking at my pant leg and growling fiercely, as if truly committed to removing my pants. I shook my leg vigorously and was about to give her a good swift kick with my other foot, when Mrs. Endicott called, "That's enough now Tesa." Tesa released my pants and stood barking until I'd reached the end of the street. Luckily, she'd put only a few pin holes in my pants. I always wore polyester suits, which I found practical, affordable and quite durable; I owned one blue, one gray and one brown. What did trouble me a bit was that Tesa had put a two-inch-long scratch in the leather of my sturdy brown shoes, the same type I'd worn since I was a boy, and on which I always maintained a flawless, military shine.

When I got on the commuter train people parted for me like the Red Sea before Moses. A woman with watery eyes, who appeared to have a sinus irritation, vacated a seat next to where I stood and moved to the front, holding a tissue over her nose. I happily took the seat and opened my paperback copy of Alma Chesnut Moore's *How to Clean Everything*, which is among my favorite works of nonfiction.

I got to the office at ten minutes before nine, as always, and began working immediately. Frank Farnsworth, whose cubicle was adjacent to mine, got in at nine twenty-three, huffing and puffing, and threw his briefcase against the wall of his cubicle that bordered mine. This disrupted my concentration on the wording of a brochure for what may very well have been the definitive text on real estate litigation. I had to submit a draft of this piece to John Hastings, my supervisor, later that morning. I'd already written and revised it several times, but I always double- and triple-checked things before submitting them to Hastings. Farnsworth made a great deal of noise shuffling papers about in his cubicle and muttering to himself. I heard him pick up his phone. Here we go again, I thought.

"Hey honey," he said loudly, "did you get Suzie to school on time?" He paused for a moment. "I know, I know, I think it's because she's still getting over that cold... No, look, now I can't be responsible for everything all the time, okay? I'm running my ass ragged trying to keep on top of things here, and I can't be expected to put everything on hold if I notice the kid's started to sniffle or—what?... Yeah I know about the goddamn wedding, I don't think your sister will let me forget about it for five minutes. Jesus, something stinks in here... Because I didn't have time, not because I forgot. Macy's isn't on my way, and the last time I was late you went ballistic. Man, I think I stepped in something on the way to work... No, listen, I called you just now because I wanted to straighten out something else and now... Okay, fine. Yeah. Okay. Alright, I'll talk to you then." Farnsworth dropped the receiver noisily, got up and left his cubicle. I could hear the clanging of metal and glass from all the way at the other end of the hall as Farnsworth molested the coffee maker. He came back to his cubicle and banged his mug down on his desk.

"Shit," he said, "God damn it." Then he was standing there in my cubicle. "Hey Damien, can I bother you for a second?" It had already been much longer than that, so I could see no reason he needed permission to continue the practice. Without moving my chair, I rotated my head to face him. Farnsworth's necktie was loosened, the top button of his shirt unfastened, his sleeves rolled up, and his hair disheveled. His demeanor suggested that rather than having just shown up at the office, he had already worked an entire day and was preparing to unwind.

"I just spilled coffee all over my stupid keyboard," he said. "Is that going to ruin it completely? Do you know?" Farnsworth's face began to look as if he'd taken a bite of a rancid piece of cheese. He began sneezing, and sneezed five times in my cubicle without once covering his mouth, though he did turn his face away from me. When he'd finished he said, "God, do you smell that? I think it's even stronger in here. Jeez, it's terrible."

Though my posture is always nearly perfect, I felt myself sit up straighter upon hearing these words. "To what smell do you refer?" I asked.

He stepped toward me and sniffed. He stepped back again and gave me a puzzled look. "Well, anyway, do you know what I should do about my keyboard?" he asked. "I mean, is it okay to just wipe it off with a damp rag or what?"

"I would do nothing without first consulting Mr. Daltry regarding the matter," I replied. Sean Daltry was the building's maintenance man.

Farnsworth rolled his eyes. "Yeah, I guess, I was just wondering if you might know."

"Well I don't suppose I do," I said. In fact, Alma Moore's book had been written before the advent of the personal computer. "And I don't suppose I really have all morning to sit here chatting with you about your keyboard, Mr. Farnsworth."

Farnsworth raised his hands, palms facing outward. "Whoa, take it easy, bud. Forget I was here, okay?" He backed out of my cubicle. I turned back to the screen of my computer. "What the hell's the matter with everybody today?" I heard Farnsworth say behind me to someone passing in the hall.

That night when I went home, I put a small portion of my dinner in a dish outside Homer's burrow. I did not try to get him to spray at me. In those first few weeks after Homer's arrival, I only allowed myself a bit of skunk musk on the weekends, and then only after I'd completed all my chores, which included going to the dump, doing the food shopping for the week and cleaning the house from top to bottom. I was always extremely meticulous in this exercise—going down on my hands and knees with a toothbrush to get the mildew that grew between the tiles in the corners of the shower, polishing the pipes beneath the kitchen sink, and so on. Then I took a shower, shaved, stretching the skin to get a close swipe at the stubble in the dip beneath my chin, and combed my hair, which is jet black and a bit too wavy. If I let it go for very long it gives me a wild appearance, which I find unbecoming. For this reason I visited the barber once a month, which I thoroughly enjoyed, because I find it satisfying to cut off loose ends. My appearance, I believed, was one of economy, efficiency. I am neither excessively tall nor excessively short. I carry no surplus flesh. My nose, the sense organ I prize the most, is straight and ends in a fairly sharp point. My eyes are as dark as my hair and are extremely weak. For this reason I have worn thick glasses since I can remember. When I worked at Grund & Greene, I still had the same pair of black frames that had served me since high school, though my prescription had changed many times. Despite the fact that I am quite capable of making my way in the modern world, I know what a miserably inadequate creature, despite my efforts, I truly am. My constitution is so delicate and my eyes so weak that I would not have survived if I had dwelt in an earlier era of history, say, in the Stone Age. I would have been one of the casualties of natural selection—either killed by a wild boar during a hunt because I could not see it coming, or maimed by one of the bigger, stronger boys of the tribe before I reached the age where humans begin copulating—and thus would have been unlikely to pass my defective genes on to future generations. Hence, the race would have continued to grow stronger, as indeed it should. I consider it an abomination that I have actually participated in procreation. I never intended to.

Anyway, only after all the previously described observations of hygiene and domestic maintenance were completed would I go out in the yard to chase Homer. I trapped him against the fence and gave him as much of a scare as I could, and in turn he showered me with that sublime scent of his. My head was sent spinning with the strength of his emissions the first few times—my sight blurring and sense of balance temporarily upset—but I began to develop a tolerance to him and by the fifth weekend I was doing my best to get him to spray at me two or three times in an afternoon. I found that the smell made me hungry and I often went out in the yard to eat my dinner in an appetizing cloud of skunk scent. After doing this a few weekends, I thought to myself, now wouldn't it be even more sensuous if I could actually taste the skunk musk, actually ingest it?

I was not about to butcher poor Homer and eat the little chap, heavens no. I was becoming quite attached to the furry fellow. He had a pleasant enough disposition and kept to himself, which was more than could be said for most people. So I began to look forward, not just to his scent, but to the sight of him when I came home from work at the end of the day. And besides, if I ate him, I'd immediately be back where I'd started, without my own source of skunk musk.

In a single blast, Homer usually emitted about half a fluid ounce of the sticky, oily, yellow substance known as musk. Getting even a small amount of this fluid into my food took some doing. For two or three weekends, when I got Homer out of his burrow and chased him about the yard, I held a hot plate of spaghetti or a vegetable and tofu stir-fry out in front of me, so that when he finally stopped to spray at me, he got at least a few drops of the fluid on the plate. After a time, even the most exquisite dish seemed incomplete without having been seasoned with fresh skunk musk.

One day, about a month and a half after Homer had joined me, I discovered the conspiracy at the office. I left my cubicle at eleven forty-five to get a drink of water. In my peripheral vision, I noticed Farnsworth glancing up at me from his desk as I passed his cubicle. He'd been giving me insinuating looks for some time now, and on returning to my cubicle, I went around the other way, simply to avoid his eyes. He must have assumed I'd gone to lunch, because after I sat down at my desk, before I could put my fingers to my keyboard, I heard my name.

"You really think it's Damien?" the voice said. It was John Schrempp, an annoying little fat person. Whatever he did for our department, it must have involved the consumption of vast quantities of Twinkies, Ho Hos and chocolate Ding Dongs, because I never saw the man do anything else. Once, he came into my cubicle to ask a question about one of my back ads, munching on something chocolate and cream-filled. He spoke while masticating, giving me a full view of the wet, brown mush in his mouth, then licked each of his fingers with a moist smacking sound and placed the copy on my desk with dark brown smears across it.

"I know it's Damien," Farnsworth said. "Didn't you notice how much stronger the smell is right around here?"

I felt the clenching of nervous fear in my stomach. I heard the clomp of Barbara Flemming's high heels coming down the hall.

"Hey Barbara," Farnsworth said, "have you noticed the stench around here?" I didn't think there was much possibililty that Flemming could have noticed any scent other than her own. She wore enough perfume to make her presence known from a distance of several yards.

"Yes, I have noticed it. I spoke with Sean about it. He thinks a skunk got into one of the walls and died. He's going to try to find it and get rid of it this week," she said.

"Well he can crawl around every crawl space and rip apart all the walls in the damn building, but Damien will still be sitting right out here in his cubicle," Farnsworth said. Schrempp chuckled. "I'm not kidding," Farnsworth said, emphatically. "I was in his cubicle the other day. The guy smells like a freaking skunk."

I was simultaneously enraged and mortified. I felt like I was in boarding school again. Imagine, people talking behind my back! How very sloppy and juvenile. It was that cootie business all over again. I wanted to say something out loud in my defense, but at the same time I wanted to curl up under my desk and cover my ears with my hands.

"Well, the smell is a lot stronger over here in this part of the office, I'll give you that," Schrempp said.

"You know, I wouldn't doubt that it is Damien," Flemming said. "There's something creepy about that guy. He's so skinny and dark, and he acts like some kind of robotic rodent." While they spoke, I quietly got up from my chair and went and crouched in the corner of my cubicle. From this position I could still hear what they said, but when the others left Farnsworth's cubicle, they wouldn't be able to see me. I remained there for the next twenty minutes.

Of course the inevitable occurred. Homer got used to me. After about three months he could no longer be frightened. When I saw me emerge from the house, he toddled over and rubbed himself against my leg and licked my hand. After all, I fed and housed him, what could I expect? So we became friends. I sat on the porch, rubbed his belly and read to him from the *Collected Works of E.B. White*. He seemed to like *Charlotte's Web* in particular, but also showed great appreciation for *Stuart Little*. He was a much better friend than any I'd ever had. But then, I hadn't had any to speak of since the day I was separated from my mother. I generally don't care for people. At best, they talk constantly about themselves, dig wax from their ears with their pinkie fingers and indulge in other repulsive habits. At worst, they get themselves involved in such hopeless entanglements as marriage, misuse one another, betray, rape and kill each other. I found Homer's nature much more agreeable.

But alas, though I had gained a friend, I now seldom got to enjoy such a rich emission from Homer as I had in the beginning of our relationship, and found myself lying awake at night wishing for the single strong whiff that would send me into olfactory ecstasy. I was able to frighten him enough now and then to get him to spray, but my methods for doing so became increasingly contrived. And I felt guilty sneaking up on him, or dressing up in costume to frighten him.

Then, one Sunday afternoon, I made my discovery. Homer and I were playfully wrestling about, as we had gotten in the habit of doing. I would lie on my back on the ground and let him walk over the length of my body until he got to my head, at which point I would grab him with both hands, pin him to the ground and tickle his belly. During one of these tickling sessions I squeezed him and he suddenly sprayed. It was one of the greatest blasts of his scent I could have asked for. When I'd recovered from this surprise gift, I tried to figure out what had caused it. I wondered if the squeezing had frightened him in some way, but he seemed quite calm, if slightly bewildered. I squeezed him again, but nothing happened. After a little experimenting, I found that if I placed both thumbs just beneath the rib cage and applied just the right amount of pressure, with a quick, down-and-up massaging motion, it invariably caused Homer to spray. If I pressed too hard, it didn't work—he merely stuck out his tiny tongue and made a gagging sound. Nor did it work if the pressure was too light. With a little practice, though, I found I could control the intensity and the length of the emission that was produced.

"Eureka!" I shouted, jumping to my feet. Homer looked up at me placidly. "Homer, do you know what this means?" I said. "Absolute bliss! No more chasing you around the yard with a Halloween mask and a plate of pork chops. No. I can simply pick you up whenever I want and squeeze a bit of that delightful seasoning onto my plate—a dash on my salad, a liberal squirt into the entrée and perhaps a drop in my tea afterwards. Oh, it is too good to be true!" Homer himself

looked pleased. He seemed to get some satisfaction out of being relieved of his musk, just as cows are known to enjoy being milked.

I let Homer move into the house and he soon became an indispensable part of the place. It was comforting to have his warm body
nestled beside me on the couch while I read at night. And I got accustomed to his habit of licking the water from my ankles after I stepped
out of the shower. I cut a hole in the bottom of the back door and
installed a little plastic flap so he could go in and out as he pleased.
And any time I felt like it, I picked him up and squeezed him for a little
of his scent. I soon gave up the rule I'd made for myself about only using him on weekends. The first thing I did when I got home from work
was pick Homer up from where he greeted me at the front door and
give him a little squeeze.

What my discovery of the abdominal manipulation of the musk
gland had done was give me the liberty to drink musk whenever I
chose. And this is quite different from smelling it from a few yards
away, or even from using a few drops of the fluid to season one's casserole. Taken with food, the musk's potency is significantly reduced.
Direct ingestion introduces one to a completely different aspect of
the juice.

The first time I took skunk musk straight, the effects were overwhelming. I held Homer over my head, squeezed a full shot straight
down my throat, and was aware of a burning sensation in my sinuses
for an instant before I blacked out. I awoke on the ground, with little
idea of how much time had passed. By overdosing the first few times
I drank musk, I missed out on much of the experience. Measuring
my dosage, I found I could administer myself just enough to induce
a sense of euphoria without passing out. Instead of squeezing a full
shot directly down my throat, I squeezed Homer over a glass and then
used an eyedropper to obtain a single droplet I let fall to my tongue.
This I immediately chased down with a glass of water.

Most people are unaware of the fact that the skunk gland is the
key to an entirely different realm of sensation. I would say the world of
a musk dream is the everyday world seen with better clarity, but this
is often said about the effect of such inferior chemicals as THC. When
embarking upon a musk dream, one graduates to a higher plane of
existence than the one people normally inhabit. I would go so far as
to say that a person who has not experienced a skunk musk dream
is like one who has seen only two dimensions of a three-dimensional
world. For such a person, I will make a comparison (though this is

probably akin to describing colors by comparing them to textures for a blind man) based on what I've read about the effects of other drugs. Skunk musk has the anesthetizing effects of an opiate and produces the sense of heightened awareness of a hallucinogen, without the disagreeable side effects of constipation, hallucination and paranoia. But what makes the musk dream even more complex than anything possible with botanically-derived drugs is the exhilaration. Research I later undertook revealed that this is the result of the large quantity of animal endorphins contained in skunk musk. The immediate effect of ingestion of the appropriate dosage of musk is at once subtle and dramatic. All the tedious pressures and concerns of daily life drop away like a suit of clothes so cheap that it actually dissolves in the sudden storm of chemicals, and one finds oneself instead wrapped in a robe of serenity. The musk dreamer's dream is one that emerges from his own subconscious and over which he has complete control.

But of course euphoria is always followed by depression. And as my tolerance for skunk musk increased, so did my need for the sensation that had not been a need before I knew the sensation existed. Developed over a period of time, a tolerance of a beloved substance, and a tailoring of one's lifestyle to the enjoyment of that substance, can enrich one's life. It is one of the tragedies of modern civilization that the tendency to cultivate such a lifestyle is, in ignorance, condemned as an "addiction" by society's sentinels, people who are fundamentally intolerant. They are the same petty, insecure busybodies who took my mother away and whom I shall never forgive or trust ever again.

2

My mother drank quite a lot of beer when I was growing up. She always drank McDougal's—an imported brand that comes in a green bottle and has a slightly skunky aroma. This was the first scent to greet my nostrils in the morning and the last whiff I sniffed before falling asleep at night. I awoke each morning to the clinking of beer bottles as my mother opened and shut the door of the refrigerator to get out her first McDougal's before starting my breakfast. Then I heard more clinking, of empty bottles, as she cleared the kitchen table, filled a large plastic garbage bag with the previous day's bottles and carried them outside to put in a can by the street.

After this, she came into my room and sat down on the edge of my bed. I always pretended to still be asleep because I liked the gentle way she had of waking me up. She sat next to me for a moment and sighed. The bed sagged with her weight. She pushed the hair back from my forehead with her fingertips and ran one finger down the bridge of my nose, over my lips and let it come to rest on my chin, which like hers was fairly pointy. She leaned forward so that her mouth was only a few inches from my ear.

"Damien," she whispered. "Time to rise and shine, my little soldier." I continued to feign sleep, scrunching my eyelids shut so tight she would have had trouble prying them open with her fingers. "I've got a little surprise for you," she always said. Then her body shuddered, the bed shook slightly, and she let out a long, deep belch she blew into my face and which sounded very much like the lowing of a cow. It went on for a few seconds while I gradually opened my eyes. And there it was—a new morning. My mother sat beside me in a yellow bathrobe, a shaft of sunlight sliced into the room from between the curtains and the skunky smell of my mother's first McDougal's of the day filled my nostrils. I threw my arms around her neck and she pulled the covers down and tickled me until I couldn't stand it any longer and jumped out of bed and ran into the kitchen to eat the eggs, oatmeal, French toast or whatever she had prepared for me that morning.

All day long I looked forward to seeing my mother again because I knew she got lonely while I was at school. I was an only child and my father had left shortly after I was born. When I opened the door to the rather rickety old jalopy in which my mother arrived to pick me up from school, I was greeted by the same comforting smell to which

I'd woken up. My mother drove along with a bottle of McDougal's nestled between her thighs, sometimes still dressed in her bathrobe even though it was the middle of the afternoon. She took long swigs of beer between asking me questions about my day at school. Before I went to sleep at night, she sat on the edge of my bed and sang to me—usually her own rendition of an Irish drinking song. "Whisky in the Jar" by the Clancy Brothers was my favorite. After she finished, she kissed me on the cheek, tucked me in, and I drifted off to sleep with that same comforting smell in my nostrils.

When I got a little older I was allowed to walk home from school on my own. Some days I went to a friend's house after school, but that wasn't often because I didn't have many friends, and whenever I asked one of them to come to my house they told me their parents wouldn't allow them to. This was okay with me, since I knew my mother would be waiting for me with milk and peanut butter cookies, and would always be willing to play any game I chose. Sometimes we played monopoly and sometimes we played quarters. My mother was an expert at the latter game and I usually ended up drinking a gallon or so of apple juice, which was my substitute for beer.

One day when I was about eight years old, I was walking home, singing "100 Bottles of Beer on the Wall," swinging my lunch box in one hand and dragging a stick with the other, making a long squiggling trail in the dirt and pretending I was being followed by a snake. All at once, I was acutely aware of the presence of my mother and I stopped walking. I pushed my glasses up the bridge of my nose, sniffed and looked around. I saw nothing but trees on either side of the road. Not a person or car in sight. I walked along a little further and the smell grew stronger, as if twelve of my mothers were standing right beside me. Following my nose, I walked away from the road through the tall weeds and undergrowth that led up to the woods. I didn't have to go far. A small cloud of flies dispersed from a furry mess on the ground at my feet and revealed a small skunk who had doubtless been run over and then tossed away from the road. I poked the carcass with my stick to make sure it was dead, for its eyes were still open, as was its mouth, which was filled with menacingly sharp, white teeth. The smell was much stronger than what I was accustomed to, but it was unmistakably the same odor that was like an aura about my mother.

Then I had what seemed at the time like a brilliant idea. I would bring the skunk home for her, because this, evidently, was the raw material out of which beer was made. How pleased she would be—she would be able to make her own beer! I put my lunch box on the ground, flipped the latches and took out my thermos. Lifting the skunk up by the tail and lowering it into the lunch box, I was careful to leave its head facing up, with its tail curled around in front of it the way a cat's often lies when it's sleeping. I skipped the rest of the way home, swinging my lunch box in one hand and my thermos in the other.

When I burst through the kitchen door, my mother was getting a beer from the refrigerator. She was still wearing her bathrobe, which she seemed to change out of less frequently as time went on. I was glad to have something to cheer her up. The kitchen table had sprouted a field of empty green bottles during the time I'd been at school, but nevertheless my place at the table had been cleared and there was a glass of milk and a plate of peanut butter cookies waiting for me.

My mother turned toward me and smiled. "Hey little soldier," she said. "Back from the wars?" In one fluid motion, she popped the cap off her beer, tossed the cap and bottle opener together onto the counter and took a few long gulps.

"Yup, back from the wars," I said. I pushed aside some of the beer bottles and placed my lunch box and thermos on the table. I didn't want to give away my secret yet, but I must have been grinning crazily, because my mother, smiling, cocked her head and said, "What are you so jolly about?"

"Oh, nothing," I said, sliding onto my chair and taking a bite out of a peanut butter cookie. "I just came across something you might be interested in, that's all."

Her smile evaporated. "Damien, what's that smell?" she asked.

I shrugged. "Just a part of my little surprise for you," I said.

She didn't look like she was in the mood for a surprise at that particular moment. "Damien, what in the world do you have in that lunch box?"

This wasn't going how I'd planned at all. I decided to just get it over with. "It's a present," I said, and with a mouth still full of cookie, I stood up, turned the lunch box toward my mother and sprang the lid. The nestled skunk stared up at my mother with its teeth bared. A shriek filled the air as my mother dropped her beer on the floor and backed away. The McDougal's bottle lay on its side, pouring beer that spread like a disease over the lime-green linoleum.

"Good God!" my mother exclaimed. I wasn't used to hearing my mother scream or swear, and I too jerked away from the table, overturned my chair and almost fell over backwards.

"Get that thing out of here," she said.

"But it reminded me of you!" I protested.

"Out!"

I whisked the lunch box from the table, ran out the door and burst into tears. It's remarkable how a certain scent can conjure a memory and return one to a whole different time and place, or for that matter, cause one to be rejected from a place. After unceremoniously burying the skunk in the back yard, I must have psychologically buried the entire incident, because I had completely forgotten it ever happened until some time during the first weeks of Homer's stay with me. Not that I had had much time to ponder it back then—only a few days after I'd brought home the dead skunk, I was taken out of school in the middle of the day and told my mother had suffered a breakdown. She had been put in a hospital and I was sent to live with my aunt. This aunt had never gotten along with my mother and wanted nothing to do with me. I could not have stayed with her for more than a couple of days, for I have only the vaguest memory of her and her home, though I have a very distinct memory of my first days at Rigby, the boys' boarding school where I was to spend the next eight years of my life. Naturally, at the time, I thought my mother had left me because she was still angry about the skunk I'd brought home, or that my actions had caused her supposed breakdown.

Whoever had had my mother taken away—relatives, neighbors, other parents from the school—I never did find out. Somewhere in a murky adult world, it had been decided that my mother was not a fit parent and she'd been extracted from my life. This noble humanitarian gesture left me without a family. My housemates and houseparents at Rigby were a shabby substitute, to put it mildly. To put it harshly, they were poor specimens of human life whose moral lapses led to cruel and criminal behavior.

The Rigby School occupied a huge, sprawling old farm and was founded to accommodate boys who were orphans of one kind or another. Most were from broken homes, on neither side of which was there adequate money or competence for child rearing. One can imagine what a happy bunch of young men we were. A married couple, the houseparents, resided in each dorm. My houseparents' strategy for managing a house full of unruly boys was to ignore them completely, keep the doors to their quarters shut and let us resolve our conflicts on our own.

I don't care to delve too deeply into this period of my life because it is irrelevant. Suffice it to say that my roommate was a twisted sadist about twice my size whose idea of a good time was to give me a wedgie, then hang me from the top of the open door to our room by my underwear and announce to the rest of the boys that it was piñata time. They then took turns blindfolding one another and whacking at me with a Wiffle-ball bat. My roommate also liked to remove and hide the wooden slats from my bed frame so that when I got into bed the mattress fell through the frame to the floor. After the fourth or fifth of these incidents I was unable to find the slats and eventually gave up looking for them and slept on the floor for the rest of the year.

Another activity that amused my roommonster and won him a higher standing among the other boys, was to steal my diary from under my pillow and read it aloud to a room full of our housemates. Of course, a high percentage of the information contained in the diary was about my mother. Organized readings of my diary were arranged, after which I was forced to kneel on the floor while my twelve housemates lined up behind me, each giving my buttocks two whacks with a paddle that one of the older boys had made in a woodshop class. There was nothing to be done about these adolescent male rituals and the random thrashings to which I was treated by my roommonster and others, since I was considerably shorter and thinner than the other boys and had no allies. Often I was too nervous to eat much during meal times and thus became even thinner and weaker while the others sprouted like redwoods around me. I treated my emaciation like an epidermal disease, attempting to conceal it by wearing heavy sweaters in cold weather and by avoiding any outdoor activities in warm weather that might require the shedding of my shirt.

There were further inconveniences. Occasionally, someone would steal my glasses and I was forced to go through an entire day without them, unable to take notes in class because I could not see the blackboard. Boys I didn't even know accosted me between classes to tease me about my mother—the "alky" as they referred to her—and everyone on campus, each of them a needy, orphan bastard himself, was relieved to know that his background, however disgraceful, was at least not as sordid as mine.

My introverted nature intensified until I scuttled furtively about the campus like a pair of ragged claws, speaking to no one, participating in no sports or other extracurricular activities. Instead, I read. I read book after book, hiding from the world among the pages of novels, usually adventure stories. On the weekends I found refuge in the world of television. While the other boys were at sporting events or relatives' homes, I had the television lounge to myself, where I became a rock of a man, a loner who blew into town after robbing a wagon train and who could vanquish his enemies with a sardonic glare, or if necessary, a few plugs of hot lead.

I returned from classes one afternoon toward the end of my first school year at Rigby and was informed by my houseparents that my mother was dead. She'd committed suicide, they said, and my aunt didn't see any reason I should attend the funeral. As I was one of the few boys with no relatives or friends with whom to stay (my aunt had let the school know she would be too busy during the summers to take me), I spent the summers working with the groundskeepers on the Rigby campus. I looked forward to those months of long, hazy afternoons when the campus was peaceful, as it might have been in the days when it had been a farm. I was left to work on my own most of the time, and occasionally, while I was weeding a flowerbed or raking the freshly-mown grass, I caught a whiff of skunk. I stopped whatever I was doing, stood there and sniffed. It made me tremble. There was something voluptuous, something forbidden about that smell. By that first summer at Rigby, I had already blocked out most memories of my mother and had completely forgotten the lunch-box incident. Loss has always been intolerably painful for me and I'd already found that the best way to deal with that pain is to do one's best to obliterate its source, memory.

⁓

I knew Mrs. Endicott was spying. She poked her nose over the fence to watch Homer and me while we spent quiet Sunday afternoons together on the back porch. He sat with his head resting in my lap while I drank tea and read the newspaper aloud. There was a little space between the bottom of the fence and the ground where I could see a sliver of the blue plastic milk crate on which Mrs. Endicott stood. Cataract-obscured though her vision was, I don't believe she could have maintained the illusion that Homer was a dog for very long.

Homer was living quite high on the hog at this time. He slept at the foot of my bed and only used the burrow now and then. He ate whatever I ate—from beef stroganoff to fruit crepes. It was quite a cushy life for such a savage skunk as Homer had so recently been. He was always a little groggy in the morning, but I woke him up when I got up and had him follow me through my morning rituals. This way I could ensure that he was fully awake by the time I left for work, that he would have the opportunity to get a jump on whatever animal kingdom business might be on his current to-do list. It wasn't until later that I learned that Homer's lethargy at this hour was not by any means due to a flaw in his character, but to an aspect of his nature that I hadn't taken into consideration because it hadn't yet occurred to me.

I set Homer beside me on a stool by the sink each morning so he could watch me shave. Even though he was now living in the house, he still seemed to have the blues, and one morning, glancing at his reflection in the mirror while I rinsed my razor, it seemed to me that he looked particularly melancholy. "What's the matter, Homer?" I asked, stretching the skin to get at the stubborn stubble along my jawline. "Domestication getting you down, old boy?" Then it struck me. I put the razor on the edge of the sink and turned to him. "Of course. How selfish I've been. Here I am, getting ready to go off to work, knowing very well that you'll be left alone all day. What you need is a friend." I patted him on the head and turned back to the mirror to finish shaving. I looked at his reflection out of the corner of my eye. "And I bet you'd like a lady friend, wouldn't you?" See, whereas I had always regarded contact with other animals of my own species as a disagreeable, though necessary, evil, Homer—a helpless little slave to instinct—might actually desire the company of his fellow creatures. I had my intellect to keep me company. Through reading, I could, at my leisure, listen to the thoughts of some of the best minds ever to flourish on this planet and I could always shut them up when I liked by simply closing the cover of the book. Homer, without this advantage, might have been experiencing bona fide loneliness. I rinsed my face, toweled it dry and then, as I'd started to do quite often in the mornings, picked Homer up and gave him a little squeeze, sweeping him across my chest as I did, and giving myself a dash under the arms, so I wouldn't have to go all day without a single whiff of skunk—it would already be on me.

I went out the door excited with the anticipation of the surprise gift I would soon bestow upon my little chum. My feet crunched the frozen ground and my breath turned into fog as I walked across the dead grass of my front yard. Winter is my favorite season. People stay in their homes, the leaves stay in their branches, everything is calm, quiet, cold. I looked forward to getting on the commuter train and burying myself in a book. My spirits were so high, I went as far as to call out a good morning to Mrs. Endicott, who was coming down her walk with Tesa, who I was happy to see on a leash. As soon as I'd called out, Tesa began yapping and straining toward me.

"Good morning," Mrs. Endicott said, and then, barely audibly, "ya stinker."

John Piper was hovering around my cubicle when I got to work. With a tense grunt meant to indicate the word "Morning," he asked to see me in his office. I followed him in and sat down. The window of his office looked out over the rooftops to the river, glittering coldly in the sunlight, a white fringe of ice along its banks. Piper sat down behind his desk. There was a framed studio photograph of his family, as well as individual photos of his four children. In each of the individual shots, the child was either smiling and holding a tennis racket or smiling and waving from where he sat in a sailboat with an orange life preserver around his silly neck. There was a large silver paperweight in the shape of a cocker spaniel sitting on Piper's desk. A sanguine man with jowls, a thick neck, and white hair that he kept swept straight back over his head, Piper himself looked something like a bulldog crossed with an East European politician.

"Damien," he said, "I've been meaning to have a word with you." Then he interrupted himself to walk across the room to open a window before sitting down to begin talking again. "Damien, you've been doing good work with us for several years now."

"Six," I said. If we were going to sit around discussing things we already knew, I thought, we might as well at least be precise.

"Beg your pardon?" he said.

"Six years, sir. Six years, three months and seven days."

"Yes, six years. Well, in that time I've had nothing but positive reviews from Mr. Hastings regarding your work. You've been quite efficient and everyone agrees that you're extremely professional."

I really wished he would get to the point. We both had a lot of work to do. He should have known that. Unaccustomed to idle chatter, my discomfort may have shown, because Piper cleared his throat, leaned forward and put his forearms on the desk in a getting-down-to-business pose.

"You're a young man, Damien, and I think there's a good future for you here," he said. He cleared his throat again. "And I'm sorry that what I have to talk with you about is a personal matter." Then he was at a sudden loss for words. He lifted the paperweight and turned it from one side to another, looking at it as if he expected it to bark a cue to him. I sat with my hands folded in my lap, waiting. Piper's pink face flushed red right up to the white of his hairline. "Um, where do you live, Damien?"

"New Essex," I said.

"Ah yes, that's a nice area," he said, setting the spaniel back down on the desk. "A very clean area."

"Yes, very. That's why I chose it in fact."

Piper looked stumped again for a moment. "I'll cut to the chase, Damien. A few people have been complaining that you have a certain odor about you they find offensive."

My back stiffened. I'd thought I was dealing with full-fledged adults in this company, not childish tattletales. Now, did I complain to Piper about Hastings's habit of picking his nose while he spoke to me? No. Or of how Farnsworth liked to make a slurpy, lip-smacking noise that sounded like someone walking through deep mud, and that he did it approximately once every sixty seconds for a full hour after eating lunch? No. Nor did I complain of the twenty-foot radius of perfume fumes that surrounded Barbara Flemming like a force field. Nor of how Piper himself left your hand reeking of some heinous cologne for the rest of the day after he shook it.

"It's nothing to be alarmed about," Piper went on. "As I said, everyone agrees that your work and your work habits are impeccable. It's just that maybe you should walk to the office by a different route if you think you're picking up a strange odor along the way. Or maybe try a different cologne."

Oh, yes, I thought—cologne. That's probably Piper's solution to all his problems: things aren't quite going your way, something's a little off? Just add a little more cologne to your life. I sat regarding Piper as before and said nothing, which seemed to frustrate him. The only movement I made was to push my glasses up my nose quickly with one finger, which I often found necessary to do when I began to perspire.

"So, whatever it is, I'll expect no more complaints," Piper said, suddenly blustering. He smiled aggressively, stood up and came around the desk to clap a cologne-soaked hand on my shoulder as I rose from my chair. "Well, I guess we'd better get to work," he said. "Enough small talk, eh?"

I nodded, turned and walked out of his office. I thought of poor Homer, sitting around the house by himself. Cute, cuddly little Homer and that magnificent aroma of his which was being mistaken by the uninitiated in my office for—for what? Some fetid thing left in a dumpster that I walked by on my way to work perhaps, or an inferior brand of cologne? And the notion that my colleagues were conspiring against me because of a personal preference was absolutely odious. It was dirty. It was a filthy, rotten trick. I was a man of few comforts. They'd taken away my mother, my diary and the slats for my bed. I'd been ill at ease in the company of other people all my life and had never found pleasure in any of the social games with which they amused themselves. But now they wanted to take this from me—my new hobby, my greatest pleasure and my only solace. Well, god damn them. God damn them all to hell.

And furthermore, I thought, is it not my own business what I do at home? Mine and no one else's? Is there no division between a man's professional and private lives? We all choose our own smells. Some choose one that comes in a can or bottle. Some secrete a garlicky odor, others a cheesy one. Some smell of coffee, some of vinegar, and some of onions. My odor was different, but not grounds for crucifixion. I tried harder than ever to ignore Farnsworth and of course I did not alter my habits with Homer in the least.

After work on Friday, I went to the pet store and bought the sort of traveling kennel one uses for cats. It was time to hunt for Homer's surprise. When I got home, I retrieved my camping gear from the basement and packed it, along with a copy of *The Last of the Mohicans,* in the trunk of my Eldorado. I went to the bedroom to change into the hiking boots (to which I'd applied a liberal amount of waterproofing gel) and khaki hunting pants with eight pockets I had laid out after making the bed that morning. When I've made my bed, one can throw a coin down on the taut bedspread and a watch it pop back up in the air like a miniature person on a giant trampoline. Homer meandered into the bedroom and stood there watching me change.

"Homer, old boy, I'm going on a bit of a safari," I said. "Now, I've left you with plenty of food and I'll be back by dinner time on Sunday at the very latest. Can I trust you to hold down the fort for me?" I paused to let the news sink in. Homer hadn't been alone for such a long period since we'd started living together. He continued to stare at me with his dark, intelligent eyes. "Good," I said. "You're a young skunk and I think you've got a good future ahead of you. So just keep a stiff upper snout and don't do anything I wouldn't do." With that, I stooped to give him a pat on the head and went out the door.

It was a couple hours' drive to the place I had in mind—not too far from where I'd found Homer. Dusk had dissolved into a lonesome darkness by the time I pulled into my site and set up camp. I cooked up some pork and beans over my propane stove. Towering evergreens surrounded me like the walls of a dark cathedral whose ceiling was a clear, starry sky. I've always found it simultaneously peaceful and un-nerving to sleep outdoors. On the one hand, it's a relief to be alone and away from the distracting noise of other human beings, but on the other hand, it *is* the out-of-doors, and there's no telling what can hap-pen. Getting in the tent and having walls around me, though they were only nylon, made me more comfortable. I curled up in my sleeping bag with my earmuffs on, reading from Mr. Cooper's *Mohicans* by the light of my kerosene lantern. Though I did not need the eye covers I usually required to achieve the total darkness I prefer for slumber, I found get-ting to sleep difficult because no matter which way I lay there always seemed to be one troublesome rock gouging into my spine.

I had my tea and toast before sunrise the next morning, packed a lunch in my knapsack and set out into the woods with my compass to guide me. I reveled in my preparedness as the frost on the under-growth began to melt and bead on the tops of my protected hiking boots. But one can revel in such things for only so long. My enthusi-asm had substantially diminished by the time I'd returned to camp at sundown, having tramped around in the wild for an entire day with-out any sign of a skunk.

The next morning I started out early again, divided the area into quadrants, and combed each of these one at a time, very thorough-ly, keeping an eye out for a bushy tail or any hole that might possi-bly be a burrow. I found a fallen tree on which to eat my lunch and contemplate the fruitlessness of my skunk hunt. Here it was Sunday afternoon, and still no sign of a playmate for Homer. I realized then that it would have been wiser to have brought Homer along and per-haps walked around with him on a leash, since he would be better than I at seeking out other skunks. Then I remembered something so blindingly obvious that I was shocked by my own stupidity: skunks are nocturnal animals. Finding Homer out and about in the middle of the day had been an anomaly. Furthermore, it was possible that what I'd interpreted as despondency and loneliness could have been the effects of sleep deprivation caused by my forcing Homer to get up early in the mornings. I threw down my cucumber sandwich in disgust. "Stupid!" I exclaimed aloud. I stood up and began slamming my head against a tree. "You stupid, stupid man!" I yelled. I banged my head until I became dizzy, stumbled over a root and rather unexpectedly found myself sitting on the ground, which was covered with frosted, crusty leaves. I gathered myself up, went back to my campsite and took a nap.

At dusk I set out again with a powerful flashlight and eventually came across the spot where I'd eaten lunch. I shined my flashlight at the base of the log, and low and behold, a skunk was devouring the remains of the sandwich I'd thrown down that afternoon. As one might imagine, it is more than a little awkward trying to hustle a skunk into a burlap sack with hands numb from the cold, while simultaneously holding a flashlight and being clawed and sprayed at by the irate little creature in question. When I got it back to camp and put it in the kennel, I discovered I'd been fortunate enough to bag a female. I clapped my gloved hands. Homer was going to be absolutely delighted. And as for me, the capture meant twice the amount of skunk musk available in the house. On the way home, I thought about what to name the new member of the household. I decided on Louisa, a name that has always appealed to me. It sounds like the name of a quiet person who does not often go out or nose about in other people's affairs. I looked down at Louisa, who was circling around in the kennel as I drove. It seemed only yesterday that I'd brought Homer home with me in a slightly less dignified fashion.

Homer greeted me at the door and followed me into the den where I set Louisa's box down and opened it. She stepped cautiously out and looked around. Homer was immediately circling and sniffing at her. "Homer, meet Louisa," I said. "Louisa, Homer." They paid no attention to me whatsoever. Louisa began exploring her new surroundings and for the most part ignored Homer as he sniffed at her and followed her about. I decided to leave them alone to get better acquainted. I put some Tchaikovsky on the stereo and went into the kitchen to bake a cake. This is how I always celebrate accomplishments. If it had been a slightly less significant event, I might have postponed my baking celebration until the next day, since it was so late on a Sunday night, but the compulsion to bake was overwhelming. So I made an angel's food cake, put two slices on separate plates and set them on the floor of the den for Homer and Louisa, then ate my own slice on the couch. After they had finished their cake I pronounced Homer and Louisa skunk and wife and took several photographs of them together in front of the fireplace.

The next morning on my way to work I dropped off the film at a shop around the corner from the office and picked up the photos and a frame on my lunch hour. Homer and Louisa had globs of icing and crumbs of cake on the fur around their muzzles in all the pictures. I chose what I believed to be the most flattering photo, put it in the frame and set it up on the desk beside my computer. Unlike the Piper types, who regularly construct shrines to their families and pets in the workplace, this was the first time I'd allowed any evidence of my personal life to manifest itself in my professional life. The effect was to cause me to be late for the Monday department meeting. I was gazing at my only cubicle decoration when I suddenly realized it was two-ten. The meeting began at two and ordinarily I was as punctual as I was punctilious, arriving at the conference room at twenty seconds before the hour with my project report up to date. Usually, I spoke about my progress while many of the others unabashedly threw their reports together on the spot, scribbling away while I talked, or gave up altogether and said by way of excuse that they had family obligations that had kept them from completing their reports. But now here I was, lost in sentimental contemplation of a photograph, late and unprepared for the department meeting. I dashed down the hall, into the conference room and slipped into an empty seat next to Farnsworth at the end of the long table.

"Jesus Christ!" Farnsworth swore under his breath the moment I sat down. He covered his mouth and nose with his hand and leaned away from me. Then Hastings interrupted his own typically self-aggrandizing Monday meeting opening oratory to say, "Excuse me, but could someone crack a window please?" Barbara Flemming immediately got up to do so. I glanced around the table. Conspiracy. I could see it in each and every smug, disapproving face. And not one of those faces dared let their eyes meet mine. But what did I care? I'd never needed the approval of these vermin. Let them air their disgust, I thought, for they disgusted me as well. My true friends, the bearers of the delicious and transporting musk, were waiting for me at home.

When I got home that night, Homer was not at the door to greet me. I called out his name but he did not come. A sudden panic overcame me and I flew through the house in search of him, going down on my knees to peer under the bed, overturning chairs, pulling back the sofa to look behind it, all the while calling out "Homer, Homer!" at the top of my lungs. "For goodness sake, they've eloped!" I cried. Then I remembered the burrow, which I'd practically forgotten existed since Homer had moved into the house. I ran into the backyard, threw myself on the ground and squinted down into Homer's burrow. And there were Homer and Louisa, somewhat startled by the sudden appearance of a huge moon of a face at the entrance of the burrow, but hardly roused out of what was quite obviously a postcoital stupor. I turned away, embarrassed and perhaps a bit jealous. But if they were happy together, I decided, I was happy. I might feel rejected if Homer stopped greeting me at the door, or never again wanted to spend the afternoon reading, but I wouldn't get in his way if he wanted to become a family man. Though I would prefer to be his closest friend, all I really needed from him and Louisa was their musk.

I read up on skunks to learn what to feed Homer and Louisa. In the following weeks, I made frequent trips to the pet store to purchase crickets, spiders, mice, etc. But this did not work out satisfactorily for two reasons: it cost more money than I cared to spend on skunk food and I kept buying out the entire store. So I took a few field trips with Homer and Louisa and observed as they foraged for their own food. Making a note of what they ate, I went on a few field trips of my own, during which I kidnapped several species of insect, arachnid and a few mice. I set up a bug zoo in my garage at very little expense, where the insects bred faster than Homer and Louisa (and later, the rest of the family) could eat them. I had two types of grasshopper and one type of cricket, a ground beetle and potato beetle. I also had a common meadow spider, two ant farms—one of black and one of red ants—as well as moths, caterpillars and white grubs. It was a veritable skunk's smörgasbord. I kept my car parked in the street, as the garage quickly became a metropolis of boxes and cages in which these various insects were housed. The centerpiece was a large, plywood mouse house with a floor of wood shavings and a wire-mesh ceiling.

It was a morbid kind of pleasure to watch the relish with which Homer partook of a furry brown field mouse. He grasped the tiny fellow between his forefeet and twisted his body until a faint snap could be heard. He then took the smaller rodent's head between his jaws, crushed the skull and gobbled the mouse quite quickly, though he always left a generous portion of the remains for Louisa if she had not been given a mouse of her own. I collected a small herd of mice, but they did not multiply as quickly as the insects, so I saved them as treats that were doled out on special occasions.

One Monday morning, a week after the department meeting for which I'd been late, I found Piper waiting for me again upon my arrival at the office. He was pacing in front of my cubicle, looking even more flushed and disturbed than he had the last time. He summoned me into his office, closed the door and opened the window.

"Damien," he said, "I thought we had an understanding that you were going to clear up the matter we talked about." I gave him as blank a stare as the one Homer usually gave me when he wasn't sure what I might be hinting at. "However," Piper went on, "I received several complaints after the department meeting last Monday, and it's obvious to me right now that you haven't done anything about it." He looked as if he expected me to say something for myself, to make some excuse—the way others made excuses for failing to complete their project reports, I suppose—but he hadn't yet asked me a question and I wasn't about to fall into the pattern of groveling obsequiousness displayed by so many of my colleagues. And besides, I was sick of all this tiptoeing around the issue, of being black-balled by my coworkers, of being ridiculed behind my back. I wanted someone to confront me head-on if he really had a problem with me.

And as it happened, Piper was willing, finally, to give me what I wanted. His face grew redder and redder, contrasting sharply with his white hair, while I refused to speak. "Is there anything you'd like to tell me about?" he tried. I shook my head. He began to tremble with rage and I found I could easily imagine steam shooting from his ears. "Are you unhappy working here? Would you like to say anything regarding the complaints of your coworkers?" Finally he exploded. "Goddamnit man, you smell like a skunk! You stink! Can't you understand that this is a professional environment, and we can't tolerate this sort of thing? We're not running a farm here—"

For one of the first times in my life I acted spontaneously. I don't believe in spontaneity as a rule; I prefer a carefully considered plan, a deliberate course of action. But the logic of the idea that popped into my head at that moment seemed infallible.

"Would it be alright with you," I asked calmly, "if I continued my work as an employee for this company but did my work at home? I have my own computer, a fax; there is no reason I couldn't do everything I do here from my own house." The red began to recede from Piper's fleshy face as he considered my proposal. He said he'd have to talk it over with Hastings, but by five o'clock I'd been given the OK and I cleaned out my cubicle and began working as a freelancer the very next day.

3

I was quite thrilled by the prospect of never again having to endure Farnsworth's revolting lip-smacking performances or Hastings' nose-picking. And come to think of it, every person in the entire claustrophobic office clicked his pen, tapped his foot constantly, or had some other irritating habit that seemed calculated to drive me out of my mind. Not to mention those soporific and inconsequential department meetings. Without these distractions I would be more productive than ever. But most importantly, I would be at liberty to give myself a dose of skunk musk whenever I liked. I could be absolutely whimsical.

So my life went on quite happily for several months. I worked for eight hours each day, maintaining a strict regimen. At first, I sat down to work at precisely seven AM, finished at three PM and had the rest of the afternoon and evening to do as I pleased. But after the first week, while working the same number of hours, I pushed my starting hour back to eight. Then after a while to nine, then ten. During the summer I found it preferable to work in the evening when it was cooler, and pushed my schedule back so far that I wasn't getting out of bed until rather late in the afternoon. Part of this may have been the influence of living with Homer and Louisa, who of course were late risers.

One afternoon, while I was sitting at my desk working, Louisa walked by and brushed against my foot. I decided I would allow myself a five-minute break, and I picked her up and squirted her musk into a shot glass I kept on my desk beside the wedding photograph of her and Homer. By this time I was beyond using the eyedropper, but I could only imbibe about half a shot of musk at a time. I held Louisa in my lap for a moment before putting her down on the floor. There was a significant bulge in her stomach, but I hadn't fed her a field mouse for days and I wondered how she could be putting on weight so quickly. As she sauntered out into the kitchen, I noticed something in her walk, that touch of pride one often sees in the way a female carries herself when she is carrying a second life within her. With this sudden realization, I got up from my chair, staggering slightly under the effects of the musk I'd just drunk, and followed Louisa into the kitchen where she stood contemplating her empty food dish.

"My dear lady," I said. "I thought you were gaining weight due to lethargy, but I understand now what you must be going through." I knelt down and took one of her forepaws in my hands and shook it. "I'd like to congratulate you and Homer in advance. May your children be as handsome and pungent as are the two of you." She continued to gaze down into the food dish after I released her paw. "Of course," I said. "You're eating for six. I'll go get some crickets right away. How about a mouse, hmm?"

She voraciously devoured the food I brought her and I made sure to give her double rations for the next few months. I also excused her from the duty of providing me with musk and relied entirely upon Homer.

I had always been a creature of habit and now I gradually began to recognize that such a creature is compatible with skunk living. I made a complete shift to a nocturnal schedule. My wardrobe changed. It felt strange at first to do my work without a necktie, but dispensing with it seemed to have no dilatory effect on my performance. It may even have improved it. I have always suspected that neckties, by constricting the arteries in the neck, reduce the amount of blood reaching the brain and thereby retard its functions. Neither Homer nor Louisa seemed to care whether I wore a tie or not. I began, now and then, to absentmindedly slip off my shoes while I worked. After experimenting a bit, I eventually discovered that I preferred to spend my working and my relaxing hours in slippers. My time was so economically managed that I seldom left the house, and when I did, I had an errand route mapped out that enabled me to drastically minimize the amount of time wasted in the world of human beings, whose company I found to be increasingly tiresome the less time I spent around them. Even a few minutes spent in conversation could drive me to distraction.

One evening, Louisa gave birth to a litter. It was a field-mouse day and I was bringing Homer and Louisa fried ant hors d'oeuvres. Since Louisa had been reluctant to leave the burrow for the past week or two, I'd started bringing their meals out to them. When I peered into the burrow to look for a good spot to put down their dishes, I found Louisa in the throes of labor. Homer sat in the corner looking perplexed, as I imagine I did, neither of us being very well versed in what to do in such situations. I cursed myself for not having been prepared for this. It was unlike me. Here was an event I'd seen coming for months and I hadn't read up on it to find out what equipment one might need to deliver a litter of skunks. Had it been out of spite that I'd decided to leave the responsibility to Homer, because lately I'd felt neglected by him, and envious of Louisa? I hoped not. I went into the kitchen and filled a large salad bowl with steaming hot water, brought it outside with a couple of fresh towels and placed these articles next to the entrance to the burrow. Homer and Louisa could use them at their own discretion. Then I went back into the kitchen where I'd left the hot water running. Steam rose up from the basin of the sink. I held my hand under the scalding stream, watched my hand turn red and tremble as I lost control of it. "You bastard!" I yelled aloud. "That will teach you, you lousy bastard!" After a few minutes of this, I turned the water off, dried my hand and slammed my head against the counter until I'd calmed down.

In the following weeks, Louisa was extremely busy nursing and looking after her young pups. There were five of them (not including Bradley, whom I had to bury in a corner of the yard two days after he was born). They were Elsbeth, Rupert, Gertrude, Nathaniel and Helga. Ugly little things, baby skunks: hairless, pale pink like little pigs, they spend the first vulnerable days of their lives blind, their eyes shut tight, suckling at their mother's teats. After a week or so, however, Rupert and Elsbeth began trying out their legs. They poked their tiny snouts out of the burrow, or stepped outside momentarily, wiggled their whiskers, and then jumped back into the burrow to hide behind Louisa. I brought all Louisa's meals to the burrow during this period, though Homer came to the kitchen to eat from his dish and seemed happy to spend as much time as possible in the house with me and away from Louisa and the children.

After a while, the pups' black-and-white fur began to grow in. They explored the yard and then, tentatively, following their parents, ventured into the house. I let them have the run of the place. At first they went nowhere without their mother. They followed Louisa from room to room, out into the yard and back again, in a pleasingly tidy single-file line. Sometimes, if I were going from one room to another myself, I had to stop at the doorway like a motorist at a crosswalk and wait for all six of them to parade by. Either Helga or Gertrude, who were slower than the others, brought up the rear. These two were the least practical-minded of the group. Helga was easily distracted. She would stop to sniff at something and Gertrude would walk right into her and they would both go tumbling over. Gertrude also had a habit of tripping over her own feet and falling forward on her snout, emitting a sound like the release of air when one opens a can of soda. Of course I had to wait until they were mature, but I must confess I tried my darndest to get some musk out of them long before they were capable of giving me any. I'd squeeze one of the little buggers over my cup until he let out a shrill squeak and I put him down, apologizing profusely and swearing not to try it again until I was certain he was old enough.

It was shortly after the children were born that I began to have real problems with Mrs. Endicott. She was constantly peering over the fence or muttering about "evil odors" as she collected her laundry from the clothesline in her backyard. One evening at dusk, while I was taking my morning tea in the backyard, I caught her. The orange glow of the sun was just barely visible over the rooftops to the west and Homer was rough-housing with Rupert and Nathaniel when I glanced over and saw Mrs. Endicott's eyes and the curly top of her head above the wooden fence. She ducked down as soon as I saw her. There had been several occasions already that month when I'd noticed similar espionage operations. I was growing perturbed.

"Is there something I can help you with, Mrs. Endicott?" I called, the next time she reared her graying head. Again she disappeared behind the fence. I took a few more sips of tea and then noticed her peeking again.

"Oh, what *is* it?" I said, not even caring that my voice betrayed irritation.

This time her face remained above the fence. "It's just that," she whined, "well, I've noticed you have some skunks over there."

"Is there a law against skunks?"

"I'm not sure," she said, and as she spoke, a strain of animosity strengthened until it dominated her tone. "But see, I hang my laundry out back, and all my clothes and sheets started to reek like skunk. That was bad enough, but now that those things have started breeding it's even worse. You've practically got a skunk kennel over there. The smell gets into the house unless I keep the doors and windows shut all the time, which makes it stuffy, which is bad for my sinuses. Do you realize I go through four containers of nasal spray every week—four every week!"

"Mrs. Endicott," I broke in, "I really do not care to sit here while you stand on a milk crate and preach to me about your overindulgence in pharmaceuticals."

"Well, listen. Now the smell of your damn skunks gets into my house no matter what I do. My friend Edna was over the other day. 'What've you been doing in here?' she says, 'cooking skunk cabbage all day?' 'No,' I say, 'it's that Damien, next door. He keeps skunks in his backyard.' 'That grumpy bachelor?' Edna says, 'I thought he was kind of strange, but I wouldn't've guessed he was weird too.' 'Well, he quit his job and started sleeping all day,' I says, 'and now he's got these disgusting skunks running all over the place and it stinks to high heaven.' 'Isn't there a law against things like that?' she says, 'A public nuisance law, I think.' 'I don't know,' I says, 'but he'd better do something about them soon.'"

"What do you mean, I'd 'better do something about them,'" I said. "Is that some kind of threat?"

"Well, you'd better, because I'm not going to be able to stand living like this for very long. You know, what you need is a good woman to take care of you. A young man like you," she shook her head. "Maybe then you wouldn't be so grumpy, and you'd get rid of those god-awful skunks."

I could actually feel my temperature rising. She was slandering skunks—and right in front of Homer and the children. I stood abruptly, letting the tea cup and saucer go clattering to the cement floor of the porch. "That's quite enough, Mrs. Endicott!" I roared. Her head disappeared from above the fence and I heard her back door slam shut a second later.

Homer and the boys had stopped playing and stood there in the yard, staring at me. The poor, trusting little chaps. What would Mrs. Endicott have me do, send them off to some wretched boarding school? My hands were shaking. I hadn't conversed with another person for quite some time, and renewing that experience had been unpleasant enough, but I'd thought I'd left behind petty reprobations like Mrs. Endicott's when I left Grund & Greene and started working at home. "Is there no end to it, Homer?" I said. Homer shook his head sadly.

Life was becoming busier and busier with such a large family in the house. By the time the children were about four weeks old, their fur was almost as full as their parents. They had even begun to venture into different rooms of the house on their own and get into mischief. One night I almost murdered Rupert by the unlikely method of washing him to death. He must have been playing in the hamper and fallen asleep among my dirty clothes. I noticed the sleeve of one of my shirts was wriggling with life after I'd already put the clothes in the washing machine and was sprinkling detergent over them. Then Rupert popped his curious little head through the end of the sleeve and looked around, blinking.

All the children had matured enough to spray by this time and for me their coming of age was the beginning of my connoisseurship. I had noticed that Louisa's musk was slightly more acidic than Homer's, but I hadn't thought much of it until after the rest of the family came along. Sampling each one, I learned that the flavor of each skunk's musk was as distinct as his or her personality. For example, Nathaniel's musk had an earthy aroma and a bold but simple flavor, while Elsbeth's had a comparatively faint aroma, though it was full-bodied, higher in acidity and had a more complex flavor. I developed a routine, by which I squeezed each of the skunks over a mason jar each evening, after they'd had the day to sleep and replenish their musk glands. They seemed to like this ritual and after a while they came into the kitchen after they awoke, loitered around their food bowls and patiently waited to be milked of their musk. I had a different mason jar for each of them, with the name of the skunk whose musk it contained taped on the side. This way I could choose from among the jars at my leisure, depending on what sort of mood I was in, or what sort of meal I was preparing, without having to go searching around the house for the right member of the family.

I usually ran my weekly errands late on Friday afternoon. I had timed this excursion and gotten it down to under two hours, plus or minus a few minutes depending on the line at the bank. That was only two hours per week I had to spend away from my house and my skunks; eight hours per month, ninety-six hours per year. Though fairly minimal, even this was plenty of time for me to get more than my fill of humanity. The grubbiness of the buying and selling of goods, the greedy expressions on the faces of people in the stores I was compelled to enter, the strangulating exhaust fumes and cigarette smoke, foul body odor and even fouler deodorants and perfumes, the nerve-grating glances, the harsh blasts of car horns, the offensive, careless shouts of greeting, the impudence and naked lasciviousness of strangers, the fearsome grinding of young people's skateboards, the oppressive neon lights, garish posters advertising films that promised further immersion in the swill bucket of greed and violence in which we were already drowning, and to top it off, the grime, the streets littered with fast-food containers, cigarette butts, bums begging for change—it all made me sick. And this was only a relatively small suburb. After a time, I wondered at how I'd ever summoned the nerve to go into the city each day. I often got migraines after my weekly outings and had to spend an hour or two in the den with all the shades down, languishing in a musk dream while my skunks climbed over the furniture and over me as I lay on the couch.

One day during my weekly tour through the Dantesque horror known as downtown New Essex, I noticed, or rather, found myself utterly galled by, a fantastically rude, brusque woman in the canned-foods aisle of the supermarket. I was just about to pick up a can of sardines when it was snatched out from under my fingertips by a hand that was wrinkled like a prune. At the same moment, I noticed a strong odor of fish. I was near the end of my errands and could already feel my head beginning to throb at the temples. My distaste for conversation had grown so strong that I almost let the incident pass, but my aggravation got the better of me.

"Excuse me," I said, "but I was just about to pick that up." The woman was so busy sweeping stacks of sardines off the shelf and into her cart that she hardly seemed to notice me at all. She cleaned out the entire section. Her cart was filled almost exclusively with canned sardines.

"Sorry," she said, "but I have to have these." She glanced at me, only for a moment, but long enough for me to notice that she had a walleye. Then she started on the canned clams and anchovies. Dumbfounded, I watched as she made her way down the aisle and noticed that, like me, she was wearing bedroom slippers. She also wore a long, grayish-white terry cloth bathrobe.

That night I had trouble getting to sleep. There was something familiar about the woman and something strangely exciting as well. Anyone seen at the supermarket in a bathrobe and slippers, buying a whole cartload of canned fish, must be the keeper of at least a few interesting secrets. I found myself longing to know what those secrets were. Over and over, I rewound and played the scene in which she glanced up at me in the midst of swiping sardines from the shelf. The frizzy brown ringlets that framed her face seemed to have a life of their own, made her look even more vital, more vigorous than her swift motions suggested. And the way she looked at me! That one walleye stared off in another direction, as if she were wary of an ambush, while the other eye, an aquamarine pool pierced by the black of a large pupil, bore into me—qualitative, distrustful, competitive and considerate all at once.

I woke up several times in the morning from dreams in which this strange woman's face appeared and I asked her for a can of sardines. Then the face became my mother's, and no sooner had I asked for peanut butter cookies and milk than the face turned into the sardine woman's and I was hopelessly embarrassed for having asked her for cookies and milk. "Mother!" I yelled, sitting bolt upright in bed and tearing off my eye covers. It was eleven AM—the middle of the night for me—but I was wide awake. I realized two things. One was that it had been nothing but the woman's bathrobe that had reminded me of my mother. Otherwise they were opposites. While my mother was slow and languid, this woman was quick and energetic. So I could dispense with the nagging notion that I was committing an Oedipal offense. The second thing I realized was that I had never had the time, or allowed myself the time, to grieve for my mother. So I sat there on the edge of my bed in my diamond-patterned pajamas and cried for the loss of a woman who had been gone from my life for some twenty-odd years. I cried for about an hour. My sobs echoed through the house and woke Homer, who came into the bedroom, lay down at my feet and fell asleep again.

I would not have noticed the woman the next week if I hadn't been looking for her. Normally, as I went about my errands, I scrupulously avoided contact, even eye contact, with other people. But this time I was on the lookout. I saw the sardine woman at the end of the canned foods aisle. I made sure to check out at the same register, just behind her. Again there were the towering heaps of canned sardines, tuna and clams. I followed her out of the supermarket and watched as she put her groceries in her car and took a large, empty plastic bucket out of the trunk. She carried out all these actions with the certainty of one who has a long-established and satisfying routine. I hurriedly got my groceries into the back seat of my own car and trotted after the woman to see what she might be doing with the bucket. It was so far out of character for me to be blatantly minding someone else's business that I would almost not have been surprised to discover someone else following me with a movie camera. I followed the gray bathrobe and curly hair, keeping a safe distance, down the street and into the fish market.

One of the men behind the counter seemed to recognize her. He was a heavily muscled fellow with a twisted nose, large hairy ears and a white apron smeared with fish scales and entrails. He nodded, and even though there were a couple of people in line ahead of the bathrobed woman, he reached across the counter to relieve her of the bucket and took it through the plastic curtain into the back room. I found I was absurdly jealous of this fishmonger. I can't be much uglier than that great big Neptunesque boob, I told myself, certainly I can't be much uglier. The great goon came back out a minute later with the same bucket filled to the brim with fish heads and tails. He grabbed a lid from a stack beside the counter and pressed it down on top of the bucket and snapped it into place.

"Anything else for you today?" he asked, as he put the bucket on the counter and slid it forward.

"Yes, I'll take three pounds of salmon and four of bluefish," she said. The man nodded and began to weigh out the fish she'd asked for. This really is something else, I thought. She must live on a diet of nothing but fish, fish, and shellfish. I noticed that she was considerably undercharged for her purchase. She thanked the man and I followed as she carried the bucket, which must have been quite heavy, and the bag of fresh fish, back to her car with apparently little exertion. Her car, a blue Tempest, was parked close to mine. I got in my car, started the engine and watched this strong woman swing a bucket of fish ends into the trunk of her car.

I couldn't say precisely why I continued to follow her. I made sure to keep at least a few car lengths between us, but she must have kept a constant watch on the rearview mirror with her walleye. I followed her into a residential neighborhood that was a few miles from my own and pulled over to the curb when I saw her pull into a driveway. Instead of taking her groceries out of her car, she walked directly over to mine and tapped on the driver's side window, a few inches from my ear. At a loss as to how to address a situation that had veered completely off course, I pretended to be deep in thought for a moment, stared straight ahead through the windshield and hoped the woman would go away. She rapped on the window again. She was bent over, looking in at me like someone peering into a fishbowl, wondering how the creature manages to breathe under all that water. I rolled down my window and my nostrils were immediately assailed by the odor of fish.

"What do you want?" she asked, staring at me with her left eye, while the right one gazed off into the back seat.

"Want?" I said.

"Why are you following me?" She had a rather husky voice.

"I'm not following... I was just driving..." I trailed off into silence, having failed to find an appropriate lie. "I live near here," I said finally.

"Did they send you from the university?" she said.

This one really baffled me. "Well, I did attend college, if that's what you mean. But they didn't give me much in the way of guidance there. In fact I despised them."

She was snub-nosed and now her nostrils began to flare and collapse rapidly as a rabbit's. "You have a skunk in here?" she asked.

I felt my cheeks growing warm, perspiration springing to the surface on my back and forehead. As she leaned forward to peer into my car, her scraggly mass of brown ringlets fell forward and the top of her robe parted to reveal a V of fair, freckled skin. The cool air had added a touch of blush to her cheeks in the area just below her pronounced cheekbones. Her scent made me think of the sea, fishing boats tied to a tired old wooden dock, lopsided pilings with seagulls perched on them in a snug, foggy little harbor somewhere on the Maine coast. She was so absorbingly beautiful I had to look away. Neither of us said anything for a moment.

"Do you have a skunk fetish?" she asked.

I was taken by surprise. I'd never thought of my hobby as fetishistic. It sounded perverse. "I suppose one could put it that way," I said.

"It's okay," she hastened to add. "I'm a fish fetishist."

I nodded, wondering if there were some underground society of fetishists into which I was about to be initiated.

"My name's Pearl," she said, sticking a hand, wrinkled as if it had been immersed in water for too long, through the open window. I shook it. Slightly slimy. "You wanna come in for a drink?" she asked.

4

I do not know what wild and daring spirit possessed me at that moment, but I accepted. I thought, fleetingly, of my work, and decided I could push my schedule back an hour or two without any dire consequences. A moment later I was standing on Pearl's porch, holding a bag of canned sardines in each arm. "I don't usually do this," she said as she unlocked the door. "But I've always trusted my instincts. Actually, they're all I've ever trusted." Pearl lugged the plastic bucket with the fish scraps into the house. I took a step inside and almost dropped both bags of groceries on the floor. The smell of rotting fish was absolutely overpowering. I staggered and bumped my shoulder against the open door. "Oh, shut that, please, quick," Pearl said. "The flies." I pushed the door shut, but it seemed to be too late; there were houseflies all around us. Pearl did not turn a light on and there was a gurgling sound in the room, as if water were boiling nearby. On the coffee table I noticed a large potpourri bowl filled with fish heads A buzzing swarm rose from it as we passed into the kitchen. I kept my head down and followed Pearl's bare ankles, afraid of what other frightening sights might appear in the gloom. I tried to breathe out of my mouth and only let the air in though my nose a little at a time to give that poor organ a chance to adjust, but the odor of fish was so strong it was almost palpable. It became a taste coating my tongue.

"You can just put those over there," Pearl said, pointing to a counter. Between the end of the counter and the back door of the house, there was a large plastic trash can filled with empty sardine tins, around which congregated another flitting colony of flies. How in the world, I wondered, can anyone *live* like this? Pearl noticed I was staring. "Oh, I've been meaning to take out the recycling," she said. "Never seem to get around to it. I'm so darn busy." The sink was filled with dirty dishes. On the counter were pots and pans, a large jar of fish oil, a stray sock and a blue t-shirt. An ancient, petrified slice of anchovy pizza lay in an open, grease-stained box on the kitchen table. The refrigerator door was covered with newspaper clippings, some of them curled and yellow, about scientific discoveries and Nobel Prize winners. I glanced over them as Pearl darted around the kitchen, putting groceries away, talking, and occasionally shooting a glance at me. Her skittish behavior made me think perhaps she regretted that she'd been so forward as to invite me in for a drink.

"I thought I'd have a martini," she said, as she got out a shaker and a pair of martini glasses. "I usually do on Fridays. Would you like one?" I said I would. Instead of vermouth, Pearl poured cod liver oil in with the gin.

"So what do you do?" I asked, while Pearl was fixing our drinks. She put the bottle of gin on the counter and studied me for a moment before she answered. I returned her gaze, sweating with nervousness and trying my best not to look like someone who'd just been following her around town. I pushed my glasses up the bridge of my nose. Pearl seemed to be making a decision as she watched me. Then she turned her attention back to the drinks. Without even using a shot glass to measure, she poured the cod liver oil straight into the metallic shaker and gave it a good rattling.

"I'm a marine biologist," she said, pouring the drinks. "Or I was. I mean I still am, but I only do independent research now." She handed me my martini. "Would you like to sit in the living room?" I thought of the dank living room with the festering bowl of fish heads and the strange bubbling sound, and was about to say I was happy to stay in the kitchen when Pearl strode past me without waiting to hear my reply. I followed, taking a sip of my martini as I did. Having never before had a real martini, and therefore no basis for comparison, I thought the cod liver oil was a nice touch. However, Pearl's disregard for accurate measurement and her general slovenliness seemed to me strikingly unscientific for a marine biologist. She flicked on the overhead light and as I looked around the living room for the first time I almost forgot all about the smell, the flies and the potpourri bowl. I felt that I'd not stepped into a living room, but had dived beneath the surface of the ocean and found myself in the middle of a tropical coral reef. Covering three walls, from floor almost to ceiling, were three enormous fish tanks. Large, colorful formations of brain and fan coral rose up from the sandy floors of the tanks. Multitudes of fish, of every imaginable shape and color, darted around us. There were orange-and-white clown fish, black-and-yellow angel fish, damsel fish, box fish, butterfly fish, rainbow fish, bottle-shaped trigger fish. There was even a giant clam the size of a suitcase in the corner of one of the tanks.

I stood there, flabbergasted. "Holy mackerel," I said, then bit my tongue.

Pearl smiled. "Very punny."

So there it was: I'd already revealed to her what a blithering idiot I am. For several minutes I said nothing while I wandered around the room looking at the fish. Pearl told me about the different species and the names she had given them. "There's Angela the angel fish," she said. "See her going behind that pink coral?" There was Sigmund the sturgeon, Toby the trigger fish, and so on.

After a few minutes of this name game, we sat down on opposite ends of the couch and fell into an uncomfortable silence, suddenly strangers again. I scratched my earlobe, then wished I hadn't. I sipped my martini and looked at the buzzing potpourri bowl in front of us. Pearl got up and moved the potpourri bowl to an end table on her side of the couch. I had the feeling I might have been the first house guest Pearl had had in quite some time, which I found sad, but surprising, too, since she was so attractive and outgoing. Then I realized that this was the first time I had been a house guest in probably a much longer time. I wondered if I'd overstepped some recently drafted law of etiquette by showing so much interest in Pearl's fish tanks. The last time I'd been invited into anyone's house was when I was a college student, but it had been ten years since that unhappy occasion when I'd crouched in the corner of a large, dim apartment strangely devoid of furniture, watching my classmates drink from a keg, smoke marijuana and exchange body fluids in front of me. I did not leave the party, for fear of being laughed at, but did not speak to anyone for the same reason. I was laughed at anyway. The boy who'd invited me (whom I did not know very well) and some of his friends stood in a semicircle passing around a joint, laughing and pointing at me occasionally. That might have been the very reason I'd been invited to that party—to provide entertainment for the other guests.

There had been a particular young woman in attendance at that party next to whom I often sat in my Anthropology lecture. She had glasses thick as storefront windows and an endearing overbite. She always wore a sweet smile and even spoke to me a couple times during the semester. During the course of the party I observed her from my corner and she glanced over at me once or twice between dainty sips of beer and nibbles of conversation with her friends. I could have tried talking to her, even if it had only been to exchange opinions about our Anthropology class, but I did not. I had regretted this for years and years—in fact, right up until that afternoon at Pearl's.

"So, what do *you* do?" Pearl asked. We both had to crane our necks to view each other from opposite ends of the couch.

"I work at home," I said.

"Oh," she said. She turned toward me, swung her legs up on the couch and folded them beside her.

"I write ad copy for a law-book publisher."

"Is it interesting?"

"Not really. But it allows me to spend more time on other things."

"Like skunks," she said.

"Well, yes," I said. I wondered what Homer and the gang were doing at that very moment. They weren't used to my being gone for so long.

Pearl raised her glass, threw back the last of her martini and stood up. "Want another?" she asked.

I'd only taken a few small sips of mine. "Not yet, thank you."

She walked into the kitchen to prepare one for herself. "Would you like to stay for dinner?" she called to me as she shook up her martini.

"I really shouldn't," I said. If I stayed, I would get home late for the skunks' feeding time. Besides, I was feeling fidgety for a shot of musk. I was up to three shots per day and I usually took a full one and a half after going shopping.

"You sure?" she said. Pearl stood in the doorway to the kitchen. I couldn't help noticing the width of her hips and the roundness of her thighs even through the terry cloth bathrobe. "I was going to cook a salmon," she said. "I've got more than I know what to do with."

After a smoked oyster appetizer, we moved to the kitchen, where we ate by the light of fish oil candles and Pearl told me about her childhood, which I've taken the liberty of reconstructing as follows.

Pearl Nickles grew up in a small fishing village in the South, where she played on the docks and helped her father repair his fishing nets. Her father was a rugged, fearless fisherman, notorious for going far offshore in weather that found most other captains in the bar, cringing over their mugs of lager at the mere thought of taking their boats out. One day, when gale-force winds were raging before he even cast off, what Pearl's father's competitors had predicted would happen much sooner finally happened and he was never seen again. Pearl and her mother, Virginia, moved north to live with Pearl's aunt in the city. They learned to live without the sound of waves pounding on the shore, the salt air, the constant smell of fish on their hands and clothes. Virginia adapted quickly to their new life. She found a retail position in a clothing store, which she preferred a great deal over the position at the cannery where she'd worked part time when her husband was alive. And she was good at it. She loved clothes and she loved selling clothes. Soon, Virginia was able to afford a tiny apartment for Pearl and herself. She often came home in flashy new clothes and talked about becoming a fashion designer. Pearl, on the other hand, cried herself to sleep each night for about a year after her father's death. She wasn't interested in clothes and had few friends at school, since all she really liked to talk about were such things as filleting tuna, repairing nets and hurricane season. On her way home from school, Pearl often lingered in Jake's fish market, watching the buying and selling of fish, letting the smells carry her back to the little village where she'd been born. Sometimes she ran her fingers over the cold, smooth scales of the fishes that lay packed in ice, while the grown-ups around her shouted out prices and pounds. Virginia began to complain that Pearl smelled when she got home in the evening.

"I don't want you bringing that smell in here any more, young lady," she said, one Friday evening when Pearl was twelve.

"Why? We used to live with that smell all the time," Pearl said.

"But we've risen above all that now. I have a new career and I don't want to think about all that mess at the end of the day." Then she seemed to realize she'd hurt Pearl's feelings. "Look, honey," she tried, "why don't you get cleaned up. My date's going to be here to pick me up in a few minutes and I don't want him to walk into an apartment that reeks of fish."

"Daddy always smelled like fish," Pearl said. "It doesn't reek."

"Honey, it's been three years since your father—" but she was interrupted by the doorbell. "We'll talk about this later," she told Pearl.

The man for whom Virginia opened the door was wearing clothes that were far too ridiculous to be anything but the latest fashion. "I hope I'm not late," he said.

"Oh no, you're right on time," Virginia said. "I'd like you to meet my daughter, Pearl." The man held out his hand, but Pearl kept both of hers on her hips, where she'd had them since the door opened.

"Is someone cooking fish?" the man said, sniffing the air.

"My dad is a fisherman," Pearl said. "And that's what I'm going to be."

"Honey—" Virginia started.

Pearl turned to face her. "I'm starting my job at the fish market tomorrow. I have to be up early, so don't make too much noise when you get in, because I have to get a good night's sleep." With that, she turned and marched off to her bedroom, which was really just an alcove off the living area with a curtain in front of it. She lay in bed and stared at the ceiling. She heard her mother whisper apologies, heard the words "disturbed," and "taking it awfully hard," then heard the door close and the lock click.

The next day, Pearl began working at Jake's fish market. Jake, Bill and Jared, who were all old enough to be her father, called her the little minnow. She worked at the fish market every afternoon after school and all day on the weekends. She got strong from heaving fish around the market and learned to fillet as fast as Jake and the others. In a voice that grew deeper and more confident over the years, she called out orders to co-workers and recommended different kinds of fish and preparation techniques to customers. At the end of the day, she pounded as many beers and was as loud and raucous at the bar as any of the big burly men she worked with, well before she was of legal drinking age. Pearl and Virginia saved money and by the time Pearl graduated from high school, they had enough saved to pay for most of her college tuition.

After we finished eating, I cleared the plates from the table and started hunting around the counter and under the sink for some dish soap. I was thinking that as soon as I did the dishes, I would go home, have a shot of musk and get started on a back-ad for which I still had to do a little research on insurance litigation. Pearl was resting her head against the wall, her chair tipped dangerously on its back legs. "Oh, don't bother," she said, waving her hand as if to dismiss the plates of half-eaten pieces of fish, the wine glasses, the pans on the stove, the dishes strewn across the counter and towering in stacks in the sink. "I'll take care of it later. You feel like some Kahlua and cream?"

I had never in my life felt like that, but nonetheless I accepted. To be honest, I would have preferred a shot of skunk musk. Though I had been fine while she was talking, once Pearl paused in the telling of her story, the craving came back. I could find no clean glasses for Kahlua on any of the shelves, so Pearl rinsed out our wine glasses, filled them, and we went into the living room. Pearl took a few throw pillows from the couch and we lounged on the floor, sipped our drinks and watched the fish. I lay on my side, leaning on one elbow, so I could look at the tanks and at Pearl. She lay on her back with her head propped up by a couple of the pillows. I tried not to notice how the slit in her bathrobe revealed her wonderfully thick, pale calves. She continued her story.

On the night after her last day of work before she was to go away to begin her freshman year at college, Pearl had a beer with Jake, Bill and Jared from the fish market. They went to one of their usual after-work spots, but everyone was uncharacteristically subdued. They normally sat at the bar, but since it was a special occasion, they'd taken a booth.

"We're sure gonna miss you, little minnow," Bill said. Jake didn't say anything. He kept his eyes cast down at his beer and only glanced at Pearl over the side of his mug when he raised it to drink. Pearl felt cruel. She'd never been out with these men without hearing Jake tell stories about his days working on a trawler, or Jared arguing politics with whoever gave him the opportunity. So she tried to fill the silence by telling them about the courses she'd signed up for at college. After downing several beers in less than an hour, Jake began to look mournful. Bill and Jared got up to play darts.

"Jake, take it easy," Pearl said, patting his hand. "I'll visit at Christmas, and I'll be back to work in the summers, just like we talked about." But she didn't go back. It took Pearl less than a semester at the university to figure out that marine biology was her field, and she spent the summers working at the aquarium or traveling with professors who needed help with their research projects in the West Indies and the South Pacific. Pearl expressed surprise and interest when I revealed that I'd gone to the same university and graduated only two years after she. I was excited to have something in common with her, even though I could not claim to be familiar with any of the various student organizations to which she'd belonged and could not say I'd heard of any of the rock bands that had played at a club near the university. In fact, I'd gone out of my way to avoid the street on which the club she spoke of was located. With its aggressive, pounding music, loud crowds of ruffians hanging around it and the smoke pouring forth, I'd always thought of it as a stalled railway car to hell.

Pearl would never have seen me around campus. I'd seldom left the dorm room I inhabited, except to go down to the cafeteria, which was in the dorm, or to go to class, which was only a block down the street. It was the first time I'd been able to live alone and in fact I'd chosen to go to that particularly large university in order to be anonymous, to hide in the back of tremendous lecture halls, to avoid being coerced into participating in the extracurricular activities in which thousands of others could take my place.

While she was an undergraduate, Pearl began the tropical fish collection that surrounded us in the living room. In her junior year she began an affair with Richard, one of her professors. He was married, but the affair lasted for several years.

"I haven't seen him for a long time. I moved a year ago, so he doesn't even know where I live now. None of those people do."

"You've only lived here for a year?" I said. "But, with all this?" I gestured to the fish tanks around the room.

"Yeah, these things are a bitch to move, believe me. And you haven't seen the half of it."

What eventually came about in Pearl's life was, looking at it now, a matter of course. Precociousness is always a handicap in human relations. Pearl's ideas were too new, her plans too revolutionary. Her colleagues at the university lab, all of whom were older and had more degrees, became jealous. But Pearl identified new species of fish by the dozens, spliced genes with the rapidity other people knit scarves, won awards for her work, and her projects were written about in *Biology Today* and *Genetic Future*. Ph.D. candidates several years Pearl's senior worked as her assistants. Gossip circulated about Pearl and Richard's relationship. The notion, countenanced if not encouraged by Richard, that he truly deserved the credit for Pearl's discoveries became increasingly popular. But he was sly about it and Pearl, who was in love for the first time, took a while to realize what was going on.

"But when I did, you better believe I gave him an ultimatum."

I drained the rest of my second Kalhua and cream, shifted to my other elbow and stretched out my legs. "What was that?" I asked. I was feeling sated, comfortable. Homer could wait. The food, alcohol and narrative had distracted me enough from my craving for musk that it was just a vague discomfort rising occasionally to the surface of my consciousness.

"I told him on a Saturday that if he didn't tell his wife about us and ask her for a divorce, he'd never see me again. He had until Monday."

"What happened?" I asked.

"He thought I was bluffing like a blowfish. He never believed that his little piece-of-ass apprentice would actually stand up to him. Fucker."

I must admit I found Pearl's vernacular abrasive at times. It was something I assumed she'd picked up early in life and, in spite of her education, decided never to put down, perhaps as a way of honoring the past. "So, um, you left him then?" I asked.

"Damn right I did. He walked into the lab Monday morning with this shit-eating grin on his face, and I knew, I just knew he hadn't done it. I didn't say a word to him. I washed my hands, walked right out of the lab, and I never went back. That was the last time I saw him."

"How do you know for sure he didn't tell his wife?"

Pearl glanced over at me. "I just know. Women know these things."
I let it go at that. Pearl was quiet for a moment and we watched the
fish. "You know what's really pathetic though? I still miss the son of a
bitch sometimes."

After leaving the lab, Pearl moved, worked alone, wrote her own
grant proposals to secure funding for her research, all without the
help of any assistants.

"I think I've actually been able to get more done on my own. All
those people just got in my way, really." She took a sip of Kahlua.

I watched two angel fish playfully chasing each other around
one of the tanks. I have read that watching fish can be relaxing, and
I truly was more relaxed than I had been in some time. In fact I was
so relaxed, I felt like leaning over and twirling one of Pearl's ringlets
between my fingers. I'd all but forgotten about the back-ad I had to
write. I was slightly drowsy and had trouble concentrating on the
conversation.

"And now I've made a breakthrough in genetic engineering
which—and this is why I'm afraid—is going to change the world."

"Hmm? How's that?" I said. I was not accustomed to speaking
with people for such long periods, nor to having cocktails and a large
meal in what was for me the middle of the day.

Pearl looked from the fish tank over to me with her left eye. She
smiled. She patted my shoulder, much, I imagined, the same way she
had patted Jake's hands before she went away to college. "Maybe I'll
tell you another time," she said. "You look kind of tuckered out."

I glanced at my watch. It was two o'clock in the morning. "Good
grief!" I exclaimed, and leapt to my feet. I'd missed most of my work
day now and my schedule would be completely awry for a couple of
days. And what must I have done to Pearl's schedule, assuming she was
on the diurnal one most people are on? I simply could not have been
a worse house guest. I thanked Pearl for dinner and shook her hand,
though she remained lying on the floor, looking rather amused. We exchanged telephone numbers and I rushed out the door to my car.

I don't know whether it was the night air that affected me, the rich
food and drink, or the disruption of my schedule, but I found it difficult to work and even more difficult, later, to get to sleep. I kept thinking about Pearl and wondering if and when I would see her again.
Was it common for people to meet by chance, spend several hours in
each other's company and then never get in touch again? Would she

think it strange of me to want to see her? I supposed I could always say that I felt I owed her a meal. As I lay in bed, scratching at the elastic band that held my eye covers securely in place, I wondered when I could contact Pearl again without seeming over-anxious. Confound it, I thought—I usually spent most of my waking hours hoping not to see another soul, and there I was, unable to sleep because I wanted to see a person. Nothing but a lousy person, for crying out loud. But the story of how she had made her way in the world fascinated me. It was even more vivid in my mind than if I had just read it in a book, which was normally the way I would have encountered such a story. I tossed and turned and got the sheets all tangled around my ankles.

5

For the next couple of days I was a bit disoriented and continued to have trouble concentrating on my work. I wondered if I were in love, then told myself, nonsense—far too early for such a drastic diagnosis. I'd spent only a few hours in Pearl's company and might never see her again. Or worse, I could see her in the supermarket and she might ignore me. There was also the possibility that, being the damned fool I was, I would get nervous and try to ignore her. So put it out of your mind, I said to myself—just carry on, carry on! But it was no use. I found myself at my desk, gazing out the window, oblivious to the work in front of me, twiddling a pen in my fingers, daydreaming about Pearl. I wondered what she was doing at the moment; I thought about her past more than I thought about my own. I imagined her as a little girl, with a wild head of curly brown hair, telling her mother to be quiet because she had to work the next day.

"Well Homer, I've got a dilemma," I said, early one evening. He was sitting on a stool while I prepared a mushroom and cheese omelet. We'd started this routine after I'd adopted his nocturnal schedule. It replaced our shaving ritual, affording us a similar opportunity, without the women and children about, to have a good, bracing, man-to-man talk. "I've been meaning to ask, old boy, how do you like married life?" Homer scratched himself behind the ear with his hind foot. He blinked twice. "I mean, there are the obvious advantages," I continued. "But doesn't it kind of disturb your routine? Turn your whole life upside down, in fact?" I flipped the omelet over in the pan to cook the other side. I sprinkled on some grated cheese and put a lid on the pan. "On the other hand, if one is going to spend all of one's time wondering what someone else is doing at a given moment and whether one is going to see him or her again soon, well then perhaps cohabitation would save a lot of wasted time and anxiety." I lifted the lid from the pan and folded the omelet in half with a spatula. "But then, children are bound to come along, right? It seems inevitable. And in addition to the fact that by passing on my genes I would in effect bequeath a curse to all humanity, I don't know the first thing about children, as you yourself have witnessed. Plus, well, good lord, children would mean people, more gosh-darned people in the world, and right here in this very house. No, no, no, that simply won't do." Homer yawned. "Ok, you're right, perhaps I am jumping the gun a bit." I removed the pan from the burner and turned off the heat. "We've only just met. I may never even see her again."

But later that very evening I was on the phone dialing Pearl's number. It had been two days since I'd been to her house for dinner. I hadn't been able to concentrate on my work, so I figured I might as well call her, suffer the rejection and get the whole silly business out of my head. Promising myself I'd only take a break of five to ten minutes, I bolstered my resolve with two drops of Louisa's and three of Homer's musk with the eyedropper, then dialed Pearl's number. As soon as it began to ring at the other end, I realized I hadn't planned what to say. I panicked. What was my excuse for calling? Was I going to ask her out on a date? Pretend I thought I'd left my coat in her living room? What? I began to bang the receiver against the side of my head. "Damn it!" I said "Damn it, you Goddamn bastard! Goddamnit!"

"Hello?" a voice said. I stopped slamming the receiver against my head and put it to my ear. "Hello?" she said again.

"Hi, ah, yes, I um, I was just wondering if perhaps you might be going shopping again this week?" I said.

"Damien? Is that you?" Pearl said.

"Yes, yes, Damien here."

"It sounded like you were fighting with someone," she said.

"Just a radio program, not a very good one. I've turned it off. So anyway, how are you Pearl?" This was going terribly. I considered hanging up the phone and going to the toilet to vomit.

"Okay." She paused. "You kind of bolted out of here the other night."

"Well, one must attend to one's work," I said, picking up the eyedropper and squeezing a couple more droplets of musk into my mouth.

"Right," she said.

To fill the silence that fell between us, I said, "By the way, I was curious about the breakthrough you mentioned. Possibly we could reconvene at some point and you could tell me about it."

"You busy right now?" she asked.

"Well, I have my work, of course, but I'm not doing it right this minute."

"Why don't you come over?"

"Over? There, now?"

"Yeah Damien—here, now—you goof. I'd rather show you what I'm doing than just tell you. You won't believe it otherwise."

I looked at the work piled on my desk, hastily performed a few mental calculations and decided that extending the ten-minute to a two-hour break would not set me back so very much. I'd just have to push my dinner hour back a little and put off brushing Elsbeth and Gertrude until the next day. I took a deep breath. "Fine, I'll be right over," I said.

Pearl came to the door in her bathrobe, a fly or two buzzing around her head. Though her hair was pulled back in a bun, a couple of ringlets on the right side had escaped and dangled in front of her walleye. Again I experienced a feeling of light-headedness as the fierce odor of decomposing fish wafted through the open door, though it wasn't quite as overpowering this time, and actually seemed pleasant and welcoming. The immediate erection I experienced at this time may have been the result of a pheromonal response to Pearl's scent, though I'm sure the curve of her hips, which flared out from beneath the tie of her bathrobe, had something to do with it. At any rate, this was when I first began to associate the smell of fish with sexual stimulation.

Pearl ushered me through the gurgling aquarium of a living room to a door which, on my last visit, I'd assumed led to a closet. However, it opened into a short hallway that led to a laboratory. The room was fairly narrow and there were counters along both walls and one in the middle. The immediate impression was one of a vast clutter of beakers, test tubes and flasks filled with variously colored liquids. A large fish skeleton was laid out on the right counter. On the left counter were several petri dishes that had brown, spongy lumps in them. Something was cooking in a little pot on a stand over a Bunsen burner. Whatever it was gave off quite a bit of steam and a fishy, sulfuric odor that was strong even in Pearl's house. There were posters on the walls that identified various types of fish. I was afraid to touch anything, or even move, for fear of knocking over a beaker full of goodness knows what sort of flesh-dissolving chemical. Pearl turned off the Bunsen burner.

"What's that?" I asked, pointing to the pot over the burner.

"Oh, just a hobby. I'm developing an extremely potent kind of fish oil. It's good for your skin."

"I see."

"And now you'll see something else," she said. She pointed to a large plastic basin on the counter. It contained what looked like a patch of leafy grass floating in several inches of water.

"SeaLawn," Pearl said, poking it with her finger. "It's the future. Wanna touch it?"

I politely rubbed one of the narrow blade-like leaves between my fingers. "Ah. Quite nice," I said.

"Have a taste," she said. She tore off a leaf, ripped it in half, stuck one half in her mouth and handed me the other. I'm not a great lover of leafy vegetables, unless they are properly seasoned with skunk musk, but this wasn't bad at all. It had the texture and a bit of the tartness of clover, though it was fairly sweet, too.

"Flip it over," Pearl said, still chewing. She gestured with a piece of leaf at the SeaLawn in the basin. There was a challenge in her tone.

I did not posses a desire to reach my hand into this messy floating salad, but didn't feel I could decline to do so either. It seemed somehow alive, like a starfish with the carnivorous habits of a Venus's-fly-trap. I grabbed the thing, which was about the size of a serving platter but several times thicker and, with some effort, for it was sodden and heavy, flipped it over.

"Oh dear," I said, for the underside of the SeaLawn was a terrible tangle of slimy Chinese noodles.

"What you have there is some phenomenally high-protein fish food," Pearl said. She ran her fingers through the brownish noodles. "These tentacle-like growths dangle down and fish can feed on them." She grabbed the patch of SeaLawn and flipped it over with a deft, effortless motion that was nothing like my clumsy performance of the same task. "This whole thing is basically a piece of algae," Pearl said.

"It looks slightly more evolved than your average pond scum," I noted.

"That's because I spliced kelp with the genes of several other plants to create what you see here. What I wanted to do was create a fish food that would enable fish to grow more quickly and provide a habitat like the kelp forests that are rapidly disappearing from the ocean—along with all the marine life they support—as we speak. The advantage of this," she said, pointing again at the contents of the basin, "is that unlike kelp, it doesn't need holdfasts to attach to something on the ocean floor. It can float around freely like clouds on the sea surface."

"As in the poem," I interjected.

"What poem?" Pearl cocked her head and I thought she might be annoyed by the interruption.

"Oh, no particular poem," I said. "The concept itself is poetic, I think I meant to say."

Pearl smiled. "You really are a kind of funny specimen," she said.

"Thank you," I said, bowing slightly. "Anyway, as you were saying."

"Well, I realized I could do a lot more than I set out to do with this. First of all, by developing these leaves that grow on the top and that will absorb a lot of carbon dioxide, enough surface area of this plant will slow down global warming. It could stop it within ten years. Obviously, it's going to mean introducing thousands of acres of the stuff into the oceans, but SeaLawn is the fastest-growing weed the planet's ever seen. And there's another way it can be used to help stop the greenhouse effect. If you grow SeaLawn in a controlled environment, deprived of sulfur and sunlight, just like any algae, it begins producing hydrogen, which can be used for fuel. The difference with SeaLawn is that it produces about twelve times as much hydrogen as they're getting from the same amount of algae they're using for the process now. And it can be used as food by land as well as sea creatures. As you know."

"Yes," I said. I was having trouble looking at Pearl now, so I let my eyes rest on the SeaLawn. Not only did I feel slightly stupid, but also embarrassingly selfish about my own aims in life.

"I've got multiple patents pending on the different aspects of this stuff."

"Well," I said, "let's say you had a salt water pool in your back yard with a good-sized piece of SeaLawn in it. I imagine you could live off the fish it feeds and also go out and mow it with your hydrogen-powered lawn mower and make salads with it. You could almost completely dispense with trips to the grocery store," I mused. "Now that certainly has its appeal." I wondered if Homer and the family would consent to SeaLawn salads.

"Follow me," Pearl said.

We went through the laboratory into the garage where there was a large, round swimming pool, partially in-ground, with transparent, Plexiglas sides that rose up about four feet from the floor. It occupied most of the three-car garage. The water, which looked to be about fifteen feet deep, was clean and clear, and the bottom of the tank was blue. About three quarters of the surface of the pool was covered by a small field of SeaLawn that was much thicker and lusher than the one Pearl had shown me in the laboratory.

Even more surprising than the large SeaLawn were the enormous gray fish circling around in the tank. Pearl said they were codfish that had been fattening very quickly on a SeaLawn diet. They were anywhere from three to six feet long. The big ones must have weighed upwards of 200 pounds and had eyes like tennis balls with which they uninterestedly looked us over as they browsed slowly around the tank, their huge mouths agape. Pearl claimed that this species of cod grew so quickly on SeaLawn that you could see the difference from day to day. She called them Morecods—a fish that would be so plentiful that, combined with the spread of SeaLawn, it would help solve the world's hunger crisis.

"That's Serge," Pearl said, pointing at one of the larger ones. "He's a real character once you get to know him."

"Um, Pearl, isn't all this a bit frightening?" I asked.

"In itself, no. But if it's stolen from me and gets into the wrong hands, yes. See, that's why I was so cagey the other day. When I realized you were following me around town, I thought you were from the university." Her face lit up suddenly. "But I could tell by how you acted that you weren't. You were so cute—sitting there in your car, in your pressed shirt and your pleated pants, pretending not to see me." She chuckled. "And then when you got out of the car wearing those bedroom slippers, I knew you were alright. But anyway, Richard knew about some of the things I was onto and I can't be sure who he's told now. It sounds paranoid, but there are jealous, devious people out there—I've worked with some of them. And it's not unheard of for scientists to be abducted by government agencies." She gazed across the SeaLawn and shook her head. "Sometimes they say it's for their own protection. I don't know."

I scratched my ear and gazed at the fish swimming around in the tank. "Pearl, what you have shown me today is, without a doubt, the most extraordinary thing I've ever witnessed in my entire life." I turned and looked at her. She smiled proudly. More hair had come out of the bun on the back of her head and several long ringlets fell about her shoulders and in front of her face. Her nostrils flared.

"How about a swim?" she said.

"A swim? Where? You can't mean in there, with them," I said, pointing to the tank where the Morecods circled like submarines. It might have been humid in the garage, or I might have begun sweating for no reason, but I found it necessary to push my glasses up the bridge of my nose several times in the next couple minutes.

"Of course I mean 'in there.' Don't worry about them." Pearl climbed onto a platform that rose several feet above the rim of the tank. "A more docile fish has never been bred, believe me. They're like sheep." She stood looking down at me.

"Oh, it's not that," I said. "I'm not afraid. It's not that at all."

Pearl loosened her belt and let the bathrobe fall down around her feet. Though a thick, terry cloth bathrobe is one of the least revealing garments a person can wear, as I mentioned, I'd noticed a certain shapeliness about Pearl. But nothing had prepared me for the shocking beauty of her body, scantily clad in a black bikini. I wanted immediately to run from the room, out the door, get into my car and drive home as fast as possible without exceeding the speed limit. Pearl had the most succulent, thick, white thighs, which looked especially pale next to the black bikini, and which were sprinkled with a handful of cellulite dimples and painted with a web of thin blue veins. She had what are often referred to derogatorily as saddle bags. But I must say that if I am going to ride a horse, I prefer a beast that has been well provisioned. Whenever I get within a two- or three-foot proximity of the wide hips on a woman like Pearl, I feel an almost overpowering urge to grab hold of them with both hands and slam her body against mine. Pearl had one of those delectable pot bellies reminiscent of a Renaissance oil painting, a galaxy of freckles scattered across her chest and strong shoulders. Cupped in the black triangles of the bikini top, her breasts looked like water balloons that would fit perfectly in one's hand.

"Well, are you coming in, or are you going to stand there all day?" Pearl said.

"First of all, I don't have a pair of bathing trunks," I said. "Secondly, I don't want to catch a chill when I get out. It's rather drafty in here, I mean, it *is* a garage. Thirdly, I have work to—"

"Oh put a sock in it already," Pearl said, cutting me off. "Come on. You can go in your underwear—I don't give a shit." She kicked off her slippers, turned and dove from the platform. I thought for a moment that she'd been trapped under the SeaLawn, but she came to the surface at the far end of the tank and flipped her hair back. "The water's beautiful!" she called out. She dove under again, dolphin style, her wonderful buttocks, then her feet, breaking the surface as she went down. I walked over to the edge of the tank and peered down at the Morecods. Well, what in heaven's name are you going to do now, Damien? I said to myself. Gotten yourself into quite a pickle, haven't you? I suppose I didn't really have much choice. It would have been far too rude simply to walk out of the house while Pearl was under water. I climbed onto the platform, knelt down and began untying my shoes. Suddenly, Pearl's head popped up out of the water next to the platform and she squirted a mouthful of water into my ear.

"Oh, my goodness!" I exclaimed.

"Oh, my goodness!" Pearl mimicked, wagging her head back and forth, her eyebrows raised in mock surprise, as she propelled herself backward through the water with her feet.

"OK, fine, we'll see about that!" I said, with exaggerated indignation. I began hastily yanking off my clothes.

"Oh, no, oh dear me," Pearl said, "I've overstepped the boundaries—look! I've unleashed a wild sea monster that was only disguised as a mild-mannered copywriter."

I finished undressing, folded my clothes, piled them neatly on my shoes on one corner of the platform and placed my glasses on top of the clothes. I can't say what on God's green earth possessed me, but it seemed appropriate to let out a yawp of some kind before jumping into the tank.

"Bonzzzaiiii!" I shrieked, and leaped, somewhat spastically (since I am not one who does a great deal of leaping in his day-to-day life) into the water. It was colder than I had expected. I came sputtering to the surface. "Su-sweet Jesus!" I said. Though I couldn't see very well without my glasses, Pearl, I realized, was laughing at me. She was clinging to the side of the tank with one arm and holding her stomach with the other.

"Oh, it's Aquaman!" Pearl said, between bursts of laughter. "This is just too much." I swam over to her, but as soon as I got close, she took a few strokes and got out of my reach. It was immediately apparent that she was a far stronger swimmer than I, and in fact seemed more in her element. It was as if with all the strength and energy she had, the resistance of the water was necessary in order to make her body's motions more fluid. She swam with the startling speed of a seal, but I tried to catch her anyway. At one point, when she'd let me get within arm's reach, she suddenly dove under. I dove under too, keeping my eyes open, and watched as she grabbed hold of one of the Morecods by putting one hand around each of the pectoral fins that protruded from its sides. The Morecod gave a few quick, powerful swishes of its tail, took off with Pearl clinging to it, and I was left behind in a swirl of bubbles. I came up for air and treaded water for a few moments, waiting for Pearl to come up. When she did, she was on the opposite side of the tank.

"You cheated!" I called to her. She just laughed. "They don't mind you doing that?" I asked.

"They try to get rid of you by swimming fast," she said. "But they get tired of that pretty soon and go back to poking along like they usually do. You get a heck of a ride for about a minute though." She dove back under the water.

I looked down into the water at the Morecods swimming beneath me. When I saw a big one, I dove down and grabbed hold of the fins on his sides as I'd seen Pearl do. As soon as my hands were on the handlefins, as it were, the beast leapt forward as if I'd kicked him with a spur and began tearing around the perimeter of the tank. His back bumped up against my chest occasionally, but for the most part it was a smooth ride. Pearl came up next to me, clinging to a cod even larger than mine. She turned to me and smiled as they overtook us, her hair streaming like ribbons through the water. I looked down at my fish, who seemed to be slowing down. I brought my knees forward and squeezed them against either side of his body. "Heeyaaa, heeyaa, giddyup!" I yelled. Air bubbles streamed from my mouth and my voice was garbled and distant. Pearl was a length ahead of us now. I squeezed my knees together more tightly and yelled some more. We began to creep up beside Pearl and her fish. My lungs were beginning to feel as if they might burst. Pearl glanced over her shoulder at us. My fish and I kept gaining until we were neck and neck with Pearl. Finally, my lungs couldn't take the strain. I let go, my fish zoomed forward ahead of Pearl, and I swam up to the surface. I made my way over to the side of the tank, which I hung on to while I gasped for air. Pearl came up a few seconds later and swam over to me. She didn't seem to be short of breath at all.

"Where'd you learn to ride like that?" she asked.

"Spaghetti westerns," I said.

"No actual horseback riding?"

"No sports whatsoever."

"Except chasing women," she said. I could feel myself blushing. Pearl laughed and splashed water at my face. "Another race," she declared. We both looked down at the large, gray bodies of the Morecods moving beneath us. "I see my steed," Pearl said. She looked up at me. "See you at the finish line." She dove down, making a little splash with her feet. I swam over to the SeaLawn. It was much thicker than the piece in the laboratory. The side of it was slippery, so I had to grab handfuls of the grass on top, but I managed to haul myself onto it and stand up. It sagged with my weight and water rose up from the leaves between my toes, yet it supported me. I took a few steps and the entire SeaLawn undulated beneath me. It was like walking on an enormous, boggy waterbed. My feet made a squishing sound with each step and I began running—squish, squish, squish, squish—across the SeaLawn to the other side. Pearl was surfaced near me after a lap and a half around the tank on her Morecod.

"That's cheating," she said, just before I leaped from the edge of the SeaLawn and did a cannon ball just in front of her. After another Morecod race around the tank, I got out of the pool, put my glasses back on and sat wrapped in a large beach towel, watching as Pearl showed off by doing complicated dives from the platform into the tank. She made very little splash when she entered the water.

"Did you ever compete?" I asked.

"A little. I was on the dive team and the swim team in my freshman year of college. I never had time for it after that, though. I was always in the lab. Now watch, this is my double back flip with a twist."

I cringed as Pearl leapt from the platform, did two somersaults in the air, then extended her body straight into a diving posture and twisted it, entering the water like a corkscrew. I was terrified that she might smack her head on the platform or do something to her back. If anything were to happen, I was certain I would panic and begin performing the Heimlich maneuver instead of artificial respiration, or find some such way of botching her rescue. But Pearl was in ab-solute control. It was like watching a professional gymnast. She was amazingly flexible and could get her body into all sorts of impossible configurations in mid-air and then untangle it again before plunging into the tank.

After she got out and put her bathrobe on, we realized that my clothes had gotten wet because Pearl had splashed them several times climbing onto the platform between dives. She got another bathrobe out of her bedroom for me. It was pink and barely hung past my knees, but quite cozy. We went into the kitchen and Pearl made some cod liver oil martinis for us. I was hesitant to accept one at first. I was thinking of the work piled up on my desk at home.

"You don't drink, usually, do you?" Pearl said.

"No, I don't. I'm not opposed to it or anything, it just doesn't occur to me to have one very often." We moved into the living room.

"It's actually good for you to have a drink or two at the end of the day," she said, plopping down on the couch and stretching her legs out in front of her.

"Oh, right, I suppose I should call it a day, then."

"Well, it's eleven o'clock at night. What do you have to do?"

I explained the nocturnal schedule I was on, and how it was the result of my living with a family of skunks.

"So when are you going to invite me over to meet the skunks anyway?"

"You certainly aren't bashful, are you?" I said.

"Being bashful is a waste of time," she said.

"Then so much for the thirty years I've put in thus far. Well, if you really want to meet them, I suppose this weekend would be alright." I waved away a fly that had landed on the rim of my martini glass. Since I'd started the drink, a craving for some skunk musk, which I'd been too busy to acknowledge since I'd arrived at Pearl's, began to gnaw at me. I also realized I was developing a tolerance to Pearl's scent. The fish odor was only noticeable when I brought the martini to my mouth, or when I was near the bowl of fish heads on the coffee table. I sat down on the floor and watched a pair of orange box fish drifting aimlessly about in one of the tanks. Pearl got up and went to the kitchen to make herself another martini. I was still in the middle of my first.

"Do you want to have some dinner?" Pearl asked, when she came back into the living room. "Or I guess it would be closer to lunch time for you. I'm practically starved from all that swimming. I think I could eat a whole tuna."

I wanted to stay, but I didn't. It would have been pleasant and relaxing to stay there and eat, but there was all the work I'd been neglecting, I hadn't fed any of the skunks yet, and my craving for musk was making me nervous. I kneaded the knuckles of one of my hands to keep from biting my nails. And yet I wanted to stay with Pearl almost as much as I wanted some skunk musk. I wondered if perhaps I'd been placing too much importance on my work schedule, my skunk-feeding schedule, and schedules in general. Even though my body had stopped doing so when I got out of the SeaLawn tank, my head was swimming. Sometimes it's difficult to sort out the things that matter from the apparatuses that help you ensure that matters are attended to. The thought occurred to me that I could invite Pearl to my house at that very moment. That way I could have everything—Pearl and musk. But that was crazy. I immediately dismissed the idea from my mind and downed the rest of my martini.

"I'd better be getting home," I said, standing up and handing the empty glass to Pearl. "Thank you very much for showing me the results of your research." I turned and walked to the door, turning around only for a second as I closed it to give a tight-lipped smile and, for some reason, a little wave. Pearl was still standing in the middle of the living room, looking slightly mystified, a full martini glass in one hand, an empty one in the other. I leaped into my car and sped home. Homer was standing in the foyer when I came in the door.

"Hello Homer. I know. I'm sorry I missed your meal time, but I was unavoidably detained." He stood there looking at me disapprovingly. It was then that I realized I was still wearing Pearl's pink bathrobe; my clothes had been left in Pearl's dryer. "Oh for Pete's sake," I said, "I am such a fool, such a God-awful fool." I grabbed the handle of the door and jerked it toward me, simultaneously sticking my head out. The door made a dull thud when it met my forehead. I repeated the action. "Fool!" I said. "Stupid—lousy—fool!" I yelled, as I smashed the door against my head. After banging my head eight or nine times, I stopped and closed the door. Homer had turned around and was waddling into the kitchen, no doubt to scratch at his empty food bowl in order to underscore his point. I went into the kitchen where Homer, Louisa and the rest of the family were standing accusingly around their empty food bowls. I got out a water glass, picked up Gertrude, squeezed a shot of her musk into the glass and gulped it down in two swallows. That steadied me a bit. I went to the mouse cage in the garage and got one for each skunk. This made them happy and helped assuage my guilt. Rupert and Nathaniel seemed to smile up at me as they munched away, the quivering tails of the field mice protruding from their mouths.

I went and sat down at my computer to get some work done, but I might as well have tried to levitate. The fact that I was too distracted to concentrate on my work enraged me. Over the years, I'd arranged my life so that distractions, particularly inter-personal engagements, were at a minimum. Yet my mind wandered back: I could have tried to kiss Pearl when we were in the tank, I thought. Lord knows I wanted to. I also wanted to squeeze that beautiful tummy of hers, bite her neck and earlobes, run my hands along the insides of her thighs and tear off the black bikini with my teeth. What a fantastic trove of nonsense! I turned off my computer and slapped the side of the monitor with the palm of my hand. "God damn you," I said. I got out the vacuum cleaner and went over the whole house. I dusted every piece of furniture and scrubbed down the kitchen and bathroom with disinfectant and steel wool. I scoured the back of the toilet and the underside of the sink. I got a ladder out of the garage, armed myself with rags and Windex, and by the light of the moon made war on the film of dirt on the outsides of the windows. Then I cleaned the entire basement. I vacuumed the cement floor and dusted the joists. After several hours my shirt was drenched with sweat and I was sore and tired. I took a shower, crept into bed as the first rays of sunlight were turning the window shades yellow, slipped on my eye covers and fell sound asleep.

For the next couple days I was able to get some work done, but not enough. There was no denying it, even to myself now—I was in love. This was the most singularly disagreeable affliction I have ever suffered. One moment I was doing a little soft-shoe routine on the linoleum floor of the kitchen and the next I was huddled on the edge of my bed with my head in my hands as tears ran down the bridge of my nose, dangled momentarily and then fell to make small, dark circles on the carpet. The telephone rang now and then, but I didn't pick it up. I'd decided that there was no room for Pearl in my life. I had my skunks and that was sufficient. But inevitably my thoughts drifted back to the warm, fuzzy scenes in Pearl's house, the constant surprises I seemed to encounter every few minutes spent in her company, the calm and tranquility of sitting with her on the rug and watching the fish flit about the coral reef that was her living room. Even when I caught myself in these daydreams I was tempted to stay there. My thoughts were like lazy workers standing around smoking cigarettes and I had to grab them by the scruffs of their necks and shove their noses violently against the grindstone to get them back to work. I needed more skunk musk than ever to get me through the day, so I kept Homer's and Louisa's jars on my desk and kept the shot glass handy in case of particularly wrenching fits of anxiety.

After three days, I felt a little more like my old self. I still wanted to see Pearl, but it was not an overwhelming need. However, there was the business of my clothes, which I'd left at her place, and that ridiculous pink robe, which was now hanging in the back of my coat closet. I'd put it as far out of sight as possible, to keep myself from thinking of Pearl. But I was feeling pretty resilient now. With a few shots of skunk musk, I'd be able to meet her somewhere; we could exchange the clothing, I would smile and not feel tempted to throw my schedule to the wind and accept if she invited me to her place for dinner. I tried to think of something offensive in Pearl's nature, some reason to shun her as I did all other human beings. Well, for one thing, she's not exactly tidy, is she? I said to myself. And there are those fish heads everywhere. Actually, she's far too slovenly to be my type, I thought. But I was grasping at straws and I knew it.

I went out onto the back porch with a cup of tea and a bowl of Cheerios that I'd seasoned with Helga. I sat down in one of my aluminum lawn chairs, took a sip of my tea, and had a thought. What if the life I was living was a little too sterile? Perhaps if I encountered more human beings on a regular basis, then this one, Pearl, gosh darn her, wouldn't be so captivating. But then, if I became more involved with people, wouldn't I become just like them, just as devious, conniving and generally vile—always using one to get something from another?

And then again, Pearl might have been fairly enchanting in any case. I'd certainly never met or read about anyone quite like her. I wanted to protect her from the rest of the world. It was absurd, I realized, because she'd been such an independent person from the time she was eight years old, but there was still something very innocent in her that I felt it was my duty to protect from the sea of corruption around us.

It was Saturday, and after finishing my breakfast, I went out and stuck the project I'd worked on all week in the mailbox, even though I knew it wouldn't be picked up until Monday. I liked to think of Hastings receiving the package. He might run into Piper in the hallway. "Just got Damien's work," he would say, proudly holding the package aloft. Piper would go back to his office and sit down behind his huge desk. "Ah," he'd say to himself, "our eccentric friend Damien, punctual as ever." Then he might sigh and look at the photograph of his son waving from the sailboat. "I only hope my own boy is some day as efficient as that young spark, Damien," he'd think. But I knew that in his eyes I was as despicable a creature as he was in mine.

Since I'd managed to get caught up on my work and had no plans for the weekend, I decided to call Pearl and get that clothing exchange over with. I couldn't invite her to the house. I'd had people in my house once before—a pair of Jehovah's Witnesses—and the experience had almost driven me batty. They insisted on touching so many of my things with hands that had been God knows where. I had to sit in my den and watch, with growing despair, as they set their drinking glasses directly on the coffee table, ignoring the coasters I'd given them, leaving rings of water I had to suppress the urge to wipe up while they rattled on about the afterlife. When one of them asked to use the bathroom, I was on the point of telling the uncouth crusader he could jolly well use the back yard. The moment they were out the door, I vacuumed and dusted the entire house, making sure to erase their footprints from the carpet. I cleaned the bathroom and washed and sterilized the glasses they'd used. No, house guests simply were not the thing for me.

As I sat in the den, petting Nathaniel, listening to Bach, and trying to decide where I might tell Pearl to meet me, a car pulled up by the curb in front of my house and turned out its headlights. I peeked through the curtains and, by the pale glow of Mrs. Endicott's porch light, watched a woman with frizzy hair get out of the car and shut the door. She was wearing a bathrobe.

6

My heart began racing. The woman started up the walk to my front door. Her car was an old Tempest—the same make as Pearl's. Of course, it's Pearl, you nincompoop, I told myself. What other woman would park in front of your house in the middle of the night and approach the door in a bathrobe? I'd forgotten that I'd told Pearl my address. Several possibilities leapt to mind: I could turn out all the lights and pretend not to be home; I could just open the door a crack and toss the pink robe out to her; or I could open the window and speak to her from there, explaining that I'd contracted some horrible contagious disease, and that for her own sake, I could not visit with her again for a long time. When the doorbell rang I practically hit the ceiling. Sharp pains began stabbing at my stomach. Nathaniel hopped off my lap and onto the floor where he joined Elsbeth and Gertrude, who were wrestling in front of one of the stereo speakers. Homer, who'd been lying on the armchair with Louisa, sat up, pricked up his ears and gave me an inquisitive look. The doorbell rang a second time. Bracing myself, I got up from the couch, pulled my bathrobe more closely about me and tightened the knot. I went to the front door and peered through the eye hole at Pearl. The curvature of the glass made it look as if she were in a little fish bowl.

"Who is it?" I called through the door. Pearl stuck her face so close to the eye hole that I stepped back, afraid, even though I knew it was impossible, that she could see in.

"Hey—Harry the Hermit. It's me, Pearl." I partially opened the door and peered out. "Don't you ever pick up your phone?" she asked. She held up a folded stack of clothes. "I brought these over. You left them at my place. Sorry I got them wet, but the salt water won't hurt them any. I washed them for you." She paused for a moment. "Well, are you going to invite me in, or are you going to stand there looking at me like the Grim Reaper just showed up at your door?"

I opened the door all the way and stepped to the side. One of the flaws in my character is that I cannot help but be polite when someone else behaves civilly toward me. It was via exploitation of this weakness that the Jehovah's Witnesses too had successfully intruded. "Yes, come in, I'm sorry. It's just that I wasn't expecting you."

Pearl stepped into the foyer and I closed the door. Her eyes widened, then almost shut completely, and she took a step sideways as if someone had pushed her. "Whoah, it's even stronger than I thought," she said. I took the pile of clothes from her and showed her into my den, trembling with nervousness. I tried to imagine what this scene might look like to someone else. The place was crawling with skunks. Homer and Louisa were lounging on the recliner, Elsbeth and Gertrude were still wrestling on the floor, Rupert and Nathaniel were crawling over the arms and back of the couch and Helga was standing on the coffee table. Gertrude got up, walked over and sprayed at us as soon as we entered the room.

I stepped in forward. "Now Gertrude, let's mind our manners. Pearl is a guest here," I said. Never having had a real house guest before, and not knowing what else to do, I began to introduce the skunks. "That's Louisa and Homer over there on the recliner, they're the parents," I said. "Rupert and Nathaniel are the ones on the couch." There was a sound behind me like someone dropping a laundry bag full of shoes. I turned around and saw that Pearl had collapsed on the floor.

"Good lord," I said. I turned to Gertrude. "Now, see what you've done, Gurty, you rude little girl!" I opened a window, then dashed to the kitchen for a cup of water and a damp dishcloth. I put the dishcloth on Pearl's forehead. It was almost a minute before she came to, and while she lay there I admired her curls and her cheekbones. I breathed in her fishy scent, an odor that undeniably excited me. Her robe had come loose and I could see the freckles that covered her chest. All I wanted to do was look at her. I could have just sat there on the floor watching her for days. Her eyelids fluttered open.

"Here, have some water," I said. "I'm so sorry about the skunks. I know the smell can be overpowering. In fact, that's what I like so much about it." Pearl raised herself onto one elbow and drank down the whole cup of water. "And I suppose that's why I'm such a solitary person" I continued. "No one else seems to understand that." Pearl was looking into my eyes, probably still delirious. "I suppose I'd change if I could, but I'm not sure I want to." I was babbling like an idiot. I didn't want to meet Pearl's gaze and I looked down at the floor as I spoke, thinking how I'd like to slam my head against it. "And if my habits are incompatible with human society, well for all it's done for me, I guess I'm just as happy without that society. I know it's—" Pearl's hand came up, grasped the back of my neck and pulled my head down to hers. I realized suddenly that we must be kissing, or she was kissing me, because I didn't know what I was doing. I quickly shut my eyes, having read that this is the proper etiquette, and let my mouth open slightly. I don't know why the tongue, whose purpose is tasting, should be such an erotogenic area of the human body, but I must say I went absolutely stark raving mad. I climbed on top of Pearl and held her head so tightly between my hands one would have thought I was afraid it might scamper across the floor. After a while, I moved my hands down her sides and squeezed those wonderful hips through her bathrobe. I kissed her mouth, her eyes, her ears, her neck. I pulled the top of her bathrobe open further so I could kiss her chest. I felt I was remembering something I had wanted to do since I met her, but only realizing I wanted to do it in the process of doing it She was wearing a red bikini with little strings that tied it together. Leaning on my left elbow, I squeezed each of her breasts and then explored further down her torso. I was beginning to think that spontaneity might not be such a bad thing. It might even be a new way of life for me.

Pearl pulled my robe down off my shoulders. "Wow," she said. "You really take off once you get started."

"Pearl, I have to tell you this kind of thing never happens to me. I've never felt, I mean, you're just such a wonderful person, and, you see, I don't even like people, but you, you're—"

She raised her head up and kissed me on the mouth. "You're very special to me too, Damien," she said. She pulled my robe open and slid my boxer shorts down as far as she could reach. I pushed them down around my ankles and kicked them off with my feet. I pulled her robe completely open. I untied the bikini top while she pulled off the bottom. She gently massaged the underside of my penis, slid it into her and the next embarrassingly few shimmying moments scooted by rather quickly. Then my body went rigid, there was a strange groan that originated in the back of my throat, there was some sort of explosion in my head, and in a far corner of my mind I wondered if I'd burst a blood vessel in my temple. But there was little time to contemplate that because a blinding light broke into billions of stars, comets whizzed this way and that, fiery, kaleidoscopic images merged and fell apart, finally all melted away and left me sinking from the surface of consciousness. I swam lackadaisically back up.

"Oh," I said. Sweat dripped from my forehead onto Pearl's shoulder. My glasses had come off at some point and I saw them now across the gray field of carpet. Pearl grasped a handful of my hair and pressed my head against her chest. I was ready to go again after a bit, and managed to last several minutes the second time, and about half an hour the third time, the time Pearl had the most intense and beautiful orgasm I'd ever—well, the *only* orgasm—I'd ever seen. This occurred when I was standing, half crouched in front of the kitchen table, the same table at which (bizarrely it now seemed) I took most of my meals. Instead of a plate of lasagna, Pearl was stretched out on her back on the table, and instead of shoving food into myself, I was thrusting myself into Pearl, my body jerking with the speed and violence of a man trying to regain control of a runaway jackhammer. Pearl moaned as her head rolled back and forth on the table.

"Oh, Damien," she groaned. "Oh Damien, you're going to—oh you..." Suddenly she wrapped her legs tight around my waist, sat straight up and threw her arms around me. The force of this embrace knocked me backward, and I staggered away from the table with Pearl clinging to me like a koala bear, raking my back with her nails and humping away like a rabbit. I clumsily backed through the kitchen doorway and into the foyer where I fell down on my back. No sooner had I done so than Pearl came.

She grabbed hold of my ears and I feared for a moment she might yank them from the sides of my head. "Aaaiieeeeeyaaaahaha!" she screamed, throwing her head back, thrusting her torso down and holding it there. Then she collapsed, panting, onto my chest. I ran my fingers along her spine. There was a faint, dew-like perspiration all over her back.

I do not wish to sound boastful, but we made love several times in a row and in every conceivable position. And we did not restrict ourselves to the house. We did it out in the back yard once, then once in the car on the way to Pearl's house. I put the seat of the Eldorado all the way back, undid my bathrobe, and Pearl sat on my lap handling the steering wheel, bouncing up and down, telling me when to hit the gas or the brake. Pearl liked to do it in the water best of all. We did it twice in the tank while the Morecods swam around us. We did it in Pearl's bathtub, where we rubbed fish oil all over each other's bodies and licked it off.

We slept all the next day, got up, ate bagels with cream cheese and lox, drank a couple cod liver oil martinis, then made love for another seven hours or so. I returned to my house on Monday evening, exhausted, exhilarated. I was a new man, older and younger than I'd ever been before. I whistled as I walked through the door and, with wild abandon, tossed my car keys onto the little table on the foyer. (I usually hung them on a special hook in the kitchen.) I pretended not to notice Homer for a moment while I shrugged off my coat.

"Well hello there Homer, old boy, how was your weekend?" Instead of hanging my coat in the closet, I walked into the den and recklessly threw the garment upon the sofa. Homer looked at me as if I'd walked through the door on my hands speaking Swahili. "Oh, don't be such an old crank, Homer," I said. "You have to just let yourself go now and then. It's not as if I've been gone for a month. And there was enough food out for you all to get by on." I retrieved some insects from the garage and filled everyone's bowls. I poured out a couple of shots of Gertrude and Helga's musk from the jars on the shelf and tossed them back. "You know what, Homer," I said, while he munched on a cricket. "I think I'll take the day off tomorrow. What the heck. I don't think I've ever taken a day off before." I tried to think of something wild and extravagant I could do. "Perhaps I'll go to the movies. Yes, that's it, I'll call Pearl and see if she wants to go too. Maybe I'll get up early and we can see one of those afternoon matinées."

I called Pearl and she suggested that, just for laughs, we dress up to go to the movie. I shaved with the overzealousness of an adolescent boy who's just discovered he needs to, put on a gray suit I hadn't worn since I worked in the city and went to pick up Pearl. She squinted in the afternoon sun as she stepped onto the porch and smiled at me for a moment before turning to close and lock her door. The image remains etched in my memory, if memory is a surface that can be etched upon. Actually, no, this image is like a photograph I take out and admire from time to time. Pearl had brushed out her hair and it exploded from her head in a great, soft mane that glistened in the sun. The red dress she wore accentuated her small waist and wide hips. A black overcoat was thrown over her arm. As soon as she got in the car and shut the door, we both burst out laughing. But it was a nervous laugh, on my part anyway, because I felt as if I had just seen Pearl for the first time again. My mind began brimming over with lascivious thoughts—variations on some of the acrobatics we'd performed a day before. Pearl looked at me as I drove.

"What?" I said, glancing over at her. She was beaming at me. She had put on some extra fish oil and as my car began to smell like a cannery, I was growing aroused.

"Nothing," she said. "You clean up nice." I shrugged and made an ambiguous noise. Pearl reached over and felt the side of my face with her fingertips. "Ooh, so smooth," she said. I had such a tremendous erection, I wondered if too much blood had left my cerebrum in favor of my penis, because another car's horn blared suddenly as I drove right through a stop sign. "You know, you must have been the most adorable baby," Pearl said. She plucked the pieces of cotton from my face I'd put there to stanch a couple minor cuts I'd given myself while shaving.

"Oh, phooey," I said. "I'd forgotten about that cotton."

Pearl laughed, and glancing over at her, I began to laugh too, though I was not sure what I was laughing about. Pearl slid over next to me on the seat and squeezed my arm.

I didn't like the movie at all. It was based on *Travels With My Aunt*, which I'd read twice, but which one could clearly see none of the actors had read even once, for if they had, they wouldn't have acted so hopelessly absurd. Not that I could concentrate on the movie anyway. There were only five other people in the theater besides Pearl and myself, but they made as much noise as a hundred. I spent most of the hour and a half watching them. A fat man to our left insisted upon guffawing at times when there was absolutely nothing humorous going on and made intermittent crackling noises with plastic bags of junk food. A woman behind us noisily slurped a soft drink through a straw. Someone in front of us kept moving around in his seat, which creaked each time he did. I gripped the armrests and joggled my knees up and down to keep myself from going berserk. I couldn't wait to get out of the place. Pearl leaned over at one point and whispered in my ear.

"The movie's over there," she said, pointing to the screen. I'd been staring over at the fat man, who'd begun his most recent ruckus with a bag of potato chips.

"These people are idiots," I hissed. I meant the filmmakers, but I'm not sure this is what Pearl understood, or that it mattered.

Pearl patted my arm, then pried my hand off the armrest and held it in her lap. For me, this resulted in an immediate and almost painful erection. Glancing around to make sure no one was looking our way, I took her hand and put it in my lap. She began to stroke my penis where it lay like a ramrod against the inside of my thigh. I reached over, slipped my hand up her skirt and returned the favor by petting her vulva. We left the theater while the illiterate actors were in the process of making an unintentional parody of the last chapter of the novel.

I drove us to Pearl's and she had her dress off not two seconds after we stepped in the door. I pulled off my necktie. She yanked open my shirt and the buttons popped off and bounced off the sides of the fish tanks and the top of the coffee table. Pearl pulled my pants down around my ankles.

"Come on," she said, "in the tank." I followed her bottom, jiggling in a pair of black satin panties as she ran through the laboratory, into the garage and climbed up onto the platform. She pulled off her bra and panties and dove into the tank. I was right behind her. I came up to the surface and immediately her beautiful, thick, white legs were wrapped around my waist. I swam to the edge of the tank, grasped it with both hands, slid into her and began thrusting as fast and hard as the water sloshing between us would allow.

That night we went out to eat. This was my second outing in public within only a few hours, and I was edgy about it at first, but somehow Pearl's presence calmed me. She took me to a sushi place she knew, where we took off our shoes and sat on cushions on the floor at a low table. We had our own little dining room, partitioned off from the other tables by walls made of bamboo and white paper. I liked this because we could not see our fellow diners, nor they us. We had only to contend with a servile little Asian woman in a blue kimono who occasionally peeked into our cubicle. To my surprise, Pearl rattled off our order in Japanese, and the woman bowed her way backward out the door.

"I didn't know you spoke Japanese," I said.

"Oh, just a teensy weensy, but I come here a lot. I hardly have to tell them anything now. They know what I usually get. I just had to tell them to bring twice as much tonight." The woman in the blue kimono brought us sake and sashimi. I had a brief anxiety attack during which I wondered what brand of sanitizer was used in the washing of the dishes, whether the fish was crawling with bacteria that would evolve into a family of worms in my large intestine, and if the chef had washed his hands between urinating and preparing the food. But Pearl claimed to eat there often, I reasoned, and she seemed to be perfectly healthy. After a few sips of sake I was trying everything on the platter.

"What's this?" I asked, pointing out a dubious-looking gray lump.

"Octopus," Pearl said.

"You don't say." I let the lump slither down my throat. I hadn't been out to eat since I was a child, I was tired and delirious from having sex all afternoon and felt like experimenting. I tried something else, and Pearl told me I'd eaten fish eggs.

"Caviar!" I exclaimed, "how extravagant we are. Say, that rhymes!" I was getting a bit punchy.

"I got a weird phone call today," Pearl said.

I picked up something that resembled a tortellini, tossed it a couple feet in the air, and caught it in my mouth, almost rolling over backwards in the process. "Weird?" I said. "I asked you to the movies. I suppose that was a little weird, for me."

"No, I got another call. Someone who said he worked for a company called NewGenetics. He wanted to know if I was interested in interviewing for a job."

"Why is that weird?"

"Well, no one, aside from you and Richard, knows about my genetics research. As far as anyone else at the university lab knows, I've run out of funding and am not doing genetic research any more." Pearl pushed a piece of sushi around her plate with her chopsticks, but didn't pick it up. "I've never heard of NewGenetics and I couldn't find them in the phone book. I even called a few other genetics companies and they'd never heard of it either."

"That is kind of strange," I said. "Well, maybe it's a very new company." I didn't really want to think about whatever it was Pearl was getting at.

"Or it's completely bogus," she said. "I just wish I knew who this was, and how he got my name."

To avoid looking into Pearl's left eye, with which she was staring at me intently, I pushed my glasses up with my index finger, and poured some more sake into both of our thimble-sized cups.

"What did you say about the job?" I asked.

"I just said I'd have to think about it. I shouldn't have given him my address though. He said he wanted to send me information about the company or something."

I reached across the table and patted Pearl's hand, as she'd done to me once. "Look," I said, "you're probably worried about nothing. A lot of people in your field know that you're a genius. So just because you've apparently, they think, stopped doing research, doesn't mean you couldn't do it again. Maybe it *is* a brand new company and they're hoping to scoop you up. It could be a good opportunity for you both."

Pearl smiled and put her other hand on top of the one I'd put on hers. "You're too cute, sometimes," she said.

I had the feeling I might float up to the ceiling like a balloon at any moment. "One does one's best," I said.

That night Pearl slept at my house, but she left early in the afternoon. We made love twice after we awoke and then she got up. I watched groggily from the bed as she slid into a pair of pink bikini bottoms and clasped a matching top across her freckled chest. "Gotta go feed the fish," she said. I nodded. After getting dressed, Pearl sat down on the edge of the bed. Her hair was frizzy from our frolicking, her lips slightly puffy, her aqua eyes tired but sparkling. She looked at me like someone who'd just won a prize. Her head was framed by the border of sunlight around the shade that was drawn over the window. She bent over and kissed me. I lifted myself up and tried to pull her down on top of me. She drew back and gave me one of her magnificent smiles.

"I'll give you a call later," she said. She bent forward again, kissed me on the cheek, and then, as she stood up, she extended her index finger and touched the end of my nose. I watched her lovely rump as she walked out of the bedroom.

I lay in bed and listened to the sounds of the front door, the engine of Pearl's car turning over, and the sound of it receding as it carried her down the street. I got slowly out of bed and wrapped a robe around myself. I fed the skunks and started some breakfast, all at a much slower pace than usual. The house seemed too quiet and these routine tasks, in which I'd taken pleasure before, seemed strange and empty now without Pearl. I went through the motions, even sat down at the computer and did my work, but with a strange sense of detachment, as if I were watching someone else do it. By about three AM the following morning I had completed more than a full day's work, prepared for myself and eaten a superb pasta salad seasoned with Helga and Rupert, and was now relaxing in the den, listening to Beethoven's Symphony Number Four in B flat minor, sipping an Elsbeth aperitif. I was unhappy. While I watched Homer and Louisa, asleep together on the armchair, I made a decision that would alter my life completely and irrevocably.

I slept only a few hours, got up, dressed, and set out for a jewelry store. It was a breezy morning and the air seemed clearer, as if it had been filtered during the night. This, in combination with my being overtired, and the nature of my expedition, made all my actions seem profound. I spent the entire day in jewelry stores, or in the car driving between jewelry stores. Nothing seemed quite right. I thought of getting something with a pearl in it, but I didn't want there to be anything corny about what I wanted to say to her with this ring. On my way to what I'd decided would be the last store, I saw huge cumulonimbus clouds building on the horizon. When I got out of my car, the first few drops of rain were staining the asphalt of the parking lot. A few minutes before the store closed, in a display case in the back of the store a ring caught my eye. It was a gold one in the midst of a bunch of silver ones. It had a stylized design of ovals that suggested fish, but not too obviously. It wasn't a proper engagement ring. In fact, it looked more like a wedding band. But it was the one. I knew it right away, just the way I knew instinctively to follow Pearl out of the grocery store that day which, by now, seemed like years ago. I asked the man behind the counter if I could take a look at the ring. It fit snugly on my pinkie finger, which I estimated to be about the size of Pearl's ring finger. The jeweler put the ring in a royal blue felt box.

"I don't need a bag," I told him, smiling, yes, actually smiling at this stranger, this rather grumpy middle-aged man whom I would have despised had I met him a month before.

It had turned pitch dark in the twenty minutes I'd spent in the store; the saplings planted around the parking lot were bent at painful angles in the wind, and raindrops the size of pebbles pelted me and danced on the hood of the car. When I opened the car door, the wind practically blew it off its hinges. I drove slowly, the blue felt box with the ring squeezed between my hand and the steering wheel, the rain making my windshield look like the glass porthole of a washing machine on the rinse cycle. Many people had pulled off onto the shoulder of the road to wait out the deluge, but I was not about to stop. Thunder rumbled in the background as lightning tore ragged cracks in the sky. I was giddy and electrified. The ring in my hand was the key to a whole new life, as surely as was the key Ben Franklin had attached to a kite.

7

There were no lights in any of Pearl's windows when I pulled up in front of her house. I held my coat over my head and ran up the side-walk to the front door with the ring clutched in my fist. The door was slightly ajar and it was dark inside. I rang the bell but got no response. "Pearl!" I shouted over the noise of the now torrential rain. Thunder rumbled in the distance, lightning flashed a few seconds later. The eye of the storm still hadn't reached me, but it was getting closer. I heard a crash and turned around to see a garbage can blowing like a tumble-weed down the middle of the street. I turned to the crack in the door again. "Pearl!" I practically screamed, hearing the desperation in my own voice. I pushed the door open and flicked on the light. Something was missing. The tanks of tropical fish were still there in all their daz-zling, colorful splendor; the bowl of fish heads was still on the coffee table. In the kitchen, empty sardine and tuna cans were overflowing from the trash can and brown paper bags by the back door. A bolt of lightning was followed by a detonation of thunder that seemed closer than the last one had. Then I realized what was missing—the flies. There were no little black, buzzing clouds over the potpourri bowl or the empty cans. The place was deserted. I walked back out through the living room and opened the door to the laboratory. I flicked the light switch on the wall but nothing happened. Then a flash of light-ning turned the lab a ghostly blue-white and provided me a blind-ing glimpse of what could not, simply could *not* have been the same laboratory I'd walked through a couple days before. I stood there in the doorway for a moment, listening to the rain as it drummed the roof, lashed at the windows and gushed from an aluminum gutter just outside the window. The shadow of a tortured tree waved back and forth across the wall of the lab, the wind making a shredding sound as it rifled through its leaves. I took a step forward and glass crunched beneath my shoe. There was a lamp clamped to the center counter. I held my breath and clicked it on: a shambles. That's what I saw. Utter destruction. The Bunsen burner and a huge microscope were on the floor in pieces, as were all the test tubes, beakers and other parapher-nalia that had formerly been on the counters. The patch of SeaLawn I'd seen in a basin lay on the floor like a saturated doormat. All the counters and the floor were covered with broken glass and puddles of liquid and the room was filled with a fishy, chemical odor.

Stepping over the microscope and kicking aside the neck of a shattered flask with a rubber stopper plugging its mouth, I continued into the garage and flipped on another light. The Morecods were there, the gray bodies moving about the blue tank as before, though more quickly, perhaps agitated by the storm. I ran back through the ruined laboratory and stopped short in the living room. A tall man in a short-sleeved polo shirt, with a square jaw and muscular forearms was standing in the middle of the room with his hands on his hips, looking around at the fish tanks. He looked like a tennis instructor, or at least the kind of person whose presence usually means there is an exclusive country club in the vicinity.

"Who in the devil are you?" I asked.

He looked me up and down and removed his hands from his hips, as if in preparation to serve. "I'm Pearl's fiancé," he said. His voice was all confidence, entitlement, natural selection, dominant gene pool and so forth. So, this must be the infamous Richard, I thought.

"Who the hell are *you*?" he asked.

"I'm, I—" I was at a complete loss. "I'm just a neighbor," I lied miserably. "I just happened to be passing by and noticed the door was open." Gutless coward that I am, I allowed the old boarding-school mentality to take over as I sidled toward the door, talking my way out. "But I suppose everything is alright, if you're her fiancé," I said. "Just wanted to check." And with that, I scurried flinchingly out the door, half expecting him to give me a taste of his backhand as I went.

I was soaked to the skin in the short run from Pearl's front door to my car. When I turned the key in the ignition, I realized I was still clutching the felt-covered box, and that I'd squeezed it so hard I'd dented cardboard beneath the felt. It had become a sad, wet, crumpled thing that looked like a prune. I tossed it in the glove box and drove home.

What I needed was some fresh skunk musk. Some of Homer, Louisa, maybe Nathaniel—heck—all of them. That would clear my head, open my sinuses, and then I could work out a course of action. I've always wanted to be a man of action, always fantasized about it, but that's not the way it is, is it? No. The truth is that I'm nothing of the sort. Instead I'm a man of reaction.

I'd expected the whole family to be huddled by the front door awaiting my return, or cowering under the furniture in the den, terrified by the storm. I stalked into the kitchen. "Homer!" I yelled. He was the responsible one, the faithful one. He knew I'd be counting on him at a time like this. I got down on my hands and knees and looked under the couch. No one. I went into the bedroom and looked under the bed. No one. "Homer!" I yelled again. Of course I was being absurd. They would all be in the burrow. Where else would a bunch of skunks go in a storm but to the burrow that dad had dug? I took a flashlight and headed out the back door. Stepping off the back porch, I slipped and fell on my tailbone. Rain slapped my face as cool mud seeped through the seat of my pants. The yard had become a bog. It took me a couple attempts to stand back up, and as I made my way to the hutch, my feet sank down a couple inches with each wet step. I called Homer's name and got down on my knees in the muck to shine my flashlight into the burrow. It was filled halfway up with water. "Homer!" I yelled. I stuck my arm in up to the shoulder and fished around in the muddy water, expecting to come up with a handful of drowned skunks. There was nothing. I stood and the wind was so strong my body wavered like a reed. Then I heard a voice calling to me from the sky. "Away!" was the only word I could make out as the sound was carried along by the wind. "Away!"

It was Pearl, communicating via radio waves on a frequency that is only accessible during electrical storms. I looked up into the sky. "You've found the channel, my love!" I yelled into the sky. "I just need about three more decibels!" I heard the voice a little louder. "Unks away!" it said. Then I realized the voice was coming not from directly above, but from my left. I looked over and saw the silhouette of Mrs. Endicott as she leaned out her window to call to me. As usual, the sight of Mrs. Endicott annoyed me. I shone the flashlight at her face through the sheets of rain while she hollered, but I still couldn't make out what she was saying so I went and knocked on her front door. She opened the inner door, but spoke to me through the clear plastic of the storm door.

"They took the skunks away!" she yelled, over the clattering of the rain on the thin aluminum roof over her porch. She was wearing the same hideous floral housecoat she always wore, the top of which she clutched to her throat, as if afraid a tentacle of cold air might slip through the cracks and strangle her with pneumonia on the spot.

"What? What do you mean? Who took them away?" I asked, even as the meaning of the words she'd spoken sank like rocks down into the pit of my stomach.

"The dog catchers," she yelled. "I called the pound. Your damn skunks were running all over my yard."

"That's not possible!" I yelled back. "The fence around my yard is six feet high and a skunk cannot jump more than two or three inches."

"They dug *under* your stupid fence!"

"Mrs. Endicott, you had no right. Those skunks were mine. You had no right!" My voice rose to a shriek. "Gosh darn you to hell!" I pulled on the handle of the storm door, but it was locked. If it hadn't been, I don't know what I might have done, aside from drip rainwater on Mrs. Endicott's carpet while pointlessly railing against the old grocery sack. Mrs. Endicott, her rheumy old eyes wide with horror, closed the inner door, leaving just a crack through which to continue yelling at me.

"It's not just me, you know. The whole neighborhood is sick of you and those stinking skunks. Mrs. Rogers says we should've called the pound a long time ago."

All I could think of was Homer and Louisa in a kind of concentration camp for animals. How long did they keep skunks around before they gassed them with all the stray cats and abandoned dogs? I could feel a lump rising in my throat. "You had no right!" I cried again, and pounded my fist against the plastic door.

"I'll call the police!" Mrs. Endicott yelled, and slammed the door in my face.

"Call them, yes!" I screamed at Mrs. Endicott's closed door. "Please do! I'd like to have a word with the authorities myself!" I was crying now. Tears mixed with the rain water running down my cheeks and off the tip of my nose as I backed off the porch. I continued raving in the middle of Mrs. Endicott's yard as the rain whipped down at me. "Someone has to answer for all this!" I yelled. "There has to be some explanation. Someone has to be held accountable! I've had about enough of this inhuman humanity, I think, just about enough!" Lightning cracked and shattered the sky for an instant and thunder boomed simultaneously. I ran, slipping and stumbling, across the lawn to my car.

8

I'm going to bust them out, I said to myself. That's the term the out-laws use, correct? Why not go the whole taco and break the laws of grammar while you're breaking others? I drove to the Animal Control Center, which was on the other side of town and, of course, closed. Continuing my tantrum, I yanked at the handle of the door of the prison camp for pets. I flung my fists, as well as bricks, stones and tree branches I found around the parking lot, against the wire mesh over the windows, all of which bounced off. However, I managed to inspire a hellish uproar among the incarcerated dogs, some of whom had already been barking at the storm. Their howls mingled with the howling wind that made the trees around the parking lot look like rag dolls that were being severely mistreated. The wind would die down a bit, only to rise to more alarming heights and snap branches from the trees while I battled the building.

It was not until a broken branch hit me on the back of the head and almost knocked me down that I came to the realization that this approach was getting me nowhere. Climbing back into the car, soaked and muddy, my feet practically floating in my shoes, I decided a new plan of attack was necessary. I considered sacrificing my vehicle—us-ing it as a battering ram to knock the doors down so I could get to my loved ones. But the door of the center was made of reinforced steel and there was no guarantee I would be able to get through. Besides, I did not want to risk ruining my car. I needed it for my getaway. Getaway to where, and for how long, I did not yet know, but an instinct to flee was gradually overtaking me. There would be no way to tolerate the be-trayal by Pearl and my neighbors if I continued to live in this habitat. My behavior in the previous few months had been reckless. I had been more pitifully blind than a newborn skunk. It was imperative that I erase the memory of Pearl, Mrs. Endicott and all the others who'd con-spired against me. The only way to eradicate these people from my thoughts was to eliminate any visual stimuli that would bring them to mind, as it now seemed that my house inevitably would, especially if I were not able to recover the family. The insect and field mouse colonies in my garage, the back door flap which would no longer be used, the deserted burrow—all these things would be excruciatingly poignant reminders. Come to think of it, so would the kitchen table, the bed, the floor of the den, or any of the other places where Pearl and I had made love. And how could I face Mrs. Endicott, or any of her neighborhood accomplices, and resist the urge to strangle them? I'd become a victim of my own folly—allowing myself to become emotionally attached to Pearl, Homer, Louisa and the others had been abject indulgence that had resulted, as I'd known in the back of my mind that it would, in pain. "You fool!" I yelled. I slammed my forehead against the steering wheel. "Darn you! Gosh darn you to hell!" I yelled, and continued to slam my head against the steering wheel. This was simply not adequate, so I opened the car door, stuck my head out into the rain and pulled the door toward me so that it knocked my head back before it could shut. I repeatedly opened and shut the car door, bashing away at my forehead until the job was done.

When I came to, I was lying across the seat of the Eldorado. I sat up and felt a tender lump that had formed on my forehead. As I peered through the painful morning light pouring through my windshield, I saw a figure open the door to the Animal Control Center and enter. I got out of my car and brushed myself off. The mud from my yard had partially dried and clumps of dirt fell from the folds in my clothes as I walked to the building and threw open the door. The first thing I noticed in the room was the horrendous smell. It was the smell of creatures living in their own feces, urine and fear, while they awaited execution. To avoid the gag reflex, I tried to breathe out of my mouth. The desperate barks of the doomed echoed through the cinder-block structure.

A woman who looked like a linebacker, wearing a long, curly blond wig and a pink silk blouse, was sitting at a computer at one of two desks in the room, eating a jelly doughnut. How anyone could eat in the midst of that foul and nauseating smell was quite beyond me. The beast was about to take a bite of the doughnut when I walked in. She put the doughnut down, sucked air through her mouth like a giant vacuum cleaner and exhaled heavily through her nose. I was seized by a strong desire for a shot of skunk musk, and realized I hadn't had one since the afternoon of the previous day.

"All right, where are they?" I demanded.

"What?" the woman asked.

Just then, another, much smaller woman wearing a brown uniform came through the door at the back of the room. The insane barking was louder for a moment until the door swung shut. The shield-shaped patch on the shoulder of this woman's uniform bore the depiction of a pine tree and the words "Essex County."

"You must know," I said, sizing her up. "You are the one in charge of the executions around here, are you not?"

The uniformed woman looked at me as if she honestly did not know what I was talking about. I imagine Nazi collaborators all wore this expression when they were confronted by Allied investigators. "Are you interested in adopting, or do you have a complaint?" she asked. Her brown hair had been sheared to a brush cut and she had the eyes of a member of a firing squad. A gold name plate on her shirt pocket identified her as "Joanne."

"I'm here about the skunks you abducted last night," I said, my voice rising with righteousness indignation. "I'm here to take them back. They were kidnapped as the result of a misunderstanding and I demand that you return them. You have no right to separate a man from his skunks without first consulting him, and I'm not about to stand by while mine are subjected to unlawful imprisonment."

"Skunks," she said, her voice hard. Everything about her was hard, whittled down. Among all her sharp, jutting bones there was no hint of the softness and roundness I associated with femininity. I thought of Pearl. Then images of the van parked outside Pearl's house, the ruined laboratory, the self-assured Richard, all flashed through my mind in quick succession.

"Yes, the skunks," I said. "What have you done with them?"

"You got a problem with skunks? You have to call Game. Which county are you in?" After all that, "skunks" seemed to be the only word that had registered.

"No, I don't have a problem with skunks," I started, "or rather, I do, but the problem is that they're missing."

Her face took on an ironic expression and the hint of a smile began to curl up the corner of her straight line of a mouth. "We don't deal with wildlife here, just pets," she said. She glanced over at the doughnut-eater, who was licking her fingers, having just finished making another contribution to her own grotesque caricature of feminine roundness and softness, some of which bulged against her keyboard. Good God, I thought, she's probably eaten Homer, Louisa, and the rest of the family for breakfast. "Would he call Game about that or Wildlife?" Joanne asked her.

"No, no, no," I broke in. "These were not wild animals. They were domesticated skunks. They were pets."

"Did you have them licensed?" the fat woman asked. "If they had licenses they would have been brought here."

"Licenses?" I said.

"I don't think skunks are even legal as pets in this state anyway," Joanne went on. "Did you have them descented?"

"Descented?" I said. "What would be the point?" This made Joanne break into a full smile. Unbelievably, in my desperation, I'd become a source of amusement for this brusque, humorless, appetite-less little Gestapo-style person. That's entertainment for them—these people with Napoleon complexes—seeing other people in a state of helplessness. I could feel my lips quivering as I spoke. "You don't understand," I said, glancing down at her name plate, then back at her face, "Joanne," I more or less snarled, "I *need* those skunks."

Her smile leaked away and she looked directly into my eyes when she spoke. "Well then I suggest you call Wildlife," she said.

I took a deep breath to calm myself. "May I use your telephone?" I asked.

She shrugged. "Sure," she said, and nodded to the phone on the unoccupied desk.

"Do you have the number for this Wildlife place?" I asked, sitting down behind the empty desk.

"Yeah, I've got it, hold on a minute," the blonde linebacker said. Her breasts were so obscenely large they quivered with gelatinous lives of their own inside her satin blouse as she flipped through her Rolodex. "Here it is, 'Wildlife Nuisance Control.'" She read the number to me.

Wildlife Nuisance Control indeed, I thought, as I dialed the number from the phone at the unoccupied desk. The real nuisance in this case was the human beings. Had there been a number I could have called several months before to have Mrs. Endicott taken away, this whole scenario could have been avoided. There was a large poster of a white kitten on the wall of the Animal Control Center, the words "Adopt Me" writ large beneath the kitten's photograph. Lying on the desk in front of me was a brochure that featured cartoon dogs and cats prancing about on their hind legs, speaking into telephone receivers. "A License Is Your Pet's Free Phone Call Home," the brochure informed me.

After listening to the various recorded options, pressing the correct number and then listening to another series of options, pressing another number and going through the whole thing again, I finally hooked a live human being on the line who told me that the state didn't deal with my problem; all they could do was tell me how many trappers were licensed by the state to trap wild animals year round.

"What do they do with them?" I asked the woman on the phone.

"I don't know. You'd have to talk with them. It depends on the animal."

"Who would I call if I had a problem with skunks in Essex County?" I asked. In my peripheral vision I saw a brown blotch that was the uniformed Joanne, opening the door to the adjoining room to return to that howling hell from whence she'd come. A fresh wave of that ghastly odor of doggy death wafted into the room, and I clamped two fingers over my nose with my free hand.

"Let's see. Essex County," the voice murmured over the line. "For Essex County we'd give you the Trappers' Workshop."

After she gave me the phone number, I hung up on her and dialed the Trappers' Workshop. There was still a faint glimmer of hope. I imagined the trappers might take the animals they'd removed from people's yards and put them out in the wilderness again. I only had to find out where they'd taken my family.

"Hey, where are you calling now?" asked the linebacker at the desk behind me. "We can't have you running up our phone bill."

I took my hand from my nose to cover the receiver while I swiveled in my chair to face the fat bureaucrat. "It's a local call," I hissed. "If it weren't for—" A man's voice on the phone said "Hello?" It sounded as if I'd woken him up. I turned away from the pink mound of a person and back to the desk at which I was seated. I clamped my nose with my fingers again and said, "Hello, how are you today?"

"Alright," the man said groggily.

"Up all night trapping and torturing helpless animals, were we?" I said.

"What?" he asked, in a tone that let me know his attention had finally been captured.

"Nothing," I said. "I'm calling from *Trappers' World*, the monthly magazine," I said. "We wanted to send you a complimentary copy, but we've got two addresses for you on our mailing list, you murderous monster. Are you located at 54 Cherry Street?"

There was a pause during which I heard the man breathe in and out twice before slowly saying, "No."

"Oh, well, I guess you moved then," I said.

"We were never at no Cherry Street," he droned, and I realized this was a continuation of the sentence that had begun with "no," but that he had paused for so long between each word, I had interrupted him. I waited for a moment before going on.

"Hey, hey you," the obese woman said, near my shoulder.

"Well, there you go," I said to the trapper. "See, we just updated our database, and a lot of people's addresses have gotten mixed up. You know—computers." He didn't say anything, although I could hear him breathing. I glanced over my shoulder at the long-haired linebacker, whose expression was a mixture of dread and anger.

"You can't do this," she said, as she rose and went through the door through which Joanne had just gone. The man on the other end of the line still hadn't said anything. He must still be half asleep, I thought. "So what *is* your address?" I asked.

"What is it you're selling again?" the man asked.

I forced a laugh. "Oh, we're not selling anything sir. We're just sending trappers all over the country a free copy of our magazine. It's a promotional thing. You don't have to pay for anything."

With an explosion of barks, the door to the dog prison opened and Joanne and the fat woman came back into the room. I turned in my chair and smiled at them as if they were old buddies. Neither of them was smiling. Joanne stood in front of my desk and put her hands on her bony little hips. The linebacker went behind her desk and picked up the telephone. "I'm going to call 911," she warned.

"So what's that address?" I said into my phone.

"My address is 33 Holly Drive... Say, it sounds like you've got a lot of dogs there." I grabbed a pen out of a penholder on the desk and started writing on the back of an envelope.

"Oh, yes, we have dogs. What's the name of the town?" I asked, smiling up at Joanne like a maniac. I just needed the town name now, and I'd have him. I'd have my skunks back or I'd have revenge. If only the trapper didn't have to take so long to think of his own address.

"Look," Joanne said, "I don't know what you're trying to pull here—

"Winchester," the man said. "zip code, oh, two—"

"And how do you spell your last name?" I said.

"You have to leave this building immediately," Joanne said. I kept smiling, pointed to the phone and shrugged, hoping to express that I would truly have liked to give her my undivided attention, but was being kept from doing so by this intrusive phone call.

"G-i-b-b-o-n-s," the man said. "oh, two, nine—" I slammed the phone down and scribbled the name of the town and the man's last name on the envelope.

"Sue's going to call the police if you don't leave the building right now," Joanne said. I looked over at the heap of Sue, standing with the receiver to her ear and her corndog-sized finger poised above the key pad.

I raised my hands and held them in mock surrender. "Okay, fine, I'm leaving," I said. I didn't fear the police. I'd done nothing wrong. On the contrary—I'd been wronged, and if confronted by a police officer at that very moment, I'd have given him a large slice of my mind regarding the justice of the situation, which I'd been forced to take into my own hands. I would have added also a speech on the violation of my privacy, supposedly protected under the Fourth Amendment of our Constitution, but which had been violated by Mrs. Endicott several times over. I stood up from the desk, folded the envelope, my hands trembling, and put it in my pocket.

"Now you're stealing state property," Joanne announced, nodding at my pocket. Her voice and mannerisms were steady. She was much better than I at handling confrontations. She dealt with nuisances, day in, day out. Nuisance animals, nuisance humans—it was all the same to her. She could dispatch one nuisance as handily as another.

"It's only fair really. An eye for an eye," I said, though I took the envelope back out of my pocket. "The state has stolen my property. Why shouldn't I do the same?"

Joanne's eyes narrowed. "Because you can go to jail, that's why."

"Threats," I said. "Vague threats are all I ever get to my front, but then as soon as I turn my back, someone sinks a knife into it." I tore open the envelope and emptied the contents on the desk. "There," I said, turning to the big blond woman, "now you have no reason to call the police." I marched passed Joanne, folding the envelope and jamming it into my pocket as I headed for the door. "Unless," I said, turning to face them one last time, "you want to report the theft of an empty envelope." I could feel their eyes on me as I made my way across the parking lot to my car. That's the way to handle them, I told myself. Just plow right through their bluffs and get on with it.

My stomach rumbled as if in response to the sound of the gravel grinding under my tires as I pulled out of the parking lot and started down the road. I hadn't eaten for almost twenty-four hours. Still, I would have passed up a four-course meal for an eyedropper of skunk musk. My hands trembled on the steering wheel and I could no longer chalk it up to nervousness. A meal, even though it would have to be one without even a sprinkle of musk, might help steady me. But I couldn't bear the thought of going back to my deserted house. Surprisingly, I found my unsteady hands guiding the wheel of my automobile into

the drive-through of a fast-food restaurant. I'd eaten at one of them
once when I was in the seventh grade. Our house mother at Rigby
had taken us to a movie and we'd stopped there on the way home. The
advantage of these places, I recognized even then, was that one could
order one's food from a talking metal box. After procuring my meal, I
pulled into a parking space in which I intended to eat. There is something fantastically wrong with a society in which a machine becomes
the extension of an individual. One says, "I pulled into the parking
space," as if the vehicle, the enormous drain on natural resources in
which one does this pulling, need not even be mentioned. Anyhow,
the discrepancy between the pitifully small, soggy little sandwich I
extracted from the foil wrapper and the enormous, colorful picture I'd
seen on the menu board was so great that I assumed they were playing some sort of joke on me. When I lifted the top of the bun, I saw
that everything that had been promised was there, but in a drastically
smaller and paler form.

I could not remember from the seventh grade what the hamburgers had been like, but certainly they must have been more substantial
than this. As I munched on the tasteless food, I noticed the restaurant was in a very new building. The franchise owners were obviously
not serving what the corporation had advertised—they were trying
to cut costs by serving less. I couldn't grasp how, with a business plan
like that, they expected to stay open for longer than a week. The company will soon discover that they're being misrepresented, I thought,
or people in the area will soon realize the nature of the restaurant's
scam, and no one in town will come in more than once. For me, it
was the last in the long succession of short straws I'd pulled since the
previous afternoon.

I got out of the car and walked into the restaurant with the half-
eaten hamburger. When I stepped through the door, the stench of
grease hit me in the face like a soiled dishrag. There was no ventilation
and the humid, oily air that hung in the place seemed to have deep-
fried the complexion of the child behind the counter. This poor boy,
whose treacherous parents, I guessed, must have opened the doomed
eating establishment, were disregarding child labor laws by forcing
him to work, because he could not have been more than eleven years
of age. This state of things fueled the fire that had been ignited within
me the night before.

The little urchin asked if he could help me. His skin, where it was
not covered with red splotches, was as pale as if he'd been under-

ground for the past several years. The name "Shawn" was pinned on his sports shirt, which drooped from his shoulders as if it were on a wire hanger. Obviously Shawn's parents did not allow him to eat any of the product.

"Help me?" I said. "I only wish I could help you, young man." I tossed the remains of the hamburger onto the stainless steel counter. The paper wrapper came open and the top of the bun fell off, exposing the shriveled, gray piece of meat that might very well have been harvested from a murdered mouse. "Shawn," I announced, "the jig is up."

The boy's mouth hung open and he gazed at me with the most vacuous expression I'd ever encountered. I realized the heavy, greasy atmosphere must have impaired his mental functions, so I elaborated for him. "I'm sorry to have to inform you; I'd have preferred to speak directly to your parents, but I don't have all day to run around warning people about the future—this is as far as my benevolence goes. You can tell your folks this place won't last another month, and that's giving you the benefit of the doubt." Shawn seemed not to comprehend the words I spoke. I could feel the blood rising in my cheeks.

"Uh, did you want a refund?" he asked, in a voice that was much deeper than I'd expected.

"A refund?" I exclaimed. "You people are going to need all your pennies," I said, as I turned and gestured toward the rest of the room, "when this place goes under." There was a young couple, an old couple and a mother with two toddlers in the restaurant. They all chewed slowly, watching Shawn and me like a bunch of cows in a hot, sunny pasture, awaiting slaughter. I turned back to Shawn. I made no effort to control myself. Rage had taken me over completely. "Do you honestly believe you'll be seeing any of these customers ever again?" I demanded, waving in the direction of the diners. Shawn said nothing. I reached across the counter, grabbed his collar with both hands and pulled him toward me. "You don't have to live in this ignominy!" I yelled. "Don't you understand? Don't let them push you around. Don't live like this! Do something!"

The boy slapped at my wrists with his bony hands. "Yo. Get off me, man," he said.

I released his collar. "Nothing is sacred anymore. Don't you see! They'll take everything from you, believe me, they will! They'll take this, this right here!" I lifted the cash register up off the counter.

"I'm gonna call the cops, you don't get outta here," Shawn said, backing away.

"Unbelievable," I said. I dropped the register back onto the counter with a thud. "That's the third time someone's promised me that in the last fifteen hours." I turned to face my fellow diners, who had all stopped eating to give me their bovine attention. I raised a finger in the air. "We'll call the cops! Of course! Whenever someone challenges our narrow view of the world, we call the cops! It's a wonderful life! We don't have to accommodate anyone we don't agree with, no."

"You're fucked," Shawn mumbled.

I whirled around to face him. "And it's all in the name of the common good, I suppose!"

Someone, who had appeared from nowhere, was now standing at my side. "Sir," he said.

"We make laws!" I went on. "We banish the people who don't fit in, or we make their lives so intolerable they banish themselves and live in self-imposed exile."

"Sir," the person next to me said again.

"What!" I said, turning suddenly to glare at him.

He took a step backward. He was dressed in blue and his tag identified him as the manager. "I'm going to have to ask you to leave the restaurant."

I looked at Shawn, who watched me the way one might watch a vicious dog that has suddenly broken from its leash. This was my thanks for attempting to rescue the starveling soul. I was suddenly very tired. My whole body seemed to get heavier while I stood there in front of the manager. "Fine," I said. "Banish me then. But I, for one, refuse to tolerate this state of affairs any longer. I know what I have to do. I'm standing up for myself. I'm going to recover what is rightfully mine and then I'm going to leave all this behind. You'll see!" I raised my voice again and directed my speech at the young couple cowering over their mouse burgers, trying to avoid my eyes. "There's only so much a man can be expected to take. Unless he wants to give up being a man and become what you are—a mouse! A mouse living in a burgh of mice." I turned to the manager and glared at him. "And you. You are the chief mouse-burgher," I said, and took my leave.

9

Though it was only forty miles west of New Essex, there had never been circumstances such as those with which I was now faced compelling me to visit Winchester. Driving west, the landscape unfurling by my windows quickly became rural. I'd begun to perspire profusely and the trembling of my hands had gotten to a point where I had trouble using the turn signal. My nausea was worsening, and the adventure in the fast food restaurant had given me a hammering headache. The recovery of my skunks meant not only a relief of these symptoms and the rescue of my most loyal friends, but also, I saw now, a kind of redemption after the demoralizing emotional violation I'd endured the previous evening. Quite a lot was riding on Mr. Gibbons. So I couldn't just barge into the Trappers' Workshop—whatever that was—and start throwing half-eaten sandwiches around. I was going to have to behave in a more civilized manner if I were to enlist anyone's help in the recovery of the family.

I'm not sure what I expected from the Trappers' Workshop. More people marching around in brown uniforms with state seals on their shoulders, I suppose. Maybe there would be a wretched, stinking kennel like the one at the Animal Control Center, only this one would be filled with raccoons, possums and skunks instead of cats and dogs. But when I got to 33 Holly Drive, I found myself pulling up in front of a tan trailer beached in a large clearing in the woods. The name "Gibbons" was stenciled on the battered black mailbox by the road, next to the short dirt driveway. "Trappers Workshop," sans apostrophe, was painted on a piece of plywood and nailed to a stake that had been pounded in the ground next to the mailbox.

I parked on the road and walked down the driveway. The storm had strewn a few tree limbs around the brown yard in front of the trailer. As I got closer, I realized it was a private residence, not just a place of business. The blinds of the large window in front were shut against the daylight. Dried rust streams trickled down the aluminum siding from the corners of the windows and over the cracked concrete foundation upon which the trailer rested. There was no doorbell, so I rapped on the brittle screen door. I could hear a television on inside, but no one came to the door. Sticking my hand through a large tear in the middle of the screen, I knocked on the main door, which looked as if it had been kicked many times over by black-soled shoes. There was an area near the bottom of the door where the paint had been completely scratched away, doubtless by the insistent paws of the trapper's best friend.

The door swung open and I had to look up to see the face of the large man who stood before me. The odor of macaroni and cheese, mingled with the scent of stale cigarette butts, wafted through the screen door. Unwashed clumps of hair hung over the sides of the man's collar. He wore a thick beard and even thicker glasses that made his eyes appear much larger than they were. A black-and-white checkered flannel shirt hung over his sagging blue jeans.

"Hello," I said. "You must be Mr. Gibbons."

"Yeah," he said slowly. "I am." I recognized the deliberate, heavy quality of speech from our telephone conversation.

"I would like to ask you a few questions." He seemed to stiffen slightly. I didn't want to put him on the defensive right away. I could very easily imagine the response, "None of your business," coming from this man. I thought it might be best to appear friendly until I'd ascertained the whereabouts of my skunks. "I was wondering if you could tell me a little about the Trappers' Workshop," I said. "I've actually just taken up trapping as a hobby."

Mr. Gibbons seemed to consider this proposition for a moment. "You wanna come inside?" he said, again speaking so slowly it sounded like a record playing at the wrong speed. He pushed open the screen door with one hand and extended the other. "My name's Jerome. Everybody calls me Jerry." I shook his hand, an experience quite like grasping a side of beef in the supermarket, except that it was warm.

"Joseph," I said, giving him a smile as fake as the name as he ushered me into the trailer. It was extremely dark and the television screen was the only thing I could see very well at first. While Jerry closed the door behind me, I noticed there was a game show in progress. When they were not being interrupted by bells and buzzers, people answered ridiculous questions posed by a man whose hair appeared to be ceramic. The light from the television gradually revealed the shapes of other objects in the dark-paneled room—a couch, recliner, and a coffee table in front of which lay a stinking bag of garbage. I noticed some movement on the couch, and was surprised to see a pair of hands knitting while a pair of eyes peered at me through the murky light.

"This is my wife, Midge," Jerry said, as he stepped around me.

"A pleasure, I'm sure," I said. The frumpy woman with a face like a puff pastry glared at me distrustfully while her hands worked the knitting needles with unnerving speed. During the occasional silences of the television, I could hear the persistent clicks the needles made when they touched.

"He's one of 'em," Midge muttered.

Jerry didn't seem to hear her and before I could inquire what I was one of, the bag of garbage rose from the floor, the blue light of the television glinting from its eyes. It stood facing me on four wobbly legs and let out an excruciated howl.

"Shut up, Sam," Jerry said. "Never mind him, he's so old and blind he don't even know where he's at." As my eyes adjusted to the light, I could see that the black hair of the mutt had been rubbed off of its backside and the skin was red and inflamed. The act of standing had stirred up the smell of rot that emanated from him. He suddenly dropped his rear and twisted his head backward to gnaw at the bald spot on his back, which must have been hopping with fleas. Then, having already forgotten my existence, Sam lowered himself the rest of the way down to the carpet like an arthritic old man, as Jerry eased himself into the green vinyl recliner that crunched with his weight.

This is the way of the trapper, I thought. He lures you in. What he lacks in speed and agility, he makes up for with cunning and patience. "Have a seat," he said, indicating a chair across from him, on the other side of a coffee table littered with open magazines, ashtrays, silverware and bowls that still contained a few stray pieces of macaroni and small orange pools of processed cheese. My stomach lurched, and for the second time that day, I had to breathe through my mouth to avoid nausea. It was all I could do to keep my trembling hands clamped on my knees as I sat on the edge of the soft chair. Both the couch and the recliner were draped with afghans. Jerry leaned forward, an effort impeded by his burgeoning belly, picked up the remote control and dropped it again. A final buzzer was truncated and the laminated-looking face and hair of the game show host disappeared into darkness. There was a crackle of static and then only the rhythmic clicking of Midge's needles as Jerry flicked on a lamp beside his chair. Midge continued to watch me. The decal on her pink sweater depicted two rabbits in a patch of grass, standing on their hind legs, hugging. She held her crocheting low enough that I could read the words, "Some bunny loves me," stretched across her stomach beneath the rabbits. Jerry picked a box of cigarettes from beside the remote control, pulled back the lid and extended it to me.

"No, thanks," I said.

Jerry took a cigarette from the box, lit it with a black plastic lighter, and then dropped the box and the lighter back on the coffee table in the same careless manner he'd dropped the remote control. He sucked his first drag deep into his lungs and then exhaled as he settled back into the recliner. I tried to hunker down in my chair, hoping the smoke would rise above me. Whenever I am forced to endure the stench of cigarettes, I have to wash all my clothes and take a shower as soon as I return home, because the odor of ash clings to the fabrics, the hair, the skin, and quite simply makes one's very existence all but intolerable.

"What dija wanna ask about?" Jerry said, in his lugubrious baritone. Now he and Midge were both staring at me intently.

I glanced at the black television screen, and then down at the carpet, which was one of those repulsive shag ordeals. It appeared to be the Halloween special—a casserole of black, orange and brown yarn that was worn away like heavily trampled grass in front of Jerry's recliner and between the couch and the coffee table. Sam had gone back to sleep, only a few feet in front of me, and he must have passed gas, because a septic smell, that I could no more avoid than I could duck Jerry's smoke, drifted up to my nostrils.

"I was wondering if you could describe for me the function of the Trappers' Workshop," I said.

"Well, the workshop end of things is kinda on hold," he said. "I teach people trapping techniques, but I haven't had a lot of people answering my ads lately."

"But you also deal with nuisance problems in Essex County, correct?"

Jerry took a drag from his cigarette and regarded me silently for a moment. Midge's knitting needles filled the silence with their furious clicking. Cigarette smoke hung in the air like a tissue-paper curtain I imagined poking holes in with my fingers. "How'd you get that lump on your head?" Jerry asked, staring at my forehead with those eyes that his glasses made look like two fish in separate fish bowls.

I put my trembling fingers to my forehead and remembered how I'd banged it against the steering wheel of my car the night before. The lump there felt like a golf ball; I'd been so preoccupied by my withdrawal symptoms that I'd completely forgotten about it. Shakily, I pushed my glasses up the bridge of my nose. I felt a bead of sweat roll from my armpit down the inside of my arm. "I-I had a bit of a spill. That storm last night, I—"

"They didn't send you from the SAFETYS, did they?" Jerry asked.

"SAFETYS? No. What in heaven's name are the SAFETYS?"

The vinyl of Jerry's recliner crunched as he leaned forward to stub out his cigarette in the ashtray on the coffee table. Small eruptions of smoke issued from his nostrils and mouth as he spoke the words, "The Society for Animal Freedom and Ethical Treatment Standards." The combination of the cigarette smoke and macaroni-and-cheese must have made his beard reek like a humidor that had burst into flames and then been extinguished in a vat of milk. I couldn't see how he could stand to wear the filthy thing on his face.

"No, I don't represent any organization." I looked at Midge. "SAFE-TYS," I said, struck by the inanity of the name. "Imagine that."

Midge opened her mouth for the second time, and the sound emitted from that gap in her puffy face was not unlike the yap of Mrs. Endicott's Chihuahua. "You a reporter then? Ya look like a newspaper man," she said, without hesitating the slightest in her knitting. She continued to stare at me unblinkingly while my hands trembled on my knees.

Though I'd come here prepared to do whatever necessary to get Homer and the family back, something in the ways of these people shook my conviction. The sense of purpose, in which I'd felt justified for dealing harshly with the people at the restaurant and the Animal Control Center, seemed to be draining from my system like dirty bath water after the plug has been pulled. I would have given my right arm for a shot of musk to relieve the increasing pain in my head and stomach. To avoid Midge's gaze, I glanced at the television set again. In a photograph on top of it, Midge, Jerry and a younger version of Midge with a son of about eight years were all trapped in a photographer's studio, looking as if they feared the camera in front of them might explode. I don't know why I should have felt such sadness at the sight of this family, determined as they were—in spite of the rusty trailer, the macaroni and cheese, the scent of stagnation that hung over their lives—to huddle together and grin for a photograph. The younger Midge looked like a supermarket employee, a bagger of groceries, and the boy, with thick glasses like his grandfather, looked like the friendless sort of child who sits by himself in the corner of the schoolyard at recess. The sort of child I had been. Still sweating as I sat there, I found myself pushing my own glasses up the bridge of my nose again.

Jerry made the moment easier for me. "I got a license from the state to trap year round," he said. "So if someone's got a problem with raccoons or whatever, they get referred to me and I can come and take care of the problem."

I looked down at the ugly carpet and the malodorous dog festering upon it. "I see," I murmured. "The problem." I thought of Homer
sitting on a stool in the kitchen, watching and listening while I cooked
breakfast and confided in him. I thought of how he'd walked right into
the hutch I'd built for him when I first brought him home, and how
he'd walked out again, looked up at me and blinked his amber eyes. I
thought of Louisa giving birth, and of Rupert and Helga wrestling on
the floor of the den while I listened to Brahms and sipped a cup of tea.
The problem.

"It sure helps sometimes," Jerry said after a moment of silence.
"Midge and I been trying to make it on our own, but I haven't had a lot
of work coming my way lately."

I looked up at Jerry. This was the face of an executioner. Not the uniformed, shaved and scrubbed militant I'd seen in the person of Joanne
at the Animal Control Center. The state had its dirty work done by this
dim-witted lummox, an outcast living on the edge of the county.

Fear, anger and sadness welled up in my throat. "How," I began in
a gargle, then cleared my throat. "How would you take care of a skunk
problem? Say someone had a problem with skunks in her backyard."

Jerry leaned forward and lit another cigarette. "I'd use a box trap.
Or two, depending on how many there was."

"What do you do with them after you've caught them?" My voice
quivered. With one hand I kneaded the knuckles of the other. "Do
you take them somewhere and release them in the wild?" I glanced
at Midge, and something in her face told me my skunks were gone
forever. Needing some other place to rest my eyes, I looked down at
the repulsive dog, then at the cluttered coffee table.

"No," Jerry said. "With skunks, the state requires that they be
destroyed."

The tears burned in my eyes but I kept swallowing to keep them
down. "By what method do you destroy them?" I asked, measuring
each word. I could not look at Jerry now. Instead, I stared intently
at the ash tray on the table. I felt that if I shifted my gaze, the whole
world would spin around me like an unsteady carousel and possibly
fly to pieces. My intensity was making Jerry uncomfortable. He shifted
his girth about in the crunching green recliner.

"They're drowned," he said finally. "They never come out of the trap."

"And did you happen," my voice cracked shrilly on the word "happen," "to 'take care' of some skunks in this manner last night?"

"Yeah, I did."

To hide my face from Jerry and Midge, I put my hand to my forehead and pretend the lump was bothering me. "And did you take them from 49 Springer Street in New Essex?" I asked.

"Yeah."

The word fell like a heap of stones on my shoulders. My body shuddered under the weight. "Oh God," I said. I tried to fight the sinking feeling. "Where are they?" I gasped.

"You can't see 'em," Jerry said. "I already buried 'em."

I looked up at Jerry. "You don't understand," I said. "They were like family to me. You can show me where they're buried, can't you?"

Midge's knitting needles continued their metronomic clicking. She and Jerry exchanged a look. "I guess so," he said, returning his gaze to me. "They're out back." He stubbed out his cigarette and heaved himself out of the recliner. Sam opened his eyes and raised himself again on his shaking stick legs and spiritlessly wagged his frayed tail once or twice, renewing the aroma of rotting garbage. "That's alright Sam," Jerry said, in a soothing tone as he walked out of the room. I followed him through the kitchen and into the back yard. The sun was low on the horizon, making long, dark needles of the shadows of the trees along the backyard. Jerry plodded slowly across the dead grass. "I didn't have no way of knowing they belonged to anybody," he said.

"I don't suppose Mrs. Endicott told you they'd come over from my yard," I said.

Jerry looked down at the ground as he walked. "No. She just told me they'd been in her yard for a while and that they wouldn't leave. She said the whole neighborhood was complaining about them."

Next to a tool shed there were several metal traps stacked up and behind the shed a large, rusted barrel filled with water. "Is this where you drown them?" I asked.

The afternoon sun glinted on Jerry's glasses, obscuring his eyes. His beefy hands dangled guiltily at his sides and he breathed heavily through his nose. "Yeah, that's it," he said.

Any of the traps stacked next to the shed, turned sideways, would fit easily into the barrel, and could be entirely submerged. The sky would have been filled with dark clouds by the time Homer reached this destination. The wind would have been picking up, and possibly the first few drops of rain were plinking on the tin roof of the tool shed. Homer might have scrambled around frantically in the trap as Jerry lowered it into the barrel and I hurried into the jewelry store. Perhaps Homer had died at the very moment I spotted Pearl's ring, or maybe later, when I was in her devastated laboratory, making my first horrible discovery of the night. There might have been a flash of lightning which constricted the pupils of Homer's eyes, and in which he got his last, terrified glimpse of the world. For an instant, he would have seen the desolate back yard, the trailer, the trees among which he would finally be put to rest, and the strange face of the trapper above him. And then nothing; the cold, liquid darkness closing over his head, filling his tiny lungs as the life was choked out of him.

I put both hands on the rim of the barrel and leaned over it, as if by staring persistently I would be able to see to the bottom; as if the inability to make sense of loss were only some temporary weakness of the senses, a kind of nearsightedness that, with determination, could be overcome. I choked on a sob that found its way out of my throat and a short string of snot shot out of my nose. I walked around to the other side of the shed, doubled over and vomited in the brown grass. There was very little in my stomach. The yellow bile that burned my throat on the way up left a sticky, acidic coating over my tongue and teeth.

When I came back around the other side of the shed, Jerry was still standing there, looking ashamed. I pitied him—this poor, oversized tool used by a society that gave him so little in return. I wanted to go to him and put my arms around him and tell him that it was going to be alright, that even though he'd had a miserable, lonely childhood punctuated by taunts and jeers, that even though he was an outcast, that even though he lived in a fetid trailer that his wife seemed determined to fill with useless afghans, that even though he knew no way of improving his standard of living, and the father of his daughter's child was not in the picture, still, everything was going to be alright. But nothing was going to be alright. Life had dealt Jerry a lousy hand and nothing short of a miracle was going to improve it. I suspected that he knew it as well as I knew nothing was going to redeem my own life.

"You still sure you want to see where they's buried?" Jerry asked.

"Yes, I'm quite sure."

"There's a spot back in the woods," he said. He turned, his large belly seeming to guide the rest of his body, and lumbered toward the woods that lined the back of his yard. We followed a vague path about thirty feet into the woods and Jerry stopped at a small clearing where the ground was raised here and there in small mounds. He pointed to one covered with freshly turned soil. "It's that one there," he said.

I went over and stood in front of it. "Could I have a few moments alone?" I said.

"Sure, yeah. I'll be in the house," Jerry said. He turned and trudged back down the path.

I imagined the smushed, furry lump of the family in the shallow grave before which I stood. I wished I could have at least closed Homer's eyes for him with my own hands. The thought of him being buried with his eyes still open to the final terror was almost as unbearable as the murder itself. "I'm sorry, old boy," I said. "I'm so terribly, terribly sorry."

As if Homer, from beyond the grave, were calling to me, I suddenly remembered a very small eyedropper jar of his musk I had long ago stashed in the glove compartment of the Eldorado and then forgotten about. My respects perhaps only half paid, still teary-eyed and disconsolate, I skirted the woods past the Gibbons' trailer, hurried across the dead yard strewn with broken branches from the storm, and got into my car. The crumpled box containing Pearl's ring rolled out into my hand when I opened the glove compartment and I immediately tossed it under the seat to get it out of my sight. I located the jar beneath the Eldorado's title and registration, unscrewed the cap and squeezed two delicious drops of musk into my mouth. The scent made me think of the first time I'd seen Homer rooting about in the woods, how I'd captured him with a burlap sack, and how happy he'd been when I brought Louisa to him. Now I would have to do my best to forget him forever.

With the sun setting and my hands finally steadying, I started the car and pulled away from poor Jerry's workshop. The shadows of trees ribbed the road and bands of light flickered across my windshield as I drove along. I kept the small jar in one hand so that when the emotions threatened to overcome me, I could sniff from it, instead of blowing, as another mourner might, into a handkerchief. So on I drove, sniffing skunk musk and stifling memories. "All that was lost in the storm," I said to myself out loud, as if my life had been a boat upon which Pearl, the skunks and I had been sailing along until the storm destroyed it and drowned everyone, leaving me a castaway. This fantasy had the pleasing effect of relieving me of responsibility. "They were all lost in the storm," I said again. Holding the jar to my nose, I pointed the prow of the Eldorado west and drove.

10

And drove and drove. I drove through the night, all through the next day and into the next night. I hardly paid attention to where I was going; what mattered was that I was going and what propelled me was the notion that with each mile I was putting the past further behind me. I intended to continue driving until I reached some kind of conclusion about my life. Sometime during the second night my eyes began drooping shut on their own. I pulled over to the side of the road and turned off the car. The engine ticked as it cooled; the chirping of crickets and the smell of the woods in the darkness around me filled the car as I curled up on the seat and fell asleep.

When I awoke, the sun was directly overhead. My limbs were stiff and I had a stale taste in my mouth. There were woods on both sides of the road and as far ahead as I could see. I got out of the car to urinate. Where I had pulled over, there was a rutted dirt road that led through the woods. Wondering where it might lead, I got back in the car and drove—bouncing up and down on the seat as I navigated the hills and gullies of the winding road—approximately a mile and a half, at which point a short driveway appeared to my left that opened up into a clearing the size of a couple of football fields. I pulled in. Crouched in the corner of the clearing near the driveway was a small log cabin with a chicken coop beside it. I parked next to the cabin and got out to survey the abandoned farm. But what a strange little farm. Not enough land had been cleared for it to be of commercial use, and the chicken coop was built only a few yards from the cabin, as if the farmer had not wanted to have to walk far to get his eggs in the morning. The trees around the clearing were so close together that they seemed to form an enormous fence. But the forest was beginning to reclaim the farm—tall grasses, a smattering of saplings and clumps of shrubs sprang up here and there. After circling the property on foot, I came back to the little cabin. There was a Winchell Real Estate sign planted in the ground in front of it that I hadn't noticed at first because it was as brown and parched as the cabin itself. When I pushed the cabin door, it swung open with a creak and thudded against the wall. The cabin was a one-room affair with a dirt floor, a Franklin stove at one end, a heavy wooden bed frame with a water-stained mattress folded on it at the other. There was a crude wooden table in between, and a rocking chair in the corner. The windows were covered with cobwebs in which the husks of ancient spiders were curled into little balls. A bowl with a spoon in it sat on the table. Somehow, it seemed there ought to be a skeleton, dressed in a flannel shirt and overalls, sitting at the table with his bone fingers wrapped around a spoon, his jaw hanging agape, staring at me from the depths of his empty sockets.

As I discovered when I drove to the nearest approximation of civilization to find the real estate office, I was in a town called Highbridge, closer to the center of the United States than I had ever been, where next-door neighbors lived miles and miles apart amid great expanses of field and forest, where combines and pickup trucks roamed in lieu of Indian tribes and buffalo. Downtown consisted of a couple of blocks of businesses on Main Street. If one had a sneezing attack while driving down this street, chances are one would miss Highbridge entirely. There was no bridge in the town, though there was a monument in the grassy square in the town center that featured a life-sized statue of John Highbridge—coonskin cap, musket, et cetera—and a plaque that distinguished him as a "Pioneer." For all the plaque let me know, he might have been a pioneer in the business of frontier fashion design.

Taking a whiff of Homer's musk to steady my nerves, I walked into the Winchell Real Estate office, where two paunchy men with the same bulbous nose, one older, and one about my age, sat in their shirtsleeves, without neckties, leaning back from their cluttered desks. They talked and sipped coffee from Styrofoam cups. One got the impression that this was an office in which the phone seldom rang. The younger of the men swung his head lazily in my direction to ask how I was doing. I told him the address of the property I was interested in purchasing. He offered to take me there, but I said I had already seen it and was willing to make an offer.

"So, you're going to buy the farm?" he said, smiling. I wasn't sure if he was trying to be witty.

"That's the old Krauthammer place, isn't it?" the older man said, looking up from his coffee cup for the first time.

"That's right," the younger one said.

"I remember that guy. God he was weird. Had this big beard and long hair. I think he wanted to grow wheat on that property. He was against the government—or maybe it was pesticides. I don't know; he was against something. He was some kinda artist, too. Played the banjo and all that. Everyone thought he was a pervert."

"Well, I can assure you I won't be doing any banjo playing," I said. Both men started laughing. "I'm just going to be subsistence farming and that shouldn't bother anyone." They both stopped laughing, glanced at each other and then down at their coffees. A familiar feeling began creeping up my spine—a feeling that reminded me of my days at Grund & Greene. I suspected there would be a discussion about me once I left the room. "Well," I said, "that's enough small talk. Suppose we get down to brass tacks."

They got out a yellow-crusted blueprint of the property. The name "KRAUTHAMMER" was written in capitals like a stamp of condemnation in the middle of the clearing. The clearing occupied the southeast corner of fifty acres of property, most of which was wooded. The property's boundaries were the dirt road I'd driven down that morning, which I could see now was called Fisher Lane, and two other lines, one of which squiggled like a snake across the page for a reason I would discover later.

When the Winchells said I could have the place for a song, I offered them my own rendition of "Whiskey in the Jar." When they changed their minds and asked for money, it was to the tune of a much smaller sum than might have been expected, which I gathered was because of vague and superstitious reasons regarding the effects of Mr. Krauthammer's occupation of the land. I put a down payment on the place and drove back across the country to New Essex. This time I stopped twice at rest stops along the way to sleep for a few hours.

When I pulled in the driveway to my old house, I was surprised that nothing had changed. I'd expected the place to have been hit by lightning and burned to the ground, leaving only a blackened foundation, a few charred lumps barely distinguishable as the bathtub, sinks and half-melted refrigerator. But the only actual evidence of the storm was a branch or two lying in the grass of the front yard. My house stood there, sad and gray as ever, behind its square green hedge.

The first thing I did was sit down and write the last document I would write on my computer. This was a letter of resignation. "Dear Mr. Piper," I wrote. "Recent events in my life have revealed to me the necessity for a dramatic change. Unfortunately, this change is going to be so dramatic that I will no longer be available to work for Grund & Greene. As you probably know, I am not one to give in to spontaneous impulses. But I can only be true to my nature, and the road my nature has led me down is one of dirt and grass, no longer of concrete and asphalt. In short, I lost everything in the recent storm and, consequently, have decided to lose myself. Consider me lost.

"I am sure you will be able to find a competent copywriter to fill my position. I do not regret the years of service I've dedicated to the company. On the contrary, I am grateful for having had the opportunity to be of service at Grund & Greene and to have made your acquaintance.

"Sincerely, Damien Youngquist."

There, it's done, I thought, as I clicked "print" for the last time and watched the letter like a tongue spitting itself from the mouth of the printer. There's no turning back now—with this course of action, I've quite definitively and finally stuck out my tongue at conventional society. If I've made a mistake, so be it. It was another consequence of the storm. Perhaps, it occurred to me, I really had been lost in that storm.

The next thing I did was call a realtor and put my house on the market. It didn't take long to sell. The neighborhood was becoming a trendy one for young families, and a series of these paraded through the place during an open house. I felt like an undertaker standing around a funeral parlor, while Janine, the realtor and middle-aged divorcée, flitted about and chirped to everyone about closet space and the wonderful location. Through her plastic smile, she kept saying, "And it's just a stone's throw from downtown," with the sprightly idiocy that seems to possess every salesperson like a poltergeist. "Just a *stone's* throw. But this neighborhood is so peaceful, when you sit in the back yard you might as well be out in cow country."

While this sort of nonsense was taking place, I went out in the back yard, sat in a lawn chair and took tiny sips of musk. Luckily, I still had a bit of each member of the family's musk left in the mason jars. Janine told people the hutch I'd built was a dog house. "With this fenced-in yard it's a perfect place to have a dog," she'd eagerly pointed out to one of the couples. There were two holes in the yard: the one Homer had used to stay in when he'd first arrived, and the one by the fence he'd used to leave by. I remembered something I'd forgotten to do. I went back into the house, took Homer and Louisa's wedding picture out of the frame sitting at my desk, crumpled it up and threw it in a waste basket. Then I was confronted with the recently married couple that eventually took the house. They told me they were thinking about starting a family.

"Oh for heaven's sakes, spare yourselves the agony," I said. The couple then subjected me to a pair of scrutinizing looks to which I felt I had to respond. "I mean don't try that in this neighborhood," I said. "They'll take the family away while you're out at the jewelry store." The young woman stepped closer to the man and he put his arm around her. Janine must have been within earshot because suddenly she appeared and wedged herself between me and the couple.

"Mr. Youngquist is just kidding, aren't you Mr. Youngquist?" She shot me a venomous smile, then showed me her back. "The neighbors are wonderful in fact," she said, as she began hustling the couple away from me. "Would you two like to meet the nice old lady who lives next door?"

Nice old lady? Could she have been referring to none other than the scuttlebutt, the ruthless kidnapper, the felonious old crone, Mrs. Endicott? God only knew the extent of the horrors in store for the newlyweds.

I had a yard sale and got rid of my furniture, computer, much of my clothing and, in fact, any of my possessions that would not fit in the trunk of the Eldorado. But the night before I did this, I bestowed a few gifts upon my neighbors. I opened each cage of the insects I'd kept to feed the family in a different neighbor's yard. There were termites for Mrs. Rogers, grasshoppers and crickets for the Wainrights, grubs and ants for Ben Finder, and spiders for the Johnsons. I saved the field mice for Mrs. Endicott. First transferring them all to a smaller cage, I carried them into her backyard. The only thing I was worried about was Tesa, the Chihuahua, whom I knew sometimes slept near the back door. I crept into the back yard so slowly, so quietly, that the sound of the mice rustling about in the cage seemed loud. The cellar door was unlocked, so I went down the steps into it before opening the mouse cage. "Please make your home within the walls of this witch's house," I whispered, as I raised the door to the cage. "Be fruitful and multiply," I said, as they swarmed out of the cage and around the floor of the cellar.

Despite my frantic busyness, I found myself thinking of Pearl. All during the yard sale, while my neighbors and their friends, like ants at a picnic, sorted through my belongings and carried them off, I fantasized about Pearl driving up to the house, expecting to pay me one of her little sex visits. I would be too busy haggling over the price of a bureau to notice when the Tempest pulled up. After sitting in her car for a moment, stupefied by my decisive action, she would suddenly realize what she'd thrown away by reuniting with her country club boyfriend. She would then cross the lawn to me. She would come up from behind and shyly tug at my sleeve. I'd turn around casually, slightly miffed by the interruption, but too well mannered to completely ignore someone trying to get my attention. "Oh, hello there,"

I'd say with amusement, as if I'd run into some casual acquaintance. When she asked why I was leaving, I'd wave my hand dismissively at the house, the yard sale, and say, "Oh, you know, this lifestyle has gotten tiresome. I can't be held down like this. It's simply time for me to be moving on."

However, at the end of the second day of the yard sale, I began to have fantasies of a much different nature. Most of my belongings were gone—only a few picked-over items remained scattered about the yard. I sat on a folding chair, occasionally taking a drop or two of musk. An older couple was looking over the cages in which I'd kept the insects and mice in the garage. There were only a few other objects left—a coffee table, a slightly skunk-scratched armchair and a porcelain lamp, and most of the cages from the garage. I gazed vacantly over the yard while entertaining gruesomely painful visions of Pearl. I saw her reunited with Richard, the two of them eating sushi on the deck of a sailboat somewhere in the South Pacific. I saw her working with him in a secret laboratory at NewGenetics. I saw her demonstrating the viability of SeaLawn for Richard, as she had for me, and then Richard, tall, suave, sandy-haired, pulling Pearl toward him. "Oh darling, you're so brilliant," he says. She blushes and looks down, flattered. "Hey," he whispers, and lifts her chin with his index finger.

"What are these for, rabbits?" I heard someone say in the midst of my daymare.

Richard lowers his eyelids, they both allow their lips to part as their faces come together in a kiss. She puts her hands to the sides of his head and runs her fingers through his hair.

"Hey," the voice said. "Hey you."

He slips his hand into her bathrobe and pulls it open to reveal her soft, white belly, her red bikini.

An older man's face was suddenly inches from mine, replacing Pearl's soft body. "Hello, is anyone in there?" There were bags of wrinkles beneath his bloodshot eyes, wiry white hair stuck out from the sides of his head, and tiny tufts of hair bloomed from his nostrils. He was hunched forward with his hands on his knees like a fatigued athlete catching his breath. "Is this your stuff here or what?"

"What?" I said.

The man sighed and looked over at his wife, who was opening and closing the door to one of the cages. He turned back to me like an exasperated parent. "I said, is this your stuff?" He waved his hand at the remaining articles standing about in my yard.

I looked them over slowly. I hadn't gotten much sleep during the five days since the storm. "Yes, these things belong to me," I said, though the words sounded as if someone else had said them. I was still half lost in my unhappy fantasy. Richard pulls the strings that tie her bikini top together. It falls to the ground between them. He and Pearl look at each other and giggle.

"What do you use those things for, keeping rabbits in?" the old man asked.

"Rabbits," I said.

He slips his hand down into her bikini bottom, penetrates the bristly little bush and crooks a finger up inside of her where it's warm and damp.

The old man sighed and straightened up. "Yeah, you know, rabbits. Little furry guys? Hop around all day and eat carrots? Like to make lots of little baby rabbits?"

"No. Skunks," I said. "I kept skunks. That is why I'm leaving here."

"Skunks?" He looked at the cages again. "Well, I'll be damned. What the hell were you doing with skunks? Now that you mention it, they still kinda smell like skunks—or *something* around here does." He threw me an accusatory glance.

"I didn't keep them in those," I said. "I kept their food in there. Those are bug cages."

"Bug cages," the man said. "Right. Well, I guess they look like they'd be okay for rabbits anyway. How much you want for 'em?"

"Just take them," I said.

"For free? I've gotta give you something for 'em."

"Twenty dollars, then."

The man smiled. "Fifteen," he said.

How absurd can people be? I wondered. As he smiled down at me, an expression of triumph on his face, I wondered how his expression would change if one were to light his nostril hair on fire. After a moment I said, "Fine, fifteen it is."

"Done," he said, cheerily.

A few days later, with no forwarding address given to anyone, I had all my belongings packed into the Eldorado and was headed out to the farm. I wouldn't need much in the cabin. My aim was to pare life down to its essentials, to get closer to nature, to become a farmer. I had two polyester suits in addition to the one I wore, three neckties and the sturdy shoes I'd always worn to Grund & Greene. I thought this would be sufficient.

I have read travel accounts, but still I fail to see how anyone could derive much pleasure from perpetual discomfort, which is precisely what travel is. Sleeping in my car at rest stops, watching the highway scroll endlessly into the distance, constantly flexing one, then the other, of my aching buttocks, enduring the grubby, unsanitary conditions of public restrooms and the boisterousness and malodorousness of my fellow travelers, I grew increasingly annoyed with the entire business. Travel is simply a grueling, tedious, filthy undertaking. How else could one explain the physical state of the majority of truckers I saw along the way, most of whom resembled Jerry the trapper? On top of all this, I was depleting my reserves of musk more quickly than I'd anticipated. I pressed steadily on the gas pedal, thinking of my cozy cabin and how soon I would be enjoying a fresh shot of musk squeezed from a real country skunk.

The night I got to the site of my future farm, I was so happy I leapt out of the car and ran to the middle of the field. The cabin, the clearing, and the surrounding woods were all mine. And best of all, there was nothing in sight that suggested the presence of human beings— nothing but the cabin, which was acceptable, since it only suggested my own presence, which though unpleasant was as close as I could hope to come to nothing. Nothing is a form of completion, I believe. And infinity can be found in a black hole.

The stars shone more brightly here than they had in New Essex, though half of them were obscured by clouds. I pulled a jar of musk from my coat pocket, unscrewed the cap and held it aloft. "A toast!" I declared, there in the middle of my plot of land. "To Homer. Your sacrifice will not be forgotten! I shall live and prosper in the wilderness as you once did, and I hereby dedicate all my acts to your memory. And henceforth, my furry friend, I shall do my best to forget you entirely. The only true and loyal companion I ever had, may you rest in eternal peace. And to myself. A toast in celebration of myself. I sing of myself. I throw off my loafers and invite the grass to tickle my soul! The grass, the grass, the grass upon which I fling myself!" I brought the jar to my lips and took an enormous draught. "Oh sweet isolation!"

Quite exhausted, I headed to the cabin. Inside, I groped the wall for a light switch, but of course did not locate one. The cabin had no electricity. What my clumsy hand did come across was a shelf from which it knocked something that landed, with a sharp jab of pain, on my foot. It turned out to be a glass kerosene lamp. (I discovered the next morning that there were three lamps on the shelf.) I filled the one I'd knocked down with kerosene from my camping supplies. The cabin seemed to have shrunk, or perhaps its single, cold, dirt-floored room had expanded in my mind during the week I'd been away. What had appeared quaint and ramshackle during the day looked primitive and depressing at night, in a flickering lamplight. The log walls were sloppily plastered together with mud. The thick, awkward, homemade table wobbled at my touch. Tiny white crops of mushrooms grew in the corners. I stumbled across the floor, which was as riddled with dips and rises as Fisher Lane. A cool breeze blew in through the west window's shattered panes and out through the shattered east window. Well, I thought, perhaps there's even more work to be done than I'd guessed. I decided it would be best to close my eyes and forget my surroundings. Daylight and rest would soon restore my optimism.

When I flipped open the mattress folded in half on the wooden bed frame, I was immediately made aware that I'd in fact lifted the roof of a home. A family of field mice harkened to the world with squeaks of alarm and scattered like a handful of marbles in every direction. There was still much I had to learn about country living. I realized right away I was going to have to give up my disdain for dirt, since I was going to be sleeping on it that very night. I could have slept in the car, but I wanted to stake my claim here. It was my cabin, after all. I'd had enough of the seat of the Eldorado and the seatbelt buckle that always found its way into my ribs during the night.

I unfurled my sleeping bag on the cool dirt floor, crept inside and balled up my coat for a pillow. I made a lot of intentional noise in doing so, hoping that the other inhabitants of the cabin would take note of where I was and avoid scampering across my chest, or making a new nest in my hair during the night. I could hear the mice scuttling about the cabin. As I drifted off to sleep, I heard them climbing the walls, running back and forth on the exposed ceiling beams, peering down at me and whispering to each other while I slept. They discussed my arrival and the destruction of their home. "Let's pee on him," one of them said. "OK," said one of the others. They hung their little wieners over the side of the ceiling beam they stood upon and whizzed down onto my forehead. It was just a few drops at first. One of them kept missing. I could hear his urine dripping onto the floor to my right while the other tinkled his few drops of mouse pee onto my forehead. I was too tired to get up and move my sleeping bag. It would be over soon enough, I reasoned; after all, he's only a mouse. I shifted my position slightly. A third mouse joined them and I felt his pee soaking through my sleeping bag near my feet. The few tentative drops of the mouse who was aiming at my forehead became a prodigious trickle. Good grief, I thought, how much can a mouse pee anyway? "My God," the mouse peeing on my head said to his friends. "I can't stop. I've sprung a leak!" The trickle became a steady stream, more like what one would expect if a horse had been up there in the rafters. I woke up spluttering, shaking the moisture from my face. Rain was drumming on the roof, blowing through the broken window pane on the west wall, and pouring through the ceiling. I took my sleeping bag from the cabin to the car, flopped down across the front seat and welcomed the seat belt buckle as it dug into my ribs.

Shafts of sunlight stabbed at me through the windshield the next morning, prodding me awake. I got out of the car and peered into the cabin. The floor had become a mudflat, with dry islands here and there, and small ponds in the deeper divots. As there was, of course, no bathroom facility, I decided that I should go into the woods and find a suitable place for an outhouse. I let my steps follow the direction of the prevailing breeze, and entered the woods in the lee of the cabin. After a few steps I found myself on what might have been an overgrown path. I wondered if Mr. Krauthammer had followed the same procedure for choosing a spot for an outhouse, and I looked ahead, almost expecting to find a rectangular shack with a half moon carved in the door a few yards ahead of me. After going only a few yards however, I heard a sound that was music to my urinary tract as well as my tongue. It was the happy gurgling and babbling of a body of water. The stream was about ten feet wide and three deep. Scooping it up to my mouth, I found it to be as pure and refreshing as it looked, and I got down on my knees and slurped up mouthful after mouthful. The bank of the stream onto which the path immediately opened would be the spot where I did my washing and got water to take back to the cabin. I walked downstream about a dozen yards, stopped, and dragged the heel of my shoe over the ground, scraping away the leaves and pine needles to make a square in the dirt where I would erect an outhouse.

I followed the stream further and found that it eventually came to a little bridge. There was a small concrete monument jutting out of the ground next to the bridge, on the far side of the stream, which I assumed marked the corner of my property. This explained the squiggly east property line I'd seen on the blueprint; the stream was the property line. I walked back down Fisher Lane to the short driveway that opened onto my clearing. I'd found a water supply and established a location for a water closet. Quite a satisfying morning's work. There were two other areas of concern that required immediate attention. The first was skunks. I was going to need some fresh skunk musk very soon. The second was the leaky roof. Call me old-fashioned, but I refuse to live in a shower stall. As it turned out, the first matter was the lesser of the two concerns. Though I didn't know it at the time, I was living in skunk country.

Since I knew I would have more luck on a skunk hunt after the sun went down, I decided to get started on repairing the roof. I fetched my toolbox from the trunk of the car and hunted around for materials. In the chicken coop, which had apparently been used as a storage shed as well, I found a weatherbeaten ladder, rusted shovels, hoes, picks, a wheelbarrow, a canvas tarp, and odds and ends of wood. I put the ladder up against the cabin and climbed up to take a look at the roof. I figured I'd use the scraps of wood from the chicken coop to patch up the holes. Simple enough. Then I'd be free to explore my property further and do some skunk hunting. With the first step I took onto the roof, there was a crunching sound, I lunged sideways and my leg disappeared to the knee. The entire roof was like the lid of a soggy cardboard box. I tore off rotted pieces of particle board, flung them aside and looked straight down into my living-dining-and-bedroom. Luckily, all the supporting beams to which the plywood had been nailed were in good condition. But it wasn't a matter of patching—I needed an entire new roof. I threw the tarp I'd found in the chicken coop over the holey roof, made up a shopping list on a slip of paper and headed into town. With a new roof and my own food and water supplies, it wouldn't be long before I was able to sever all ties with the outside world.

~

I didn't know which one of the group of loafers occupying the area around the cash register of Jud's Country Store, if any, was Jud. But there was a weathered man in his mid-sixties whose relaxed, confident posture seemed to indicate that he was their leader. Thumbs hooked in the straps of his overalls, he leaned back in his swivel chair behind a desk littered with invoice receipts, doodled-upon yellow legal pads, coffee mugs, various tools, scraps of metal and a carburetor for a small motor. Another man, of middle age, wearing an oversized mustache that looked like it belonged on the face of a nineteenth-century police officer, sat slouched in a sagging brown director's chair. This fellow's hands, folded and resting on his midsection above a metal belt buckle, were so large and knobby that they seemed to have a number of extra knuckles. Abutting the desk was a higher counter, behind which an overfed young man in his early twenties was perched on a stool like a trained sea lion. All three of the men wore baseball caps, though none of them looked like athletes of any kind, and regardless of the fact that the store provided more than adequate shade. When the bell hanging from the top of the door announced my entrance, all three of their heads turned in my direction. I ducked down an aisle lined with shiny new shovels and rakes.

"So anyway, he says to Jimmy," I overheard the man I later learned was Jud saying, "'You ain't never gonna get no decent harvest like that. And with that son a yurs runnin' things...'" I walked halfway down the aisle and stood there trying to concentrate on what I had to buy. The amount of merchandise was astounding. There were post-hole diggers, rakes, hoes, huge spools of rope and chains, sprinkler attachments, clippers, and so on. I went further into the store, dug the slip of paper out of my pocket and looked at my shopping list. It seemed to represent a child's idea of gardening—some foggy conception of a vegetable patch—and here I was in the world of grown-up farming with all of its tremendous, complicated and alien paraphernalia. Beside Roman numeral one I'd written, "Seeds," and then beneath it, in outline format, "A. potatoes, B. corn, C. beets." Since I was in the tools section of the store, I skimmed the list to Roman numeral three, "Tools." I read the first subheading, "A. trowel." The men in the front of the store all broke into raucous laughter at once, and for an instant I imagined that they were laughing at my list rather than some joke of their own. I quickly shoved the paper into my pocket and glanced down the aisle to make certain I could not be seen. If indeed they did see this little shred of evidence of my incompetence they'd be laughing and telling stories about me for weeks. The bell over the door tinkled as another customer entered, and noises of greeting issued from the group of loafers.

Standing there, absorbing the scents of lime, potting soil, pesticides and herbicides, I wondered what, exactly, one needed to begin a small farm. There were little metal things that looked like back scratchers. "Cultivator," it said on the edge of the shelf. Would I need one of those? Would I need a grass hook or a dandelion digger? A five-tine fork or a digging fork? It was difficult to say. Off the top of my head, I could think of no use for the three-strand nylon amalgamated twisted rope, nor the chicken wire, though there were impressive rolls of both and, since they were here, they must have had something to do with farming. There were large coils of hose, pulsating sprinklers, dual outlet valves, adjustable nozzles, picks, drain spades and a frightening object identified as a garden claw. My head swam. The simple life was turning out to be far too complicated for my taste. I'd imagined planting all the seeds I'd need in one afternoon, then sitting back and watching them grow while I sipped a skunk musk cocktail. Obviously in over my head, I was stricken with a sudden panic and desperately wished I were back in New Essex in my comfortable old house.

The heck with it, I decided, the only real necessity was seeds. There were enough tools back in the chicken coop. I spotted the seeds at the end of the aisle, on a spinning rack at the front of the store, right in front of the baseball-capped congregation. Standing sideways to the men, I picked out the seeds I wanted. There was a discussion going on between Jud and the man who'd entered the store while I was in the back.

"I don't think you can afford to lose another Ben," I heard Jud say.

"Lose?" the newcomer said. "I ain't gonna lose. Your Ben Franklin is gonna join my Mr. Franklin, and then the two of them are gonna help buy me a new twelve gauge."

I picked a few packets of radish seeds from the rack. There was a tension in the store's atmosphere that had arrived with the new customer.

"Well, see now Matt," Jud said, "I'd rather see you make a purchase in here instead of just coming into my store and giving me money like this. Anyway, you probably shouldn't be gamblin'. Yuh seem ta get into enough trouble as it is."

"You ain't even heard the latest," the fat boy said. "Statutory rape. That Swanson girl."

"Shut the fuck up Doug, yuh fat fuck," Matt quickly spat at him.

"What's this about, Matt?" Jud asked.

"Nothin'. Bullshit. They ain't proved nothin' and it's nobody's Goddamn business. Anyway, look here Jud, yew ain't gonna win. It's the law a averages. It's my turn to take back what yew lucked out on last week."

While eavesdropping, I picked out seeds based on the names on the packets. I collected packets of Detroit Dark Red beets and China King cabbage seeds and soon had a pile overflowing from my arms.

When I turned around, Matt, a man about my age, was shuffling through bills in his wallet. If the other men resembled lethargic barnyard animals, this one was more like something that had crawled out of a swamp. His hair looked like a collection of black snakes trapped against his head by a grease-stained, powder-blue baseball cap. He turned his beady black eyes on me for a moment, giving me a full view of the week's worth of black stubble and a couple of detonated and scabbed-over pimples on his cheeks. A scar bisected his right eyebrow. He glanced over the length of my navy-blue suit, a neutral outfit I'd worn because it usually served as camouflage in any public place. "The fuck're yew lookin' at, candy ass?" Matt inquired. "You some kinda fuckin' Bible salesman or what?" Before I had time to formulate an answer, Matt, seeming to forget my existence almost as soon as he'd registered it, turned back to the counter, took out a hundred dollar bill and tossed it on the desk in front of Jud. This apparently represented some sort of challenge. The sea lion wiggled his feet on the stool, rubbed his fleshy chins vigorously, and shot a look at the middle-aged bag of bones, who shifted his weight in the director's chair and began fiddling with his drooping mustache. Standing there, my arms full of seed packets, I might as well have been invisible.

Jud looked at the bill on his desk as if it were a little turd left by some vermin. "I dunno Matt. You keep callin' it luck, but see, there's somethin' you're overlookin'."

"What's that," Matt said. Violence seemed to be trembling just beneath his skin.

Jud looked up at Matt now for the first time. "You's in my domain here, Matt." Jud lifted his cap and, as if they were invisibly attached to it, his eyebrows also went up, making him look somewhat bewildered as he scratched at the top of his gray crew cut. The bony man looked as if a smile might have formed behind his mustache as he began to rock back and forth subtly in his chair. He glanced at the fat boy on the stool and winked.

"See, this here's my turf," Jud continued. His voice was overly soft and gentle, as if he were speaking to a small child. "I been here a long, long time. My daddy owned this store, and before that, my granddaddy owned the land. Now how long you been here, Matt?"

Matt shrugged. "Don't make no difference," he said. He made an unconscious jerking motion with his hand, then withdrew a tin of tobacco from the breast pocket of his flannel shirt.

"Your folks moved here when you was just startin' to get that peach fuzz that's all over yur face now, if mem'ry serves. That makes it, what, twenty year?" Jud asked.

Matt didn't answer. He stuck a gob of tobacco between his front teeth and his bottom lip and brushed his fingers off on his jeans. The skinny, mustachioed man let out a short cackle. "I'd put that bill back in my wallet if I's you, Matt," he said.

Matt looked over at him and snorted. "Don't matter. I ain't superstitious."

"Well now look, Matt. You can call it what you want, but I been winnin' at this game for years, specially 'gainst you, and after a while, you start to wonder if it ain't for a reason."

Matt lifted his baseball cap from his head, ran a hand through his tangle of black hair, then clamped the cap back on like a lid. "Cut the shit, Jud. Yew gonna match me for threes, or's yew afeared?"

The bony man slapped his knobby knee and guffawed as if Matt had just told him the best joke he'd heard in a long time. He leaned forward and slapped Doug's knee, too. I wondered if Jud made the majority of his money by using his establishment as a gambling parlor rather than a store, because he certainly ignored me, the only actual customer in the place.

Matt turned his head on in my direction and spit a brown stream of saliva to the floor, just missing my feet. If Jud's hadn't been the only store in town I would have dropped all the seeds right then and there and walked out. "Aw Jesus, Matt," the fat boy said. "I gotta clean that. Here." He bent over and took a paper coffee cup from a waste basket next to him.

Matt took the cup from him, without taking his eyes from Jud. "Guess yew'd rather give me another of yer sermons about spirits watchin' over yew and your territory than play a game a threes," he accused. A smile opened like a gash in his scruffy face. Packed with tobacco, Matt's lower lip protruded like that of an Ethiopian woman who'd cut hers open and inserted a plate. He seemed to feel he had the upper hand now. Whatever this "threes" game was, it certainly incorporated the standing about, the macho posturing and the psychological intimidation of a game of baseball. The hats began to seem appropriate.

Jud sighed and shook his head slowly. "I'm sorry you wanna do this to yourself, Matt, but if it's what you want..." He shifted his weight and extracted a wallet from the seat pocket of his overalls. Thumbing slowly through the bills, he pulled out a hundred, leaned forward and tossed it on the table next to Matt's. It flopped over in half along the crease. "Roy, you wanna do the honors?" Jud tiredly asked the mustachioed man. Roy began to rise from his chair.

"No, not Roy. Roy done it last time," Matt said. His shoulders were hunched and his back was tense.

Jud narrowed his eyes. "Who's superstitious now, Matt?"

Matt ignored him. "Doug, you flip." The fat boy got off of his stool, sucked up his gut, and fished a quarter out of his pocket. "An it's gotta land on the table. If it falls on the floor it don't count," Matt said, rather agitatedly.

"We all know the rules, Matt," said Jud. "Whatta you want?"

"Heads," Matt said. Roy got up from his chair and he, Matt and Doug all stood around the desk. Only Jud seemed unconcerned, tipped back and slowly rocking in his chair. Doug flipped the quarter in the air, let it drop to the desk, and everyone except Jud hunched over the desk and peered down at it as if they were trying to see the bottom of a deep well.

"Tails!" Roy announced.

"Yeah, yeah, let's get on with it," Matt said. He lifted the paper cup, spat into it, and wiped his mouth on his sleeve. Doug flipped the coin a second time and it landed heads up. The tension in Matt's back seemed to ease slightly. Doug picked up the quarter, placed it on the nail of his thumb, and was about to flip it for the third time, when Jud leaned forward and grabbed his arm. His eyes were pale blue pools. "Now Matt, I want you to remember where you are. Okay? Whatever happens, I want you to think about that."

Jud released Doug's arm and settled back in his chair. Matt's back tensed again and he watched Doug flip the coin, his head bobbing up and down like a dog's following the path of a biscuit tossed in the air. "Tails!" Roy shrieked.

"Goddamnit!" Matt yelled. He slapped his hand on the counter while Roy and Doug burst into peals of laughter.

Jud rose slowly from his chair, shaking his head in disapproval and picking up the two hundred-dollar bills as if cleaning up a couple of candy wrappers. I sincerely wished he'd clean up the rest of the mess on his desk. "I'm real sorry, but I do feel a little safer knowing you won't be buying another gun anytime soon." He stepped around Doug and punched a key on the cash register. It opened with a ring of victory among Doug and Roy's hoots and cackles. Jud deposited the bills in the register with the care of a priest placing a communion wafer on the tongue of a parishioner, shut the drawer, and then looked up at me as if I'd just walked into the building. "Help you, partner?" he asked.

Despite the evidence of nepotism I'd just heard described, Jud had the integrity of a man who has carved out his own place in the world. Or maybe it was just the confidence of a man who understood his own place in it. He later told me he'd worked on a farm for thirty years before taking over his father's store. I unburdened myself of the seed packets, leaning forward and letting them slide from my arms onto the counter.

"Well, looks like somebody's startin' a garden," Jud happily proclaimed. He flipped the seed packets over in his hands and punched in the prices while Roy, Doug and Matt continued to discuss the game of threes.

"It's the law a averages, he's bound to lose to me real soon," Matt said. I glanced over at them. Matt glared at me as he spat in his cup, seeming not to notice the brown juice that dribbled down his chin.

"Don't look like it Matt," Roy said. "How many Franklins is that he's took off you this month, anyhow?"

Jud ignored his cronies as he punched the keys of the register. His hands were large and veiny, and the skin over them was as tough as dried, cracked earth that had been worked and reworked over the years, then finally given a season off to soften a bit. "Yeah, guess you'll be wantin' to get these in the ground pretty soon," he said. Because of the way he paused between sentences and made frequent eye contact, I felt I should say something conversational, but he hadn't asked me a question so I just waited to be asked for the total. Jud's yellow cap bore the John Deere insignia with its antlered deer in mid-leap. The cash register was one of those old models, scarcely found anywhere these days, in which the numbers pop up in the window on black squares like a little puppet show, and a noise like the action of a gun being pumped bursts from the machine each time a price is rung in.

"Ah," Jud said, turning one of the packets over in his hands. "See you knows your greens—Green Pearl Brussels sprouts, now them's the kind you want." He looked up into my eyes for an instant. I raised the corners of my mouth in an expression meant to signify a pleasant confirmation, but more likely indicating a discomfort verging on nausea, which was closer to the truth. No words came to me. I leaned forward and made a brief bow in the manner of a tourist unfamiliar with the language and customs of this particular region. Of course I knew nothing about vegetables and had only picked those Brussels sprouts because the name was appealing. Jud punched in the price of the last packet. "So, you new in the area, or just passing through?" he asked, looking me right in the eye again in that disarming way.

I looked down, pushed my glasses up the bridge of my nose and fished the money out of my wallet. "New in the area," I murmured.

"You didn't happen to buy the old Krauthammer place up on Fisher Lane there, did ya?"

I didn't see what business it was of his, but I felt I would have diminished myself in his estimation by refusing to answer and I didn't want to shrink, in his eyes, to Matt's size. "Yes, actually, I did recently purchase that land," I said.

"Thought that might be the case. Heard it'd been bought. I never thought nobody'd want the place. Well, 'cept maybe one person, an he couldn't afford it. So, how you plannin' on cultivatin' the soil up there anyhow? 'Magine it must be pretty overgrown there by now."

Good grief, I thought. Here's another confounded Mrs. Endicott, and I've only been living here less than twenty-four hours. I straightened my posture and said, a bit guardedly, "I have a shovel."

"A shovel," Jud said, raising his hat and eyebrows simultaneously, as I'd seen him do before, scratching his head, and replacing the cap. "My man's got a shovel. Well, that's good." As he took my change from the register he nodded seriously, as if the savvy displayed by my ownership of such a utilitarian object were not something he would have suspected. He handed over my change and got out a bag to put the seed packets in. "But I don't know, that land's kinda tough if yur gonna be turnin' a lot of soil. I got tillers you can rent if you're innerested." He nodded to the front of the store where the tillers stood next to seed spreaders, push mowers and riding mowers, all lined up like army tanks prepared for their perennial battle against nature. The tiller was a shiny fire-engine red. It was (I learned later) a rear-tine tiller, and its tines, glinting in the light from the front windows, looked like savage metal teeth, ready with the yank of a cord to commence chomping up the earth. Like its predecessor, the mule-drawn plow, the handles stretched out behind it, forming a V.

Jud watched me expectantly. I saw what he was up to, oh yes—the country mouse capitalizing on the inexperience of the city mouse—it was an old one. "No. That's fine, thank you," I said.

"Hope you got something to clear the underbrush with, too," he remarked.

I nodded as I wracked my noodle. Had there been something in the chicken coop with which to tame the brush or not?

"Okay, suit yurself, partner." He smiled. "Name's Jud." He held out his dry, callused hand.

"Damien," I said, well aware, as my hand disappeared into his, that he could probably break every bone in it with a firm squeeze. "One thing I do need, come to think of it, is roofing materials."

As Jud smiled, one corner of his mouth pulled up higher than the other and deepened the crosshatchings of wrinkles beneath his eyes. "'Spect you do," he said. "I 'member when Krauthammer—we called 'im Crazy Kraut—first built that thing. He went around bragging to everybody how he'd built a log cabin. You never seen a man so damn proud. He'd been living on that property in a tent for about a year or more before he got it built, but then he took off before 'e got a chance to do the roof."

"I see," I said. Well, I thought, the particle board hadn't nailed itself to the roof. But I didn't mention it.

Jud had his own little lumber yard behind the store where I found everything I needed. I filled the back seat of the Eldorado with shingles, tarpaper and roofing nails, and tied several sheets of plywood to the roof. Though they continued talking, I could feel the eyes of Jud and the rest of the men following me out the door when I left. As the door swung shut, cutting off the sounds of the men's voices behind me, I thought: I've made one of my last stops in the world of men. I'd bought the seeds of my freedom with those packets. With my own sources of sustenance, I would never again have to interact with other humans and play the petty little power games in which people are constantly engaged.

There were a couple of last stops I had to make in civilization, however. I needed food to last me until my own crops were harvested. Also, I needed books. Books were my only entertainment, and now that I was not going to be keeping skunks as pets, but using them, emotionlessly, as musk machines, I would need books more than ever. Books are the best sort of companion and most people would do well to emulate them. I had done my best to treat them as such. I'd closed the cover on them all. Only one continued to bother me. Pearl was like a disturbing novel one wants to read completely through to the end, even though one disagrees with the premise, the characters' behavior and, essentially, everything about it.

About half a mile down the road from Jud's, I noticed a large orange sign with black Western-style lettering (it would have been the unusable "Mesquite" font on my computer) that announced Highbridge Guns & Ammo. I could see the shotguns lined up in front of the barred windows of the place. There was something raw and vulgar about this large display of weaponry. I didn't imagine that one day I'd enter the place as a customer. Further down the road I turned into the parking lot of the grocery store, where everyone was humongous. Normally, I did not observe my fellow shoppers, but since I was unfamiliar with the layout of this grocery store, I was forced to look around for the things I needed. I didn't recall having seen such corpulence in New Essex. Here, tubby children waddled along behind their billowing mothers, or rested their chubby bodies in the shopping carts, from which their plump little legs protruded like inflated marshmallows. The cashiers were fat. The baggers were fat. The bacon was fat. The fat was fat. Talk about living off the fat of the land. I was almost afraid to purchase any food. I was in what is called the heart of the country and could only conclude that it was in danger of suffering massive coronary thrombosis.

I bought as much bulk food as I could, thinking I wouldn't have to come into town again. I'd be living off the fruits and vegetables of my own labor soon enough. I bought enough foodstuffs to last until my first harvest. All I need now are books, I thought. Books to keep me company after the planting, while I wait. I decided I might also buy some books about gardening. Just as I preferred the company of books, I preferred learning skills from books rather than people. When one learns a skill from a person, such as Jud, one never knows whether he is showing you a certain way of doing things because he will profit from it. Jud would have had me use a tiller rather than a shovel so I could fill his pockets for him. Nice try. I wasn't one of these bumpkins like Matt, willing to throw Jud a hundred dollars as if throwing money away were a kind of sport. I would prove to be a tougher customer than that.

11

When I plopped my books down on the counter, the young woman didn't even look up from her newspaper. Though no one seemed to use it, the library, which I'd had to visit because I was unable to locate a bookstore, was housed in a small but handsome granite building with Doric columns. It had originally been the town hall. John Highbridge, marooned on his grassy island, stared across the road at the building as if confused by this turn of events and wishing he'd learned to read.

The woman behind the circulation desk had her chair tilted so far back she was practically lying down, her feet propped up on the back counter. I was fed up with this slower-than-molasses, down-home, deep-fried country service I'd been administered everywhere I'd gone in Highbridge. I brought the palm of my hand down sharply on the silver service bell on the counter, which made a loud PING! The librarian looked up from her paper with a start. Judging from the lugubrious reluctance with which she set down her coffee mug and withdrew her tangle of legs from the counter, I gathered that she was not overly excited to find a fellow fan of literature in her establishment. Her reaction was closer to that of someone who'd been interrupted at home on a Sunday morning. She took an elastic band from her wrist, made a ponytail of her hair, tossed it over her shoulder and flipped open the cover of the first book from the stack. "Got a library card?" she asked. It hit me like a slap in the face—despite the long, shimmering, golden brown hair, the necklace that hung over the t-shirt and the thin, almost hairless forearms—this was not a woman at all. The deep voice betrayed her. She was, in fact, a man. Upon closer inspection of his face, I detected the faintest shadow of a beard and mustache. He had somehow escaped the plague of obesity visited upon the land and was almost painfully thin.

"No," I managed, in spite of my shock. "I suppose I need one."

The librarian yawned without covering his mouth, and bent down to poke around under the counter between us. A curious silver pendant dangled from his necklace; it was, I dredged up from the scanty and remote Art History section of my memory, the Egyptian symbol for life. "Ah, shit," the young man said. "I don't know where they put those damn forms." This dilemma was, apparently, call for refreshment. He turned around and went over to where he'd left his coffee mug and took a few gulps, then surveyed the shelves beneath the counter. "There they are," he said after a moment. He put down his mug and crouched down to pull a piece of paper from one of the shelves. He stood up quickly, paused for a moment to look at the form, then put both hands to his temples, as if what he read pained his mind. "Whoa. Head rush," he informed me. He shook his head, wagging the shiny ponytail back and forth, and took a second look at the piece of paper. "Oh, this isn't even it," he said.

Needless to say, I didn't care to spend my afternoon with this essentially somnambulistic librarian who stood around swearing at inanimate objects, and I had half a mind to take my literary pursuits elsewhere. The problem was that there was not an elsewhere within several hours' journey.

"This is it," he said. He pulled a sheet of paper from another one of the shelves and glanced over it. "Shit," he said, rubbing his eyes. He didn't seem fully awake yet, though it was the middle of the afternoon. "Dude, I'm sorry, man, but they musta moved stuff around and decided not to tell me. They did a hell of a good job of hiding those damn forms—oh, there they are." He stepped forward and pulled a piece of paper from a shelf under the counter in front of which I stood. "Bingo," he said. "Last one." He put the piece of paper on the counter between us, and while I filled my name and address in the blanks, he shuffled through the books I'd picked out.

"*The Organic Farmer's Handbook,*" he said. "I bet nobody in this town's ever checked this out before. Bunch a subsidized bullshit is all that goes on around here." He opened my book and began flipping through the pages as if he were the one checking it out. "Yeah man, this is the real thing though. This is what I'm gonna be doing soon. I'm not gonna stand around while America feeds me a bunch of crap. Damn Department of Agriculture. Pay these farmers not to grow. Shit. They stockpile corn and wait for the price to go up. It's enough ta make you puke." By the time I'd finished filling out the form he seemed to be fully awake. He spun the form around on the counter and squinted down at my handwriting. His mouth fell open. "Dude," he said, his voice sinking deeper with the weight of profundity, "no way." I could scarcely understand the young man's sloppy rhetoric at times, but he was, I had to admit to myself, entertaining. He looked into my face as if recognizing a long-lost comrade who'd showed up in disguise. "You bought the place on Fisher Lane?"

"It seems to be as public a fact as the weather, at this point," I said.

The librarian held the form up in front of his face and then let the hand that held it fall to his side, as he took a step back from the counter and looked me over again. "*Dude,*" he said, more emphatically this time, and then, pausing between the next two words, and enunciating them as if he were tutoring me in a new language, "*no... way.*" He pulled his ponytail around the side of his head, stuck it in his mouth, chomped on it a couple of times as if it were a gag he used to prevent himself from divulging secrets, then spit it out of his mouth and tossed it back over his shoulder. He exhaled heavily, filling the air with the smell of stale coffee. "Well, I guess we're gonna be neighbors then," he said.

"Pardon?" I said.

"My name's Robby," he said, springing forward and extending a hand, "Robby Krauthammer." He squeezed my hand and pumped it vigorously. In motion, Robby's body gave one the impression of a handful of pipe cleaners loosely twisted together and animated by an electric current. "That's my dad's old place you bought," he said, turning his hand around in mine, changing the grip of our handshake to an arm-wrestling position, then withdrawing his hand enough to grip the ends of his fingers with the ends of mine, then withdrawing his hand altogether, making a fist, and punching my hand. I stared at my hand, baffled by the process it had just undergone, and wondered if this were the Highbridge secret handshake. Robby laughed aloud. "Dude, this friend a mine told me somebody bought the place, but I figured he was pulling my leg. He knew I've had my eye on that land for a long time. I never thought anybody else would actually buy it. People around here are so superstitious. They think the land's cursed 'cause of my dad. But I *definitely* never thought some businessman interested in organic farming would scoop it up—that's what I was gonna use it for." He suddenly got a sober look on his face. "You're not gonna buy the property next door too, are ya? That was gonna be plan B in case I never saved enough money for my dad's old land."

"I wasn't planning on purchasing any other property in the area, no," I said. "But what do you mean, next door? You aren't planning on living near there, are you?" I said.

"Well, pretty near. I mean, we won't be so close that, like, you'll hear my stereo or anything, if that's what you're worried about."

Stereo, I thought. Good gracious. I imagined the sound of screaming electric guitars filling the wilderness around my cabin. That would certainly send me right over the edge. And who could he have meant by "we?" He looked too young and disorganized to have a family. "Um, where is this other, 'next door,' property," I asked.

Robby pulled the elastic band out of his hair and put it in his mouth, shook out his mane and then began energetically pulling it back behind his head again. "Right up the road," he mumbled, his mouth full. He took the elastic band out of his mouth and wrapped it around the ponytail again. "Just over the stream past my d— your place. You didn't check that out yet?" I shook my head. "There's a building down there. Used to be a hunting lodge, but the bank owns that now, too."

I winced. How was it possible for such an irretrievably stupid, nearsighted creature as myself to have been born? I'd been so excited about my discovery of the farm that I had not made sure that Fisher Lane was completely private. I left the library in something of a huff and drove home. I'd been in a cantankerous mood when I'd entered the library—having realized that I was not yet quite self-reliant enough to say good-bye to society forever. By checking books out of the library, I'd conceded to at least one more return to town. I drove down Fisher Lane past my driveway, crossed the bridge over the little stream, and after a quarter mile or less, came to the clearing in which the road ended. And there it was. Just as Robby had told me: The Highbridge Gun Club, read a sign on the front of the building—a low, oblong, cinder block structure resembling a bunker, with windows spaced uniformly along the walls and a chimney poking through the roof. Two posts the width of telephone poles were sunk in the ground in front of the building, with another post across the top of them about eight feet from the ground: a rack for hanging dead deer, it took me a moment to realize. The door of the building was locked, so I rubbed the dirty window and peered in. There was a large stone fireplace at one end of the room. At the other, the head of what must have been an extremely large deer stared stoically across the barren room. "Idiot!" I yelled. I banged my head against the side of the building ten times, then took the small musk jar from my pocket and had an eyedropper full.

I drove back to town and burst through the door of Winchell's Real Estate. There they sat, necktieless, their Styrofoam cups of coffee before them, as if they hadn't budged from the position in which I'd found them a week and a half before. I was quite worked up and didn't know exactly what to say. Both of the Winchells looked at me as if I'd just stepped off an alien spacecraft while they sipped tentatively at their coffees—pathetic caffeine addicts that they were.

I wanted to scream, but I kept my voice low, steady. "Why didn't you say anything about the hunting lodge at the end of my driveway?" I demanded.

"Your driveway?" the older Winchell said. "That's not your driveway. That's a county road."

"Whatever!" I snapped. I stopped myself and rubbed my forehead—the bump from the night of the storm had all but disappeared now—before beginning again. "You failed to mention that there is a piece of property bordering mine, which is apparently for sale. When I asked if the property was secluded, you said it was."

The older Winchell looked over at the younger and then back at me. His fleshy face with its bulbous nose was beginning to look to me like some sort of gourd. I tried to remember if I'd bought squash seeds at Jud's. "Well, it is secluded," he said. "I mean whuddaya want? It's not used any more. And even if it was you'd hardly ever see 'em."

"Why did you not mention that property before, and that there are certain parties, as I'm sure you are aware, interested in purchasing it?"

The older man set his coffee down now, and leaned toward me across his desk. "You didn't ask," he said. He then leaned back in his chair and put his hands behind his head in order to air his armpits where his shirt was darkened by saucer-sized perspiration stains. Apparently pleased with himself for having come up with such a clever rebuttal, he went on, "I don't know what you're complaining about anyway. I knew the Krauthammer kid was interested in the place, sure, but I still gave you a good deal. Truth is, I didn't want him to have the land. I think he's just as much of a weirdo as his dad was."

"But he could still buy the land next door to me," I said.

Winchell shrugged. "I can't help that. I wouldn't worry though. The kid won't ever save up enough money to buy himself a haircut, never mind a piece a property over there."

This failed to satisfy me. I simply couldn't have neighbors—that had been my whole reason for moving from New Essex. Yet I now found myself surrounded by all these "neighborly" types, who either wanted to know how I planned to till my fields, or wanted to move in next door to me. Even though I doubted I'd be able to afford it, I asked how much it would cost to buy the land the hunting lodge was on. I suspected Winchell had all along been planning to swindle me into buying more land, just the way Jud had tried to get me to rent some unnecessary farming equipment. The amount Winchell wanted for the lodge land was about twice as much as the remainder of my savings, which I would need to feed myself and buy the necessary equipment and food until my farm was supporting me. I had no choice but to risk it. If Robby moved in next door, I'd simply have to build a big gate in front of my driveway and shut him out.

After getting home from Winchell's, I began work on the roof. I cast aside the tarp and began tearing off the rotten plywood. The task was simple enough, and I thanked my lucky heavenly orbs that I'd had the presence of mind not to sell off my tool box when I had my yard sale in New Essex. I hooked the claw of the hammer into the first rusted nail holding the mushy particle board on the roof. The nail creaked crankily, then slid the rest of the way out like a rotted tooth from the gums of an old man. The work immediately centered me. In searching for my skunks, in driving back and forth between Highbridge and New Essex, I'd existed in an uncomfortable limbo, unconsciously craving the routine of work almost as much as I'd craved musk. Now I could examine things rationally. The old skunks and the old home were gone for good. I'd be starting over. The farm, like anything else, would only truly be mine once I'd worked for it. I threw a rotted board down to the ground. It twirled like a huge, square Frisbee and came to rest almost noiselessly between the cabin and the chicken coop. Now, grounded by work, I had a clear vision of my future. There were steps to be taken to provide the essentials—food, shelter, musk. The steps were vivid and each followed the other in a reassuring logical progression: One bought supplies. One climbed up onto the roof. One stuck the claw of the hammer under an old nail and wrenched the nail out. One took a new piece of wood, banged a new nail into it until it was pounded flush with the surface. When the wrenching memory of a certain woman popped up, one banged one's head against the beams of the roof, and kept banging until the memory was pounded back down beneath the surface. In this way, shelter was provided.

As the afternoon wore on, the partially stripped beams of the cabin made it look like the ribs of a half-skinned animal. Resting on my knees, I looked west. The air was getting cool and the sun was turning into a tangerine on the horizon, casting orange rays through the leafless trees. It wouldn't be long before dark, and I intended to hunt all night until I found a skunk. By the time I climbed down from the roof to have dinner, I'd torn off all the old plywood, gotten most of the old nails out of the beams and put a few new pieces of plywood on. I broke down the pieces of the old roof, fed the scraps that were sufficiently dry to a fire in the Franklin stove and cooked some soup.

A ribbon of smoke rose from the chimney. Looking up through the naked beams of my roof, I ate and listened to a chirping cricket being joined by another and then another, their sounds filling the woods around me while the stars punctured the deepening blue of the sky with points of white. Once it was completely dark, I fetched my flashlight and the trusty burlap skunk sack from the Eldorado and headed into the woods. An old hand at skunk hunting by this time, sniffing one out did not take me long. Besides, as I soon discovered, this was the most populous region in the country for the pungent polecat.

I came upon a young couple foraging for insects, stunned them with the beam of my flashlight and ushered them hastily into the sack. When they sprayed directly into my face, it was an experience quite like what, I understand from books, it is like to re-discover love. This couple's musks, and the others I encountered later, were quite different from those of my skunks back east (considerably richer, I was forced to concede, my loyalty to Homer notwithstanding). This fact I attributed to differences in diet, the effects of climate, etc. There was simply more space and food available out here. They were also bigger than any skunks I'd seen before; the male was like a fat house cat. He had a diamond-shaped spot of black in the middle of the V of white fur on his forehead. Though I was determined not to become emotionally attached to these skunks, and had resolved, therefore, not even to assign them names, I began thinking of this individual, if not that night, then very soon after, as Spot. Though I tried not to compare them, he reminded me of Homer; he had the staid disposition and that singular devotion to family life. The female, I can't say precisely why, looked like a Roxanne.

I deposited the skunks in the abandoned chicken coop. I'd been prepared to hunt all night, but finding these two had taken little time and had been easy, wonderfully easy. Realizing that Spot and Roxanne probably had some pups, I went back into the woods to where I'd picked them up and quickly located the burrow. As I'd suspected, there were several young skunks in residence. I prodded them out with a stick, chaperoned them into the sack and carried them back to the chicken coop to reunite them with their parents. Their parents sprayed again at the sight of me, catapulting me straight to olfactory nirvana. I slammed the door on the whole family, threw the wooden latch into place and rested my back against the coop. The air was cool and I could see my breath in the moonlight. I resolved not to look at the skunks, not to watch the little ones nuzzling their mother, curling up for warmth and protection. These skunks I would use indiscriminately and solely for their musk.

The night was still young and there were more skunks out there to be had. Why limit myself to one family? This chicken coop could become a skunk coop. But was this tyrannical? Well, gosh darn the little beasts, I was the more highly evolved being here—the bigger, the stronger, the more cunning—let me use and abuse nature as man has always done. I was taking advantage of no one, not even the skunks themselves; their meals would be provided and each day they'd even get a little stomach massage from their captor.

I dove back into the woods to search for more skunks. Under the influence of more musk than I'd had for weeks, and the fiendish greed for more that musk induces after such a long hiatus, I reasoned that stockpiling skunks would help ensure that I did not become attached to the little bastards. They would simply be one anonymous furry mass in the skunk coop. It wasn't long before I'd found another skunk, been sprayed at, then bagged him and brought him to the chicken coop. I immediately plunged into the woods again. And again, and again, and yet again. I ran blindly, staggering under the effects of the musk, slamming into trees and tottering around until I'd regained my balance, then dashing off again, branches whipping my thighs and slashing at my face.

Drunk with musk and running amok, this is the way I rejoiced. I'd lost everything, so why not reward myself? Things would be fine—no—better, better than ever before, because I was completely and utterly alone. Here, I was God. There was no one to complain about my skunks or about how I smelled. No one for me to love, to become dependent upon, only to have her stab me in the heart and leave me for someone else. To heck with them all. "Fuck them!" I yelled aloud, as I ran to the skunk coop with another struggling skunk in my sack, using for the first time in my life the expression that sharpens to the point of hate a word used to describe an act of love. I found it quite cathartic, so I did it again. "Fuck them all!" I yelled.

I opened the door of the chicken coop, untied the top of the sack and threw the skunk in with the others. He fell out onto the dirt floor on his side, scrambled to his feet and ran to the corner. I let the beam of my flashlight play over the scene. The coop was now teeming with skunks. Some were curled up in corners, some were scratching themselves, some crawling over others, a couple was rutting in the corner. Now it occurred to me that I was less like God than like Noah before the flood—collecting animals in preparation for my journey into the seas of solitude. The difference was that I was acting of my own volition, not in accordance with the request of some vain and hypocritical God who tended to destroy whatever He created. How do the believers accept these contradictions inherent in the concept of God? "Well then," one might ask them, as I did that afternoon I entertained the Jehovah's Witnesses in New Essex, "you mean to say that even if there is a God, then He's completely irrelevant?" courteously leaving out allegations regarding His incompetence. The believers always somberly shake their heads, bow them, stick them in the sand and pray.

Swaying as I stood in the doorway of the coop, I waved the beam of my flashlight over the skunks. A thick musk mist humidified the air in the skunk coop, a mist by which one could quench one's thirst merely by breathing with an open mouth. Dark eyes glinted in the beam of the flashlight. The floor undulated with waves of black fur and white stripes. I was through for the night. The sky was already growing gray with the light of dawn, and outside I could see well enough without the flashlight. My evening romp was over. Facing my forsaken house of skunks I felt that some sort of benediction was in order. "God damn us," I boomed to the house of skunks. "God damn us, every one."

12

I woke up and scratched the side of my head. It seemed the activities of the night before had been an outlandish dream. I'd turned into some sort of marauding, skunk-hoarding monster during the night. Or had I? The sun was already well up. It must have been ten o'clock or so. I got up from the bed of green, leafy undergrowth into which I'd apparently flung myself, in the midst of my musk dream, neglecting even to use my sleeping bag. Another good thing about skunk musk is that even when one overdoses, there is never a hangover to be suffered. My legs stiff from all the running around I'd done the night before, I hobbled over to the chicken coop and peeked in. It was indeed packed wall-to-wall with skunks. As I stood there in front of the door yawning, stretching, scratching my back and chest, I counted sixteen of them. An amazing catch, by any standard. They were all asleep; some had curled up on the floor, some had climbed up to the shelves where chickens had once roosted and curled up in nests of straw. I realized that if I wanted to feed them properly I'd never be able to feed myself—I'd spend all my waking hours trapping mice, collecting insects and whatnot. I decided I'd let them share the food I'd bought for myself until I worked out something else.

There was an assortment of tools at the back of the coop that I would need for the day's work. Leaving the door ajar, I made my way among the sleeping skunks like one trying to cross a stream by stepping on widely-spaced dry stones. As I gathered a bunch of tools into my arms, a shovel clanged against a metal bow rake. The noise awoke Spot, who got to his feet and stood looking at me for a moment. I silently cursed myself for leaving the door open. Spot could wake the others and they would all go streaming out of the coop. It would be a mutiny before their journey aboard the slave ship I'd created for them even began. I didn't move or breathe. I stood with the tools in my arms and stared back at him. Spot's eyelids drooped, heavy with sleep, but also, it seemed, with obeisance—as if he were acknowledging that I was his master. I'd learned with Homer and the others that if you look directly into a skunk's eyes he will reveal his emotions, for skunks are extremely honest creatures. This is why they lead solitary lives. When I looked into Spot's eyes, I saw that he was a skunk I could trust. After our exchange, Spot sat back down, curled his fluffy tail around himself and closed his eyes. I made my way back out, softly closed the door, flipped the wooden latch into place and breathed freely again.

I stood in front of the cabin and did a few calisthenics to limber up while I thought over what I was going to do. "Head. Shoulders. Knees. Toes," I chanted aloud to get myself into a rhythm. I'd planned to divide the day into two parts. First, I wanted to clear the land and begin to till the soil. It was already springtime, and the sooner I got my seeds in the ground the better. I had a lot riding on those little grains. I thought fleetingly of the tiller I'd seen in Jud's store, and how it would expedite the cultivation process. But no, I told myself, that would be giving in. Part of my reason for moving here had been to establish a more primal relationship with the earth, to do things simply, so what was wrong with using a shovel and a little good old-fashioned elbow grease? The second chore I wanted to tackle was the roof, and if not complete it by the end of the day, at least have the plywood and tarpaper down so I'd be able to sleep in it without being rained on. I thought I would have the shingles on by the end of the next day. Oh, but how lamentably naïve were my conceptions of farming, roofing and manual labor in general. The only time I'd spent in the outdoors in the past fifteen years, aside from the occasional window-washing and lawn mowing I'd done at my home in New Essex, was limited to my previous skunk-hunting, and insect-collecting expeditions.

Once I'd gotten them in the sunlight, I saw that all the tools from the chicken coop were severely corroded by rust. My arms still sore from my work on the roof of the cabin the day before, I took the grass hook to the corner of the field opposite the cabin and began hacking away at the tall, straw-like clumps of grass, the little saplings and bushes. But the grass hook was so dull it served as little more than an extension of my arm. I swiped, the grasses bent over, then sprang back to a standing position like zombies rising immediately from the grave to mock their murderers. With the saplings, my luck was even worse. Upon my first swipe at one miniature tree—essentially a thick-stemmed weed—the grass hook bounced off with as little effect as if I'd whacked the trunk of a giant redwood with a rubber spatula. A little ragged, yellow gash that looked more like the work of an infant beaver than anything else was the only evidence of my blow. As I hacked away, I stirred up quite a bit of pollen and dust, which began to form a little cloud around me, causing me to stop every so often and sneeze or scratch at my head, face, arms, torso and legs, which all became increasingly itchy as I perspired.

After a couple of hours, what had initially seemed a small farm now looked like the vastness of the Great Plains stretching before me. The result of two hours' steady labor was a clearing that looked as if it had been made by a rodent that had experienced a conniption fit and thrashed about, managing to flatten down some of the undergrowth and turn up clumps of dirt here and there in a area the size of my den back in New Essex. I scratched at my arms and back as I looked across the field, then suffered a long sneezing attack.

Enraged by my lack of headway, I swung the grass hook around like a mad batter, ripped brush out of the ground with my bare hands, kicked at saplings, stomped on the undergrowth. After another hour, I hadn't even managed to double the den-sized area. I stopped, panting, and scratched my arms and legs. My throat was parched. I felt as if I'd been force-fed handfuls of dust for the past three hours. The palms of my hands were pink and tenderized. My skin was speckled with blood from a dozen superficial cuts and scrapes and a rash had flushed the undersides of my forearms and raised the skin in small bumps. I idly scratched at these as I looked over my work. Since my hands were so sore and I seemed to be having a strange epidermal reaction to the pollen, I decided to take a break from clearing and see if I couldn't do a bit of tilling. I would just turn the soil of the area I'd cleared, I thought, and then return to my flailing about with the rusty grass hook. I sunk the shovel into the ground, jammed it as far down as it would go with my foot. When I pulled up, expecting to remove an oval of earth, there was a cracking sound, and I stumbled backward with three quarters of the handle in my hands. The head of the shovel remained stuck in the ground, a splintered stub of the dry-rotted handle standing up as if I'd just planted a thick, branchless little sapling to fill the area I'd finished clearing. Very well then, I thought, I'll leave the field for the time being and work on the roof of the cabin.

I went to the chicken coop, scooped up the handiest sleeping skunk, held it aloft, and before it even knew what was going on, I'd squeezed the startled skunk's abdomen and squirted its musk into my mouth. The young fellow immediately closed his eyes and emitted something like a purr as I lowered him to the ground. This would be how I lived—on a diurnal farmer's schedule, keeping a strictly professional relationship with my skunks. I would come to them like a thief in the night and relieve them of their musk without their even knowing it. For them, it would be like turning over in their sleep, perhaps waking for an effluent instant in the midst of a dream, only to settle back into a deeper slumber.

After a quick lunch, I climbed up on the roof with plywood, nails and hammer, and embarked upon my brief career as a roofer. This, like the cultivation of the field, turned out not to be as simple as I'd anticipated. For one thing, my hands were sore, and the hammer's vibrations against my palm as I pounded in nails felt like flames licking at exposed nerve endings. For another, the pieces of plywood did not fit the roof exactly, and I had to saw them using the only saw I had in my possession—a small hacksaw with teeth about the size of a baby squirrel's. This was extremely slow, tedious work, during which I stopped often to scratch my itchy back and arms. I tried not to think of the plywood being laid across a table saw, the blade zinging through it in a matter of seconds. By nightfall, I had not made nearly the progress I'd intended. I went and soaked my burning palms in the stream for a while before having supper and turning in.

I lay down in my sleeping bag and stared up through the rafters of the roofless half of my cabin at the stars. Luckily it was clear again, and I wouldn't have to sleep in the car. I scratched my ear. I closed my eyes and the shiny red tiller flashed across the inside of my eyelids. It was plowing through my field on its own, turning up the soil while I sat in a lawn chair sipping from a shot glass of skunk musk. I dismissed this image from my mind and thought about the next day's work. I scratched my ankles and my calves. Those seeds, still sleeping in their packets, piled up on my table, had to be gotten into the ground. I scratched at my chest and neck. I was itchy all over. Running my fingers over my forearms, I felt how dramatically the lumps there had grown. It was as if someone had poured boiling water over the skin, making it bubble up with welts. Every time I tried to concentrate on sleeping, I began to itch in a new place. This is strange, I thought, I've never had this reaction to pollen before. I scratched my face and my neck, where there were more welts. As I wriggled like a worm in my sleeping bag, I began to perspire, causing pinpricks of itchiness to sprout all over my body. It was an itch that was almost painful, and scratching only made it worse. I thought of how peacefully I'd slept the night before. Then I remembered the drooping, shiny green leaves of the plant in which I'd passed out. Poison ivy. Of course I wouldn't have recognized it in the dark, and in the morning I'd been too stunned by the fact that I'd spent the night outside to examine the plant on which I'd slept.

Probing myself in other areas, I found smaller bumps that would later become gum-ball sized pustules. My entire epidermis was turning into an aggravated volcanic terrain. I walked through the woods behind the cabin and down to the stream, took off all my clothes and dipped my body into the cold water. I lay there shivering, submerged except for my nose and mouth, and let the water run its icy fingers over my sore, itchy body. After a while I turned numb and I thought I'd cured myself at least for long enough to get some sleep. I put my clothes on and started making my way through the woods to the cabin. Before I'd even reached the clearing, I itched severely where the clothes chaffed my skin. It was worst in places such as the crooks of my arms and backs of my knees where the infected skin rubbed against itself. Mind over matter, I told myself, mind over matter, you silly man! You darn fool! I went into the coop and took a few shots of musk, which helped temporarily, then I banged my head against the door frame several times before reentering the cabin. I lay down on my sleeping bag and after keeping my arms at my sides for fifteen minutes that seemed like fifteen hours, I jumped up and ran back to the stream, tearing my clothes off as I went. This was how I spent the night—running back and forth among the stream, the cabin, and the coop. And in rare moments when I did doze off for a moment or two, the shiny red tiller rose up in my mind like the toy a child hopes Santa will bring the next day. I dreamed I was lying down in the field, letting the tiller run over my body, cutting and gouging into the itchy lumps of pus that bulged from my skin, then woke up clawing at my chest with my fingernails. By morning, my joints were so swollen it hurt to bend my arms and legs. My clothes felt like sandpaper. I was diseased, sore, itchier than that flea-bitten mongrel I'd seen at the trapper's house, overtired and hungry. Instead of conquering nature, it seemed that I was being conquered by nature. Like a decrepit old man, I lowered myself into the seat of the Eldorado, started it up and turned down Fisher Lane.

The bell above the door to Jud's tinkled like miniature church bells tolling for a funeral. Matt was sitting in the director's chair Roy had occupied the last time I'd been in the store, and Matt's unshaven face, just above the level of the counter, looked like a weasel's as it pokes its snout up from a hole in the ground. Doug had perched his girth upon the stool again.

Matt stood up when he recognized me. "Well look here, if it ain't the city slicker who decided to take up farming. How's it goin' Old MacDonald?" He squinted meanly as I approached the counter, lifted a Styrofoam cup to his distended lower lip and spat brown juice into it. Then he started laughing. "Jesuz Christ. What'd you do, go roll yur crazy ass around in a bed of poison sumac?"

Opting not to respond to this, I looked around for Jud, but his swivel chair was empty and I didn't see him anywhere. The gleaming tiller sat waiting in the front of the store.

"Goddamn," Doug said. "Smells like 'e 'ad a run-in with a skunk, too."

Matt came around the counter and stood between me and the tiller. "Hey, asshole," he said, raising his voice, "we're talkin' tu yeew."

I heard footsteps behind me and turned around to see Jud emerging from one of the aisles, his arms full of bags of peat moss. His eyes brightened with recognition, then his brow furrowed and he paused for a quick diagnosis. "calamine lotion, aisle three," he said, then continued out the front door and dropped the peat moss into the back of a pickup truck. Another man emerged from the same aisle Jud had, his arms likewise full of peat moss, and followed Jud out to the truck.

I went down aisle three as I was told, twisting my arm behind my back to scratch as I looked over the merchandise. I'd raised my opinion of Jud another notch or two, since he'd been right about the tiller. I also had a hunch that in a tiny town like Highbridge it might not be a bad idea to maintain a good rapport with someone like Jud. I walked back up to the front of the store with the bottle of calamine lotion as Jud was coming back in from outside. He and the other man had made several trips, because there were stacks of peat moss in the back of the truck. Jud was panting. "Well, don't just stand there, scratchin' like an old hog," he said, "go git that stuff on." He put his hands on his hips and shook his head as he looked me over, his lips pursed with pity. "Gawd, you look like you been through a damn war. Git some overalls; they're in aisle six. If you're goin' into the farmin' business you might as well be dressed for it. You can use the bathroom in back."

I looked down at myself as I walked down aisle six. It was true. My clothes were as riddled with holes as if I'd been shot at. Briars had tugged at the material, drawing out dozens of little blue polyester clouds on my pant legs. My white, button-down oxford shirt had smears of dirt all over it, and there was a large tear at the seam of the left shoulder so that the half-severed sleeve hung down my arm. Many of the buttons had come off and the front of my shirt was open, exposing my lumpy and inflamed chest.

In the bathroom I stripped and looked at myself in the mirror. Had an outsider hazarded a guess as to the variety of warfare in which I'd been engaged, they would likely have said that it had been of the chemical variety. My normally pale, thin arms and legs were a mottled red and yellow, misshapen with swelling. My eyes were bloodshot, circled with dark rings, and one eyelid was half-closed by a poison ivy welt. I swabbed calamine lotion over my body with a paper towel, then put on my new overalls, which was a sartorial disaster. From the loose draping of excess denim dangling from my bony shoulders sprouted a pair of thin arms that were turning pink as the calamine lotion dried.

"Oh mah gawd, it's a plucked chicken dressed up as a farmer," Matt said when I came back up to the front of the store. He and Doug both guffawed and slapped their thighs. Plopped on the stool like that, the quivering rolls of fat pressing against his white shirt, Doug called to mind a melting mass of vanilla soft-serve ice cream towering from a cone. Jud was outside, talking to the man climbing into the peat moss-laden pickup. "Wait a minute, wait," Matt said, looking around the store. He spotted what he was looking for, went over to a rack of handkerchiefs and snatched off a red one. "'Ere we go," he said. He folded the handkerchief into a triangle and then tied it around my neck.

I didn't wish to make enemies on my fourth day in this town, but enough was more than enough. I yanked the handkerchief from my neck and dropped it to the floor. "I really am not in the least amused by your antics," I said.

Doug laughed, but Matt's smile disappeared, his face darkened and he stepped up close to me, his beady eyes glittering with a deep, irrational hatred. Tobacco had fouled his breath and given each of his yellow teeth a brown frame. "I don't give a flyin' fuck what amuses yew," he hissed, "city slicker." There was suddenly too much saliva in my mouth and I needed to swallow, but didn't dare. Nor did I respond. Matt probably took my silence for fear, which is precisely what it was. My heart pounded in my throat and I'd forgotten all about the tiller. "We don't like yew here," Matt said. "In fact, I think you're just like old Krauthammer was. Some highfalutin' city slicker with fucked-up ideas doin' somethin' perverted up there in the woods. I know when I smell a skunk. An' boy, yew reek. I'd just as soon fill yuh fulla buckshot as look at yuh. So don't even *think* you can come in here an' start sassin' me." He took a step back, pointed at the handkerchief on the floor between us and said, "Now pick that up."

Well, the laws of civility, by which I'd tried to conduct my adult life, had been revoked once again and I was back in boarding school, where bullies amused themselves by exercising their superior physical strength. "Yuh better pick it up," Doug warned. Matt said nothing more, and the store seemed very quiet. I heard the pickup truck's engine turn over, whining lazily at first, then spluttering to life and roaring. Matt shot a stream of tobacco juice out of his mouth that splattered down the knee of my new overalls and onto my shoe. I glanced over at Doug. The look of simple-minded amiability that usually appeared on his flaccid wad of a face had been lifted to reveal an expression of dumb cruelty that signaled he would advocate what came next.

Matt stepped forward, a vein standing out on his grizzled neck, clapped his left hand on my shoulder—almost in the manner of a hearty welcoming—and sunk his right fist into my stomach with considerable force. Doubled over, my face almost touching my knees, I gasped for air. My face was now quite close to the red handkerchief. The little bell over the door tinkled behind me like a parody of the bell between rounds of a boxing match. I put my hands on my knees and began to breathe.

"What's goin' on here?" Jud asked. I'd never in my life been so relieved to hear the voice of an old, dried-up farmer.

Matt walked back around behind the counter. "Old MacDonald here was just pickin' up his new neckerchief," he said, spitting into his Styrofoam cup. For Jud's sake, I suppose, I picked up the handkerchief and put it back on the rack.

"So is there anything else we can help you with today besides the itchy business, Damien?" Jud asked. I might have said no, cleared out of the store, never to return, gone home and cultivated my land with my bare hands if Jud hadn't added, "You have second thoughts about that tiller?" He nodded toward the front of the store.

"Yes, actually, I thought that might come in handy," I said. "There are a few other items I might like to purchase as well."

"Well, I gotta be gettin' goin', in case what Old MacDonald's got is catchin'," Matt said, shrugging into a dirty, khaki-colored jacket.

I ignored him and spoke to Jud. "For one thing, I was interested in buying some traps," I said. I was thinking of setting them out to catch field mice and other rodents I could feed to the skunks.

"Need a license for that, city slicker," Matt said, walking around the counter. I did not do him the honor of looking in his direction. Matt bumped me with his shoulder as he walked by, hard enough that I was forced to take a step sideways. Jud gave him a curious glance.

"You see," I explained to Jud, "there are some mice eating away at the walls of my cabin."

"Ho! mouse traps," Matt said, turning before he went out the door. "Old MacDonald's not only a farmer, he's a trapper, too—a mouse trapper." Jud, looking annoyed, glanced over at Matt, who laughed and pushed through the door.

"I was wondering if you might have something bigger though," I said. "Something in which I might catch several mice at once and maybe even some bigger things." Matt was gone. I sighed inwardly as his maroon pickup pulled out of the parking lot.

Jud raised his baseball cap and his eyebrows to scratch the top of his head. "How 'bout a bear trap?" he asked.

"I don't suppose I'll be needing anything quite so large as—"

Jud broke into a grin, but when he extended his arm to give me a friendly pat on the shoulder I couldn't help flinching. "Kiddin' ya," he said. "I got just what ya need." He led me down one of the aisles and showed me some traps that looked big enough to contain a raccoon. "Just load whatever you need into your car, and when you're done come on over to the register and I'll ring ya up. I'll give you a hand loadin' the tiller in yer trunk." He winked. "I'm trustin' you not ta pinch nothin' from me, okay?"

I nodded like a boy scout trying to impress the troop leader with his sincerity. I loaded all the tools and supplies I thought I'd need into my car, including a brush hook, shovel, weed cutter, bow rake, hoe, kerosene for my lamps, bedding—Jud's had everything. On my last trip through the store, I brought to the register a case of mason jars and a case of gallon jugs I intended to use for skunk musk storage. I reported all the other stuff I'd taken. Doug slouched in the director's chair, reading, or, more likely, looking at the photographs, in a copy of *Hot Rod* magazine, occasionally eyeing me over the top of the page.

There were three bottles of calamine lotion on the counter next to the register. "Thought I'd throw these in, on the house," Jud said. "Make your initiation here as easy as possible. Good tu see yur plannin' though." He tapped the case of mason jars with a thick, leathery finger. "Y'already know how much you're goin' tu be cannin', huh?"

"Canning?" I said. "Jud, these are jars."

Jud looked puzzled for a moment and then burst into a laugh. "Gawd you crack me up sometimes, mister," he said. Then, registering my lack of complicity in the joke, he cut his laugh short with a cough. "Think this'll be enough jars, Damien?"

"For my purposes, yes, I believe so," I said. I didn't see how he could have guessed how many I'd need.

"I dunno, judging from the amount a seeds you bought. You ain't gonna be able to eat nearly as much this summer as you think. An' winter can seem to drag on for a long, long time." He looked into my eyes as he spoke. It finally dawned on me—canning vegetables, yes of course. I was so angry with myself for not thinking of this, it was all I could do to keep myself from slamming my head repeatedly against the side of the cash register. I could feel the heat rising in my cheeks, and wondered if a blush would be visible through the coating of calamine lotion, which had dried, making my face feel like the lumpy crust of an apple pie that has been taken out of the oven and left to cool.

"Perhaps you are right," I said. "Why not ring me up for a few more cases of Mason jars."

Jud nodded in a polite way that made me think, in another time, in another place, he would have made someone an excellent butler. "So what're you using to keep pests out? You got a fence around the garden?" he asked off-handedly.

Perspiration broke out on my forehead. "Oh, yes, I meant to ask you, where do you keep all the fencing hidden around here anyway?" I noticed Doug looking up at me from his magazine, a smirk smudged across his pasty face.

Jud smiled. "I'll ring you up for some chicken wire." He punched a few buttons on the register. "Oh, and I was wondrin'," he went on, "what *did* old Krauthammer use for irrigation up there anyhow? I know you ain't got runnin' tap water up there, so a sprinkler system's outta the question."

My poison ivy was beginning to itch terribly again, probably as a result of the flood of perspiration induced by Jud's line of questioning. I pushed my glasses up the bridge of my nose. "I'm not sure what he used. Perhaps I'll find out and report back to you once I've discovered it."

"Yeah, thanks," Jud said. "I'd appreciate it. Guess my curious nature just gets the best of me sometimes." His blue eyes sparkled beneath the bill of his yellow cap.

"I was also wondrin' what kinda pH level that soil might have," Jud said, while I held open the door and he wheeled the tiller out to my car. Together we lifted the tiller into the trunk, which prevented it from shutting. Jud produced a small coil of rope and began lashing down the door to the trunk so it wouldn't bounce while I drove.

"Oh, by the way, don't mind Matthew too much," Jud said.

"Mind him?" I said. "Certainly not. I mean, though he was obviously not minded by his elders when he was a child, it would be perfectly futile for me to take up the task now." I intended to shut Matt Baxter and his fetid breath permanently out of my mind.

"You may have a point there. His pop sure didn't mind him. Now *he* was a wild one. Bad apple, real bad. Matthew ain't quite as bad." Then added through gritted teeth, as he pulled the rope tight with a grunt, "unless ya got a young woman around."

"Pardon?" I said.

"Oh, nothin'," Jud said distractedly, as he fastened the ends of the yellow rope with a square knot. "Oh, an' Damien? A little tip for ya." Jud grinned. "When a skunk turns around and raises its tail up in the air? That's a good time to clear the hell outta the area."

13

There lay Robby Krauthammer, peaceful as a babe in an empty nursery—his feet resting on the circulation desk, torso cradled in the wooden swivel chair, a single page of the *Highbridge Herald* draped over his features, a faint gurgling sound audible as the paper rose and fell with his breath.

The slight chill that had been in the air when I first arrived in Highbridge a few weeks before was gone now. My peas had just shot their green sprouts through the damp, chocolatey soil and my spirits were soaring straight up through the clouds like a wild beanstalk. Spring had brought the land alive with scents of rebirth and I had more skunk musk at my disposal than I'd ever had in my wretched life in New Essex. Buds were bursting from the tips of the branches of the dogwood tree that stood just outside the Highbridge Library. Birds were singing in the afternoon sunshine. Someone had put a wreath of flowers in front of John Highbridge's memorial, and as a result of my mood, I fancied that in the visage of the eroding old pioneer was evidence that he was savoring the taste of a recent triumph. The air was so full of pollen I'd had to brush a dusty yellow layer of it from the windshield of the Eldorado that morning. The world was literally bursting with life all around young Robby, and there he lay, in a stuffy, musty, unused library, asleep.

My body felt new; in my work on the farm, I was developing muscles I'd never used before. I felt strong enough to pick Robby up and use his scrawny body to hoe the ground. I brought the palm of my hand down on the service bell five times in quick succession—PING, PING, PING, PING, PING! Robby's arms shot out from his sides and he wriggled spastically in his chair as if someone had plunged a stake through his heart. He tore the newspaper from his face and swung his feet from the counter, knocking his half-full coffee mug to the floor as he did so.

He jumped up, his eyes wild with terror, and proclaimed, "Jesus Christ!" although he himself more closely resembled one of those ubiquitous soft-focus images of the supposed savior. He dropped his body back into the chair the way one might drop a sack of garbage into a can, and rubbed his temples. His hair hung over his hands and face. "I thought there was a goddamn fire or something, shit."

"Good to see you hard at work, Robby," I said. I was so elated by the turn of events in the last two weeks since I'd been to town to rent the tiller, I could hardly contain myself. My farm actually resembled a farm now and I'd decided on an irrigation system. I'd been to Jud's that morning, where I'd dropped off the tiller, arranged with Jud for several hundred yards of plastic piping to be delivered to my property, and loaded the back seat of the Eldorado full of plastic pressure tees, ball valves, and elbows. "Remember," I told Robby, "as ye sow, so ye shall reap—not sleep!"

"Good God, I can see you've settled right into Highbridge," Robby said. "Starting to sound like you lived here all your life."

I laughed aloud. It occurred to me that Robby, just as he seemed to have less flesh on him than most Highbridge residents, also had less of the unsavory drawl in his speech. My mood got the better of me, and though I'd sworn off the human race, I decided, what the heck? I hadn't spoken to anyone (besides Jud, that afternoon) for a couple of weeks, and within the hour I'd once again be squirreled away by myself and would not see anyone again for months. "So when did you decide to go into the library business, Robby?" I asked.

"Right after I dropped out of college," he said. He looked up at me defensively, suddenly very much awake. "But this is all temporary, man. I'm only twenty-three. I've got other plans." He stood up again, took an elastic band from his wrist, stuck it in his mouth, and then, tossing his head back, began vigorously tugging at the silky brown strands, holding them behind his head with one hand and combing them back with the other. It was quite a performance. "Dude," he mumbled, and then took the elastic from his mouth and fastened the ponytail with it, "I don't believe in this society." He gestured toward the door behind me, the beautiful spring day outside. "I've seen enough to know it's all a big lie. I'm just biding my time right now, but I'm gonna make my move soon. See, my dad was on the right track. He turned hermit a little after I was born, started subsistence farming like you're doing." Robby paused to give me a knowing, respectful look. I was almost sorry I'd awoken this sleeping fount of ideology. Once you turned Robby on, the only volume level he had was maximum and the only speed was one hundred RPMs. "But my dad wasn't realistic. He didn't realize that it takes money to beat the system. Dude, man," he said. This habit of redundantly following the word "dude" with "man" turned out to be a frequent one. In this case, he said it with a certain venom—born, perhaps, of his frustration with "the system"—and the corners of his mouth turned down, as if he'd taken in a whole mouthful of sour grapes, and a pugnacious look crept into his eyes. "I'm not gonna hide out from the world—I'm gonna change it. I'm gonna start a revolution."

The phrase "turned hermit" echoed in my mind. The way it rolled so easily off Robby's naïve tongue gave me a different perspective on my own activities. "Turning hermit" was what I was in the process of doing, although that phrase hadn't occurred to me. Two weeks before, I'd pulled out of the dirt parking lot in front of Jud's Country Store, feeling like a plaster-of-Paris sculpture, the joints of my arms and legs cemented together with calamine lotion. I was overtired and suffered a sore stomach, compliments of Matt Baxter. I bounced uncomfortably down Fisher Lane, and as I turned into my clearing, I considered simply making a loop, driving back out, getting on the highway and heading back east. What did I have here? A bedroom-sized log cabin that lacked running water and electricity, with an unfinished patchwork of a roof. I also had a tiny clearing that had taken me the better part of a day to make. What in the world had I been thinking? That I was actually going to become a farmer overnight and provide all my own food? Now I had to think of an irrigation system for this wasteland. And there was that matter of the soil's pH level—pH level for goodness sakes! What in heaven's name might I, a displaced copywriter, know about such things? Nothing, that's what. And I saw with hideous clarity what I was here: a lost babe in the woods; a Hansel without a Gretel or even a trail of bread crumbs to follow.

I wondered if Piper would agree to give me my old job back. The wage-slave life hadn't been that bad, had it? Could anything be worse than the misery I experienced now? Everything was against me. Nature was against me—the forest was reclaiming this farm and my attempt to beat it back had been laughable. People were against me—Matt Baxter was bullying me and Robby Krauthammer wanted to destroy my solitude by becoming my neighbor. And I was against me—I hadn't the slightest idea what I was doing.

Exhausted, I pulled the Eldorado up next to the cabin and hauled my brittle body out of the driver's seat. Despite my pink frosting of calamine lotion, I still itched everywhere, especially in the crotch, crooks of the arms, and backs of the knees. It felt as if microscopic organisms with pincers were trapped beneath my skin, trying to dig their way out.

My scratching only encouraged them to light the little bonfires that made my skin bubble and burst and then led to more itching.

I heaved the tiller out of the trunk and set it down heavily on the ground. It looked out of place—some twenty-first-century contraption dropped from the sky into the middle of an eighteenth-century farm. As I stood there, sweat trickled down my arm and dripped from my fingertip. Scratching absently at my shoulder, I noticed that the sweat on my fingers felt thick and sticky. I thought I'd burst open another poison ivy pustule, and when I glanced at my shoulder was surprised to see my shirt smeared with red. I turned up the palm of my hand and saw that it was filled with blood. Blood drenched my forearm and dripped onto the leg of my new overalls. It didn't look real. It looked more like a blob of crimson oil paint spilled on my arm. But there was no denying the gap between the two sides of the long gash in my arm. I pulled gently at it with my fingers and immediately more blood gushed forth. Even the machinery is against me, I thought. One of the tines of the tiller had slashed my arm as I was setting it down.

I took a towel, some fishing line and a sewing kit and went down to the stream. I knelt by the bank and soaked my forearm. I was losing quite a lot of blood. It swirled into the water, around rocks, dyeing the water pink before becoming too diluted to see. Light-headed, I thought of lying down in the stream and letting the life seep from me. Everything could go unresolved. Wasn't this what I wanted after all? Oblivion? Perhaps this was the moment for which I'd been preparing myself all those years I'd spent living alone. Avoiding ties to other people made death simpler; there was nothing to sever but my own flesh. And wasn't this what the skunk musk provided me—little tastes of death in my daily life? I'd moved to Highbridge for nothing. Nothing was what I wanted, and in death there would be even more nothing than there was in Highbridge. With death I would extinguish all my failures. The memories, the pain, the betrayal—all would be permanently washed away. I could cease my struggle for solitude and, in death, achieve the most complete seclusion.

I imagined them finding what would be left of me after a couple months. Jud would remember the tiller and come to the farm to retrieve it. By then, scavengers and the rushing water would have nibbled, torn and washed away most of my flesh, and there would be only my ragged bones lying in the stream bed, empty sockets staring up into the sun-pierced ceiling of leaves above me, the eyeballs long ago plucked out and carried off by birds, my jaw bone hanging agape as if in laughter. The joke would be on them. I would be gone. Pearl would never know what had become of me, which, after all, was what I wanted.

I'm still not sure what made me decide to live. If I knew this, perhaps I could make sense of everything that followed. It was as if I were standing by, watching helplessly as my body healed itself. I resurrected my dripping forearm from the stream. A precise incision ran almost the entire length of the underside of my forearm. I toweled it off, then, fingers trembling, threaded some fishing line through a needle and plunged it into the flesh at one end of the cut.

The animal wail of pain was so sudden that, for a moment, I thought there was someone or something else in the woods screaming out to me. I pushed the needle through to the other side, forced it back up through the flesh and pulled the line tight, closing the gap in my skin. And so I went, pushing and pulling the needle through my forearm. My hands shook so violently at times it was difficult to stick the needle in. About halfway through, I put one of the stitches too close to the edge of the wound, and when I pulled it tight, the fishing line ripped clean through from the rim of the wound to the opening, making a secondary wound. Of the successful stitches, I made a total of thirty rather crude ones, and the meandering, stream-like aspect of my scar attests to the fact that I probably should have used twice as many. When I'd completed the operation, I tied the towel around my forearm, stood up, and for a second before the darkness closed in on me, thought I might vomit. Probably no more than a minute later I came to, lying face down on the ground. I rose slowly and made my way down the path to the clearing.

Knowing that I needed to get my blood level up again, I ate as much canned food as my stomach would hold. The skunks needed to be fed as well. But before I did this, I wanted to establish the routine that would become part of their lives. I took a case of mason jars into the chicken coop, picked up the sleeping skunks one by one and squeezed a shot from each into a different jar. Still determined not to give them proper names, I looked for some definitive characteristic of each skunk and wrote this down on a piece of masking tape with which I labeled each jar. Some, like Spot, were easy: Tiny was the smallest, Tripper had only three legs and Whisky had extremely long whiskers. However, it is more difficult to pinpoint why some of them seemed deserving of names like JoJo and Dr. Bigglesworth. Each of them awoke for a startled instant while I executed the old hoist and squeeze, then drifted back off into their skunky dreams.

My forearm throbbed with pain. A thin red line spread and darkened on the towel until I looked like a waiter who'd spilled a good deal of wine on the napkin over his arm. The pain kept my mind from the poison ivy until, now and then, it came rushing back like a memory that every cell of my epidermis shared with the others. It was all I could do to keep from grabbing my new garden claw and raking it across my skin, which oozed in places with a sticky pus that looked like pine sap. For the pain, I drained four of the jars right away.

I decided to use a trough that had originally been used for chicken feed to put the skunks' meals in. So distracted was I by pain and itching, so addled by the large dose of musk, that I hardly knew what I fed them. Leftover scraps of meat, loaves of bread, opened cans of pork and beans, chickpeas and soup all found their way into the trough. I stumbled out of the chicken coop and into the cabin. Though it was the middle of the afternoon, it seemed to be a very good time to go to bed.

For the rest of that day and the next I convalesced, rising from the bed only to get a shot of musk or swab on some more calamine lotion. Then, on the third day I awoke feeling hungry. Despite all the fantasizing about death, and even if a part of me—the part that had given itself to Pearl—had died, my body was, like it or not, through a series of chemical processes, still functioning. There was nothing to do but rise from my bed and get to work.

I headed out to the corner of the field opposite my cabin, where I'd made my first attempts at clearing the land with the rusted grass hook. If before I'd behaved like a deranged baseball enthusiast, I now moved with the fluidity of a ballerina performing a pantomime of a golfer. As I danced through the field swinging the new weed cutter, clumps of tall, yellow grass fell to the ground like handfuls of hair dropped to the floor of a barber shop. Saplings flew to the left and right like silent exclamation points sliced from their periods. By lunchtime I'd cut half the field down to size.

There was a pair of wooden crates in the chicken coop, which I converted to lawn furniture by putting them in front of the cabin and using one as a table, one as a chair. Chewing a sandwich, gazing over the field and patting myself on the back for making such tremendous headway, an idea occurred to me. Examining the huge spool of chicken wire Jud had given me, I guessed there was enough to fence in the whole clearing. The chicken wire could be used not only to keep pests out, it could be used to keep things in, as well—black things with white stripes, four legs and a distinctive odor. This would make life more comfortable for them, I was sure, and make me feel less like a jailer. That was a solution to one problem, but there was another. Jud had raised the question, and it had become a riddle, nagging as persistently at my mind as the poison ivy nagged at my flesh. How was I going to irrigate my crops? I envisioned a nightmarishly Sisyphean summer spent trekking back and forth from stream to field with buckets.

That afternoon I worked on the roof and by nightfall I'd finished nailing down the plywood and stapling the tarpaper, and had started on the shingles. The excitement and pride aroused by the notion that I would soon be living from the land began to swell within me again. But as for that—and I've noticed this to be the case with any image of the future—the unattained, sterilized ideal was preferable to what was finally accomplished. Later that night, while sitting in bed reading *The Art of Organic Farming* by the light of a kerosene lamp, I paused for a moment and looked around the cabin. Since he'd done a decent job on the rest of the cabin, it seemed strange that Mr. Krauthammer had done such a shoddy job on the roof. Though it was primitive—there was still bark on the walls—it was sturdily built. After replacing the broken windows, I noticed that no drafts seeped in from anywhere else.

The greatest challenge in those first few weeks was getting accustomed to the lack of indoor plumbing. I made a tap for a fifty-gallon holding tank I found at Jud's, and I used metal brackets to rig the thing up to the outside wall of the cabin. Beneath it I placed a metal tub on a stool to serve as a sink. After a while, I found I cared less and less about bathing and domestic cleanliness. I often wore my overalls two or three days in a row without a cleaning, I gave up shaving, and sometimes went to bed at night with dirt blackening the rims of my fingernails. I invented a philosophy to support this change in lifestyle, a change I might have regarded months before as a deplorable decline in standards. We are of the earth, and we eventually return to the earth, I reasoned, so what difference does it make if we carry bits of it around with us, on our skin and clothes. If cleanliness is godliness, then godliness betokens death, because dirtiness is a sign of life. And I had chosen, after all, to live.

That night, however, while the organic farming book lay open on my knees, this philosophy was still simmering on a back burner in my mind, and the flow of my thoughts was continually interrupted by a single obstacle: irrigation. I thought of farms I'd driven by in my car, the pipes stretching through the fields to a sprinkler that shot jets of water in long, slow-motion blasts. I flipped to the section of *The Art of Organic Farming* that dealt with irrigation, but running water seemed to be a prerequisite.

The next day the itching had subsided quite a bit. When I went down to the stream to dress my wound, I found that my stitches were holding my arm, albeit sloppily, together. Possibly these conditions may have seemed to improve only in contrast to a newer one. I was so sore it felt as if all night someone had stretched my muscles like elastic bands, twanged away on them until they'd snapped and then, embarrassed by what he'd done, had hastily stuffed them back in my body, not bothering to see if they were in the right places. With each movement I made, I was reminded of the day before—of each swooping stroke I'd taken with the weed cutter and each jolly swing I'd made with the hammer. Nevertheless, after a few calisthenics, I went back into battle against the field, armed again with my weed cutter, though I swung it with a rather circumscribed range of motion and atrophied enthusiasm. Worse than the aching of my muscles was the soreness of my hands. Holding onto the handle of the weed cutter was like wrapping my hands around a hot iron poker. When I shifted my grip, the fingers were reluctant to release the handle; they were crimped around it as if they had never known any other position. Blisters rose on the palms of my hands—one of the only areas of my body that was not already lumpy with poison ivy pustules. I wrapped rags around my hands and continued working.

After a couple of hours I decided to take a break to swab some calamine lotion over myself, since the perspiration had caused another outbreak of itching. The tiny little monsters beneath my skin were still trying to escape. I gave the skunks their squeezings into their respective Mason jars, and took a straight shot from Spot, whose musk, perhaps because it had been the first one I'd tried the night of the skunk hunt, appealed to me the most. Then, filling the tiller with gasoline, I pulled the cord of that dangerous, shiny beast and began tilling the soil. This was considerably easier on my aching muscles. The odor of gasoline mingled with the rich scent of soil as the tiller sunk its teeth into the earth, tore it and chewed it. I went over the land I'd cleared, following this wonderful, masticating machine until I'd tilled it all. As I worked, I settled into a Zen-like trance. I imagined Jud watching, smiling at my progress and nodding as if to say, "See, I told you so," although I knew Jud would be too polite to utter those words.

Another day later, despite having put myself through a quite extensive stretching routine the evening before, my muscles were in even worse condition, and my hands were so raw and cramped it hurt to extend my fingers. The evidence of spring all around me lent a sense of urgency to my mission to get the seeds in the ground. Only a week before, there had been frost on the ground in the mornings. Now there was dew. Shoots of green burst from the tips of branches around me as I made my way down the path to the stream to perform my morning ablutions.

I decided to begin digging the hole for the outhouse. I decided I would soak my hands in the stream for a while before beginning this task. Blisters had swollen and burst on my palms, and the pus had dried, pasting the rags to my hands. I cleaned and rewrapped my cut, then let the cool water run over my blistered hands. Wait, I said to myself—the water is running over my hands. Running over the rocks and sand. *Running* for goodness sake. It was running water! I had no need for sprinklers.

Abandoning the outhouse project for the time being, I chopped down two small pine trees, cut them into six four-foot lengths and sharpened each at one end. With a sledgehammer and the six spears under my arms, I headed into the woods and found a suitable spot for a dam, ten or fifteen yards northeast of the clearing, and waded into the middle of the stream. The only time in my life before this that I'd used a sledgehammer was when I was in the ninth grade. This was at a carnival, on another outing with my housemates from Rigby. The sledgehammer was one of those fat, padded instruments that the carnival-goer pays a dollar to throw down with all his might in an attempt to send a chunk of metal up a post, ring a bell and win a stuffed pink elephant for his girlfriend—the existence of either of which, in my life, was equally implausible.

Though I've attempted to eradicate the memory, I know why I was swinging that hammer at that carnival. I'd been forced into it for the amusement of Dan Lander, one of my bullying housemates. He and the others wanted to see me fail, and they got their wish. Each time I lifted the hammer, which was as big as I, and hit the pad at the base of the pole, the piece of metal barely rose a few inches from where it rested before falling back down again. My housemates hooted and laughed, and strangers began to cluster about until a large crowd had gathered around to laugh at me while I impotently flailed the over-sized sledgehammer. I became the biggest attraction at the carnival. Dan kept giving tickets to the man who operated the thing so that I could keep trying. It cost Dan nothing, since he was using tickets he'd stolen from me. Finally, the carnival man, perhaps taking pity on me, told me to stop. He might have noticed that I was crying, though I'd kept my head down, pretending to look determined, pretending to be wiping sweat from my forehead when I lifted my sleeve to wipe the tears away.

Things were different for me now. I'd had a girlfriend, although Pearl had turned out to be too good to be true. She'd joined that crowd at the carnival, had become one of the legions of laughers stretching in a long line through my past while I clubbed my way through life. I could forget her. I knew I could. Just as I'd forgotten those people at Rigby, the people at college and the people at Grund & Greene.

I brought the hammer down, wishing that with my first blow on the top of the pine post I could detonate a bomb that would blow them from my memory and leave me alone forever. At the carnival, the mark I'd had to hit was quite a bit bigger and did not wiggle back and forth in the current of a stream. That first violent swing I took missed the mark entirely; the sledgehammer entered the water with a sad plop, splashed water in my face, and sank into the sandy bottom of the streambed. I missed smashing the bones of my right foot by only a few inches. After a few less ambitious but more accurate taps, I began to sink the post into the ground beneath the stream. I spaced the posts roughly a foot and a half apart, used two-by-fours to give them further support and plywood left over from the cabin roof to form the walls of the dam. The center panel of this wall could be raised and lowered from the bank with the use of a lever made from a long tree branch.

Later in the week, I began planting, but as I pushed the seeds of potatoes, beets, radishes, peas, broccoli and cabbage into the soft, loamy soil, it seemed impossible that they would do anything besides rot there. I'd learned from *The Organic Farmer's Handbook* that succession planting was the key to maximizing the use of soil and space. It would not be for another month that I would begin to sow the seeds for my green beans, tomatoes, peppers, and corn. Sowing seeds was the least strenuous work I'd done thus far, but the most exciting. Never in my life had I watched anything grow, or nurtured it from its birth—with the exception of Elsbeth, Gertrude, Nathaniel, Helga and

Rupert. But they had been nursed and brought up by Louisa, and depended only indirectly on my support.

The work began to change me. As my poison ivy disappeared, I noticed the muscles and veins were beginning to stand out in higher relief on my dirty arms, which already were beginning to look more like those of a farmer than a copywriter. And work of one kind seemed to lead naturally to other work. Though I fed the skunks regularly, often giving them freshly baked bread I baked in the Franklin stove, I worked assiduously on the chicken wire fence, looking forward to the day when I would be able to release them without the fear that they might disappear into the woods. Though I did not know it at the time, this would not be a problem. Since they are creatures of habit, skunks can be quickly conditioned. One example of this is that as a result of my daily extraction of musk, their glands were forced to produce twice as much of the substance in order for them to be armed for emergencies. I realized this had to be the case a month or so later, when they began to congregate outside the coop each morning, waiting for me to milk them before they went to sleep for the day. Spot was always the first, and if, as happened one or twice, I overslept, he came into the cabin, climbed onto my bed and licked my ear to wake me up. When I came outside, there they all were, waiting. Some of them would come over to me and scratch at my pant leg, or, to show their annoyance, waste a shot of musk by shooting it straight into the air. We'd formed a bond of mutual dependency, and though I tried to maintain a professional relationship with them, I couldn't help myself at times. After relieving Whisky of her musk, I'd nuzzle my face in her fur, or drape her around my neck like a boa. Sometimes I'd wrestle briefly with Tripper. Sometimes I'd just pretend to oversleep, and when Spot crawled into my bed to rouse me, I'd pounce on him and tickle his belly. But this was not until a month or two later.

By the end of my first two weeks the farm was a different place from the one I'd driven up to in a state of trauma, where I'd found a washed-out real estate sign in front of the cabin in the midst of tall weeds. Where before there had been a particle-board sieve, there was now a shingled roof that looked, if not professional, at least serviceable. The untamed wilderness was now a field of dark, cultivated soil, with long, straight, mounded rows of seedlings, stretching lengthwise from one end of the rectangular clearing to the other. The trenches between the rows were there for a very definite reason. I'd decided—and I'd be happy to announce the fact to Jud—that furrow irrigation would be my irrigation system of choice. After two solid weeks of struggle, I stood in the twilight, exhausted from a good day's work, a shot glass of musk in one hand, a rag with which to mop my brow in the other. My poison ivy was gone, except for a few scattered blotches and scabs. The muscles in my arms and legs were no longer sore. I felt strong. I had created my own self-sufficient world where I could pursue my passion for musk without interruption. However, I could not help the fact that I wanted someone to see this expression of my will, someone to appreciate this marriage of farm and function. And that someone, I knew, was Pearl.

The next morning I spent some time driving my handmade posts into the ground for the fence and stapling the chicken wire to it. I had about three quarters of the field surrounded, and figured I'd be finished before the sprouts were out and in danger of being nipped by rabbits and squirrels. Around noon, I took a bath in the stream, loaded the tiller into the trunk of the Eldorado and headed off to Jud's.

When I swung open the door, Roy and Doug swung their heads in my direction almost as slowly as a pair of sunflowers following the path of the sun across the sky, and with as much expression upon their faces. My stomach muscles contracted at the sound of the bell tinkling over my head. Round two with Matt Baxter. I hadn't seen his maroon pickup in front of Jud's, but I supposed he could have gotten a ride there with someone else. I half expected him to call out "Old MacDonald," like a war whoop and shatter my jaw with a roundhouse punch as soon as I stepped through the door. This was why I pushed the tiller ahead of me and barreled into the store prepared to mow down anyone or anything in my way. Jud happened to be stepping out from an aisle near the door at that moment, and had to leap back to avoid having his legs clipped out from under him by his own tiller.

"Whoah!" he said, as I slowed down. Matt Baxter didn't seem to be in the store. "Gawd Damien, you scared the bejeezus outta me." Roy and Doug sat eyeing me and the tiller from beneath the brims of their baseball caps as if an unusual-looking raccoon had come sniffing around their garbage, and they were not sure whether to shoot it, or let it eat and move on. I wondered why neither of them ever seemed to do anything at all. I was pretty certain that Doug was employed at the store, but all he seemed to do was periodically produce a bag of tobacco from which he extracted the dark brown leaves he packed into his fat face. This process was most disagreeable to observe. The strands of tobacco dangled from his fingers like earth worms as they made the journey from the pouch in his hands to the squirrel-like pouch in his cheek. Roy, who didn't appear to work at the store, did even less than Doug.

"Just returning the tiller, Jud," I announced. "Thanks for recommending it to me. It proved to be indispensable, I must say. Quite a handy piece of machinery." Jud looked at me with surprise. However absurd, I was, for all intents and purposes, a farmer now, and it made me exuberantly, ridiculously happy. "Oh, and in answer to your question of a couple weeks ago, I was unable to discern what sort of irrigation system it was Mr. Krauthammer used, but I've decided that for myself, furrow irrigation is just the thing."

"I'll be damned," Jud said. He lifted the John Deere cap, scratched his stubbly gray crew cut, and then clamped the cap back on. "I didn't know you was capable of that, Damien."

"What do you mean?" I snapped. "Of course I'm perfectly capable of manual labor."

"Oh no, not that." Jud smiled. "Me'n the boys here," he nodded in the direction of Roy and Doug, "we didn't reckon you could say more'n four words at a time. You're gettin' to be a regular chatterbox livin' up there on your own."

Roy and Doug both laughed as if this were the wittiest comment they'd ever heard, which, considering their circumscribed realm of experience, was quite possible. And though I do not usually appreciate jokes made at my expense, I shook my head and chuckled as Jud relieved me of the tiller and wheeled it to the back of the store. For a rare moment in my life, I was just one of the boys. I could afford to laugh. Yes, for the moment, I felt rich. The sun was shining, Matt Baxter was not around, I'd made myself a farmer, and I'd earned Jud's respect.

"I'll be needing some piping, Jud," I said, when he'd returned to the front of the store. "I've built a dam, you see."

Jud stood in front of the counter, looked me over and cocked his head. "You get in a fight with your cat?" he asked, nodding at the bandage on my arm. "I'd guess it was a polecat by the smell of ya." Then he knitted his eyebrows. "Hey, you smelled last time you were in here too, didn't ya, when ya had that poison ivy real bad? What're you startin' a skunk farm up there?"

Half an hour later I was in the Highbridge library, where I'd awoken Robby Krauthammer, whose apparent disregard for the spring

weather that had so invigorated me had inspired me to ring his bell
with such enthusiasm and then tease him a bit. But now I found myself being talked to at an astonishing velocity by a young man whose
mind hopped from one topic to another like a leprechaun on amphet-
amines. "See, everyone doesn't have to live this way," Robby said, waving his scrawny arms at the shelves of books as if they represented
the status quo. "The two point three kids," he gestured at the Fiction
section, "the two-car garage," he waved a hand at the History shelves,
"satellite dish, bowling club membership—"

"Robby," I interrupted, "I'm just returning these books here," I
tapped the stack of books with my index finger, "and I would like to
know if there is a bookstore nearby where I could buy some books so
I don't have to come in here anymore."

"Oh, yeah, yeah, sure, man, sorry," he said, bobbing his head up
and down like a pigeon. "I go off on a tangent like that sometimes.
It used to happen to me in college all the time. Professors always
got pissed at me. School was such a *drag*, man. I don't know what's
worse—work or school." He bent down to pick up the coffee mug
and the newspaper that had wound up on the floor as a result of my
suddenly awakening him with the bell. Shaking his head at the *Highbridge Herald* as he folded it in half, he said, "This is crazy, this stuff
about Matt Baxter, isn't it?" At the mention of the name, my stomach
lurched, scrotum sack shriveled tight, and I stood up straighter. "Rat
Bastard—that oughta be his name," Robby said.

"What? What stuff about him?" I asked, trying not to sound too
concerned, though I experienced a sudden craving for a shot of musk.

"About how he raped his niece. They haven't pinned it on him yet
though. Probably won't." Robby tossed the newspaper on the counter,
yawned and stretched his arms over his head with his fingers inter-
locked. "So anyway, how's it goin' up there on my dad's old place?"
Then, before I had a chance to answer, he pulled out a book from the
middle of the stack, spilling the other books across the counter, and
held it up with two hands like Moses raising his stone tablet of the Ten
Commandments. *The Organic Farmer's Handbook* blocked our faces
from one another. "Dude!" Robby exclaimed. Then, his voice deepening with reverence, he said, "Now this is a *good* book." I wanted to
know more about what Matt Baxter had done, but I was almost afraid
to look at the newspaper. Robby's eyes were wide with awe as he lowered the book to the counter. "Did you read the section about interplanting in here? Now *that* is the way to go. No way they can tell what

you're growing, even if they fly right over. Even if they walk up to the edge of the field and look at it."

"What do you mean? Who can't tell what you're growing?" I heard the door swing open behind me and Robby's face suddenly became serious.

"So, just returning these books, sir?" he said. "Do you have your library card?"

A fiftyish woman in a brown flannel skirt with a matching jacket walked around the circulation desk. I could not help noticing her wide hips and plump buttocks, which seemed to move independently of the rest of her body as she bustled around the desk. There was a stirring in my trousers that had not occurred since the last time I'd seen Pearl.

"Hi Margaret," Robby said.

"Hello Robby." The woman put a bag on the counter, from which she unloaded a sheaf of papers. "Excuse me, I want to put these away before I forget." Robby moved aside while she stooped down in front of me to put the papers in one of the shelves beneath the counter. "I just ran off a few copies of the library card form, not that we get hordes of new members knocking down the doors every day." Her blouse hung open, and I could see a dark line of cleavage plunging down into a white brassiere. She straightened up and smiled at me, wrinkles gathering in little bouquets at the corners of a pair of hazel eyes. "You must be the new member. You took our last form," she said, and gave me a wink. She was absolutely succulent—the way I imagined Pearl would look in about twenty years, the time only adding to and refining her beauty. It was obvious from her accent and her industriousness that she was not from this part of the country; she was from the Northeast. I could easily picture her as the owner of an apple farm who liked to go out and pick apples all day despite the fact that she'd hired plenty of migrant workers. Her ruddy cheeks and even her hair seemed to radiate her personality—as if vigor and determination had made it wiry and gray. She was also the first reasonably articulate human being I'd encountered in Highbridge. "I'm Margaret Percy," she said, extending a hand that was soft, gentle and warm. I suddenly felt foolish standing there in overalls and a flannel shirt and was embarrassed by my rough, soiled hands.

"Damien Youngquist," I managed to make audible. Almost before the name was out of my mouth she turned to Robby, and I was left staring at her panty line, her deliciously bulging hips and rump.

"I have to do some work in the back," she said, and bustled out from behind the circulation desk and went to the back of the room. I followed her with my eyes and continued to look at the door through which she'd gone.

"Old Peg," Robby said. "Square old peg in a round Highbridge." He rolled his eyes. "If it wasn't for her, this job would be a total blow-off. She's always givin' me projects while she does God-knows-what in that back room. Old bitch. Anyway, I was wondering, could I come up there to your place one day and see how you're doing things up there? It would help me out a lot, since I'm plannin' on getting a similar gig goin'."

"Robby, I do not care for visitors," I said, rather distractedly, as I could not help glancing continually at the door at the back, hoping Margaret might reappear. That woman had winked at me! I was quite certain of it. And now I was much less certain I wanted to stop visiting the library. "I do, however, want to know where there is a decent bookstore in the vicinity," I said to Robby. "Perhaps Ms. Percy would know where to find a good one," I said, then added casually, "Is it Ms. or Mrs. Percy?"

"Nah, don't worry," Robby said, waving his hand to dismiss Margaret from the conversation. "I can tell ya where there's a bookstore, but first, lemme tell ya about this idea I got. You ever hear of *The Organic Gardener*?" His eyebrows were raised hopefully.

"A friend of yours, I presume?"

Robby smiled and gave me a light punch on the shoulder. "Yeah, heh, heh, right. The *magazine*, man. I'm gonna write an article for them." He paused, lowering his chin and glaring at me in what I supposed was a sardonic, literary look, and said, "I'm a *writer*." He managed to infuse the word "writer" with the flavor of danger, as if he were letting me know he worked as a hit man in his spare time. "I was wondering if I could come up to visit your farm, and use you, I mean, your farm, in my article?"

"Oh, certainly not. Goodness. I could think of nothing more vulgar and intrusive. And besides, magazines exist almost exclusively for the promulgation of an obscene culture of vanity and greed. The last thing I'd want would—"

"Alright, okay, man, okay," Robby said, taking a step back from the counter, and waving a hand around as if to erase his words from the air. "Forget it then, forget I mentioned it, dude," Robby said. "Nothing to get hung up about. Listen, I like really respect what you're doing, that's all, and I thought I could learn from you. Listen, can I come up there and just check it out? I mean, I could give you a hand. Help out with the hoeing or whatever."

This gave me pause. As much as I detested the presence of other human beings, it was true that I could have used another pair of hands to help me on the farm, especially to help lay all the piping I'd just bought that day.

"I might even be able to give you some advice," Robby said. "I mean, I never actually farmed before, but I've read a lot about it. Like, for example, you didn't plant any hybrid seeds, like they sell down at Jud's, did ya?"

"Well, yes, actually, I did."

Robby gave me a desperate look, then swung his body to the side, slumped his shoulders, dangled his helpless arms and exhaled heavily. It was the most physical display of exasperation I'd ever seen. "*Dude*," he said emphatically, "you're playing right into their hands, man. Did you look at the names of the companies on the backs of those seed packets?"

"Robby, would it be safe to assume that you intend never to reveal the secret whereabouts of a bookstore in this remote corner of the world?"

"No, I'm serious, dude. You look at those packets. They're put out by the same companies that manufacture the fertilizers and the pesticides. They breed those hybrids so that they're vulnerable to all kinds of shit, get it? So you *need* to buy their products. These are multinational corporations, man, they want con*trol.* They wanna make everyone dependent on their seeds and poisonous chemicals. Lemme ask you this, did Jud try to sell you some pesticides and fertilizers?"

Now that I thought of it, Jud had asked me if I'd wanted to buy some pesticides that very afternoon. He'd showed me a pump sprayer I could wear on my back. He'd also asked me, in that manner of an inquiring chum he often employed, what I intended to use for fertilizer. I'd sidestepped his questions, opting to try things on my own first, as I had before renting the tiller. Now I began to wonder if behind Jud's benevolent smile was the agenda of evil garden-seed-fertilizer-pesticide conglomerates.

Robby must have seen the realization creeping across my face. He slapped the counter, then shook his hands in front of himself once, as if flicking water from them. "Goddamnit," he said. "See, it's the government—it's controlled by big business. Nobody listens to me.

The Department of Agriculture is in cahoots with all the big farmers. They're ruining this country, man, serious. It's the biggest scam goin'." He was beginning to hyperventilate.

"Robby, despite what Jud and the United States government may have going, I've got other plans as to how to deal with pests on my farm." I did, too. That was one problem to which I knew I had the solution.

"Oh, really, what?"

"I'll tell you, if you tell me where the bookstore is," I said.

"Well, can I come up to your farm? I got the day off on Friday, I'll give you a hand."

I thought of the trench I would have to dig to lay the piping, the weeds that had already begun to sprout everywhere, and the tedious task of collecting mulch from the woods. I glanced at Robby's skin, so pale it almost matched his white t-shirt. He would burn to a crisp after an hour in the sun. "Bring your work clothes, and consider it a deal," I said.

"Cool," he said. "Alright, dude, see you on Friday."

"And where might I find a bookstore?"

"Oh yeah, there's one at the mall." He raised his hand above his head and pointed toward the Children's section of the library. "You go up Marlborough Road about three miles, you can't miss it."

14

I shall not bother to enumerate the series of olfactory offenses I endured at the Highbridge Mall. Nor shall I complain of the cacophony of human voices, amplified by the cathedral-like acoustics of the building—fitting, I suppose, for a culture that worships commerce. But I will take issue with the assault upon my vision, the barrage of colors and the neon signs that imprinted themselves on my sight after the most cursory glance, so that I saw the names of several stores floating before me as I made my way, and which were responsible for the ensuing twenty-four-hour headache which required several shots of musk. What with the overload of sensory input, it's a wonder people don't constantly stumble, stagger and collide with one another in shopping malls. Instead, they participate in the raw insanity of it: though shopping is not a particularly athletic undertaking, I saw many people wearing sweat suits that featured fluorescent colors and the most disturbing fabric patterns. Is this a sort of armor, I wondered—are they fighting garishness with garishness? The swirl of colors, lights and noises is so disorienting, I can easily see how a shopper could become delirious and spend more than he intended. In fact, I believe that shopping malls are designed with this purpose in mind. The consumer, intoxicated by lights, sounds and colors, is trapped like a mouse in a maze, deprived of parking garage signs and forced to spend his way out of the trap. Thus, in hope of purchasing his freedom, he falls victim to a spending frenzy in the throes of which he will buy unnecessary, overpriced accessories as well as food not fit to serve a skunk. And such flailing only tightens the consumer's entrapment within the system's web, for he becomes a slave who toils solely for the plastic card he mistakenly believes to be his key to happiness.

The selection of books was abysmal. Though the bookstore was small in comparison with the stores that sold far less important commodities, space was wasted displaying the books as if they were merely the fashionable ones for the current season. The books themselves looked more like cereal boxes, with bright colors and catchy titles designed to capture the interest of young children. I have tried reading the contemporary novelists. I have. The problem is that there are so many of them that seem to have had, at some point in their lives, a little dribbling of inspiration. Recognizing this, they decided to announce to the world that they'd had such a dribble, and had fully expected the world to share in a celebration of their dribbling. No doubt this is all well and good for these authors, their friends, the publishing company, other companies with which it does business, the many people employed by them, and the economy in general. However, for the hapless reader who'd hoped the dribble of inspiration would become a stream as the book progressed, and then a river, and finally open into a great lake in which he could immerse himself, paddle about, or dive beneath the surface and encounter new and interesting creatures, then emerge at the far shore, refreshed, with a new perspective from which to view the world—for this reader, the experience is more akin to slogging through a sewer pipe, wishing he'd been warned to wear hip boots as he works his miserable way to the light at the end, where he finally sees that the dribble of inspiration had merely been what rose to the surface of not a lake but a plastic wading pool filled with untreated fecal sludge.

For this reason I tend to stick to the classics. One might presume that world civilizations, having relied to some extent upon the written word for the past couple thousand years or so, would have produced a larger collection of works considered classic than could fit on the front seat of a pickup truck. So far as the residents of Highbridge were concerned, this was not the case. The "Classics" section was the size of a cupboard. Given its contents, if one had been looking for a literary square meal—in terms of representation of different time periods and countries—it would have been difficult to cobble together the most minuscule of appetizers. I bought everything I hadn't read in this section, as well as books from the History, Travel, Mystery, Gardening, Fiction, Thriller and Cooking sections.

When I got home and unloaded the books from my car, I realized I would need a bookshelf. I also intended to make a floor, to cover the dirt, which got stirred up occasionally and made me sneeze, and onto which I was always dropping things that I wanted to keep clean. But first there were more pressing matters. Namely, the fence, the outhouse, the pipeline and the root cellar.

On a Tuesday morning I began digging behind the cabin. The cellar would be a square, eight feet by eight feet—a little less than half the size of the cabin—deep enough to ensure that the vegetables would stay cool and large enough to warehouse the food that would see me through the winter. I'd planted enough potatoes to yield about twenty bushels. They would be my main staple, along with the corn, which I would process into a meal and keep in large sacks. I would also be cellaring squash, carrots, onions and a bushel or two each of radishes and beets. I would make pickles, can tomatoes, beans, and peas.

The fence around the field was completed by Wednesday evening, and just at twilight, when the skunks were beginning to rouse themselves from their slumber, I threw open the door to the skunk coop, "Be free," I said as they all blinked at me from the shadows. "Or at least roam within these fenced-in acres to your heart's content, and try to gather some grub for yourselves." I doubted they would be able to completely support themselves, since most of the land had been cleared. To supplement what they might find, I intended to make some food for them and leave it in the chicken coop each night to ensure that they would return. They all came ambling out of the coop, yawned, exposing their needle-like teeth, stretched their legs, lay down on the ground and wriggled on their backs, then began to explore the farm.

I sat in front of the cabin, sipped skunk musk from a martini glass and watched them for an hour or so in the fading light. What could it hurt to watch, I wondered, as long as I kept my distance and did not become emotionally involved? A couple of young males wrestled with each other in front of the coop. Three young skunks followed their mother in a singlefile line as she walked along, sniffing at the ground, occasionally stopping to eat an insect. In spite of myself, I began to revise their names in my mind to suit their personalities, and later, changed the names on their jars. One female, who always came up to me and rubbed against my leg, I named Constance. There was another who always avoided me. I named her Inconstance. There was a particularly pugnacious male who always instigated fights with the other males. I named him Nasty. Dopey yawned incessantly and never quite seemed to wake up. He lay down while the others played, or came over to where I sat, rested his snout on my boot and fell asleep. I have already mentioned Spot, whose even temper and ability to get along so well with all the others quite impressed me. I watched him making his rounds, interacting briefly with each of the skunks, the way a priest maintains relations with his parishioners. I decided to rename him Father.

That night it rained and I was happy. Snug in my new sheets and blankets on my new mattress, I lay awake listening to the rain tapping on my new roof, thinking of the seeds snug in their beds of soil, soaking up the water, splitting open and pushing up through the ground. On Thursday morning I found most of the skunks sleeping in the skunk coop again. With profound satisfaction, I admired the rounded rows of dirt stretching from one end of my farm to the other. At the end of each row was the seed packet with its picture of what would soon be growing there. I had already made a little trellis for the bean stalks to climb and divided the plots of different vegetables with strands of white string. Yes, everything was in place, neat, orderly, and on time.

But what was this disturbance in the soil of my farm? Here and there, large clumps of dirt seemed to be moving. I removed my glasses, rubbed my eyes, replaced glasses, and looked again. Squinted. Yes, unbelievable as it was, the earth was coming alive and mounds of it were quivering, wriggling, even getting up and walking several yards to wriggle in another spot. There had been nothing mentioned in any of the gardening literature to prepare me for such a phenomenon. I walked slowly and quietly out into the field. As I got closer to them, I saw that the moving clumps were all about the size of my boot and darker than the rest of the ground. In fact they were black. I came right up to within a few yards of one, when it suddenly flew straight up into the air, flapping its wings and cawing. Immediately, the rest of them—there must have been twenty or more—rose up into the air cawing and screeching, and flew off toward the woods. I was astonished, and then, looking down at the holes where the crows had dug out the seeds which I'd engaged in so much industry to plant, enraged.

All around me the ground was punctured with little divots, as if a few helicopters had flown over and the gunners had opened fire on my field. They'd flown off with at least a quarter of my plot of corn, plus what would have become several bushels of potatoes, wheelbarrows full of radishes and beets. I jumped up and down yelling, flinging my fists at the air, swearing death upon each of the invaders, their families and friends.

I suddenly realized a new purpose for my polyester suits, which had been rendered useless by my purchase of overalls, flannel shirts and work boots at Jud's. There was work for them now, by golly. My suits would go to work without me. They'd done it before, more or less, in my life as a copywriter. Each morning in New Essex, as I'd slipped on my jacket and straightened my tie, I'd felt myself slipping out of my body. I left my true self at home by the umbrella stand and sent the suit to work. I suspected that the majority of suits I saw each day in the city were likewise acting of their own volition. People left their true selves in the dreams from the previous night or others they hadn't visited since school, before the suit had commandeered their bodies and begun to drag them through lives that became more deadening with each day they did not spend cultivating their dreams.

I hacked down a few small trees, lashed together three crosses, martyred my suits upon them and placed them strategically around the farm. They were the best-dressed scarecrows I'd ever seen. I spent the rest of the day replanting corn and potatoes. The time I spent replanting and making scarecrows set my schedule back, and I was thankful that Robby Krauthammer would be coming to help me the next day.

The next morning, walking through the woods near the stream, I trampled on a weed that released a most delicious odor. Looking around, I seemed to be in a patch of these plants with yellow spathes sticking up from a gathering of large cabbage-like leaves. I knelt down and breathed in deeply. It was skunk cabbage, and I was already envisioning the most delectable salad and a sweet steam rising from a pot of skunk cabbage soup on my stove. I dug all of them up and transplanted them along the inside of my fence. Taking their seeds, I planted enough to go almost around the entire perimeter of my field. By midsummer, I would have a hedge of skunk cabbage surrounding the farm.

By eleven o'clock on Friday morning I'd assumed that Robby had forgotten his offer of assistance. I was standing in a hole behind my cabin, digging the root cellar when I wasn't swatting at the black flies swarming around me. They were out in full force and had begun a blood feast on my back. My perspiration seemed to enhance their attraction; I felt like a piece of honey-glazed chicken sitting out on a buffet table. From a distance came a strange, whining, chirping sound that turned out to be the engine of Robby Krauthammer's VW microbus fighting its way over the hills and gullies of Fisher Lane. It continued past the opening that led to my clearing, faded into the distance and then stopped, I assumed, at the hunting lodge. I guessed Robby had missed the turn and was now sitting in his vehicle, running his fingers through his shimmering hair, admiring the unattainable lodge. Twenty minutes or so later, the engine started up again and grew louder as it approached my land. Then it poked its nose into the driveway, came lurching into the clearing and stopped next to my Eldorado. On the side panel that had faded from red to pink, a large peace symbol had been painted in blue and next to that, a large, green marijuana leaf. Rust ran in a blistered fringe along the bottoms of the doors and around the wheel wells. It reminded me of my poison ivy outbreak and I began to scratch needlessly at my chest and neck. The engine shut off with an exhausted groan, then started itself up again for a second like a dying man awakening for one last shuddering, gargling gasp, then went silent. Robby burst from the door of the vehicle—his hair tossing about like a pom-pom—a happy clown leaping from his clown car. He didn't see me at first. He looked around, tugging his hair into a ponytail, then walked up to the front door of the cabin and knocked.

"Yes?" I called out from where I stood in the hole behind the cabin.

"Damien. Dude. It's Robby. I was gonna help you out, remember?"

"Yes, Robby, I remember," I called.

"Is it alright if I come in?" he asked. I could hear him swinging open the door of the cabin as he spoke. The door thudded against the inside wall. I heard Robby take a couple of steps into the cabin. Then came his voice, confused, muted by the wood of the structure in which he stood, "Damien?" he asked. "Where are you, man?"

"Back here burrowing behind the cabin."

Robby came around to the back of the cabin looking perplexed. Then his face lit up and he chuckled. "Don't mess with my mind like that, man. What're you doing, building a bomb shelter or something?"

"Root cellar, Robby, root cellar. One who plans for the future does not find himself living in the past."

"Yeah, that's cool. Hey listen, guess what? A friend of a friend of mine came into some dough, I mean, we're all gonna pitch in, but he's got the bulk of it. We're buying that land next to yours. We already talked to Winchell about it. He was worried about us being able to make the payments, but I said, man, don't worry about *that*, just let us have the land and we'll make the money." I began to clamber out of the ditch and Robby extended a hand to pull me out. "Hey man, we're gonna be neighbors." He continued to hold my hand after I was out of the hole. Smiling, he pumped my hand like a politician, then performed that bizarre handshake routine with which he'd manipulated my hand when I first met him at the library.

I felt like falling backwards into the hole and telling Robby to make good use of the shovel by burying me and saving us both a fair amount of hassle. I felt my solitude slipping away; I imagined rock concerts being held at the former hunting lodge, the noise finding its way into my cabin while I sat in bed, huddled by my kerosene lamp trying to concentrate on a book. "When will you be moving in?" I asked, weakly.

"In a couple weeks," Robby said, still beaming. "You gotta meet my friends. I can't wait. I was just up there checking out that lodge. It's gonna be a total party house."

I needed to sit down and have a shot of musk or two. "And how many of you will there be?"

"Let's see, there's me and Terry—he's my best friend, really cool dude—and then Beazly, he's the one who's got the cash. Terry knows him better than I do. And Fiona, my girlfriend, is gonna live with us, too. And maybe Beazly's girlfriend. Her name's Star, I think. Is that it? Maybe it was Moon or Venus—it has something to do with planets and shit. Parents musta been hippies. Galaxy? No. Maybe it was Luna. God damn these black flies." He waved a hand in front of his face. "Well, anyway, whatever. So that's four of us, maybe five."

I hung my head and began walking toward the twenty-foot lengths of plastic piping I'd stacked next to the cabin. A few days before, I'd tied a tin cup to the water tank on the side of the cabin. I filled the cup now and took a drink. This neighbor news was the worst news I'd had in a long time. Winchell, that good-for-nothing, swindling, two-faced, real-estate monger, had sworn Robby would never move into the hunting lodge.

Robby followed me. "Hey, don't worry, man, we won't bother you or anything. We'll be busy doing our own farming. After all, we gotta raise the money to keep the place. God*damn* it smells like skunk around here. Lousy things are all over the place this time of year."

I started thinking about building a large stone wall around my property. "And how do you plan to raise the money?" I dropped the tin cup, letting it clang against the side of the cabin.

Robby gave me a puzzled look. "Dude man... I... wuddayou think—we're gonna grow ganja."

"By 'ganja,' I suppose you mean that plant depicted on the side of your van," I said.

Robby smiled. "You're getting the picture." He slapped at a black fly that had landed on his arm. "Hey, you got any bug dope? Oh, never mind, I got some." He went over to the VW and got out a plastic bottle.

"Look, Robby, I don't want to know anything more about what you plan to do at that hunting lodge."

Robby shrugged. "Okay dude, whatever." He tossed me the bottle of insect repellent. "There's nothing to get paranoid about. I don't know where you're from, but the shit goes on around here all the time."

I applied some of the insect repellent and tossed the bottle back to him. "Could you grab the other ends of these top two pipes?" I asked.

We didn't talk while we moved the pipes, spacing them along the path I'd cleared through the woods from the dam to the field, and then along the lines I'd drawn in the dirt. The pipeline branched out in three directions when it entered the field and then emptied into the furrows I'd dug between the rows of crops. When I wanted to water the field, I would simply close the sliding middle panel on the dam, thus raising the water level until it reached the pipe and drained out into the field. Once water had trickled down through every channel in the field, I would go back up to the dam and re-open the gate.

We began digging a trench in which to lay the pipe—Robby a few yards behind me. He started talking after we'd been working fifteen minutes or so. "I like those scarecrows," he said. "Really sharp." I said nothing. "Saw the roof on the cabin," he said. "Looks pretty good. My dad never did get around to putting a roof on the place."

"Well, he did, just not a very good one," I said, heaving dirt from the trench. I spoke to Robby without turning to look at him.

"Oh, you mean the plywood?" he said. "Nah. Me and some friends put that on in high school. We used to come up here all the time. It was a cool spot to party." Robby seemed to be in much better physical condition than I, because his voice was not strained at all. Streams of sweat flowed down my cheeks, through the forest of my beard, down my back, joined other tributaries and funneled right down into my boots. I'd gotten to love the feeling of sweat in the past few weeks. Once I'd begun to sweat, I knew I was working in earnest.

"Yeah," Robby said. "I don't think my dad lasted here more than a year. Wasn't much of a farmer, I guess. Had the right idea though. I'm not saying it was cool of him to walk out on my mom after she'd just had me, but like, at least he believed in individualism. I do too. That's why I've got such a problem with society and all its dumb rules."

I was puffing and panting, but making some real headway on the trench. "What happened to your father, anyway?" I asked between gasps for breath.

"He went to Canada during Vietnam. I hitchhiked up to Canada one time when I was in high school to try to find him. I don't blame him. Dude man, that war was the worst Goddamn scam. Do you know that our country is the biggest imperial aggressor in the history of the world?"

I stopped digging for a moment and turned around to look at Robby. His shovel planted before him, one arm resting on top of the handle, the other on his hip, he gazed through the mists of the past wars with narrowed, nonconformist eyes. I straightened up and stood there panting, sweat dripping from the end of my nose. I spent so much of my day sweating that I'd tied a piece of string between the ends of my glasses, so they wouldn't slip down my nose and fall off my face. Not that my glasses seemed to help me a great deal these days. I guessed I needed a new prescription, because even now, squinting through the sweat stinging my eyes, I couldn't see Robby's features very well. What I *could* see was that he'd only dug about three feet of the trench, while I'd dug over thirty. I had half a mind to slap the side of his head with my shovel.

"Oh, sorry, man, sorry," Robby said, when he noticed I was staring. He bent over and started digging quickly, sloppily tossing shovelfuls of dirt too far from the trench.

"Robby, follow my example. See how I've piled the dirt next to the hole so we can cover the pipe back up?" I wondered if it would turn out that Robby was to impede rather than expedite the farm's progress. He handled a shovel awkwardly, failing to get very much dirt on it with his feeble scoops. And his flimsy leather sandals didn't seem very practical for farm work.

"Yeah, so I never got to know my old man," Robby said, continuing to talk while he dug. My mom never wanted to talk about him much, but what do you expect?"

"Not much Robby, I've never expected much, and I've received even less." Though I pretended not to be interested, I wondered whether Robby had found his father. For one thing, I was curious about my predecessor on the farm, and for another, I'd never sought out my own father. In my case, I'd been given no clues about him or his whereabouts, and had decided long ago it would be better to let a dead skunk lie.

Robby seemed not to notice my rudeness. "I've got a picture of him, from when he was around my age. You know, someone told me he was friends with Bob Dylan? That's why they named me Robert, I think. My mom won't tell me anything about it." Robby had caught up to my section of the trench, and now walked past me to begin digging a few yards ahead. I'd just reached the corner of the field, so we both had to step over the fence. Now that we were out of the shade of the woods, the sun beat directly down on us and the sweat made my shirt stick to me like a second skin. "My mom's turned into this idiot now. When she's done her shift at the drugstore all she wants to do is sit on the couch with Daryl and a can of beer. It's fuckin' pathetic, man. That's another reason I at least gotta get my own place."

"You live with your mother?" I asked. I wanted to take a break and get a shot of skunk musk, but I had never done this in front of anyone and I thought that doing it in front of Robby could, in effect, be like broadcasting it over the local radio station.

Robby began digging again. His ponytail, darkened and limp with sweat, flopped around on his back like a dead snake. "Well, yeah, I mean I haven't always lived with her. It's just a temporary thing. But now that son-of-a-bitch Daryl is always there with his smelly fuckin' feet on the coffee table, giving me advice like he really knows his fat ass from a meteor crater. Well, it's a long story. So anyway, I've always wanted to buy this place. It means something to me; it's where my dad made his final stand against the establishment. I wanna pick up where he left off." Robby stopped digging and sunk his shovel into the ground. He raised the lower portion of his t-shirt, exposing his pale skinny torso, and wiped his face with it. "Speakin' of beer, I could go for a coldie myself right now."

"So did you find your father?" I asked. I jammed my shovel in the ground and stood with my hands on my hips. We'd finished about three-quarters of the digging.

"Yeah, I found him alright." Robby breathed heavily, his mouth open as sweat ran down the sides of his face. "But he wasn't much of a conversationalist. He was six feet under." Robby looked down at the trench and the white pipe lying beside it, waiting to be buried. His knobby shoulders made it look as if his white t-shirt were hanging from two rounded posts stuck in the ground close together. "I went to the address I'd found in some papers of my mom's, and the people there were other draft dodgers from the States and their girlfriends. They told me my dad died of colon cancer. The funny thing is, if he'd gone and gotten the physical when his number came up, not only would he not have gotten drafted because of the cancer, they might've been able to save him."

"Ironic," I said.

Robby looked up from the trench. "Huh?" he said. His eyes were moist. A stream of sweat ran along his collar bone and followed his leather necklace down his hairless chest into the loose neck of his shirt. He seemed not to notice the flies on his cheek and neck.

"That's irony," I said, feeling much more than seven years his senior. I resisted an urge to put an arm around his sad, frail shoulders, to pat his bony back.

"Yeah, I guess so. I never thought of it like that until I said it just now." He ran his tongue along his lips. "Dude man, I need some water." We went back to the stream, knelt down and slurped the cool water from our hands. This seemed to rejuvenate Robby and he began talking at an impressive rate while we finished the digging and then began laying the pipeline. Or rather, I finished the digging and began laying the pipeline while young Mr. Krauthammer smoked cigarettes, waved at black flies and expatiated upon the evils of "the establishment." After learning the fate of his father, I felt less inclined to reprimand Robby for his lack of interest in physical labor.

"See, they got this system worked out for you from the minute you're born, man. It's all based on institutions. Before you know what's going on, you get sent to the first institution, elementary school, where you learn two things: how to stand in line and how to swallow. Then you go to the next institution, high school, where they make sure you've learned to swallow really good and then they feed you a bunch of shit. Then there's college, where one professor tells you all the shit you swallowed for those first eighteen years was meaningless, and then the next class a different professor tells you there's some magical design in all the shit. Then you join the next institution, the great American work force. You work for some company where you've got no way to express your individuality, not that you even know how to do that, because ever since you went to kindergarten they've been stamping individuality out of you like a wildfire and filling you with shit. And dude, this country was not founded by shitheads." Robby stood with his hands on his hips and shook his head at the shovel he hadn't taken out of the ground for over an hour. "It's gone, man. The individual has been replaced by belief in one institution or another. Big business, that's all it's about anymore. And if you don't fit in their mold, well then you're just screwed. You're an outsider and you don't count. It's fucked, man, it's just totally fucked."

We had lunch sitting on the crates in front of the cabin. Robby shared some of the bags of granola and sunflower seeds he'd brought along. If this is what he dines on, I thought, munching on a few of the dry seeds, it was no wonder he was so thin. I offered him some of my bread. "Wow, you made this yourself?" he asked. I said that I had. "Dude, that's way cool, but I wouldn't touch the stuff; wheat is bad for you man, and this bleached flour is the worst. If rice was the main staple in this country, we'd all be a lot better off, in a lotta ways."

"I see," I said.

Robby spit a sunflower seed shell out of his mouth, took a cigarette from a red-and-white package and lit it. I hadn't followed all of Robby's discourse, because my mind was occupied with how to get at the jars of skunk musk in the coop without him seeing. Robby took a drag from his cigarette. The smoke was beginning to annoy me. It reminded me of the city. It was one of those odious odors—along with exhaust fumes, urine, perfume, feces, rotting vegetables, colognes and body odors—that I thought I'd escaped. Freedom is not to have to smell other people. I'd had that freedom for the past month.

"Yeah, it's the big industries that're ruining this country, taking power away from the little guy," Robby said, while cigarette smoke brought to him by one of the world's largest corporations poured from his nostrils and mouth. "That's why what you and me're doing is so cool. This is how the world is gonna change, man, on a grassroots level. And everybody loves grass." Robby grinned. "Irony, dude. Gotta love it." Suddenly, something behind me caught Robby's attention and he stopped talking, dropped his cigarette on the ground and put his heel down on it, still focused intently on whatever was behind me. "Dude man, you *do* have a problem with skunks."

I turned around and saw Constance walking out of the chicken coop. She sometimes came out in the middle of the afternoon and walked around, blinking in the sunshine. I'd written it off as insomnia. "Oh," I said. "But that's just Cons—"

Robby grabbed my arm. "Shht," he hissed. "Don't move. I know how to take care of this."

"Really," I said.

"I need a stick, a long-ass stick. You can't get too close to 'em."

"Oh, I believe one can," I said.

Robby looked at me with a mixture of confusion and annoyance. Still speaking in a hushed whisper, he said, "Dude, you're from the city, there are some things you just plain don't know." He glanced around the ground outside the cabin. "This should do it," he said, picking up a switch about four feet long.

"You don't intend to flog her, I trust." I could see no reason to whisper.

"What?" Robby hissed. "No, no—I just have to keep it at a distance." While he spoke, Constance turned around and ambled back into the coop. "Shit, this is gonna make it a pain in the ass. Now I have to get it out of there. You can't corner 'em." He began to approach the skunk coop with the stealth of a hunter.

I rose from my crate. "Robby, just a moment," I said, too late. "There's something I'd better tell you." Ignoring me, Robby disappeared into the coop. As soon as I reached the door, he came flying back out and almost knocked me off my feet. He grabbed my arm and tried to pull me away from the coop as if it were in danger of exploding at any second.

"Dude!" he shrieked, "come on!" His eyes were wide with horror. "The place is infested with skunks, man."

I wasn't accustomed to dealing with hysterical people and doing so put me even more in the mood for a shot of musk. "Robby," I tried to say gently, but firmly, "it's quite alright. I keep them here for a purpose."

Robby's eyes darted around the yard as if he expected to find himself surrounded by a skunk firing squad, their rears pointed at him, tails up. "We'll smoke 'em out!" he exclaimed. He didn't seem to have heard my last remark at all. He pulled out the plastic red lighter he used for his cigarettes and began fumbling with it. "That's it. Get some kindling together Damien dude, we'll smoke 'em."

I grabbed both of Robby's shoulders, which felt more like wrists, and shook him. "Damn it man, get ahold of yourself. Didn't you hear what I just said?" Constance came waddling back out of the coop just then, looking a bit miffed, and gazed up at us with her head cocked to one side, as if to say, "Hello, what's all the racket about? Can't you see I'm trying to sleep, and I'm having a bad enough time of it, what with my insomnia, without the two of you brawling outside my bedroom?" My frustration had mounted to such a point that the need for a shot of musk was all-consuming, and what I did next, on impulse, served to illustrate my point to Robby. Picking up Constance and holding her over my head, I squeezed a shot of her musk down my throat. I put her back down, gave her a little pat on the back, and she moseyed back into the coop.

Robby drifted momentarily out of focus, but I could see that his mouth was hanging open. He looked from me to the skunk coop. "Dude, no way. I mean, *no... way.*" Then he took a couple of steps backward, scrunching up his face. "Ugh, God," he waved a hand in front of his face and coughed a couple times. He turned and went to where he'd left his cigarettes on the crate we'd used as a picnic table. Lighting a cigarette, then turning back to me, his face still bunched up in disgust, he said, "Like, how come you're not puking or anything? God, I can hardly stand it. And you—it went right down your—ugh, man! That's fuckin' gross. Anybody ever tell you that?"

I was quite calm now. Robby's distress did not matter in the least. In that musky moment, I wouldn't have cared if he'd immediately gone and told my secret to everyone in town. "No one has ever seen me do what I just did," I said. "So no, no one has ever had the opportunity to inform me that it is gross." I walked over to one of the crates, sat down and gazed out over the field. Green shoots and leaves sprouted everywhere out of the dark soil, white strings neatly segregated one crop from another. It wouldn't be long before I had some of my own fresh vegetables and could stop eating out of cans.

Robby sat down on the other crate and observed me. "Dude man, you look stoned," Robby said. He turned and looked at the coop then back at me. "Hey, Damien," he said. But I wasn't paying attention to him. He got up and left for a little while; it's hard to say for how long, since I was half lost in a musk dream. I was beside myself with joy. My own farm. I had my own farm and could do as I pleased here. I could sit in the sun, warming my blood all day like a lizard on a rock. No one to tell me what to do. No sitting in front of the computer for hours. No reports to get done for Mr. Hastings.

"Hello, anybody in there?" Robby said. He'd sat back down on the crate next to me and was leaning forward with his elbows on his knees, peering at me as if I were at the bottom of a hole much deeper than my root cellar. I turned to him and smiled. Poor, confused, fatherless Robby. He took a plastic sandwich bag of marijuana and a pack of rolling papers out of his back pocket. "You get high off those skunks, is that it? That's why you keep those jars of their juice in the chicken coop."

"Robby, I won't mention the marijuana if you don't mention the skunk musk to anyone. Mum's the word."

Robby's brow wrinkled as he crumpled a couple of buds into one of the creased papers and began rolling a joint. I'd tried marijuana once in college, but it hadn't agreed with me. "People grow pot all over this state, man," Robby said. "Second largest crop. And besides, what're you worried about, there's nothing illegal about skunks is there?"

"No, but I wouldn't want everyone to know. Margaret, for example, if you—"

"Peg? The old bat at the library? What's it matter if she knows?"

Old bat! How could he degrade her so? She was beautiful, intelligent, and in no way resembled a nocturnal flying mammal. Nor was she old. "I'd just prefer she not. And other people. I've had problems along these lines before."

Robby lit his joint, held in his first hit for several seconds and exhaled a large cloud of smoke. "I think you're sweet on old Peg."

I sat up straight on my crate. My cheeks warmed. "It's not that. I just, well, you see, Robby, I'm a rather private person. Today has been an unusual experience for me. I think for some reason I feel obligated to you because this was your father's land."

"Hey, no sweat, man. But if you've got the hots for Peg, go for it. Her husband died about ten years ago, and it's not like there's a huge line of guys waiting to bag the Highbridge librarian." Robby held the smoldering, torpedo-shaped cigarette out to me.

"Robby, don't—" I cut myself off. I wanted to say, "Don't you dare talk so abusively about that woman again," but was afraid that would be too close to a confession of my affection. "No, thank you," I said to the joint. The smell was not as offensive as the commercial cigarettes he'd been smoking; it was actually somewhat pleasant. I considered taking a couple of hits just to be polite. But besides the fact that I did not care to spend the rest of the afternoon in a state of giddy paranoia, followed by hours of depression and self-loathing, I could not stand the idea of tainting my lungs with the filthy stuff. People really ought to think about their drug choices before using their bodies as disposals for all the THC, nicotine, alcohol, caffeine and sugar society pushes on them. In more highly evolved human societies, people live in grass huts and use more civilized drugs, such as kava root, which calms them after a stressful day rather than making them loopy.

"I don't hold it against you or anything." Robby said, taking another drag from his joint. "Shit. You get high off skunks, I get high off weed—whatever." He looked out over the field. "I think what you're doin' here is great, man. I think my dad would've done it about the same. And I'm happy with the other place. Actually, it's better, because at least the lodge has electricity."

We finished laying the pipeline that afternoon and got it all covered. It was time for the big test. Robby and I went to the dam, lowered the gate with the lever I'd installed, and watched the pool fill up. Like an overflowing sink, the water began to trickle into the only outlet, the pipe, and as the water level grew steadily higher, the trickle became a gush and we knelt by it, listening to it echoing down the pipeline.

"Come on," I said, and dashed through the woods, out into the field. Robby ran behind me. Water was already pouring from the end of the first prong of the forked pipeline and forming little streams in the furrows between the rows of vegetables. I ran to the end of the second prong and then the third. Water poured from each of them. The field began to fill with water.

Robby ran over to me, trampling a few potato sprouts. "Dude, we did it!" He held his hand up in the air as if saluting someone far off in the distance. I turned and looked. There was no one but one of my scarecrows, then the woods at the edge of the field, so I turned back to face Robby. "High-five, man," he said, his arm still extended over his head.

I'd heard the term before and now connected it with the action I'd seen performed by other young men when I was in college. "Oh, right," I said, "high five, of course." I raised my arm and slapped his hand.

⟨~⟩

Over the next several days, everything seemed to fall into place. I finished digging my water closet and root cellar. The irrigation system worked splendidly. Later, I added another line that ran through a filtering system and into the holding tank on the side of the house, so I didn't have to carry water to it. Also, between swatting black flies, I collected leaves and pine needles from the woods for mulch and pulled the weeds from around my seedlings.

Spring and the mischief in me were in full swing. The leaves had started from the trees like little green handkerchiefs and I imagined Margaret Percy naked, on all fours, giving me horseback rides around the dirt floor of my cabin. A honeysuckle bush near the entrance to the field was in bloom, as were the skunk cabbages all along the fence. So that the skunks could come and go as they pleased, I cut a section of the fence and made a door that swung open when a small lever on either side was depressed. This the skunks could easily do with a stomp of a paw. One day, I gathered them together and demonstrated several times how it worked. The door flew up, they walked through, and the door swung back down. This way, rabbits and other creatures who were not in the know would be kept from my crops, while the skunks could take trips into the woods and once again hunt for their own food, relieving me of that responsibility.

What with the skunk-cabbage hedge and the skunks roaming freely over the grounds, my farm was the muskiest world one could visit. Not that I anticipated any visitors other than Robby, occasionally, when I wanted him to help out with some of the chores around the farm. However, if perchance Margaret happened to come to my neck of the woods, say, to retrieve an overdue book (she'd be forced to pay me a visit, since I had no telephone and no mailbox), there were a few things in the way of comfort I might want to have. Among these were the improvements I'd been procrastinating on: a floor, an outhouse and a bookshelf. Every time I looked at the books stacked up on the table I wanted to put them away and thus suffered a perpetual frustration of my tidying-up impulses. I needed more wood and nails, for which I decided to go to Jud's. Since I would be in town, I might pay a visit to the library, simply to be neighborly. It would be good of me, I thought, to drop by, for her sake—to let her know there was another intellect in the area.

If I could have guessed that my next visitors, as uninvited and unwanted as a flock of crows, would be Robby, a couple of his friends, and, of all the foul beings to stalk the earth on two legs, Matt Baxter, I would have spent less time worrying about amenities and would have taken some pains to make the place less accessible.

And so, oblivious, I set off for Jud's at about noon one bright spring morning. I looked over the corn fields divided by the long, flat stretch of the country road on which I drove. The stalks were as high as a dog's eye, which I was comforted to see, as my own had reached more or less the same height. I didn't recognize the approaching pickup truck and I wasn't thinking about Matt Baxter. As it got closer, I noticed that the truck was maroon, but even then I did not register the significance of this fact.

My thoughts bulged with the brown-skirted hips of Margaret Percy. I was picturing her in my cabin, the kerosene lamps turned down low, an orange light from the coals and waning flames in the Franklin stove filtering through the side vent and playing on the walls. I was picking a treasured volume from the bookshelf. (I'd have mentioned during dinner that I'd built the bookshelf myself—and what could make a librarian feel more at home than a bookshelf?) Holding the book like a dove in my hands, I described how it had provided me a window to another world. With a shrewd smile, perhaps a wink, I said she could borrow it, but that if she failed to return it on time, I would have to think of some suitable fine. Margaret blushed and glanced down at the newly-installed floorboards as I took a step closer to her. Our fingertips brushed as she took the book from my hands. She lowered her glasses and let them hang from their silver chain on her pillowy bosom. We looked into each other's eyes. She raised her chin, her mouth inches from mine.

A horn blared. Shaken from my fantasy, I realized I was staring at the grill of a truck not a car length in front of me. I swerved and skidded onto the shoulder of the road, missing disaster by inches. As I did, for a split second, Matt's face flashed by mine, so close I could have grabbed his nose. His head was sticking out of the window of his pickup as if he were straining to get it into the window of my car in order to bite my head off. For many nights afterward I would replay that instant in my mind, so it's possible that memory may have colored it more vividly, but I swear I could smell the beer and tobacco on his breath, see the fillings in his stained teeth. "Chicken shit city slicker!" he yelled. When I'd gotten my bearings again I realized that I'd driven past Jud's. I turned into the parking lot of Highbridge Guns & Ammo to make a U-turn, my heart thumping away like a jackrabbit trying desperately to kick its way out of my chest. For a few moments, I sat there in the parking lot collecting my scattered wits, admiring the guns lined along the barred window of the store before I headed back to Jud's.

Jud stood up from his swivel chair behind the desk, put his hands on his hips and looked me over. Roy, the broken-down slouch, remained in his director's chair. His red baseball cap announced, stupidly, "Diesel."

"Yuh look like you just seen a ghost!" Jud said.

"I only wish," I said, not realizing, until the words left my mouth, that murderous was the most appropriate adjective to describe my state of mind at that moment.

Jud raised his cap and eyebrows. His lips formed a circle as he emitted a low whistle. "Well," he said, looking down at Roy and then back at me, "it looks like somebody got a bee under his bonnet."

"I've never been partial to bonnets, Jud," I said, "nor to any other women's accoutrements, in case the implication is that I have some secret penchant for cross-dressing."

Jud's eyebrows knitted themselves for a moment. "Whoa, easy there boss," he said. Then in a lighter tone, "Hey, I see the calamine lotion worked. And if I'm not mistaken, you've maybe even put on a few pounds."

It was true. There was no trace of the lumps that had formerly covered my body, and the shirt I wore beneath my overalls felt tight in the shoulders, as if it'd shrunk. My arm muscles bulged from the digging, hammering, lifting, pushing and pulling required to get my farm up and running. I recognized that without Jud's guidance I might not have made it, and I was suddenly ashamed of my rude entrance and petulant attitude since Matt, not Jud, was the source of my annoyance.

"So, what can we do you for, anyway?" Jud asked. I told him my plans and he instructed me as to which kinds of lumber I should use for which projects, all the while speaking as if only reminding me of what I already knew, saying things like, "Course, you'll want a good number of two-by-fours for studs for the outhouse." He helped me load all the lumber onto the roof of the Eldorado and tie it down. "So, you need any insecticides while you're here?" Jud asked as he rang me up at the register for the nails and lumber.

I scrutinized the man, remembering what Robby had said about the conspiracy among multinational companies. Jud stared back at me, the blue eyes like two clear pools in the parched, cracked desert of his face. He had nothing to hide, although I suspected he easily could have if he'd wanted to; his were the eyes of a cardsharp. But on the other hand, he didn't look like the kind of person who would be used as a tool in some corporate conspiracy. It was on the tip of my tongue to ask him about Robby's theory and I probably would have, had Roy not been sitting there, like a hunter eyeing a deer, waiting for me to make a wrong move so he could shoot me one of his bitter, gaptoothed smiles and produce one of those hideous cackles of laughter. Buzzard, I thought, looking at him. The man is transmogrifying into a buzzard right here in Jud's Country Store.

"No, I don't think I want any chemicals on my plants," I said.

Jud shrugged, not at all the way I imagined a multinational conspirator would shrug. "Suit yerself. But by the middle of summer, you'll find yerself up to yer ears in every kinda pest imaginable."

"Oh, I realize that," I said, thinking of Robby and his friends. "They've already announced that they're on their way."

Jud gave me a puzzled look as I began to back away from the counter. "Uhuh," he said. "Well, I guess that's to yur advantage." Just before I turned around to leave, I glanced at Roy, who was staring at me with a muddle of hatred and incomprehension on his vulturine face. "Don't be a stranger, now, Damien," I heard Jud say to my back as I walked through the door.

Robby was not at the library, which was just as well, since I'd really wanted to see Margaret. There didn't seem to be anyone about at all when I first entered, and I was alone for a moment with the deliciously musty, mildewy smell of old books. This scent I've always associated with the secret worlds writers invent, then leave to be discovered by their readers. When I was a boy, sometimes, in the middle of reading an especially good book, I pressed the volume to my face, wedged my nose right into the seam and inhaled, as if the scent of decaying paper were part of the atmosphere of the new world I encountered, as if I could crawl nose first into a novel, befriend the characters and live among them.

There was a rustling among the stacks. I walked over to the rather small Fiction section, and was rewarded with a view of Margaret's tremendous rear end as she bent over to tuck a book into one of the lower shelves. The lines of her panties were visible where her buttocks pressed against a gray flannel skirt. As painful as it was to do, I turned away from this stunning vista, feigned interest in the titles on the spines of books on a shelf above my head, then coughed lightly.

"Oh, hello there Mr. Youngquist. You startled me." Margaret had turned to face me. The glass of her horn-rims reflected the fluorescent lights overhead and her round cheeks glowed. There is nothing quite so exciting, when one has been living alone on a farm for over a month, as the sight of a hardy, well-proportioned and intelligent woman. Margaret's breasts strained against a tight-fitting white blouse. I detected a faint hint of perfume, something floral.

"Oh, hello Margaret," I said, as if I'd just noticed her. "Please, call me Damien." Unable to think of anything more to say, I glanced down and, once again, regretted my hastily trimmed beard, my shoddy overalls and the brown dirt stains stiffening the denim at my knees. I'd thought of hundreds of things to say over the last week and rehearsed them while I pulled weeds and pushed wheelbarrows full of mulch into my field and spread it around my sprouts, and while taking skunk musk aperitifs, watching the sun set over my land. But somehow, the eloquent phrases I'd conjured, and the keen observations, indicative of a rich literary background, had all suddenly dissolved in the rush of the moment.

"So, is Robby working today?" I asked, and wanted immediately to take the heaviest available book from a nearby shelf and bash myself over the head with it as hard as I could.

"No, I let him have off today. He usually takes Friday and Saturday, but he said he had something very important to do." Margaret rolled her eyes.

"Hah! Well, boys will be boys!" I declared. What a confounded, blustering fool I was. The most appropriate thing to do would have been to promptly exit the library, return home and drown myself in the stream.

"Yes, and unfortunately some boys think they're writers before they've become very good readers," Margaret mused. "He doesn't seem to realize that most of his ideas are not terribly original."

"Ah, yes, he mentioned something of his literary pursuits to me," I offered, realizing I was happy to know something about Robby, to have anything in common with this voluptuous woman. "I think he's got it mixed up somehow in his mind with folk music—Bob Dylan and so forth."

"Yes, well, he's got a good heart." Margaret sighed. "He's so much like his father." She looked down at her patent leather shoes, scratched her cheek and chuckled to herself. "People in Highbridge did not understand him at *all* when he came along. He was certainly a child of the sixties." She looked back up at me.

And there I stood—a mute, grinning skunk farmer, listening while silence fell like snow around us, pleasant and cozy at first, but after a while very difficult to dig oneself out of.

"So, can I help you find anything?" Margaret asked.

A few minutes later I was driving back to the farm with three books I'd already read on the seat next to me. "Idiot!" I yelled, "Goddamn worthless idiot!" I slammed my head against the steering wheel as I drove. I'd asked Margaret for *The Quiet American, Robinson Crusoe* and *Walden,* because I hoped she would make some unconscious associations between me and the heroes of those works. Did I ask her to lunch, as any normal man would have done? No. Instead I'd taken the imbecilic approach of attempting to manufacture an image of myself in her mind that was utterly absurd.

And whence had I excavated the gall to imagine that I was one who could "pick up," as they say, a woman? I was an ugly man, feeble of mind and body, who spent his leisure hours lost in books and musk dreams. Not exactly a hot date. It dawned on me that I knew very well where I'd gotten the gall—from Pearl. Pearl, God damn her, had made me feel worthy of a woman's company, capable of giving and receiving love. I'd told her about books I'd read, had described what a musk dream is like, and I'd listened to the story of her life and her love of fish. With Pearl I'd shared the story of Homer and Louisa's courtship, tales of Nathaniel's wrestling prowess, Gertrude's tendency to trip on the carpet. But Pearl had only been feigning interest all along. It had all been a lie. But lies or not, her memory would not cease to plague me. What a waste of flesh and blood you are, Damien Youngquist, I thought, as I bumped down Fisher Lane to my property. The plywood made a shushing sound like a skier taking sharp turns as it shifted around on the roof of the car and the long two-by-fours bounced up and down in front of the windshield.

When I first saw the maroon pickup parked in the radish patch, I thought I was suffering a paranoid hallucination. The chicken-wire fence had been run over and the neat rows of little sprouts had been mashed down by the truck's tires. Then I saw Robby's faded micro-bus parked next to the cabin where I normally parked the Eldorado and four—no, five—figures in front of the cabin. This was the largest public gathering I'd seen in Highbridge. At first I was too shocked to feel anything, then, as I drove up and parked next to Robby's van, fear began to creep up my spine. I felt like a settler who'd gone ahead of the group to scout out possible trouble, returning only to find the wagon train being hijacked by tribe of Apaches. Then, as I got out of the car and approached the gaggle of invaders, my hands began to tremble uncontrollably as the fear within me was transmuted into nervous, seething rage.

15

Everyone was quiet for a moment. Robby and Matt were squared off in front of the cabin. Doug stood behind Matt. It was the first time I'd ever seen him off his stool. He looked sullenly from Matt to me, then down, past the flabby belly that hung over his blue jeans, to his untied basketball sneakers. A young man with wavy blond hair stood behind Robby. He was dressed entirely in black, including a long black trench coat, and wore a large, complicated camera slung around his neck. As I made my way toward them, he raised the camera and took several photographs of me. A young woman in a brown flannel shirt and partially bleached, disintegrating blue jeans stood beside the fellow with the camera. She had long, straight brown hair, very much like Robby's. Though it was the middle of their sleep hours, several skunks had left the coop and were wandering around. Inconstance and her little ones were inspecting Robby's microbus. Father, always the mediator, stood near Robby and Matt, looking from one to the other, as if he wished to get in a word of reason amidst this irrational, bipedal bickering.

"Well 'ere's the freak himself," Matt said. "Old MacDonald," he said, slowly, making the name sound sinister, "eeyyiii, eeyyii, yo." His eyes were dark pits in his rat face. In his customary, territorial form of greeting, he spat. I noticed there was a blue cylinder on the ground near his feet.

"This bastard came up here to snoop around your place," Robby said. I'd never seen Robby angry before. The cheeks of his smooth, hairless face—such a contrast to Matt's stubbled one—were flushed, and a vein throbbed in his scrawny neck. The young man dressed as an undertaker stepped to the side and took several profile photos of Robby, lending to the scene the atmosphere of a prizefight.

"Fuck yew, yuh long-haired hippie bitch," Matt said, turning to Robby again, "Even if I wuz a bastard I'd be better off than yew. Everybody knows who yur faggot father was, an' he didn't want nothin' to do with—"

Robby shoved Matt, who took a step backward, then, grunting the words "Mother fucker," lunged at Robby and knocked him into the fellow in black, whose camera fell from his hands and dangled on the strap. Robby quickly regained his balance and took a wild swing. His fist missed Matt's jaw and glanced off his shoulder. Before things could get any worse, Doug stepped forward and encircled Matt in a bear hug, forcing both his arms to remain at his sides. The black-cloaked photographer put a hand on Robby's shoulder and pulled him back.

"Listen here!" I yelled, my voice so loud it surprised even me. "I want you people off of my property immediately, or I'm reporting you all to the police and pressing charges of trespassing and willful destruction of property against every one of you!"

"Yew got no reason to be pissed at me, weirdo," Matt said, still wriggling to free himself from Doug's arms. "This turd here," he jerked his head in Robby's direction, "wuz snoopin' around here before I was. Why doanchew ask him what he was doin' with whatever the hell kinda moonshine you got in them fuckin' Mason jars."

"Fuck you," Robby said, then turned to me. "If we hadn't gotten here before this sonofabitch, he woulda burnt the place down. Why don't you ask him what he was gonna do with that fuckin' blowtorch." Robby pointed at the blue cylinder on the ground between Matt and himself. I squinted at it, but still couldn't tell what it was, and honestly, I didn't care. If it had been a bomb, I would have been happy to see it explode and blow them all to kingdom come.

I picked up the blowtorch and heaved it at Matt's truck. I hadn't intended to hit it. What I really had in mind was to physically demonstrate to Matt that I wanted him and his belongings out of my sight. It may have been wiser simply to say that this was what I wished. With the sound of a far-off explosion, the blowtorch smashed right through the passenger-side window. This proved to be a true conversation stopper. We all stared at the truck as if the vehicle had just made an announcement. Matt, whom Doug had released in his surprise, was the first one to speak. He turned to me, his eyes beadier, squintier than ever. "You fuckin' city-slickin' son-of-a—" He never finished the sentence, because at that point, he dove at me, clenched the strap of my overalls in one fist and would have punched me in the face with the other if Doug hadn't grabbed his arm. Robby grabbed the arm that had attached itself to my overalls and he and Doug tried to pull Matt away. He raved, swore, and strained close enough for me to smell the fetid little latrine rimmed with a crust of yellow spittle that was his mouth. We finally disengaged when he ripped the strap on my overalls and it slipped from his grasp. Doug and Robby wrestled him down. Each of the boys pinned one of Matt's arms to the ground, but he continued to squirm like a lizard until he'd tuckered himself out. "Alrahht!" he gasped, finally. "Alrahht, I said, I ain't gonna kill nobody." Doug and Robby released him and rose slowly. "Least not today

I ain't," he muttered, picking himself up and brushing off his jeans. His baseball hat had fallen off and sweat pasted black strands of hair to his forehead.

I stood with my fists clenched, still ready for anything. The adrenaline was coursing through my system, my heart pounding in my throat, my hands tingling. Matt seemed unsure what to do. Avoiding my eyes, he snorted, hawked, and spat a large phlegmy glob into the dirt.

"Let's get outta here," Doug said, in the whine one might expect from a swine.

Matt turned ferociously on him. "Don't tell me what the fuck t' do, ya fat worthless shit." Then he spun around and stuck a finger in my face. "An don't think I ain't onta yew, yuh fuckin' pervert. We don't like yew city freaks around here, Old MacDonald, an I don't know what the hell yuh think yer doin' with all them skunks, but it sure as shit ain't natchrul." He spat at my feet, then for good measure added, "Yuh fuckin' weirdo," turned and stormed off to his truck with Doug galumphing along after him, carrying Matt's blue cap. Matt started the engine and began to pull away while Doug was still sweeping the crumbs of glass from the passenger seat. The rest of us watched as Matt stomped on the gas, spun the truck around 360 degrees, and sent dirt, pebbles and baby radishes flying out from under the tires like water from a rotating sprinkler. Clumps of dirt fell around us and a small rock hit my leg. The truck careened toward the driveway, the tires still spewing dirt, and smashed through another section of the fence, snapping several of the posts and flattening the chicken wire to the ground. I was too relieved that Matt was gone to be angry about the destruction right away.

"Oh my God," said the young woman. She was looking at the doughnut the truck had torn in the field. I learned later that this woman was Fiona, Robby's girlfriend. In contrast to Robby, who was always jittery and effusive, she remained placid and spoke dreamily, as if words floated in the air around her like dust particles and occasionally drifted into her mouth. I followed Fiona's stunned gaze. The white strings I'd used to divide the plots of different vegetables had been tangled and scattered on the brown ground by Matt's truck. Then I noticed the dark clump. I squinted as I began to make my way over to it. The smell had already begun to fill the air. I was reminded of the first time I'd ever had this experience, when I was a little boy, on my way home from school.

Father lay in a twisted, crumpled little heap like a discarded sweater. There was a large red ball stuck in his wide-open mouth. I knelt over him and put a hand on his little chest, just to make sure there was no heartbeat. I realized nothing was stuck in his mouth, but that a large portion of his innards had been forced up through his throat when he'd been run over. There was a brown pouch that might have been his liver, and the intestines were drenched with blood. The whole business looked rather like scrambled eggs and sausage smothered in ketchup. I closed Father's eyelids with my palm.

"Damien." Robby's voice startled me. I hadn't heard him and the others come up behind me. Now they stood around in a semi-circle with the dazed expressions of people at the scene of a gory car accident, which was exactly what they were. "I'm really sorry about all this," Robby said. The undertaker's camera began whirring and clicking.

A lump rose in my throat and the tears sprang to the rims of my eyes. I bowed my head back down to Father. I held a hand up in the air to let Robby know to stop talking. I was sorry enough for myself, without his pity. I stroked Father and breathed in the last of his scent—the first one I had enjoyed on the farm. There was something special about him, as there had been with Homer, simply because he was a first. And the pain it caused me was an awful new burden. Each death lived through brings one closer to one's own. It is another weight added to the load that forces one to hunker down closer to the earth, gradually bends one to it in old age, and eventually sinks one into it. The emotion I was experiencing was just the kind I'd hoped to protect myself from by purchasing the farm and keeping a coop of anonymous skunks. I'd failed. Miserably.

"Uugh, man, I don't know if I can take this stench," the photographer said after a moment.

"Shut up, man," Robby said, through clenched teeth.

The left knee of Fiona's pants was patched with a flower. A daisy. How nice, I tried to think—a daisy patch. A nice daisy patch. I tried to cling to the image.

Robby said, "Look, if there's anything we can—"

"Robby!" I interrupted, my voice becoming shrill. I kept my eyes cast down at Father and continued stroking him slowly. "For once, could you shut your—" my throat constricted suddenly, and I had to stop and swallow. "Yes, there is one thing you could do, incidentally," I said, with more control, "you could get off my property. As I asked earlier." I kept my eyes down as they walked away. Behind me, I heard rusty hinges complaining as the doors to the microbus opened and closed. The engine started up and I continued to listen, head bowed down to Father, as the microbus rumbled and chirped out the driveway, faded down the dirt road and finally dissolved into the silence of the woods. Then I got up off my knees, took Father into the woods and buried him.

Desperately in need of musk, I went into the skunk coop and pulled the case of Mason jars from its shelf. Father's jar contained perhaps four shots. These I would have to savor. I noticed there seemed to be less musk in all the jars than I'd thought. This struck me as quite odd. I'd thought they'd all been nearly full. Apparently, I'd been mismanaging my musk, probably as a result of being unaccustomed to having such an abundance of it on hand. I squeezed a shot from each of the skunks into their jars and resolved not to be so indulgent in the future.

Two days after the murder, my ears were again assaulted by the chirping of Robby's microbus—a sound that would, over the months, continue to penetrate my consciousness like a recurring nightmare. The day before, I'd reshaped the mounds and furrows disturbed by Matt's truck so that the water would drain properly again, replanted the radish sprouts and fixed the flattened fence. I used a rake to erase the tire tracks and the footprints in front of the cabin where we'd had our scuffle; I'd picked up every last crumb of glass from the window of Matt's truck, and put them in a brown paper bag which I buried in the woods near Father. Despite one's efforts, the obliteration of the memory of any serious violation is never completely finished. I've never seen this as a reason to stop trying.

Upon hearing Robby's microbus, the whole horrific scene—the rumble, the hit-and-run murder of Father—all came rushing back in gruesome detail. I had just lowered the gate on the dam and had reemerged from the woods at the far corner of the field. From a distance, the microbus was a blur. It looked like a dried scab moving in front of the trees as it pulled in and stopped next to the cabin. Just then a deer, disturbed either by me or the noisy microbus, leaped out of the woods not six feet in front of me, bounded across the field and disappeared into the woods again. After getting over my surprise, I was suddenly seized by hunger. It took me a minute to figure out why. Since I had no way to refrigerate meat, I hadn't eaten any since I'd moved onto the farm. To me, the young buck was nothing but an ambulatory cut of venison. These woods, I mused, were probably filled with deer meat I already owned, more or less. I could salt it, smoke it, jerk it and keep it through the winter. This would be a tremendous boon to my diet. It would also be a good excuse to purchase a gun, something I'd contemplated since Matt's visit.

Robby jumped out of the VW, and before I could open my mouth to tell him to get off my property, he was talking a mile a minute, begging my forgiveness for the events of two days before and promising to leave me in peace forever if I would only give him an hour of my time. His friend, the wavy-haired young undertaker with the black overcoat, came looming around from the other side of the microbus and stood silently behind Robby in a fair imitation of a shadow.

"See, we're gonna be starting our own farm over behind the hunting lodge, and we wanna learn from you. You're doing the real thing, subsistence farming—it's like, the ultimate rejection of society man." Robby took a notebook and pen out of the back pocket of his jeans. "So what would you say is like the first thing somebody should know who wants to start subsistence farming?"

"Robby, it's the middle of May. The first thing you have to do is get your seeds in the ground at the right time. Have you even begun cultivating the ground behind the hunting lodge?"

"Well, no. But just kind of talk about subsistence farming in a general way." Robby stuck his pen behind his ear for a moment to take a cigarette out of the pack in the breast pocket of his t-shirt. The shadow also lit a cigarette, then turned his attention to loading film into the large camera dangling from his neck.

"The first thing I recommend you do is rent a tiller," I said. "Cultivate the land and then plant the seeds. There's not a lot to it. The back of the seed packets will tell you when and how to plant the seeds. But you'd better be prepared to sacrifice your lower back; elbow grease is what it's all about with this business, Robby—it's not like being a librarian. You can't afford to spend the day snoozing in a chair, or thumbing through the *Highbridge Herald*."

Robby scribbled furiously in his pad. "Great, great, this is good stuff. Go on."

"Well, you need some sort of irrigation system, as you know, and then you just weed, mulch, weed, mulch, weed, weed, weed and wait. Now please take your terrible van and get off my property."

"Oh yeah, yeah, the irrigation system. Uh, you think we could show Trent that dam? By the way, this is Trent. Trent, Damien."

I looked at Trent, who glanced up at me from his camera, squinted through his cigarette smoke and nodded. "How's it goin'?" he said.

"It's going well, thank you," I said. Then turning to Robby, I said, "and now, I trust, *you* will be going?"

"Damien, man, c'mon, I mean, I helped you put those pipes in the ground and everything. Dude, my arms are still sore from all the digging we did that day."

"It's a wonder your jaw never gets sore."

"C'mon, just let me show Trent the dam and then we'll be outta your hair." Robby dropped his cigarette butt on the ground and stamped it out with the sole of his leather sandal.

"Now you're littering. Honestly Robby, sometimes you're about as considerate a guest as your friend Matt Baxter."

"Aw, sorry man, I wasn't thinking," Robby said, bending to pick his cigarette butt from the ground. "But please, don't compare me to that bastard."

We walked up to the dam, where Trent began snapping photographs like an obsessive-compulsive tourist. "Now tell me again how this thing works," Robby said.

"What is he doing?" I asked, pointing at Trent, who had gone a little further upstream and crouched on the ground to take photographs of the dam from across the pool.

Robby smiled broadly. "Taking pictures, dude, what does it look like?"

"I know he's taking pictures, but why? Are the two of you collaborating on a school project or something? He's making me nervous." He was. There was something sneaky about the young man. My palms sweated whenever he was around. I imagined he must also have been sweating quite a bit, since it was sunny, well over seventy degrees, and he was still wearing his black overcoat.

"I told you I quit school, and Trent here graduated a couple years ago. He's just taking pictures 'cause he likes to. Just like I write. We're artists, man."

"I see." I had no intention of hosting an artists' colony, so, in order to get them off my property as soon as I could, I quickly re-explained the principle of the dam to Robby while he scribbled away in his notebook.

"So why this type of irrigation?" Robby asked.

"It was simply the best way to make use of what the land had provided for me. There are a couple advantages to furrow irrigation, though. The soil between the furrows stays dry and for this reason weeds are less of a problem. Also, because the leaves of my plants don't get wet, they're less susceptible to leaf diseases. You can find all this in any of those books I took out from the library—the ones you claim to have read."

"Great, great," Robby muttered as he scribbled along. He looked up from his pad for a moment. Can you show us some of your plants?"

The field had gotten enough water for the day, so I opened the gate of the dam. Trent's camera whirred and clicked like mad. We headed back, and Robby began tramping through the field as regardless of where he set down his big, sandaled feet as the deer that had bounded through earlier.

"Could you please watch your step, Robby," I said. He'd already squashed several sprouts. I knelt down to stand them up, and again I heard Trent's camera. I looked up at him and he stood there shooting right down at me with that huge lens projecting from his face like a growth. "And would you please not aim that thing at me, Trent," I said. "It makes me nervous."

Wordlessly, he lowered the camera, then gazed down the furrowed rows toward the cabin. I believe Trent instinctively put a frame around everything he saw to determine how it would look in a photograph. He knelt down to take a shot of the field from a cat's-eye view. The way his black overcoat fanned out around him, I was reminded of how the crows had plundered my field until I'd chased them away. After a few shots down the rows of vegetables, Trent moved on to take close-ups of a scarecrow. I kept an eye on him, though he seemed to choose where he placed his feet carefully enough. Robby pestered me all the while with questions about things like harvesting and how I planned to make it through the winter without going to the grocery store. I finally turned to him and said, "Robby, this is the first year I've done this. I know about as much about subsistence farming as you do. And honestly, all this about rebelling against society and big business, and the agricultural crises you speak of are all news to me. I'm simply doing what I feel I have to do."

Robby scribbled away in his pad. "Great, great," he mumbled. "Great stuff. OK, can you show us the root cellar now? Hey, Trent!" Robby called out to his friend, who was taking a photograph of a knee-high corn stalk. "Root cellar!" he yelled.

I followed them across the field, making sure they didn't trample anything else. While they were behind the cabin I quickly ducked into the skunk coop to throw back a shot of musk. When I rejoined the microbus brothers, Robby was lifting the boards I was using to keep the root cellar temporarily covered. This was rather irksome, and if I hadn't just had a shot of musk I would have ordered him to replace the boards immediately. But in my dreamy state of mind, I felt like helping Robby and Trent, since they were, Robby claimed, planning to follow in my footsteps.

"I put a bed of rocks on the floor of the root cellar, so moisture can trickle through," I explained. "Then I put a floor of boards upon that. Those boards you're holding, Robby, are the roof. I plan to cover them with dirt and leave a small hatchway so I can climb down in there and get what I need in the winter."

Robby dropped the boards and began writing again in his notebook, while Trent took photographs of the exposed cellar. "Cool. It'll be like a little bomb shelter," Robby said.

"Yes, it should stay quite cool down there," I said. "It will be almost completely airtight, and will keep the sunlight from the vegetables." Then, remembering the deer, I added, "And meat."

Robby promptly stopped his scribbling. "What?" he demanded, knitting his brows at me. "Dude man, tell me I didn't hear you say what you just said."

"I didn't hear you tell me say what you just said," I said.

Robby gave me a withering look, turned sideways to spit and slapped his notepad against his pant leg in frustration. "Do you realize," he said, turning on me like a prosecuting lawyer, "that cattle farming is the most destructive, evil practice ever foisted on the American people, and that the red meat craze in this country is the most savage, cannibalistic—"

"Oh Robby, please," I said, a chuckle unintentionally erupting from my mouth.

"You laugh!" Robby said, and pointed at me across the root cellar. "You laugh while at this very moment, hundreds of acres of rainforest are slashed and burned in Brazil every day. *Every day!*" Trent had stopped taking photographs and was now listening to Robby, nodding solemnly in agreement. "And for what?" Robby angrily yanked a pack of cigarettes from his breast pocket and shook it open. "To raise a few cows so they can sell some beef to McDonald's, that's what. The fat morons in this country are willing to sacrifice the ecosystem of the whole planet for a few hamburgers. The U.S. imports 200 million pounds of meat per year from countries like Costa Rica, El Salvador and Nicaragua." He paused to light a cigarette and exhale loudly. "But never mind that. In this country, the cattle are force-fed, shot up with steroids to increase beef production. The gases destroying the ozone layer that protects us from the sun's UV rays, you know what fifty percent of it's from? Cows. That's right, cow farts are ripping a hole in the ozone layer. It's fuckin' disgusting, man."

I'd never heard of a young man bearing quite as many crosses as Robby Krauthammer seemed to bear. Here he was, a small-town librarian's assistant, who'd taken it upon himself to fight against all the havoc being wreaked upon the world by such forces as the United States Government and the multi-national corporations controlling it. One could not help but admire his bitter passion.

"Fact," Robby said, fumes shooting from his nostrils, "colon cancer, the second leading cause of cancer deaths in this country, is directly related to a carnivorous diet. Fact: the nutritional information taught in schools—the four food groups—is sponsored by McDonald's and the USDA, the biggest promoters of animal products. Fact: veal calves live a twenty-week life confined within a windowless stall in which they cannot even turn around, and only see light when an electric one is turned on so somebody can give them an anemia-producing, quick-grow formula. Fact: 260 million acres of U.S. forest have been cleared to create cropland to produce a meat-centered diet. Fact: Eighty-five percent of U.S. topsoil loss is directly associated with livestock raising. Fact: topsoil depletion has been the reason for the downfall of most great civilizations throughout history." Robby stopped to breathe.

"Well, Robby," I said, "call me a killer of God's creatures, a wrecker of the biosphere, or what have you, but I still plan to do a bit of dear hunting on my own property. During deer season, that is."

Robby's mouth hung open slightly. He put his cigarette in it and glanced down at the root cellar. "Oh," he said, and was silent for a moment. "But there's another thing. Fiona told me about this. When you eat the meat of an animal, you swallow a lotta bad karma," he said.

"Oh, really," I said.

"Yeah," Robby said, still staring meditatively at the open root cellar. "A lot of people don't know it, but when you eat the flesh of an animal that's died a violent death, the fear they experienced in their last moments releases chemicals into their bloodstream that you ingest. You know what they do in a slaughterhouse? They shackle the pig by one leg, hoist it upside down, then cut its jugular while it's still conscious."

"Then I suppose we should keep them around and wait for them to die of old age?" I asked. Robby looked up at me quizzically. "Or when we eat the flesh of an animal who's died of old age, do we absorb some of its geriatric qualities, do we, in effect, age more quickly when we eat the flesh of an animal that's died of natural causes?" Robby came around the root cellar toward me. "It introduces an interesting dilemma, doesn't it?" I went on. "If one were to eat the flesh of an animal who happened to be a narcoleptic, would he then take on its sleepiness for the rest of his life? It seems to me that by the logical extension of your hypothesis, we become, in a way, the animal we have eaten. Which, when you think about it, does make some sense. Most of the people I've seen around Highbridge resemble cattle, and when I was in the supermarket, it was indeed mainly cow products with which they were filling their shopping carts."

Robby was standing within a couple feet of me now. He wrinkled his nose. "You've been at it again, haven't you? I thought you were acting funny. You don't usually talk so much. Man, I just don't see how you deal with the smell." Then his eyes lit up. "Hey, show Trent what you do with the skunks."

"Robby, I thought we spoke about keeping that confidential."

"Aw, it's just Trent, man," Robby gestured at Trent as if his silence denoted insignificance.

"No, Robby. And if you've no more questions, I suggest you get on your way, and get some seeds in the ground." I thought of my own difficulties in the first weeks of my farm. "A stitch in time saves several in the arm."

"By the way," Robby said, smiling, "we'll be moving in next week. I gave my two weeks notice to Peg. I'm through with the establishment, man. I'm on my way."

16

The arrival of Robby and his friends is forever mixed in my mind with the appearance on my farm of the Colorado potato beetle. Like Robby, the potato beetle showed up with an entourage, which included spotted cucumber beetles, Japanese beetles, root maggots, cabbageworms, cornborers, cutworms, flea beetles and corn earworms, to name a few, and for all of whom I was to be the host. In my mind's eye, I saw the packed root cellar's contents being nibbled down to one bushel of potatoes, a few ears of corn, some beets and a carrot or two huddled in the corner of what I'd imagined would become a subterranean cornucopia. I saw myself growing thinner as the winter wore on. I would sit huddled by the Franklin stove, pulling up the strap of my overalls that would continually slide from my shoulder, and consider going into town to shoplift at the grocery store. I'd spent more than I'd anticipated on such things as the tiller rental, building materials, tools, fencing and plastic piping. So the threat posed by such miniature invaders as the potato beetle was quite real.

It was on a clear, sunny morning while I was weeding in the potato patch that I noticed the leaves of one of the plants had turned into a fine green doily. One might say I was struck by its very leaflessness. So holey was it that how it even maintained a leaf's shape was a puzzle, for it was more hole than leaf. I noticed the same fate had befallen other leaves on the same plant, and I hurried over on my hands and knees to examine the next plant and the next, and saw that this lacy condition had occurred in many of the potato leaves.

Then one of the ravenous culprits emerged into the sunlight from the underside of one of the leaves. He had a black-and-white body and an orange head with antennae like two long black eyelashes. He began to scurry down the stem of the plant. At just that moment I heard the staccato chirp of the microbus as it bobbed up and down the hills and gullies of Fisher Lane like a bathtub bobbing along on the sea. I grabbed the beetle between my thumb and index finger, felt the wriggling of its little legs for an instant as it squirmed to get free. Robby's microbus buzzed past the driveway and he hit the horn which played the first several notes of "Dixieland." Without looking up to have my vision assaulted by the bloody blur of Robby's microbus as it passed, I squeezed the beetle between my fingers until I felt the life ooze from it. "Pests," I said aloud. I deposited the tiny corpse into the front pocket of my overalls.

After a brief investigation, I found evidence of the other invaders in other vegetable plots, and I wondered about what Robby had said about hybrid seeds. I imagined asking Jud about conspiratorial seed and pesticide companies and then watching as he burst into honest laughter, slapped me on the shoulder and said, "Yeah, that's a good one, Damien, you sure bust me up sometimes." Then he'd show me to the aisle in his store where a plethora of pesticides was shelved. But the use of pesticides would mean an umbilical cord to the outside world. I wanted this even less than I wanted to spend the money. I wanted self-sufficiency. So I decided to marshal the forces I had at my disposal. As I'd mentioned to Jud, I did have a plan for dealing with certain pests.

Earlier that morning, as usual, I'd picked up each skunk as he filed into the coop to retire and squeezed a shot of musk into the appropriate jar. "Good night," I said softly to each of them, though it was actually morning. The only other time I saw them was around twilight, when they rose from their slumber and came blinking out into the yard. I was usually sitting in front of the cabin on one of my crates, yawning at the sunset, a shot of musk in hand, thinking over the next day's work before I retired for the night.

But this morning, though they'd retired only a few hours before, I threw open the door to the chicken coop and awoke all of the skunks, sticking my arm down into some of their burrows to get them out, and suffering several angry little nips on my hands and forearms. However, the pain of these wounds was soothed by the effects of the musk fired at me. I tied a leash around each of their necks with a length of twine, tied the ends of each of the leashes together and dragged them all, bleary-eyed, scratching at their necks, into the sunlight.

Disgruntled and inquisitive, their fur rumpled with sleep, the fifteen skunks stood in a line outside the chicken coop. A couple of them turned and sprayed at me. Having had more than my share of musk for the morning, my vision blurred and I experienced a sudden giddiness as I stood before them. Finally, the ones who'd sprayed turned back around to give me their full attention, all of them recognizing that there was no chance of getting back to bed until I'd had my say. After all, they were harnessed by the neck and the reins were in my hand. Once I'd composed myself, recovering from the slight overdose of musk, I spoke.

"You're probably all wondering why I've gathered you here during your sleeping hours. Of course, I would not have taken such a drastic measure as rousing you from your beds unless I believed that what we have on our hands here is a full-blown crisis." As I spoke, I walked back and forth in front of the assembly, and since all of their leashes were in my hand, one end of the row was forced to take steps toward me as their leashes were pulled taut. I twirled on my heel, and began pacing in the opposite direction, and the skunks who'd been forced to step forward now had to step backward to avoid my feet while the skunks at the other end were pulled forward. It kept them on their toes. "Perhaps 'crisis' is not a strong enough word, ladies and gentlemen. I should say a war. Yes, a war. And we must protect ourselves from the onslaught of these parasites. As you are all aware, we have already had one casualty in this war. One casualty which no doubt has wounded each of us deeply." I paused in my pacing and allowed a moment of silence for Father, then turned on my heel and resumed. "However, this is no reason to be discouraged. On the contrary, we should feel chastened, more determined than ever before to defend our way of life, so that Father may not have died in vain." I held up my free hand, palm facing outward. "I do not speak of vengeance. Nay, our interest does not lie in those quarters. Father died valiantly, yes, and with dignity. We should all be proud to die such a death." I did not say so, but I myself would hardly be proud to have been run over by a pickup truck. "But we should see this death as a lesson. We cannot allow ourselves to be overrun by pests. That's correct. It was a form of pestilence that resulted in our brave comrade's demise." My voice began to rise. "A pest, different in size, but no different in character, from this one." I whipped the crushed beetle from the pocket of my overalls and held it aloft. "This new threat cannot be tolerated," I boomed. "And as the larger pests are my concern, these other pests—smaller physically perhaps, but just as clear and present a danger to our existence—are your concern." I squatted down, and working my way down the line of tethered skunks, held the crushed beetle's cadaver in front of the nose of each male, female and pup, let them look, sniff, and lick at the squashed body on my open palm. "That's right everyone, take a good look. This is our enemy. We will go forth now, and crush this enemy—I with my fingers, you with the sharp incisors many of you sunk into the skin of my forearm this very morning." I did my best to sound venomous when I said, "Comrades, we shall eat our enemy for dinner."

With that, I strode into the field, dragging the unwilling ranks along behind me. I found a couple more potato beetles and a couple of Japanese beetles which I crushed between my fingers and fed to the skunks. Marching them up and down the rows of vegetables, with one skunk in each lane, I was able to keep somewhat of an eye on all of them. Most of them caught on to the assignment quite quickly, especially the older ones. Some of the pups imitated their mothers by snapping viciously at the leaves, even when there was nothing on them. The mothers occasionally spit out one of the beetles they caught for their children to eat, and in this way, the young ones eventually came to understand the nature of the task.

After about an hour of this, during which Robby's microbus went out Fisher Lane and came back again, followed by a moving truck, I led the skunks back to the chicken coop and unleashed them. "Now then. You've all done a splendid job. That field, as you have seen, is not only a source of corn, asparagus and so forth, but a battlefield as well. I trust you'll all continue this effort during your normal waking hours." They headed back into their burrows or curled up in their nests. "Thank you and good night," I said, and closed the door.

"Next order of business," I said, getting into my car. As I pulled out of the driveway, I was almost broadsided by Robby's microbus, which came whizzing by with another blast of "Dixieland" and a flash of Robby's triumphant, laughing face behind the wheel with Trent and Fiona next to him. After they passed, the scent of burning cannabis trailed behind them like a long tail. Terrific, just terrific, I thought. They'll turn this into a freeway. The gosh-darned-freeloading-potato beetles' freeway.

Though I have never been violent, except with myself, entering the gun store was the first step in the fulfillment of a lifelong fantasy. It had been eighteen years or so since I'd last watched one of those gunslinger films in boarding school, but I don't think I'd quite shaken the romance from the image of a gun-toting lone wolf who destroys his enemies with one flick of the wrist and click of the trigger.

In a cloud of dust, I skidded to a stop in the parking lot of Highbridge Guns & Ammo. I noticed a flier taped to the door announcing a supper to benefit the Highbridge Fireman's Fund. It occurred to me that thanks to Matt Baxter I'd come quite close to requiring the services of that very organization the week before. This calcified my anger about Robby & Co. moving in next door and almost running me down in the process. I threw open the glass door at Highbridge Guns

& Ammo a bit more aggressively than I'd intended, stalked in, put my hands on my hips and looked around.

A man with a beer belly and a mustache that resembled a woman's hairbrush was sitting behind the counter reading a magazine. He dropped the magazine on the counter and held up his hands in mock surrender. "Hey man, it wasn't me," he said.

"Oh I know it wasn't," I said. "It seems everyone's responsible but no one's accountable these days. Potato beetles. Potato beetles everywhere I look."

This seemed to confuse him adequately for the moment, and I began browsing around the store. I'd never seen such an arsenal. Guns were lined along the walls and the barred windows; racks of guns crowded the floor in long rows; guns were encased in the glass counter. Picking one at random, I lifted it to my shoulder and looked down the barrel at the sight as if I'd been going around buying guns every day of my life.

"The American Arms Brittany," a voice said over my shoulder. "That's a nice gun there. Always did like them side-by-sides, myself. 'Swut muh dad always used. Makes me nostalgic I guess." I lowered the shotgun from my shoulder and looked at the man who'd come out from behind the counter. The mustache made him look like a walrus. It covered his mouth completely, and I was reminded of how whales use a similar device to filter plankton into their bellies as they swim along. The buttons of his shirt were doing quite a bit of work to hold the front of the garment together and I wouldn't have been surprised to see one of the lower ones pop off and zip across the room like a BB. "What're you gonna be usin' it for, bird huntin'?"

"No, bigger game," I said. "Deer, actually."

"Deer?" The man chuckled. "Yuh might give a deer a serious limp with somethin' like this, but yuh wouldn't be able to put 'im down unless yuh got close enough to whack 'im over the head with it." He snorted. "Naw, sumthin' like that'd only be good for varmints. By the smell of yuh, this might be a gun you could use."

I looked at him with the blankest of skunk stares. It was the same stare I'd given Piper when he'd suggested I use a different brand of cologne. This overfed marine mammal was beginning to annoy me already. I doubted I'd get out of his establishment without a raging headache that would take two to three shots of musk to cure.

"Heh, just kiddin' yuh buddy," the walrus said, nudging me with an enormous elbow. He lumbered by me and around to another rack, took a key out of his pocket and unlocked a gun that was much larger and more lethal-looking than the one I'd picked up. "I'd recommend the Remington 11-87 SPS Deer Gun," he said. "Can't go wrong with this baby. Semi-automatic. Twelve gauge. Yuh got yer Monte Carlo stock, an' a Cantilever scope mount." He tapped the top of the gun with a beefy finger, then passed it over the rack to me. It also had a strap on it and I imagined myself stalking around the woods, predatory, alert, with the large shotgun slung over my back. If Matt Baxter's truck pulled onto the farm, I'd whip the gun from my shoulder and level it at the windshield. I took a look at the price tag of the Remington: 749 dollars.

I passed it back over to him. "That's nice," I said. I made my way over to a rack with a red magic-markered "used" sign. I looked over the guns and picked one up that said "Marlin" on it. This, no doubt, was the gun Pearl would choose, were she to buy a gun.

"The Marlin," announced the shopkeeper, putting the Remington back on the rack and drifting over to me. "Now there's a gun. I can see yer more the traditional type, eh? Well you don't get more traditional than this. This here's the oldest shoulder firearm still bein' made anywhere in the world. This is *the* American huntin' rifle." The man lowered his voice and leaned toward me, as if there were anyone else on the store to hear us. He said, "Did yuh know Annie Oakley used a Marlin?" Then he stepped back from me, and held up his hands, surrendering for the second time since I'd seen him, his eyes wide with amazement at his own claim. "No lie," he said, though I hadn't contested the point. "Hey, that's the gawd's honest truth." He took the gun out of my hands, put it back on the rack and picked up another. "But this is the one you want for big game. Yuh always know you can depend on a Marlin. Reliable Marlins, I call 'em. I got one muself. As yuh know, the Marlins are famous for their lever actions, got that pure Old West look, these beautiful Maine birch stocks," he said, rubbing his hand lovingly over the dark wood. "'An this one's got this purdy mother-of-pearl inlay, here." He flipped the rifle over in his hands to reveal a shiny, iridescent scroll of shell on the stock. I was sold. It was a handsome gun, and I liked the notion of its being the oldest. Older is almost always better in my book. And it was only three hundred dollars.

The man glanced around the store again, though there still was no one about. "Say, you wanna give 'er a test run? I got a couple targets out back." He grabbed a box of shells from behind the counter and led me out the back door. "By the way," he said, as he opened the door, "name's Ken, Ken Conover."

"Damien, Damien Youngquist," I said. There was a field behind the gun store. Ken loaded the Marlin, lifted it to his shoulder and fired into the field. "Hah! Would yuh look at that. Damn old thing's still as accurate as they come." I squinted into the field, but I didn't know what he'd shot at, so I couldn't agree with him. "Here, yew give 'er a try." He ejected an empty gold shell from the side of the gun, and reloaded.

I hefted the rifle to my shoulder. Not wanting to kill any unsuspecting forest creatures, I aimed at the tops of the trees that lined the back of the field. "Whoa!" Ken exclaimed, "Hold yur horses Hiawatha." He reached out and pulled the barrel of the rifle down. "Shoot et the target."

"What target?" I asked, looking at the trees.

"Raht there," he said.

I squinted in the direction Ken was pointing and noticed a few thin smudges of white against the dark trunks of the trees. "Those white things?" I asked.

"Thur black an' white, yeah, a course. Doncha see the one shaped like a deer? I just put a hole in its heart."

I looked again. "No, I don't."

"Whuter ya, blind?" Ken said, then muttered something which remained forever lost in his mustache. "Wait, I know. Just hold up a second." He hurried back into the store and came back out a moment later with a black cylinder that looked like a telescope. "Here lemme see that," he said. I handed him the gun. "Scope should make it show up real nice for ya. I'll throw this one in with the Marlin for seventy bucks. It's a hunurd, regular. There," he said, clicking the instrument into place on the top of the rifle, "take a look through that."

I raised the rifle to my shoulder, looked through the scope and saw a miracle. At the end of the field, there were three targets. Three black silhouettes—two of deer, and to the right of them, the silhouette of a man—were depicted in life size on large pieces of white paper. There was indeed a bullet hole in the chest of one of the deer. I could even see the little rips like spiders' legs radiating out from the hole. I was able to distinguish the individual needles of a pine tree behind one of the targets. I looked around at the leaves of some of the other trees, then at some of the wispy clouds that hung in the sky. The world was suddenly a much clearer and sharper place. "There yuh go aimin' at the sky agin',' Ken said. "Yuh sure yuh don't want a bird gun after all?"

"This is amazing," I said. "Fantastic. I've never seen like this before."

"Yeah, Bausch an' Lomb come out with them new scopes—" Ken started saying. I swung the gun around to look at him through the scope while he spoke. I could see every hair on his mustache and a red pimple with a white center on his forehead just above his right eyebrow. "Jesus H. Chrahst!" he yelled, suddenly ducking down, then grabbing the barrel of the gun and jerking it up into the air over his head. He could move with surprisingly speed and agility for such a large, portly fellow. Thinking the gun might drop to the ground, I automatically grabbed at it and accidentally tugged the trigger. It went off, shooting straight up into the air, then was out of my hands. Holding the rifle like a kayak paddle, Ken slammed it against my chest, knocking the wind out of me and forcing me to stagger back a couple steps. "You wanna freakin' kill me? God *damn*!" He popped the live shell out of the rifle and then aimed the gun at my head. "There, how the hell do *yew* like it!"

I apologized and explained that I'd only been surprised by how well the scope worked. After several deep breaths he settled down and eventually handed the rifle back to me. I loaded it and pointed it down the field at the targets. I looked at the deer. The little altercation had gotten the adrenaline coursing through my veins and I thought of Matt Baxter. I moved the barrel slowly to the right past both deer targets until the scope was filled with the dark image of a man. I imagined a soiled blue baseball cap on it, greasy jeans and a week's worth of stubble. I fired. I was a natural. I put a nice round hole in the very center of the chest. As the ringing faded from my ears I heard a low whistle coming from Ken.

He looked at me thoughtfully for a moment, while I bent down and took another shell out of the box. "Yuh know," Ken said, "if yer in'erested, I got a couple real nice handguns I could show you."

Handguns—now we were really talking showdown. It was too irresistible. "Sure," I said, nonchalantly, raising the rifle to my shoulder again, "I'll take a look at them."

My nerves were a little frazzled as I pulled out of Highbridge Guns & Ammo with my big-game Marlin, two handguns, a 20 gauge gun for bird hunting that Ken had thrown into the bargain for almost nothing, and a couple cases of shells. I hadn't meant to buy so much. I felt dangerous just driving down the road with all that firepower in the back seat. I was headed for the library to return the books I'd checked out to impress Margaret. It really takes a desperate fool to check out books he's already read, but very impressive, oh yes, very impressive; no doubt Margaret thought of me as a modern-day Robinson Crusoe. What a dolt I was. And now what was I going to talk to Margaret about? Guns? Ask her if she'd like to come out to the farm for a little skeet shooting perhaps? Then I had it. After expressing my discontent with the selection at the shopping mall to which Robby, in his limited wisdom, had directed me, I'd ask her where there was a good used bookstore, which might result in a literary conversation of some sort.

While I drove, I took out the scope, which I'd detached from the Marlin, and looked through it down the road. Incredible. I could see cars far in the offing. Looking to the side, where before I'd only seen a blur of trees or a blur of corn, now I could see individual trees and leaves, rows of individual corn stalks stretching into the distance.

As usual, I was the only person patronizing the library. I put the books on the counter, took the scope out of my pocket and peered down the Nonfiction aisle where Margaret was standing on a stepstool, wiping dust from some half-empty shelves. The skirt she wore came to just above her knees, and I admired the fullness of her calves, the thickness of her ankles. She glanced over and I quickly put the scope back in the pocket of my overalls.

"Hello, Damien," Margaret said. She climbed down from the stepstool and walked toward me. How dull the world was without my scope. Whereas a moment before, I'd been able to see a small run in her stockings, the individual links on the chain that held her glasses around her neck, the titles of the books, now the anonymity of the soft-focus world I normally inhabited was restored. "Checking out some more books?" she asked.

Once she was close enough for me to admire the way her belly pressed against her white summer skirt and the way her hips flared out from her waist, another bulge began to rival the one made by the scope in my pocket. "Yes, yes," I said, as if I were in a terrible hurry. "Actually, I was wondering if you would know where I might find a good used bookstore." I tried to keep my eyes on her curly gray hair, but even that aroused me. "You see," I rushed on, "Robby directed me to a bookstore at the shopping mall, and I went there, but there wasn't such a great selection, and I thought, you being the librarian, might know where to get some good books."

Margaret scratched lightly at a mole on her chin. I noticed she used clear nail polish and that she also still wore her wedding band. I wondered if Robby had been misinformed about her husband dying. "You know, there isn't really anyplace," she said. "Now and then people have yard sales, and you can usually find some interesting things. The only thing I can think of is the books we have. We get donations of books and sometimes they're duplicates. Come into the back room with me," she said, turning around. I followed her, penis first, trying my damnedest not to look down at her bottom, which, snug in the white skirt, reminded me of a pillow.

On the floor in the back room there were three large cardboard boxes which had at one time held oranges from Florida. "You can take whatever you want from there," Margaret said, looking down at the boxes of books. She picked her up glasses from around her neck, slipped them on, and knelt down to pick out one of the books. "*The Chocolate War*," she said. "Now, I thought our copy of this had gone missing." She looked up at me. "I left Robby in charge of this, so I'm not even positive they're all duplicates. I'd better check for this one."

"Robby's not exactly the most dedicated worker in the world, is he?" I said. Here I was talking about Robby again, without a single more interesting idea in my head to use as a topic of conversation.

"Well, no, we couldn't very well say that," Margaret sighed. "He speaks quite highly of you, though," she said, brightening up. "He said your farm was—now how did he put it?" Margaret looked down at her shoes and, smiling, momentarily placed her index finger on her lips. "Oh yes, 'A small but significant battle won in the war against the agricultural establishment,'" she quoted.

Leaning forward, and lowering my voice to give the word the significance it seemed to hold for Robby, I appended, "'Dude.'"

"Yes, exactly," Margaret broke into a giggle that made her breasts quiver beneath the white blouse and I felt the blood rising in my cheeks. "I'm kind of sorry he won't be around here much longer. He definitely keeps things lively." Then, with a sniffle, she placed a finger thoughtfully under her nose and said, "Well, I'd better go check on this." She raised the copy of *The Chocolate War*. "You take whatever you want from these boxes."

As she stepped toward the door, still holding a finger beneath her nose, I asked, "How much do you want per book?" I meant to say, "Are you still married?" I could feel the moment slipping away and there seemed to be nothing I could do about it.

"Oh, they're free. I really just need to get them out of here." She turned again and put her hand on the doorknob.

"Margaret!" I blurted, as if the doorknob she were about to grasp had an electric current running through it.

She froze and turned around slowly. "Yes, Damien?"

"Does your husband read very much?" I asked, stupidly.

"No, I'm afraid not. He's been dead for five years. It was a farming accident."

"Oh, I'm very sorry. I was just wondering, because I thought he might want some of these books." I was babbling like an idiot and couldn't stop. "But, I suppose in that case he wouldn't be interested in any books, well, yes—I'll let you get back to work."

As the door closed behind her and I knelt down to sort through the books, I thought, Yes, I have a chance. Thank you! But at what a cost I'd uncovered this information. "Does your husband read?" What an obvious, pathetic moron I was. I picked up the heaviest hardcover volume available and began repeatedly slamming it against my forehead.

"Damien?"

I dropped the book and looked up. Margaret had partially opened the door and was peering in at me, clearly a little alarmed.

"Ah, I was just going to say, you're welcome to take the cardboard boxes, too—to carry the books...um, are you alright?"

"Fine! Oh, fine!" I adjusted my glasses. "Never better." Margaret managed a tepid smile, then let the door swing shut.

I began sifting through the books. A lot of them were earlier incarnations of precisely the same pulpy trash I'd seen in the shopping mall, but there were a few interesting titles. I wondered, even if I could think of some place to meet with Margaret besides this library (where it seemed Robby Krauthammer was the only topic I could think of), whether she would want to see me ever again.

I could ask her if she would be attending the fireman's supper on Friday, hinting that I wanted to discuss literature. No, no, no. I could see it now. We'd be surrounded by a bunch of overfed, noisy louts like Mr. Conover; we would eat macaroni salad with too much mayonnaise from Styrofoam plates and quickly succumb to indigestion and possibly food poisoning. It would be virtually impossible to engage in any sort of intellectual discussion under such circumstances. I placed in my discard pile a book with the title *Quickie*, whose cover featured an illustration of a woman in a garter belt lounging on an unmade bed. *Oh, what a gal was Quickie!* read the subtitle. Besides, I thought,

I am repulsed by the sight of human beings, especially when they're feeding. And what was I doing entertaining fantasies about Margaret? Didn't you learn your lesson, I asked myself, when Pearl betrayed you? Are you interested in more pain at the hands of some female of your species, simply because of her alluring hips? I filled one of the boxes with all the books I wanted and left the library. Margaret was poking around in the Children's section, but I said nothing to her as I went out the door.

In my car, I put the box of books in the passenger seat. Yes, books, I thought, with something like relief, books—the only dependable companions—will always occupy the passenger seat of my car. Then I took the scope out of my pocket and spied on Margaret through the front window of the library. She was bending over, poking around one of the lower shelves of the Children's section, and her behind stuck up like a great white flower in full bloom. It felt as if a great hole were opening in the middle of my chest. Margaret straightened up rather abruptly and turned toward the window. I immediately put down the scope, started the car and drove home.

17

After Robby and the other potato beetles moved in, there were only three disturbances on the farm over the next couple of months. The first came one day while I was weeding around the beans. My back was soaking with sweat in the afternoon sun. I'd gotten into the habit of lowering my overalls to my waist and working with only a white cotton t-shirt on top. A faint breeze occasionally drifted through the field. I would hear it rustling the leaves of the surrounding trees with a sound like small waves flattening on a beach. The breeze would temporarily relieve the oppressive weight of the sun and blow the scent of skunk cabbage across the field.

During one of these brief intermissions from the heat, the breeze brought to my nostrils the scent of mildew mixed with a burnt, ashy smell, and I turned and spotted a figure entering the gap between the trees that opened onto Fisher Lane. I pulled the scope out of my pocket (I had begun to keep it on my person at all times) and peered through it at Robby Krauthammer, who was walking toward me, hands jammed into the pockets of his blue jeans, which were stained dark brown at the knees. His t-shirt was likewise stained with smudges of dirt. Well, well, well, I thought, it appears that our fun-loving young neighbor is in the process of unearthing the knowledge of work. I put the scope back in my pocket and continued weeding. I listened to Robby's footsteps as he strode up and stood beside me. He breathed through his mouth, watching me weed for a moment before he said anything, as if he'd run out of breath during his short walk. He sniffled a couple of times. His sinuses sounded badly clogged. "Hey Damien," he said, slowly, nasally.

I leaned back, resting my buttocks on my heels, and shaded the sun from my eyes with my hand. Robby looked terrible. There were dark rings under his eyes and though I would have thought it almost impossible, he seemed to have lost weight. His t-shirt was like a white flag of surrender hanging limply from a battered stick. "Hello, Robby," I said. "How's the revolution coming?"

The corners of his mouth turned down, he swung his head aside, hawked and spit into the dirt. "Fuckin' allergies," he said. I suppose I should have felt triumphant, should have suggested he cut his losses, move back with his mother and leave me in peace. But it was quite dispiriting to see the young chap in such a state. Usually he was so full of life, bursting of fun facts and threatening theories. Now he looked as if he'd been forced to run a marathon after being drained of a couple quarts of blood. Slowly, he drew a cigarette out of the pack in his breast pocket, which pulled the neck of his shirt down like a yoke on an ox. He looked over the beans, the corn, tomatoes and squash with which my farm was burgeoning, lit his cigarette, shook the match out slowly and let it fall from his fingertips to the ground. "It's lookin' good, man," he rasped. After the second drag from his cigarette, a cough from deep within his chest rattled his entire frame, forced him almost to double over as he clutched at his stomach. He spat again. Something that looked like a clam hit the ground with a slap. Robby wiped his mouth with the back of his hand. "I'm startin' to think maybe I shouldn'a quit my job at the library," he said.

This was not the Robby Krauthammer who'd spoken so passionately on the ills of modern civilization a couple of months before and who'd sworn he was going to change the world. This was a wilted half-brother of the real Robby. "Is there something I can do for you?" I asked, with a mind toward getting this suffering specter out of my sight. "I doubt that you came all the way over here to compliment my farm and complain about the path you've chosen in life."

"Actually, yeah, there is somethin' you could do," Robby said, adding a nervous sniffle to the end of the sentence. "Could you come over and take a look at my plants? I don't know what's the matter with 'em."

At Rigby we were required to go to chapel on Sundays, and I remember nothing but one line from all the many sermons I listened to in that drafty little building with the slate roof and the dark wooden rafters. The priest was talking about the Garden of Eden. He said our lives were begun as unspoiled gardens. "The question each of you must ask yourselves," he said, "and not just today, but each day of your life, is this: What have you done with the garden entrusted to you?" All the years I'd spent in the employment of Grund & Greene, I'd thought of myself as a sharecropper. My cubicle was my own little patch in a large communal farm, which, if cultivated well, would help the whole farm prosper, and in turn I would prosper. The problem with this arrangement, I could see now, was that the relationship between garden and cultivator was too indirect to hold any meaning for the sharecroppers. This was why I'd been able to walk out on it with no feelings of guilt, or even curiosity about who had succeeded me in my copywriting position. This was also why, rather than working,

Farnsworth spent his time talking on the phone, Schrempp stuffing his fat little face with various forms of maltose, dextrin and glycerol. (Glycerol—now *there's* an interesting one. What conclusions might be drawn about a society in which people use the same substance for food preservation and the manufacture of explosives? What have the destructive creatures responsible for the production of chocolate Ho Ho's and weapons designed for large-scale devastation done with the garden entrusted to them?)

Well, with the garden I was entrusted now, I made all my own food. I'd never felt more in tune than when I ate the first tomato I'd grown myself. Twisting it slightly, feeling its weight in my hand as it loosened from the vine, then lifting it, red and ripe, to my mouth and taking a juicy bite of it—not many experiences can match that one. A lot of my vegetables I did not even want to eat at first. After digging them from the earth, or plucking them from the vine, I would decorate the cabin with them. I placed them on the table and the bookshelves like trophies so I could admire their color and natural perfection.

Ah, but what had young Robby Krauthammer done with the garden entrusted to him? If only I'd known the whole of it. If only I hadn't been such a blind fool.

The soil around the plants behind the hunting lodge was so saturated that when I knelt down in it, a little moat immediately formed around my knee. It was water mold; I could see that right away. "Robby, you've practically drowned these plants," I said. The thin, spiky leaves fanning out from the stems of Robby's plants had turned yellow and droopy.

"Really?" Robby said, genuinely surprised, as he squished through the soil to where I was.

Fiona lingered behind him. She'd emerged from the hunting lodge as soon as we'd entered the field behind it. I wondered if it had been her spasm of inspiration that had led to the wrapping of multi-colored Christmas lights around the poles of the deer rack in front of the lodge.

"But look at the leaves," Robby said. "They look like they're drying out."

"You obviously did not read much in those books you loaned to me when you worked at the library, Robby. The leaf symptoms of water mold are almost identical to those of drought, and the most common mistake gardeners make is to over-water their plants and make the disease even worse." I got up and walked around, looking at the other plants that filled the clearing behind the hunting lodge, an area about the size of a baseball diamond. Robby walked behind me, puffing away on a cigarette. His plants were all between knee and waist height, and most of them only partially infected. Drying out the soil for a while would probably save most of his crop from ruin. "I thought you were interested in interplanting, Robby."

"Oh, yeah, I am," he said. "That's the only way we're gonna save the country from turning into a desert at the hands of the soil-mining corporate farmers." The delivery of this pronouncement was so dry and rehearsed, I was sure he'd wrung all the meaning from it long ago. It had all the hollowness of a PR manager's response to questions regarding his company's exploitation of factory workers in third-world countries. Robby broke into a sneezing fit and Fiona pulled a tissue from the hip pocket of her jeans, the ones with the daisy patch, and handed it to Robby before he could wipe his nose with the back of his hand. He blew, and my ears were accosted by the revolting sound of snot being discharged from his nose.

"But you're not growing anything here besides cannabis," I said.

"I will, I will," Robby said, wiping his nose. "Maybe next season. The reality of the situation right now is that we need to raise money or the whole thing's off." Fiona came up and put her arm around his shoulders. "Beazly made the first couple payments," Robby said, looking at the ground, shaking his head, "but, dude, we're really gonna be just scrapin' by, and those Winchell bastards would just love to take the place away from us."

Robby stood there looking at the ground, Fiona encircling his frail shoulders like a mother heron enshrouding her ailing baby with her wing. In that moment I saw Robby as Fiona must have seen him: a boy with bony shoulders and a leather-string necklace trying to play the part of Atlas. It was too much for him—his delusions of grandeur, the absurdity of his attempt to change the world with a farm, his father's ghost, his mother's despondency. Robby was breaking down beneath the weight of it all. It made me want to disappear. "Well, I suggest you lay off the water, as far as these plants are concerned," I said. "Most of them should make it." I turned and started to walk back to my own property.

"Damien," Fiona said. Her voice was soft, supplicating. "Would you like a cold drink? I know you don't have a refrigerator over there."

"Thank you very much, but I've got work to do. I really should be getting back." In fact, I wasn't planning to do much more than take a nap that afternoon to avoid the heat, and maybe go for a little dip in the stream to cool off. I turned again to leave.

"I'm sorry about your skunk," Fiona said, in a voice so airy it seemed to float into my ears from the surrounding woods.

It stopped me in my tracks. I turned around. "Thank you," I said. "But it really doesn't matter. I've suffered greater losses."

"That doesn't make the little ones hurt any less, though," Fiona said.

I was at a loss—a little loss, I suppose—for words. I didn't even want to think about poor Father and his grizzly murder, much less argue with this silly waif about the importance of the death of one of my favorite muskerteers.

"Why don't you just come in for a pop," Robby said. "Get outta the sun for a minute. You still haven't seen our place."

Against my better instincts, I agreed, mainly because I was uncomfortable with the position Fiona seemed to have maneuvered me into. I would have felt more than rude turning my back and walking away after an expression of empathy such as hers.

It was dark in Robby's den. I tripped over a dead body in a body bag just to the right of the doorway when I stepped inside. As my eyes adjusted to the gloom, I saw that the lodge's one long room had been partitioned with tapestries that hung from the ceiling. Tapestries had been tacked over the few windows, and very little sunlight was able to find its way through. A gauze of smoke filled the air and the scents of cannabis and tobacco mingled with those of patchouli, vanilla incense, mildew, body odor, coffee and garbage. Most of the light in the lodge came from a television screen next to the fireplace, where someone was sitting in a lawn chair with a cigarette in his mouth, playing a video game. The body bag I'd tripped over moved, groaned, and I realized it was a sleeping bag which in fact contained a body that was more or less alive.

"Come this way to the kitchen," Fiona said. I followed her past two tapestry-partitioned areas that had little nests of blankets and pillows in them, which lent the lodge the flavor of a low-budget harem. The kitchen windows let in more light, which was unfortunate, because the place looked as if it had been bombed in an air raid. The most impressive aspect of the whole disaster was the number of beer cans and wine bottles, which were overflowing the garbage can, stacked in cardboard boxes on the floor, littering the counters, and even the top of the refrigerator. The table was so cluttered with dishes, overflowing ashtrays, cans, bottles, coffee cups with cigarette butts floating in them, it looked like a sculpture by some postmodern artist out to make a statement about the decline of Western civilization. The sink was clogged with murky water that looked capable of spawning brand new life forms. The smell was that of a landfill. Only the seagulls were missing. I wanted to leave and tell Robby to invite me back when he'd cleaned and sanitized the place.

"Welcome to the Krauthammer commune," Robby said, forcing a smile up one side of his mouth.

"Thanks Robby, I'm sure your father would be proud." I immediately wished I could take the words back. Robby looked down at the orange-and-brown linoleum, sniffled, scratched at his forearm and then coughed into his hand, his whole body shuddering in a way that made me think what I'd said was enough to make him literally fall apart, cause his arms to disconnect and fall to the floor, his head to tumble forward off his shoulders and his scrawny chest and legs to collapse into a knobby pile of Robby parts.

"I gotta take a leak," he gasped. He shuffled through a door next to the refrigerator and closed it behind him.

"That's kind of a sensitive topic with him," Fiona said, pulling a two-liter bottle of soda from the refrigerator. I took a seat on the edge of one of the chairs and tried not to look at the depressing table. "You know, he looks up to you a lot. All he ever talks about is how great it is that you're doing what his father tried to do on that farm." She handed me a glass of soda and I wondered when was the last time the glass had been washed, what had been in it before, and who had drunk it. I said nothing.

We heard the toilet flush and Robby shuffled back into the kitchen, blowing his nose into a long streamer of toilet paper. I tried not care that this pathetic waste of a boy looked up to me. I told myself I only wanted him to leave me alone. But there I was in his kitchen, drinking a glass of soda.

"You want more of that cough medicine, honey?" Fiona asked, handing Robby a glass of orange juice. He shook his head, took a sip from the glass and started to cough, blowing a mouthful of orange juice back into the glass. He set it the glass down, hawked and spat into the stagnant sink, then leaned his back against the refrigerator. The effort of coughing seemed to have robbed him of what little energy he'd had left for the day.

Fiona went over to him and ran a hand up and down his rib cage. "Why won't you let me call a doctor? You know it's too late in the season for it to be allergies. You've got some kind of infection."

"Can't afford to see a doctor," Robby mumbled.

"I told you I'll pay for it," she said. Robby snorted. "Will you at least lie down for a while, honey?"

I took this as my cue. I finished my glass of soda, then found a small clear surface on the table and wedged my glass between two beer bottles. "Well," I said, standing, "I'd better be off then."

"Thanks for taking a look at my plants, dude," Robby managed.

"You're welcome." Least I could do for a dying man, I thought. Robby closed his eyes and nodded slowly. I shook his limp hand and made my way back to the door through the submarine light of the front room and squinted out into the sun and fresh air.

The second disturbance during that two-month period came about a week later. I awoke in the middle of the night to the clattering of farm tools being knocked over. My shovels, rakes and hoes were all kept in the skunk coop, near the door, below the shelf on which sat the case of Mason jars. At first I thought I must have imagined the noise, but then I heard another clang and some hushed swearing. I grabbed my flashlight from the bedside table and headed for the door. Then, hesitating for a moment during which Matt Baxter's vile visage leaped to mind like a rodent from a hole in the ground, I grabbed a pistol—my Heckler & Koch semi-automatic .45. After buying them, I'd mounted the pistols, the bird gun and the Marlin on the wall by the door.

"Who's there?" I said, as I stepped out of the cabin, swinging the flashlight around. Two figures burst from the chicken coop and ran east, toward the stream. I couldn't see them very well at all, and they were almost to the woods by the time I yelled again. Fear gripped me and I fired two shots into the air, to let them know I had a gun and wasn't afraid to use it—hoping this would be enough to prevent them from coming back. No damage had been done to the coop.

The third interruption came on an afternoon in the middle of August, when the heat was at its worst. I was sitting outside on a crate in the shade of my cabin, my back against the wall. The air had the deadness of desert air. It was so hot the mosquitoes had taken the day off. I had a shot of musk in one hand and a straw hat I'd bought at Jud's to keep the sun off my head in the other. Jud had offered me a free baseball cap before I purchased the straw one, but I'd turned it down. With my eyes closed, I fanned myself lazily, felt the tickle of sweat trickling down the side of my face, and considered taking a dip in the stream. But that would have meant actually moving.

The odors of patchouli oil, mildew and dirty ashtray preceded Robby, borne along, I suppose, on the waves of heat he pushed ahead of him as he walked. "Hello, Robby," I said. "How does your garden grow?" I opened my eyes and he was standing before me, shirtless, the leather necklace dangling over his hairless pigeon chest, a case of bed head puffing the hair out from the side of his head.

"Hot enough for ya?" he asked.

If there were such a thing as seasonal laws, certainly the first on the list under "Summer" would be a ban on such fatuous colloquialisms as, "Hot enough for ya?" The punishment for violation of this ban would be that the offender would have to dress in ski pants and a down overcoat and sit in the attic of the oldest, most poorly ventilated house in the area for a period of two to three days.

Robby pulled a pack of cigarettes and a book of matches out of the pocket of his cut-off khaki pants.

"How can you strike a match in this..." I trailed off, waving my hat toward the surrounding woods and heat.

"Oh, I always forget it bothers you," he said, and stuck the cigarettes back into his pocket. "I gotta say thanks, dude, thanks a million. The plants are doing way better. We ended up losing maybe a quarter of them." He shrugged. "But we woulda lost all of 'em if it wasn't for you." The old Robby was back. His sinuses were unclogged, he wiggled his toes happily in his sandals. He pulled a pack of chewing gum out of the pocket of his ragged shorts. "Piece?" he asked holding the pack out to me. I shook my head, Robby put a stick in his mouth and continued talking. "We're gonna get some mega buds outta some of those plants, man."

"Robby, I really don't care to hear about that," I said.

"Oh, right, right, sorry, yeah, see no evil, hear no evil, all that." He chomped his gum as he looked down at me. "Whatcha drinkin' there, anyway?"

"Robby, it's none of your—"

"Okay, okay, forget it man. I was just tryna make a point. Look, I'll cut to the chase. We're havin' a party tonight, and I was wondering if you'd wanna come. We were gonna have a harvest party later on, but then it didn't look like we were gonna have a whole lot to celebrate, and we never did have a house-warming party. So we're having it tonight. Whudda you say?" He paused and looked at me. I continued to fan myself slowly and said nothing. "Do you wanna come?"

"Thanks anyway, but I don't think so. I've never cared for parties."

"I didn't think so. I mean, I want you to come and all, but I thought you'd rather not be bothered. But Fiona said I should invite you anyway." He shook his hair and began pulling it back in a ponytail. "Well, if you change your mind, things'll be getting started around eight." He turned and began to walk away, then stopped and turned back to me again. "You know man, you shouldn't be so, so... curmudgeonish."

"Why, Robby, you surprise me. I didn't think your vocabulary was very extensive and I certainly never suspected you might even be an inventor of words. I believe the one you want is curmudgeonly, not 'ish.'"

"Whatever dude. I told you I'm a writer—I make up all kinds a shit."

"Yes, I see. Well in that case, carry on, do carry on," I said, extending my arm and waving my hat in the direction I wanted him to walk. I imagined myself sitting in bed, trying to read while the cars began groaning down the dirt road and the drunken voices and loud music began to sift through the woods and penetrate the walls of my cabin.

"Oh," Robby said, turning back to me again before he left, and adding, as if it had been an afterthought, "I invited Peg from the library. I thought you might want to know." I opened my eyes all the way for the first time since Robby had walked onto my property. He smiled at me, chomping his gum in triumph, then turned around and walked off.

Oh, but things had been going so harmoniously! My crops had begun to yield enough food that I didn't have to go in to town for anything. The skunks marched out of the chicken coop every night at sunset (while I sat watching, floating in a foggy musk dream) and waged war on the beetles and bugs. Now and then, I thought of going into town to visit Margaret, but I really had plenty of books to last me through the winter. And besides, I was afraid of making an ass of myself again. Though Margaret and I both read books, the words did not flow freely between us, so there was little probability of fluids flowing between us either. This is what they mean by chemistry, I suppose, and given my increasingly musky ways, I doubted that there was any chance of my finding another Pearl. The short and bitter chapter of my life entitled "Love" was closed, and I had no desire to reopen it. This would have been difficult anyway, since its pages were so drenched with melancholy they'd gotten stuck together and become a soggy little loaf of wood pulp. Pearl had been a mirage, a minor character popping up in scenes in which she had no business in the first place. And she'd been upsetting enough to make me consider closing the book forever.

Aside from some weeding, adjusting the neckties on my scarecrows, and turning the irrigation system on and off, the farm ran itself. Where before there had been a dark field of soil and seeds, invisibly working their magic beneath it, now a neat, orderly jungle was rising up. The beans climbed the rows of trellises, the tomato plants overflowed from the cylindrical cages I'd made out of chicken wire, the corn rose up taller than I, and the skunk cabbage was knee-high all around the perimeter of the farm.

And so I was able to take a couple hours' siesta in the middle of the day when it was too hot to do much besides enjoy a meal and a shot or two of musk, and also I was able to devote time to other projects. I built the outhouse—the first entire structure I'd ever completed on my own—which was a considerable source of pride and satisfaction, until it tipped over one night during a rather blustery thunderstorm. I came by the next morning to make my regularly scheduled movement and found the little building, which was only a bit bigger than a telephone booth, lying on its side. I'd neglected to give the thing a proper foundation. But it hadn't suffered much from having been knocked over, so I poured a small footing for it and felt much better about it after that.

I built a bookcase, which occupied almost one entire wall of the cabin and which I sanded, stained, and filled with classics, trash, history, etc. I also put a floor in the cabin, and by tying some long, stiff grasses to the end of a tree branch I made a broom. Thus I was able to enjoy a bit of housekeeping.

Yes, everything had been going so very well. But because of Robby, it came to pass that I found myself sitting in the Highbridge ex-hunting lodge with a perspiring can of cheap beer in my hand, while I too perspired, and hoped Margaret would not notice. Pretending to have an itch, I wiped the beads of sweat on my forehead with my fingertips before they ran down my face.

You see, I'd convinced myself that afternoon that I might still have a chance with Margaret. In desperation, I'd exchanged my overalls for the tattered shirt, pants and necktie of one of my scarecrows. The shirt had been light blue, but was now bleached white on the front, the tie was a bit threadbare and there were holes in the pants, but I'd decided I didn't have much choice in the matter. It was a party, after all—I couldn't very well show up without a necktie.

All the while, I was telling myself that I really did not want to attend the party anyway, and in fact would probably not go. I was only washing up and dressing in these clothes in case I had to go over there to tell them to turn the music down, in which case Margaret would see me, plead with me to stay for at least one drink, to which I would modestly capitulate, by saying yes, perhaps I could stay for a few minutes. I spent the afternoon perspiring, pacing back and forth in my cabin, and by the time eight o'clock rolled around, decided I might as well go over to Robby's and perhaps warn him in advance to keep the noise down.

I was the first one at the party. I became increasingly embarrassed for the rest of the people to whom I was introduced before Margaret arrived, for there was obviously not one among them who knew even a very well-dressed scarecrow from whom he could borrow some clothes. I met Beazly, who physically resembled a keg of beer; Zack, a pimply young man who wanted to know if I'd attended a recent Screaming Samurais concert; Sue, she of the purple Mohawk, combat boots and enough eyeliner to last a year. I kept my eye on the clock and every five minutes or so considered sneaking out the back door. I fanned myself constantly and glanced down at the dark blotches of sweat expanding beneath my arms. To hide these, I tried not to move my arms very far out from my sides, which made such movements as handshakes and the passing of drinks rather robotic.

The mongrels had cleaned up the hunting lodge somewhat. Most of the tapestries had been taken down so that there was a good deal of open space. The kitchen, where I'd gone with Robby to retrieve a beer before Margaret arrived, looked like a different place. The bottles and cans had been taken away and the top of the table was actually visible. But as the evening digressed, the kitchen gradually returned to the state of squalor I'd encountered a couple weeks before.

The lodge seemed to fill up all at once with quite a collection of oddities at about nine o'clock, as if they'd all come together in one busload. In addition to Robby and Trent—two case studies in disaffected youth, if one ever cared to spend one's time so frivolously as to study such a thing—there was a young man who, when I got close to his face, I saw had pierced virtually every available flap of skin upon it, including ears, tongue, eyebrow, nose and lip. Robby told me this was Jocko, apparently an old school chum visiting from California.

There were two main factions at the party with some members who were more moderate and seemed to form subgroups. The first faction had hair of varying lengths that came spiked, unspiked and in a couple of cases completely shaved off. They favored black t-shirts with jagged lettering that spelled the names of rock bands, or such enjoinments as "Fuck You." The second faction consisted entirely of people with long hair, who wore tie-dyed t-shirts and buttons bearing more soothing slogans such as "Peace," and "Love Heals." The stereo was an object of contention between these two groups, but the volume was always somewhere near the maximum level despite which group had gained control over it.

Margaret arrived at eight forty-two. She held her gin and tonic with two hands and glanced nervously around the room. With her gray hair, linked-chain horn rims, and floral-print sundress, she looked as if she had been suddenly transplanted from an English garden party, where, over tea and cucumber sandwiches, she'd been discussing Oscar Wilde with an acquaintance from her book group. I couldn't blame Margaret for being uncomfortable. I was too. I hadn't been so uncomfortable since I'd had poison ivy. I was the only man in a necktie, which I loosened, undoing the top button of my shirt to allow the sweat to trickle down my throat.

"So, did you find anything interesting in those boxes at the library?" she asked, raising her voice to be heard over the music.

"Yes," I said. "*Quickie*," and then, quoting the subtitle, "'Oh what a gal was Quickie!'"

Margaret, breaking into a smile and a polite tinkle of laughter in exchange for my lame sense of humor, reached over and touched my arm lightly. "I remember seeing that title, too. Gracious. Can you *imagine*?"

No, I could not imagine. I could not even imagine a single thing further to say, except perhaps that her hips and bosom looked exquisite, pressing against the light, filmy material of her sundress, or that I would have liked to take her back to my cabin, take her dress off and nibble at her flesh.

We were not hitting it off. Our conversation drifted between observations about the guests (some of Margaret's observations I could not appreciate until I'd taken the scope out of my pocket and looked through it at the person whose appearance she was criticizing) and attempts at discussions of books we'd both read. They went something like this: "Have you read *Heart of Darkness*?"

"Yes."

"Fascinating, wasn't it?"

"Yes, extremely."

Then there would be nothing to say for a moment, while both of us looked down at our drinks or around the room at the strangely plumed people filling it, until one of us said, "Have you read *Moby Dick*?" and the rest of the exchange would be repeated with slight variation.

At some point I was introduced to Ralph. I believe it was Trent who introduced me to him. He stuck out in my mind because he seemed to belong to neither faction of rebel revelers, but mingled with both of them. It was difficult to pinpoint exactly what it was, but he did not fit in. For one thing, he was suspiciously neat. His were the only new-looking pair of blue jeans in the place, and his tie-dye was store-bought, not homemade like the others, and he wore it tucked into his pants, though later I noticed he had untucked it. His hair was short and tidily parted on the side. He looked like a fastidious boy scout someone had dressed up as a hippie.

I drank my beers quickly, which I found to be a good excuse to get up often and retrieve another, and to get a breather from the stifling conversation with Margaret. Each time I went into the kitchen, before getting my can of beer, I ducked into the bathroom, locked the door, and while the noise of the stereo pounded at the walls, gulped down a shot of musk from the hip flask I'd brought along. I quickly became drunk, and in my drunkenness, began to take more musk than I should have.

After a while I felt more comfortable. It mattered less and less that these obnoxious strangers around me were clouding the room and my lungs with cigarette and marijuana smoke, dropping beer cans on the floor, bumping into me and splashing me with a toxic red punch. This punch was being served in the middle of the room from the type of large metal tub in which one might wash a dog. Everything was fine, except that Margaret kept sliding her chair a little further away from me every time I came back from the bathroom, which resulted in my having to lean forward and yell to be heard over the music. Though I can't imagine now what I'd been going on about, once my tongue had been loosened by the alcohol, it seemed I suddenly had quite a lot to say to Margaret—had, in fact, whole volumes I'd been waiting to divulge, and for some reason I felt compelled to get them all out in one sitting. I was conscious of saying the wrong word occasionally, although I had so much to say there was no time to stop and correct myself, and sometimes my tongue slipped and ran two or more words together into one. I could tell from the expression on Margaret's face that she was updating the card catalog in her mind—under Damien: *see also* Creep; Depraved Chatterbox.

The beer can kept coming to my lips, which were in need of constant lubrication. Someone handed me a cup of punch after I dropped one of these cans, and whoever it was continued to fill the cup each time it was drained and then pass it back to me, the way people along the side of the road hand cups of water to runners during a road race. I paid little attention, as I hurried along through my marathon speech, to what was being handed to me or by whom. At one point, I was surprised to see a fat, torpedo-shaped marijuana cigarette between my fingertips as I gesticulated to emphasize some point, and even further surprised when I casually brought the joint to my lips for a few puffs while I talked recklessly on. Once, when I'd paused for breath, and Margaret was sitting back in her chair, hands gripping the armrests like someone preparing herself for death by electrocution, Robby caught my eye. Behind him, a barbaric, howling voice accompanied by a screaming guitar blared through the stereo speaker. Robby hoisted his can of beer and gave me a wink.

The room was swimming around me. I took out my scope and looked through it at the deer head mounted on the wall. Someone had put a baseball cap on its head and stuck a cigarette in its mouth. I got up to go to the bathroom again, but the hunting lodge had become a small boat tossed around in high seas where it should never have ventured to begin with. In the bathroom, my stream of punch urine almost missed the toilet entirely. I hadn't urinated in a toilet for a few months, and I remember thinking that toilet bowls must have gotten smaller or farther away, as I splattered all around the rim. After this catastrophe, I took out my hip flask, began to pour a shot into the cap, but was distracted by my reflections in the mirror. I could not focus on just one. There were three of me. They had deep sunburns from long days at sea. Unkempt beards. My body was pitched forward, then backward suddenly with the surge of a large swell that lifted the lodge and sent it careening into a trough between waves. I grabbed roughly at the sides of the medicine cabinet to keep myself from toppling over backwards, dropped my flask into the sink, and watched helplessly as several shots of musk poured down the drain. The door to the medicine cabinet swung open and several of the syringes stowed there also fell into the sink. The squall was apparently mounting into a gale. I picked up the needles with the exaggerated and inaccurate concentration of the very drunk and stowed them back in the cabinet.

Neither the long-haired young man in the Moroccan shirt, nor the young woman with whom he was engaged in conversation, looked up at me as the door to the head banged the wall and I staggered out into the galley. They must have been having an earth-shatteringly profound conversation. "The tree of life," I heard him say languidly, his fingers spread in front of his face, "continues to grow." I had to grasp the handle of the refrigerator to support myself. I was still trying to get my flask to fit into my pocket when I stepped from the galley into the front room of the lodge, which was probably why another rogue wave so easily threw me off balance, slamming my shoulder against the door frame as I tried to make my way through.

A familiar smell greeted my nostrils as I entered the room. It fit with the seafaring motif that had become the hallmark of the party soon after we'd cast off at about nine-thirty. But for some reason this smell also aroused me sexually. It was like an ocean breeze. No, it was more like a harbor breeze. I looked around. Robby was sitting Indian-style in the corner, an acoustic guitar in his lap. Fiona and another woman sat in front of him, giving him their undivided attention, though his strumming and singing were completely inaudible due to the volume of the stereo and the raucous voices of the other sailors. I didn't see how Robby could hold the guitar steady in such a gale, much less get his fingers on the correct strings, what with the deck rising and falling so suddenly and unexpectedly beneath us as we crashed through the waves. I was getting an erection, for no reason I could yet understand. I took out my scope and eyed Margaret through the haze of smoke, over the heads of the other seafarers. Her hands were clasped firmly in her lap and she looked around as if she'd just been taken hostage by a band of cannibals. I swung the scope around the room. There was someone new at the party. She'd just come in the door and seemed to be interrogating Trent. I recognized the scent now. It was fish. It was the smell of a fresh catch. I couldn't believe my scope, which, because of the violent heaving and rolling of the vessel, I had to keep swinging back and forth to glimpse the new passenger near the bow. It was Pearl. And even though she wore a thick bathrobe it was obvious that she was pregnant.

18

I was far beneath the surface of the ocean. The ship was lost, I was sinking steadily toward Davy Jones's locker and would have reached it if there were not something the matter with my guts. Kicking, flailing my arms, I struggled up through the water, finally broke the surface and found myself gasping awake in my own bed, only to discover that the alternative to remaining drowned was to return to the seasickness of the night before. The ceiling of the cabin spun around like a top. My mouth flooded with saliva and my stomach ordered me to sit up. My head, in violent disagreement with my stomach, began pounding and spinning more wildly than before. From the light that pierced the window of the cabin and burned like a laser into my sweaty chest, I could tell it must have been ten-thirty, possibly eleven. Normally, I was up with the sunrise. Somehow I'd gotten back to my cabin the night before and taken off my clothes. Lurching from the bed, I took one step and was forced to grab the back of a chair for support.

"There's a bucket by the bed," a slightly husky woman's voice informed me. Then I saw Pearl, sitting in the rocking chair, a book propped up on the bulge in her bathrobe. Though I knew it was she, and there were only a couple yards between us, I could not make out her features, just the general shapes—the frizzy hair, the belly, and the bathrobe. I dropped to a sitting position on the edge of the bed and retched the meager contents of my stomach into the bucket. Bile burned my throat. I dry-heaved and a long string of saliva stretched from the tip of my tongue down into the putrid contents of the bucket. My stomach was trying to push itself up through my throat. All the blood rushed to my face, which felt it might fall into the bucket with a plop. I wondered if this was how Father had felt in the last terrible instant of his life.

As I raised my head, I felt a hand on the back of my neck and my face was met with a damp towel. Pearl wiped the saliva from my mouth and chin, then handed me a glass of water. "Drink a little of this. Just a swallow." My entire body shivered and shook as I gulped down the cool water. "Hey, hey, not too much," Pearl said, pulling my arm down. "Jeez Louise, that must be the arm you were drinking with last night."

I sat on the edge of the bed, looking up at her. "Pearl?" I croaked pathetically. I shivered again and goose bumps spread from my back all over my body even though it must have been eighty-five degrees. Pearl sighed. She put both hands on my shoulders and looked fixedly at me with her left eye while her right stared off at the south wall of the cabin.

"Yeah, it's me. Now lie down and get some more rest."

I did as I was told. Pearl pulled a light blanket over my quaking body, and with the corner of her powder-blue bathrobe, one I hadn't seen before, she wiped the sweat from my forehead and planted a kiss there. I sunk into a deep sleep that could only have lasted fifteen minutes before I was brought struggling to the surface again by the fury of my stomach and barfed up the half glass of water I'd drunk.

Sleeping in fits and starts, a few of the events of the previous evening came back to me in a lurid blur: staggering across the noisy room. Pearl confronting me, gesturing at Margaret. "Is this your new girlfriend?" she'd said. Margaret looking like a trapped animal and saying she had to get home, she'd just remembered she had a busy day tomorrow. My inebriated attempt at nonchalance when I said to Pearl, "So, what've you been up to?" as if she and I were merely acquaintances who often bumped into each other at parties held in hunting lodges. Meanwhile, as I spoke to her, I attempted to pour myself some punch without looking at what I was doing and thus ladled the awful red stuff onto my sleeve and all over the floor.

"Are you angry with me, Pearl?" I said, now, raising my head from the pillow some time in the afternoon and looking across the cabin. The room had stopped spinning, had succumbed to the gentle swells of the doldrums.

Pearl moved slowly back and forth in the rocking chair. "No, I'm not angry, Damien. Get some more rest. We can talk later."

At one point I thought I heard voices above the surface. Opening my eyes, raising myself woozily onto an elbow, I saw Pearl's back blocking the half-open doorway, and Robby's face peering over her shoulder. There was someone else with him. I couldn't hear what Robby was saying. "No, I don't think he should be bothered," Pearl said. I closed my eyes and thankfully nestled my head into the pillow. "Nice of you to stop by," she said, "but I'm looking after him. He'll be alright."

By dinner time I was feeling well enough to sit at the table, sip some water and nibble the dry toast Pearl set before me. My tongue had the flavor and texture of a sweaty gym sock. "Well, looks like you got yourself a regular skunk farm here," Pearl said, sitting across from me and sipping a cup of coffee. I wondered where the coffee had come from. I never drank coffee. Pearl was having toast too, except she'd covered hers with sardines.

"Yes, I suppose I do," I said. Despite the fragile condition of my stomach, my proximity to Pearl's hips combined with the smell of sardines started my member pumping itself up like a bicycle tire.

"I'm on my way to San Francisco where I've got a lab job lined up. I'll get back on the road tomorrow. I just wanted to see how you were doing. I'd have just called, but," she gestured with her toast at the wall of the cabin as if a phone were mounted there, "seems your phone's out of order. You know, this cabin is something. I mean, your house in New Essex was pretty Spartan, but this place," she looked around, as if hoping to find the right words hung on the log walls or lying on the floor, "this place is absolutely monastic."

Tomorrow, I thought. All this upheaval and in less than twenty-four hours it would be as if she'd never been there. "How did you find me, anyway?"

Pearl leaned over, extracted a magazine from a duffel bag on the floor and tossed it onto the table next to my plate. It was a copy of *The Organic Gardener*, folded open to an article with the title, "Subsistence Farming—The One-Man Revolution." On the facing page there was a large photo of a bearded man in blue overalls squatting in the dirt with his hands around a green shoot, squinting up inquisitively at the camera. I did not recognize myself until I'd read my name, which followed the quote in the caption beneath the phottgraph. "'There's not much to it,' says pioneering subsistence farmer Damien Youngquist, 'just weed, mulch, weed, mulch and wait.'" I flipped the page. "Good God!" I said, dropping my toast to the plate. There was another photograph of me pointing across the field, and another of me raising the center panel of the dam.

"You mean you haven't seen this before?" Pearl asked.

"Heavens no!" I said, "I would never have agreed to..." I left my sentence unfinished, flipped back to the first page to see what I already knew: "by Robby Krauthammer," and beneath that, "photos by Trent Argile."

"Why, Robby Krauthammer," I said, "that little." My voice trembled. My heart raced. "That little p-p..."

"Twerp?" Pearl offered, "Sonofabitch?"

"P-p-pest," I spat out. I got up from the table to use the bucket, which Pearl had cleaned out three times already. Small, damp chunks of toast plunked into the bottom of it. I sat back down at the table, shuddering, and like a dog too stupid to realize that the consumption of its own feces is making it ill, I picked up the magazine again and skimmed through the article. A quote was extracted from the text and blown up in the center of the second page. "'Be prepared to sacrifice your lower back,'" says Mr. Youngquist, "'It's not like being a librarian.'" Though it had made sense to make certain statements for Robby's sake, taken out of context, my words sounded like the most pompous collection of non sequiturs ever printed. I skimmed along until I saw another quote. "'It was simply the best way to make use of what the land provided.'"

"Why do you hold the magazine so close to your face?" Pearl asked.

I was too engrossed in what I was reading to answer her. The first paragraph of the article began: "Deep in the heart of the United States, there lives a man who has taken the first steps necessary to begin the subversion of the establishment."

"Damien, can you see alright?" Pearl asked.

I ignored her and read on. "If every American took these steps," the article read, "we'd be on the road to a better world, a world where large corporations would be powerless, because no one would have any use for them. A world where people would live in harmony with the earth, instead of destroying it with modern farming methods by which farmers are strip-mining the soil for mass production and quick profit. A world where people would not have to live in fear of herbicide-contaminated drinking water, pesticide-tainted vegetables. People like Mr. Youngquist are the sowing of the seeds that will blossom into revolution..." On the second page, beneath the photograph of me opening the dam, in which I looked like an underfed Quasimodo struggling to ring the bells of Notre Dame, was the quote, "I'm simply doing what I feel I have to do." The words of Damien the simpleton on display for the entire world to see.

I dropped the magazine to the table. "Goddamnit!" I said. I began slamming my forehead against the table top, bringing it down repeatedly on the magazine. "Damnit, damnit, damnit," I said as I slammed it down. I felt a hand grab me by the hair on the back of my head.

"Hey!" Pearl shouted, jerking me around in my chair to face her. I'd forgotten for the moment that she was there.

"I'm an idiot, a lousy idiot," I babbled.

Pearl slapped my face. Hard. "Get ahold of yourself, for God's sake." I stopped talking, and when Pearl seemed convinced I wasn't going to do any further injury to myself, she let go of my hair and went back around to her side of the table. I notice how her belly seemed to lead her forward when she walked, as if the baby controlled her legs from inside like a crane operator. She'd never been so beautiful. I already knew instinctively that it was my child she carried, which meant I'd broken the pact I'd made with myself longer ago than I could remember. I knew any child of mine could be nothing but a miserable disgrace.

Neither Pearl nor I said anything for a moment. I took several deep breaths, slightly mortified that I'd lost my composure in front of Pearl. But what a monstrous back-stabbing Robby had given me. How could one have guessed he'd be such a conniving little whelp? "I never intended to be exposed in such a way. I'm sure he knew that," I said.

Pearl shrugged. She was sitting with her legs spread apart, resting her elbows on her knees like a linebacker on the sidelines. She held her coffee mug with two hands and scraped something from the side of it with a fingernail. She leaned back in her chair, her legs spread in what seemed to me a horrifying implication that she might give birth right then and there.

"And besides," I said, "the writing is so poor. I'm embarrassed about appearing in such a feebly-written article."

Pearl snorted to stifle a laugh. "Oh Damien, do you realize how funny you are? You go from self-loathing to superciliousness in a heartbeat."

"It is a terrible article, you have to admit." I was narcissistically obsessing about myself because I didn't have the stomach to go into the real issues that needed to be discussed. "Robby told me he was a writer. I would have thought he could do better than this."

"Well, if he hadn't written it, I wouldn't be here." Pearl looked up at me from her coffee mug. "Or would you have preferred that?"

I thought of the reasons I myself was there. I recalled the night of the storm. "You really should not be drinking coffee, in your condition," I said, nodding at Pearl's belly.

"It's decaf. You didn't answer my question. Here's another: why did you run away?"

It's always safer to be alone, I might have replied, if I'd wanted to be thoroughly honest. This was the belief I'd returned to at some point the previous evening when I realized things with Margaret would never go as I had envisioned, and that it was probably for the best. I'd been perfectly at ease in solitude. Now, with Pearl there, I was uncomfortable in my own house, fidgeting in my seat like a schoolboy who'd been caught peeking into the girls' bathroom. My stomach groaned and if there had been anything in it, I would have had to use the bucket again. "I did not run away, Pearl."

"Well, what would you call it?" she asked. Her voice was cold.

The memories came rushing back: Homer sitting on a stool watching me shave, Louisa giving birth, Mrs. Endicott and her Chihuahua, swimming in the fish tank with Pearl, Richard standing in Pearl's house while I clutched a useless ring in my hand. "I would—I—you," I stammered. "You were the one who—" I had to stop and swallow. This was not supposed to be happening. Everything had been lost in the storm. "What did you expect, anyway? You ran off with that, that Richard," I said, biting off the name and spitting it out.

"What?" Pearl said, cocking her head and looking truly surprised for the first time since she'd seen me.

A lump rose up in my throat and I could hardly get the words out. I looked down at my plate. "He was there. In your house." My eyes became watery and the half-eaten scrap of toast on my plate became suddenly clear, then blurred and quivered like an object at the bottom of a pond when the surface is disturbed.

"You mean, you came by the night of that storm, and he was—oh, Jesus Christ—Damien, I'm so sorry." She leaned forward, reached under the table and clasped my hands in hers. "I see how it must have looked. What did he tell you?"

"That you were his fiancée," I gargled, still looking down at my plate.

Pearl let go of my hands and put her arms over the top of the table and lifted my chin up so I had to look at her face. "Listen. He was full of shit, okay? The reason I wasn't there that night was because when I saw his van pull up outside I knew what he was up to." Pearl released my chin and I looked back down at my plate while I listened. "All he wanted was my research. And he knew he'd only have one chance to try to convince me to join him. I'm sure his career started going down the toilet after I left the university and he couldn't take credit for my work anymore. When I saw his van pull up, I was just so pissed that he'd found out where I was living." Pearl got up from her chair and began pacing around the cabin. "He would have tried to kidnap me that night if I refused to help him. So I locked the door, trashed my lab, took the notebook that had all my research results in it and ran out the back door."

I wondered how much of this I could be expected to believe. I remembered how she'd talked about conspiracies before. Even then I'd thought some of her theories were a little far-fetched. Was it possible she regularly used these convoluted stories to cover up love affairs? In light of Robby's betrayal, anything seemed possible.

"He searched the place," Pearl went on, "but there was nothing for him to find."

"What about the SeaLawn?" I asked.

"He would have had no idea what it was. I had to hide for a while. I went and stayed up in Vermont for a week or so—I kept trying to call you—and when I came back you were gone. I sold my house and moved into a women's shelter in New Hampshire." Pearl picked her coffee mug up off the table and sat down in the rocking chair. It was the only spot in the cabin where she really seemed comfortable.

"Women's shelter?" I asked, looking up at Pearl.

She was leaning with her head against the back of the chair, rocking slowly back and forth. "Well, yeah. I wasn't sure I wanted to keep the baby, and they're pretty good about letting you hide out from the world at those places."

The baby had slipped my mind for a moment. The fact of Pearl's pregnancy was as mind-boggling to me as the vastness of the universe, and therefore as easily dismissed. I looked over at the stove. Orange coals glowed through the vent. "You've decided to keep it now, though? That is, not to send it away to a boarding school or something?"

"Yeah," Pearl said. I could think of nothing to say. Pearl continued rocking. "You look pretty tired," she said. "Why don't you go back to bed. You'll be better by tomorrow. We can talk more then."

"I think you ought to have the bed," I said. "You need it more."

"I'm fine in this chair actually; it's just for tonight. I'm not here to put you out."

"Pearl, I refuse to sleep in a bed while a pregnant woman sits by in a rocking chair."

She smiled. "I think there's room for both of us in there," she said. "I mean, all three of us."

I got into bed. Pearl came over with one of the kerosene lamps, put it on the bedside table and turned the flame down low. I lay rigid as a man in a coffin, watching her in my peripheral vision while she untied her bathrobe and let it drop to the floor. Her belly was so dis-

tended it almost looked painful. She was wearing a black bikini I recognized and when she slipped into bed next to me, her knee grazed
my thigh and my penis began slowly lifting the blanket. I rolled over
onto my stomach and peeked at Pearl's bare back as she leaned over
to turn the wick of the lamp down until it went out.

"What does it feel like?" I asked.

"Just what it looks like," she said, lying down on her back and
pulling the blanket over her. "Like you swallowed one of those medicine balls you used to play with in gym class. Except that it kicks now
and then."

"Can I touch it?"

"Sure."

I moved my hand under the covers and put it on top of Pearl's
firm mound of a belly. I didn't see how it would be able to withstand
another couple months of growth without tearing open. "It's warm,"
I said.

"Mmhhmm," Pearl mumbled. It sounded like she was already
drifting off to sleep. I withdrew my hand. "No," she said. "Put your
hand back. It felt good there for some reason."

I put my hand back on her belly. "How did you happen to see that
article?" I asked. I was feeling bold now that it was dark.

Pearl yawned. "I searched for your name on the internet. I figured
it was someone else with the same name when I came across that
magazine's website until I saw one of the photos they'd posted." Pearl
chuckled. "There you were, the 'Revolutionary Farmer.' I could've shit."

I wished we could stay there talking in the dark forever. In New
Essex we'd spent hours and hours lying in bed, talking. We see each
other better in the dark. Our individual consciousnesses can occasionally intermingle as they drift toward sleep. "What do you think
happens when you die?" I asked.

"I think you become part of something else," Pearl said.

"The soil?"

Pearl scratched her forehead. "Mmm, well, that's part of it. But
that's just the physical part."

"Well, what, you think we become part of some collective consciousness?"

"Not consciousness exactly, or not consciousness as we understand it."

"Then what?"

"Something bigger. This is the only way I can explain it. You know how when it rains, a lot of individual droplets collect in a pool, or a droplet falls into a stream, the stream connects to a river, and then it flows into the ocean."

"Mhmm." There was enough moonlight for me to see the rafters. I shut my eyes again.

"Well, what can you say happened to that droplet? It's not gone, really, but it's not itself any more. It's part of something else." Pearl shifted her weight around.

"So you think we dissolve?" I said.

"I guess you could think of it that way." Neither of us said anything for a while. I listened to the crickets chirping. "What do you think happens?"

"Nothing," I said.

"Nothing?"

"I think death is the end. The end of life, the end of consciousness. We become fertilizer."

"But Damien, something has to go on."

"Why? We'd just like to think something goes on, because we're vain, we can't tolerate our own insignificance."

Pearl raised herself up on one elbow. "Do you really think that?"

I opened my eyes. Pearl was peering at me in the moonlight, as if to make sure I were not someone else. "Yes, that's what I think," I said.

Pearl lay back down. "That's too bad," she said.

"Why?"

"Well, because it's just sad. Not to mention that it doesn't make sense. You have energy—energy can't be created or destroyed, but it takes different forms."

It had never occurred to me that my theory was sad. I was simply taking an empirical approach to the matter. Now, set beside Pearl's analogy, it seemed a rather flat way of thinking. "Perhaps I need to think about it more," I said. We were quiet for a while. I listened to Pearl's breath. "When are you due to start your job in San Francisco?" I asked.

"About two weeks. Don't worry, I'll split tomorrow. I've still gotta find a place to live when I get there."

I was silent for a moment. It seemed unbelievable that though Pearl was here now, tomorrow night I would be lying alone again in this very spot, staring at the ceiling. "Could you stay for longer?" I asked. "I mean just a couple days. I could show you my farm."

She chuckled. "Sure, I'll stay. I've been wondering what the heck it's like here since I read that article. When I first read it I was still pissed. *God* was I pissed at you. But then I started thinking about what you're doing here. It's pretty interesting. I've even got some ideas to help you."

"Really? That would be great. What kinds of ideas?" I asked, like an excited child.

Pearl yawned again and patted my hand. "Let's get some sleep. I'll tell you in the morning."

Now I was almost too excited to sleep. Pearl is here, I thought— Pearl is here, Pearl is here, Pearl is here. I snuggled closer to her and breathed in the fishy aroma of her hair. Even if it would only be for two days, it was two days I would have her all to myself.

The next morning I made toast and tea, my usual breakfast, which Pearl ate in seconds flat. Then she went out to her car and came back in carrying a large Styrofoam cooler, which she set next to the stove, and a plastic five-gallon bucket, which she put on the floor next to me. I was still working on my toast. She took a fish fillet the size of a Frisbee out of the cooler and began to fry it on the stove.

"What is this?" I asked. I grabbed the handle of the bucket and tried to pick it up so I could read the label. I had to put down my toast and use two arms to lift it to the table. I'd forgotten how strong Pearl was. She'd walked in, swinging the bucket like a basket of flowers in one hand, the cooler in the other.

Pearl shifted her weight to one foot. A naked knee protruded from the split in her bathrobe. She took a sip from her glass of cod liver oil. "Why don't you take a look?" she asked.

I took off the cover and a smell of fish rose up to my nostrils, a smell more concentrated than the smell coming from the fillet frying on the stove. The bucket was filled with a flaky white powder. I hadn't noticed it a first, but on the lid was a piece of masking tape that had been marked with a red felt-tip pen. Now I squinted at it. "Hydrolyzed fish powder," I read.

"Do you really have that much trouble seeing those letters?" Pearl asked.

"They're awfully small. I think it has something to do with the color of this print. It's red. I'm used to reading things in black and white. So what do I do with this stuff? It sounds like something you'd put in your bath water."

Pearl laughed, flipped the fillet in the air, caught it in the skillet and put it back on the stove. "Yeah, I actually did. But it's to put on your plants. I thought you'd have heard of it, Mr. Organic. It's one of the 'staples of organic growing,' according to the person I talked to at the gardening store." She shrugged. "It has a lot of nitrogen the plants need. I also made you some fish emulsion and kelp extract. Oh, and a fish meal fertilizer."

"Made?" I said. "You made this?"

Pearl dumped her fillet onto a plate, made her way over to the chair at the table and sat down. The fillet covered the entire plate. "Yeah, what'd you think? I'd have to *buy* something that's made from fish? The other stuff is out in my car on the front seat. You can get it if you want."

I went outside to Pearl's Tempest. Her back seat was crammed with cardboard boxes full of cans of tuna and sardines. On the front seat were two one-gallon containers and another five-gallon container, which I carried inside. I read the labels, opened each one and sniffed at it. It was like Christmas. "Pearl, this is wonderful. I've read about these things in books, but I didn't know where I'd be able to find them. Jud's Farm Market certainly doesn't carry this sort of thing. And you made them your*self!*"

I looked across the table at her. Three-quarters of the enormous fillet was already gone. The sun was streaming through the east window of the cabin, giving Pearl's frizzy hair a border of light, turning stray strands into flames. She put down her fork and took a sip of coffee. "Don't mention it," she said, smiling. She tucked a long ringlet behind her ear. "Let's just consider it my contribution to the one-man revolution."

I showed Pearl around the farm—the rows of carrots, asparagus, broccoli, potatoes, the trellises of bean stalks, the caged tomatoes. We walked together through the rows of corn. I talked giddily about everything, starting with how I'd gotten poison ivy, rented the tiller, made scarecrows. It was as if I'd done it all only so one day I'd be able to tell her about it. I demonstrated the use of the lever in opening and closing the dam. Pearl looked at the pipe at the edge of the pool. "This is where you can put it," she said.

"Put what?"

"The fish emulsion. You can just pour it in here and let it mix with the water. It's the easiest way."

We walked out of the woods, following the buried pipe back to the field. "Robby Krauthammer helped me put this irrigation system in, actually," I mentioned.

"Why do you hang around with that guy anyway?" Pearl asked. "He's bad news."

"I don't 'hang around' with him," I said, slightly irritated by the implication. "I feel slightly indebted to him, perhaps, since his father once owned this land, and he comes along here to pester me now and then. I needed an extra pair of hands to help me with the pipes and he'd said he wanted to help. That was the beginning and the end of it."

"Which was why you were at a party at his place."

"That was... I felt obligated. I—"

"And was why you let him and his friend come over here and use you for their magazine article."

"I had no way of knowing. I just—they said they were interested in subsistence farming, in doing what I do."

Pearl snorted. "Yeah right. A couple of drug addicts like them."

"Drug addicts? No, no, no. You've got them all wrong. They smoke some marijuana. That hardly makes a drug addict, does it?" She knitted her brows as she walked along, her eyes cast down at her slippers, which had a brown fringe of dirt around them now. I wondered if she were annoyed with me.

"What about the track marks in their arms?"

"Track marks?"

"Yeah, track marks. You probably can't even see 'em. But they've all got them. Robby, Trevor, and Robby's girlfriend, and Beastly, too."

"Beazly," I corrected. "And Trent, not Trevor."

"Whatever," she said, giving me a pointed look. "You shouldn't let people take advantage of you like that." The color was rising in her cheeks. We'd done a complete loop tour of the farm, and were now standing in front of the cabin. Pearl looked down at the ground and bit her lip. "Sorry. I don't mean to tell you how to run your life."

I had no idea how to respond. I thought of the weeding I had to do. There were also a lot of ripe tomatoes hanging on their vines, waiting to fall into my fingers. "Well, I've got some work to do for a couple hours. Do you think you could entertain yourself for a bit?" I asked.

"Yeah, sure," Pearl said. "I'll be down by the stream."

Well, I thought to myself, once I was on my hands and knees, yanking handfuls of crabgrass from around the potato plants, it looks like you're going to be a father, Mr. Youngquist. I wondered if it would be a boy or a girl and wished I could be there at the time it was born to see for myself. But that was impossible, since Pearl was going to San Francisco. Unless... No, no, that would be idiotic. I tossed a handful of weeds into an empty bucket. I couldn't even suggest it. Pearl was a professional woman, a woman who said what was on her mind, called a spade a spade, a drug addict a drug addict. She would have suggested it herself if it had been an option that interested her. Not that I needed the opportunity to expose myself to another emotional flogging, as I'd suffered at her hands before. Just who was she, anyway, to come along and tell me who my friends were? I jabbed my trowel into the earth, ripping through the roots of another weed that was threatening to strangle one of my potato plants. This was the reason you came here, Damien—I told myself—to escape the grasping, weedy tendrils of human beings, who would only drag you down in an emotional straitjacket, force you to your knees in the dirt. I threw another handful of weeds in the bucket and pushed them down to make more room. But from what Pearl had said, we'd both simply been the victims of miscommunication. Ah, but that was only what she'd *said*. Perhaps she'd only come here after things did not work out with Richard. Or perhaps Richard was waiting for her in San Francisco—how had she gotten a job lined up so easily? I put down the trowel and jabbed at the ground with my weeder, with which I could delve more deeply. But then, what about bringing another orphan into the world? Another fatherless child. Suppose I had a son that grew up to be as pathetic, indecisive, ineffectual and worthless a specimen of humanity as myself?

By the time I stopped for lunch I'd soaked through my shirt and the band of leather on the inside of my straw hat. I'd weeded with extraordinary vigor, filling the bucket and emptying it into the woods several times. I filled the bucket with tomatoes and brought it back to the cabin.

"By the way, I forgot to mention how chic you look in the straw hat," Pearl said, as I removed it and mopped my brow with a handkerchief. "Is that Highbridge haute couture, or just your own style?" She'd taken off her bathrobe and was sitting on a crate in just her bikini, munching on a long piece of smoked salmon. She held the fish in one hand with the plastic wrapper peeled back as if it were a candy bar. The sight of Pearl in her bikini, in full daylight, awoke my neglected member, who now rose and stood at complete attention. I sat down on the other crate and tried to hide him, casually laying one arm across my lap. When Pearl turned to watch some birds flying by, I surreptitiously slipped out my scope, examined her pale thighs, the intricate web of blue veins. I remembered squeezing her thighs, remembered how I'd held her breast, cupped in my hands. As far as I was concerned, Pearl's protuberant belly was simply an enhancement of her curvaceousness. When she turned back around I shifted the scope and pretended to be following the flock of birds. I put the scope down and mopped the back of my neck with a handkerchief. Pearl held the salmon out to me in offering and wiped her mouth with the back of her hand.

"No, thank you," I said. I'd been looking forward to a light lunch of water, skunk musk and a fresh salad. I took off my boots and wiggled my toes around. I considered taking a dip in the stream during my siesta hours.

"Hey, listen, Damien. I'm sorry I kind of blew up at you this morning."

I shrugged. I hadn't thought of it as an explosion, exactly. "Well, I suppose you are probably right about those people," I said.

Pearl shook her head. "No, I was just being bitchy. I get that way sometimes when I'm hungry. Look, you've got to live your own life. It's out of line for me to be sticking my nose in."

It took an extraordinary amount of effort to say what I said next. I probably wouldn't have said it at all, if it hadn't been so hot and I hadn't been a bit tired from the weeding that morning. I stared into the field as I spoke. "Well, I'm sorry I left New Essex without contacting you first," I said, then glanced over at her.

She grinned happily through a mouthful of salmon, then swallowed. "Hey, it's alright. I forgive you."

After lunch, I poured out a shot of Roxanne's musk from her Mason jar into my shot glass. I might have been imagining things, but it seemed that the level of musk in her jar had been a couple of inches higher the last time I used it. While I sat back down on a crate and sipped the musk—Roxanne's was always good after a meal; it had a subtle sweetness and a floral aroma—Pearl dug around in the trunk of her Tempest, then came back and sat down next to me with a metal box, which she put on the ground and flipped open. She took out what looked to me like an empty spool and began making strange little motions with her fingers.

"What are you doing?" I asked.

"Going fishing, wanna come?"

"Fishing?" I said. So, she was tying fishing line. "Where?" I asked.

"In that stream." She jerked her head toward the cabin to indicate the stream beyond it. The fact that I'd never thought of fishing there myself provided further evidence of the fact that I was hopelessly un-equipped to rear a child and that it was only by some freak of nature that I'd evaded the process of natural selection which should have eliminated me from the gene pool by this time. However, the musk was going to my head and the placid congeniality that overtook me at the beginning of a musk dream had set in.

"You have any worms?" Pearl asked.

"Worms," I said. "Do I have worms. This land is positively writhing with worms," I said.

"Good. My guess is that that stream is teeming with trout."

Digging around in the compost heap, it took very little time to collect a can of worms. Pearl only had one rod. She let me use this, while she spooled her line around a stick.

"Stand back some," Pearl said, putting a hand on my chest and pushing me back from the stream. A little thrill ran through me while her hand was on my chest. "If they see your shadow, they won't go for the worm."

We stood back and waited. And waited. Becoming drowsy, I sat down and leaned back against a tree. I didn't know I'd been asleep until I was being awakened by something rubbing against my leg. I opened my eyes and saw the fishing rod being jerked from my lap and tugged across the ground toward the stream. "Hey," I said, grabbing at the rod. I looked around but Pearl was gone. I took my scope out of my pocket, held it up to my eye and scanned the woods around me. I felt something tugging at the front of my overalls. I looked down and saw the stick with Pearl's line wrapped around it stuck in the chest pocket of my overalls. The line was pulled taut. "Hey!" I said again, removing one hand from the rod and slapping it against my chest to hold the second line. Without Pearl I had no idea what to do next. I looked down helplessly at the bucket and net Pearl had brought to the stream, as I was tugged closer to the bank, clutching the rod in my left hand and the spool in my right hand. "Pearl!" I yelled.

She came bounding into the small clearing near the bank, as well as a seven months pregnant woman can bound, took one look at me, put a hand on her belly, threw her head back and burst into peals of laughter.

"Pearl, what's going on here?" I demanded, as my left arm was yanked around by the fishing rod.

"You look like a big puppet," she said, wiping the tears from the corners of her eyes.

"Yes, very amusing I presume. All very amusing, for *you*," I said.

Pearl picked my pocket of the wooden spool and began eagerly winding it up. "It worked. I can't believe it worked. I remember my uncle telling me when I was little that he used to do this when he went trout fishing, but I thought he was pulling my leg." She glanced over at me. "Reel it in, reel it in!" she said.

I began to do so—slowly, awkwardly. Pearl knelt down, picked up the net and then, in one swift motion, jerked a flapping fish up out of the water and scooped him up with the net. He was more than a foot long. Pearl held him in one hand, yanked the hook out of his mouth and dropped him in the bucket, which was full of water. Then she helped me land my trout, which was only slightly shorter. "So what did you do?" I asked Pearl.

"Well, see, the reason trout won't bite a lot of times is because they don't know it's time to eat." Pearl took a worm out of the can and re-baited her hook, carefully impaling the worm in two places so it would be less likely to fall off. "They're used to seeing earthworms that wind up in the stream after it rains, so what you do is simulate a rainfall. I went upstream, to just below the dam, and did a little rain dance. I just kicked and splashed around for a few minutes so that the water got all churned up and cloudy the way it does when it rains." Pearl cast her line back into the water. "And you saw what happened." She nodded to the bucket where the fish made small splashes, flicking water out with their tails as they turned from side to side, thrown into a panic, I imagined, by the vast reduction of their swimming space.

"They thought it was dinner time," Pearl said.

"I wouldn't have believed it if I hadn't seen it," I said.

"C'mon, hurry up and get your line in the water before they all forget it rained. If we don't get any bites in the next fifteen minutes, it's your turn to do the rain dance. God, I am absolutely starving."

We caught eight good-sized trout, and beside the cabin where the water tank was rigged up, Pearl showed me how to clean them. It made me a little queasy at first, lopping off their heads and then slitting them up through their bellies while they flapped and wriggled on the cutting board, but I got used to it. The first time I scraped the head off the cutting board onto the ground. Pearl said, "No, no. Put them in here." She picked up the head and put it in a bowl with the one she'd cut. Once we'd finished cleaning the fish, she put the bowl of eight trout heads on the table in the cabin. I sipped the cod liver oil martini Pearl had made for me while she fried up the trout fillets. She'd brought her own martini glasses ("I never go anywhere without these," she'd said as she got them out of the trunk of her car, along with a pair of fish oil candles.) She told me about the women's shelter where she'd stayed. She claimed not to have gotten along with any of the women there. "They were all so prissy," she said. "You wouldn't have believed it. They all complained about how my room smelled and I couldn't enter a conversation without some bitch making a fish joke."

Pearl's scent only bothered me in the sense that it made me hot and bothered. However, I wasn't sure how keen I was on having a bowl of fish heads on the middle of my table. They were not particularly pleasant to look at, and already a few flies had begun to buzz about. More pests—the common housefly with his whole repertoire of viruses and bacteria. "I think I'm going to go get a shot," I said. I wasn't much in the mood for a martini anyway. The smell of it brought back the memory of my dry heaves two days before.

"Okay," Pearl said. She took a sip of her cod liver oil—she wasn't drinking alcohol—and adjusted the tie on her bathrobe.

Once out of the cabin, I tossed the remains of my drink onto the ground, and slipped into the chicken coop. Whisky and Tripper had just woken up and were climbing out of their burrows. I picked up Whisky and squeezed a shot of musk down my throat. There's nothing better than a fresh one. My eyes clouded, my sinuses cleared. I filled the shot glass with musk from one of the Mason jars and tossed that back. Then I poured a double shot in the martini glass and went back inside.

"How do they look?" Pearl asked, as I dropped into my seat at the table. She was holding a plate piled with what I assumed were the fish we'd caught that afternoon.

I squinted at them. "Let me see," I said. I stood up, took a step closer, leaned over and peered down at the plate of fish. "They look great," I said. "And they smell delicious."

While we ate, the light of the candles glistened on the scales and wide, glassy eyes of the fish heads in the bowl. With their mouths frozen open, their expressions seemed to suggest that they'd been caught by surprise. Pearl had tied her hair back, but a few ringlets had escaped, as they always seemed to do, and hung at the sides of her face. After catching the fish that afternoon, we'd gone swimming up by the dam. Pearl had stood on the edge of the dam to leap into the pool. Her belly prevented her from doing the acrobatics she'd once shown me in the SeaLawn tank. Now she only did cannon balls, but managed to make quite a splash with the extra weight she carried.

I ate my dinner slowly, savoring the tender bites of fish that seemed to melt in my mouth, washing them down with musk, as if by eating slowly, in a musk dream, I could make the moment last longer, could postpone the hour of Pearl's departure indefinitely.

"Have you ever thought that that stuff might not be too good for you?" Pearl asked. She was already almost through with her first two fillets.

"The musk?"

"Yeah, the musk. I mean, granted, I'm into fish, but that musk is something else." She scooped two more fillets onto her plate with the spatula.

"Yes, I've told you about the musk dream. It's something of a mystical experience." I took a sip from my martini glass and glanced out the west window. The sky was orange and pink above the trees.

"Have you gotten your eyesight checked lately?" Pearl asked.

"No, why?"

She shrugged, finished chewing and swallowed. "You might want to do that sometime. Soon."

Lying in bed that night, my hand on Pearl's stomach, I fretted about the baby, about Pearl's departure, about how empty the cabin would feel in a day. But that was what I wanted. I didn't need this buzzing bowl of fish heads on my table, this expanding body taking up more and more space in my bed. She'd told me she planned to leave the next afternoon. That meant only seventeen hours or so left. Already it seemed she'd always been on the farm. The couple of days she'd spent there were somehow more substantial than all the many days previous to her visit.

The next morning at breakfast Pearl announced she wanted to help me in the garden. It was the first week of September; a lot of things needed harvesting, a lot of weeds still needed pulling. I took a sip of tea to wash down my toast. "I don't think it's the kind of labor that should be undertaken by a pregnant woman," I said.

Pearl rolled her left eye. The walleye didn't move. "Very funny, Damien."

I hadn't intended the pun. "Well, you don't even have the proper clothes," I said.

She sat down at the table and stabbed a fork into a jar of pickled herring. "A bikini is fine. It's so damn hot anyway, I don't know how you can wear those overalls."

"Protection, Pearl, protection. That's what it's all about with this farming business. First of all, you'll get the worst sunburn you could ever imagine," I said, gesturing at her pale chest with a scrap of toast. "And second of all, considering your smell, the flies will probably gnaw you right down to the bone in a matter of minutes."

"Flies," Pearl said, waving at a couple that were buzzing around her at that very moment, "I'm so used to flies I hardly notice them until I breathe one down my throat."

"Pearl, please. I am attempting to eat my breakfast."

"I know, I'll swap my bathrobe with one of the suits on your dapper dummies out there. And I'll borrow some of your bug dope."

So there Pearl was, weeding beside me on her hands and knees in the dirt. She was only in her bikini. She'd exchanged the black one for a green one that glittered in the sun. The sight of Pearl on all fours, her thick legs and buttocks quivering slightly as she moved about on the ground, resulted in a most profound stimulation and, eventually, pain. She'd promised to put on my extra pair of overalls when the sun got stronger, and I wished that would be soon because I couldn't concentrate at all. As it was, I helplessly followed her around on my hands and knees, always weeding directly behind, whether there were weeds to be weeded there or not.

"Have you ever wondered how seedless grapes got to be seedless?" Pearl asked. I was so consumed at the moment by the activity of my own hormones that I did not hear her the first time. "Well have you?" she asked, turning around.

I immediately tore my gaze from the curve of her rear, put my head down and stabbed my trowel at a clump of crabgrass on the ground near me. "Hmm?" I said, looking up, as if I'd been too absorbed by my war against the weeds to have heard what she was saying. "Sorry, something about grapes?"

"Have you ever heard of a plant growth hormone called gibberellin?" she asked. I shook my head. Pearl turned back to her weeding. "It was discovered by a Japanese professor named Kurosawa, who extracted it from a fungus he isolated, some fungus that was causing a disease that threatened rice plants, I think. Anyway, Kurosawa found that this growth hormone, administered in the correct dosage, caused young rice plants to grow abnormally tall." She paused, struggling to get her trowel into the ground.

"You don't say." I was appreciating the slight rippling effect her struggle with the trowel had on the dimpled skin of her thighs.

"Yeah, Damien—I say. The plants grew ridiculously tall. They produced several times more rice than they could have otherwise. It was a terrific discovery. Now, you're probably wondering what this has to do with the seedless grape."

"Yes, I'm wondering," I said. "I was wondering, what does this have to do with the seedless grape?" Actually, I was wondering what Pearl might do if I reached out, put my grimy hand on one of her soft white buttocks and gave it a little squeeze.

"I thought you might be. Well, for different reasons—religious, superstitious—no one really took advantage of Kurosawa's discovery in Japan, but an American got hold of it and used it to produce the seedless grape."

"Wonderful," I said.

"Wonderful for him—he made a big wad of cash and never did much of anything else in his life, at least not with gibberellin."

I was suddenly nervous. What in the world had Pearl done with this gibberstuff? Pearl was the most inventive person I'd ever met. I remembered the SeaLawn; I remembered the chaos of her lab the night of the storm. This woman was without a doubt the single most creative and destructive force I'd ever encountered. It was humbling at times. "Pearl, I'm getting the feeling I had that day when you were talking about regeneration and showed me the SeaLawn and the Morecods."

"Yes, and you should, because the research I did then comes to bear on what I'm leading up to now." She dropped a handful of weeds in the bucket and then leaned back, resting her buttocks on her heals, her knees in the dirt. She wiped her forehead with the back of her hand. I noticed a line of sweat running between her breasts and over her belly.

"And what about the SeaLawn?" I asked. "Are there plans afoot for its introduction into the oceans?"

Pearl knitted her brow and gazed down at her belly. "The thing about SeaLawn," she said, "is I don't know how to control its growth. The way it is now, if you unleashed it, it would grow so fast and cover huge areas, blocking the sun and devastating extant ecosystems." She shook her head. "No, I've still got a ways to go on that before it's viable.

But," she said, perking up, "you know what I did to make the SeaLawn grow so fast?"

Showed it your sexy thighs? I thought to ask, though I didn't. "I can't imagine," I said instead.

"Well, I used an animal growth hormone I'd taken from a seal. With the combination of gibberellin and the animal growth hormone, administered in the correct doses, I can make the biggest damn vegetables you've ever seen—anybody's ever seen." She smiled. Her cheeks were flushed. "All this is unnecessary." She waved her trowel expansively, indicating the long rows of vegetables I'd nearly broken my back to plant and care for.

"Oh. I see." I nodded. I rested on my heels too, and looked down at my hands. If someone like Robby Krauthammer were sitting there telling me this, I would have told him to shut his trap and get the heck off my property.

"I'm not trying to say that you've been wasting your time," Pearl said. "I think what you're doing is great. But if you're interested, I could mix up a little cocktail you could pour into the water supply for the plants, or just some of them, if you want. You'd have to alter the dosage according to the rate of growth. I made up a little growth chart you could use to monitor them."

It seemed Pearl was ahead of everyone, no matter what he was doing. The next time I turned around she would tell me she knew of a better use for skunk musk. "So this was one of the ideas you mentioned you had for me," I said.

"Yup."

"I'd thought it was just the fish powder and all that."

"Nope."

"Well, I'll have to think about it," I said.

Pearl said she'd leave after lunch and a dip in the stream. I hardly said a word all through lunch, or while we swam. My stomach was in knots. I kept counting the hours and the minutes until she would be gone for good. I'd be alone at last. Utterly alone. I would entertain no unrealistic fantasies about a relationship with Margaret—my behavior at the party and Pearl's arrival had put an end to that. There would be no tentative friendship with Robby, who, Pearl had shown me, was no friend at all, just another link in the long chain of betrayers in my life. No—I would be alone, as I'd always wanted to be. I would harvest my vegetables alone, hunt deer alone, watch the sunset alone, eat alone, read alone in my bed by the light of a single lamp.

After lunch, I sat in a shallow part of the pool with the water up to my shoulders and watched Pearl do cannonballs off the dam, watched her surface-dive as gracefully as a dolphin and swim around the pool under water.

"Look, guess what I am," she said. Pearl floated on her back, with her belly above the surface like a drifting isle of white. She sprayed a mouthful of water into the air, then rolled over and dove down beneath the surface. I would remember that, I told myself, every detail of it. When I came up here each day until the end of the growing season to open and close the dam, I would look at the pool and remember this last afternoon with Pearl.

Her head popped back up to the surface in front of me and she shot a stream of water into my face. I wiped the water from my eyes and tried to smile. "Whale," I said.

Pearl was about to spit another mouthful of water at me, but stopped and spit it down into the water in front of her instead. "What's the matter, Damien? You look like someone just stole your dog." She dipped her head backwards into the water to get the hair out of her face. "Skunk, I mean."

"I think I just need a shot of musk," I said. Or maybe fifteen or sixteen shots, I thought—maybe today would be a good day to see if an overdose of skunk musk can be fatal.

Pearl sighed and put a hand on my thigh. "I'm not saying this because of anything personal—actually, I like the smell; it reminds me of you—but to be perfectly honest, I don't think the stuff is very good for you. No, correction. It's definitely bad."

"What are you going to name it?" I asked.

Pearl grinned. "I've been kicking around a few names." She rested her hands on the bottom of the pool and with her head just above the surface, extended her legs behind her and her butt became a buoy as she paddled the water with her feet. "If it's a boy, maybe Homer. If it's a girl, maybe Louisa." I must look quite comical when I'm surprised, because Pearl burst into a laugh and splashed water in my face.

My heart began thudding heavily. I knew I was going to ask what I'd been meaning to ask for days, even though I knew it to be a ridiculous proposition. I began stammering. "But those are the names of—did you know that—"

"Of course I knew," Pearl said, rolling her good eye. "Did you think I could forget your adopted family? A pungent clan like that?"

It was absurd. There was no chance of her accepting. But I knew if I didn't ask, I'd spend Lord knows how long fretting about it after she'd left. It would be better to just get a slap in the face and get over it. Looking down at the water in front of me as I spoke, I blurted it out. "Pearl, I know you have this job lined up in San Francisco and that you're a very established scientist and, well, maybe that's enough reason that they might take you on at a later date, isn't it? I mean, I suppose they'll be giving you a maternity leave soon after you start, so maybe starting later might not be so unacceptable to them anyway. I can't say. I don't know about these things."

"Damien, what are you babbling about all of a sudden?" Pearl asked.

I glanced at her—she looked truly puzzled—and then back down at the water. "Yes, yes, that's a good point, and I'm glad you brought it up," I said. My heart was still pounding in my throat and my hands were shaking so much I had to shove them under my thighs and dig my fingertips into the sand. "I was just thinking, what with this new style of growing vegetables and so forth, I mean, perhaps I might botch the whole thing somehow. I'm really not in the least bit comfortable with any sort of scientific procedure. I could probably use some help in conducting this experiment and I thought you might want to see how it works yourself, since you, after all, are the inventor here. And then there's the matter of, well, the forthcoming Homer, or whatever it turns out to be. As you know, I never had a father, and I don't know if I myself would make a very good one, but, well, the Homer is part mine you know, I might like to see him come into the world..."

Pearl spoke slowly, as if to someone just learning the language. "Damien, are you trying to invite me to stay here?" she asked.

"I know, I know, it's ridiculous," I said, still looking down. My face was close enough to the surface of the pool for me to see a little water skeeter between us, gliding around like a figure skater. "And I didn't really expect you to accept. But I wasn't talking about a great time commitment. Perhaps just until the, um, the Homer is born, or well, I thought we could have seen how things work out and then, maybe, I don't know, but of course it was just an idea, a silly one at that, and you are your own person, I know you're right not to—"

Pearl interrupted me by squirting another mouthful of water in my face. I looked up and she was smiling. "I'll stay," she said. "I never thought you'd ask."

My heart was still pounding like a jackhammer and I breathed as if I'd just run several miles. Pearl moved toward me, walking with the palms of her hands on the bottom of the pool, until they were between my legs. She kissed me on the mouth, prying mine open with hers and darting her tongue in as I closed my eyes. My penis sprung to attention like a sleeping soldier yelled at by a senior officer. Pearl put her hand around it, and then, gracefully, swung her legs around in front of her. I slipped off her bikini bottom and she wrapped her legs around me, settled down on my lap, her belly pressing gently against me. She was warm, wonderfully warm inside. I hadn't thought I'd ever feel that again, that marvelous sense of completion.

19

We didn't get up the next day until we were awakened by a pounding on the door. Though we'd been in bed for quite some time, we'd been asleep for only a few hours. I guessed by the light that it was about ten or ten thirty. I groped on the bedside table for my glasses, pulled on my overalls and made my way to the door. Assuming it was Robby, I called out to the closed door, "Can't you leave me alone?"

"Maybe, Mr. Youngwurst, once you've stopped torturing others, then you yourself can be left alone," a voice called back from the other side of the door. It was not Robby.

Now I was even more irritated. Not only was someone at my door, it was not someone I knew. It was some ridiculous religious group that wanted to convert me and take my money. The time I was visited by the Jehovah's Witnesses in New Essex, though I repeatedly alluded to the fact that I had other business to attend to, the God-fearers kept hanging around until finally I began shrieking and slamming my head against the coffee table, which precipitated their rather hasty departure. I'd learned later that a simpler method for dispatching such potato beetles—if they already knew you were at home (which these apparently did)—was to open the door for the two seconds it takes to say, "I'm not interested," and then slam it shut again.

When I opened the door to the cabin I was immediately blinded by the flash of a camera. A foot leaped forward and jammed itself against the bottom of the door to keep me from shutting it. Someone yelled, "That's him!" The voice was familiar but I couldn't place it right away. It came from the back of a crowd of about twenty-five people, who all began yelling at once. I felt like a cornered skunk. This was more people than I'd hoped to ever see again when I moved onto my land. Some of them held large cardboard signs and I took out my scope and read one of them. "STOP THE INSANITY," it said.

"Damien Youngwurst?" demanded the man closest to me, who seemed to be the leader.

"Quist," I corrected. "Damien Youngquist."

"We are all God's creatures, Mr. Youngtwist, and we, as concerned citizens, want to know why you think you can play God with the lives of other creatures." He was a shortish man, about my age, with a couple of large rolls of spare flesh around his middle and straight brown hair he parted very neatly on the side, then folded a sheet of it back on itself and sprayed firmly into place. I doubt he realized that the over-attentiveness to his hairdo resulted in an impression similar to what might be given by an otter that had chosen to don a fedora.

I looked past him at the other people milling around and decided I could be reasonably certain that someone would get into the garden and trample something. Most of the crowd looked as if they'd just stepped out of one of those catalogs of outdoor wear for urbanites. They sported brightly colored running shoe/hiking boot hybrids, khaki shorts and plastic jackets with name brands stitched on the breast.

"I'm not interested in your religion," I said, "and I'd like you to get all these people off my property." I tried to shut the door, but that foot, which belonged to a tall rawboned goon, was in the way. Someone else was spying through the west window of the cabin.

"Religion!" the rotund little leader exclaimed incredulously. "The only religion we represent is the religion of humanity. We are here to demand that you liberate those whom you keep here for your sadistic pleasure."

Despite his denial of religion, his intonation and fervor were those of a deranged, pontificating shepherd who expected each of his sentences to be followed by the adamant "Amen!" of at least a hundred of his sheep.

Pearl had gotten out of bed and put on a robe. She came over and stood beside me. "Hey, they're in here!" someone yelled. "Set them free, set them free!" someone else shouted.

I stepped out of the cabin and saw two people standing by the chicken coop holding their noses. A couple of the skunks had been roused from their sleep and stood outside the coop. Raising my scope, I saw that it was Whisky and Constance, both of them looking ruffled and perturbed. "Get away from there!" I yelled.

"Oh for God's sake," Pearl said. She'd come outside and was standing beside me. "It's the SAFETYS."

"What?" I said. "What in the devil are the SAFETYS?"

Before Pearl had a chance to answer me, the tidy-haired leader said, "Mr. Younguest, we demand that you stop this insanity." Someone yelped and people began running away from the chicken coop. Whisky had sprayed at someone. Now Constance was stamping her feet and hissing. She, too, would spray any second. SAFETYS. Where had I heard that before? A couple of people were in amongst the carrots before I could say anything. They weren't leaving. With the scope, I could see a yellow school bus parked in the driveway. In spite of

Whisky and Constance's spraying, no one was headed back to the bus. They swarmed around the cabin and the chicken coop. The people who had knocked down the fence were now going over to examine a scarecrow. Some woman was bent over, peering into my cabin with her hands cupped around her eyes. Two people were helping themselves to a drink from the water tank. More pests, I thought, that's what they are—another bunch of gosh-darned potato beetles. The leader was still hovering around me like a hornet. His excitement increased, as if the chaos surrounding us were an affirmation of whatever it was he believed. He said, "We demand—"

"*I* demand," I roared, "that you all get off my property this minute!" And then, as if to punctuate my sentence, there was a loud explosion behind me. The pudgy man's face paled and his mouth fell open as he stared over my shoulder. Everyone stopped talking. The people in the field froze a few yards from the scarecrow. Whisky and Constance scurried back into the chicken coop. I turned around as Pearl lowered the barrel of the Marlin. She walked past me, stopped in front of the head potato beetle, planted her legs at a wide angle and leveled the gun at his head.

"You can get right the hell outta here," she said. "You know Logan would never condone this and you're on private property and so help me, I'll blow your stupid head right off your shoulders if you don't move it."

The man was now completely discombobulated. "Pearl Nickels?" he said.

"Get the hell outta here," Pearl said, down the barrel of the Marlin. "You know the rules. And get that damn bus off the property too." She swung the gun around at the tall man who was still standing near the cabin door. "All of you!" she yelled.

Their signs over their shoulders, talking in hushed voices, the human potato beetles herded over to the driveway and stood on Fisher Lane while the man Pearl had threatened got in the school bus and backed it up until it was off the property, too.

"Idiots," Pearl said, as I watched them leave, the scope held up to one eye. "It's sad, really. Not one of them has ever had an original idea in his head."

"But how did you know that unpleasant little potato beetle?" I asked.

"That's George Frehse. He's the overzealous protégé of Logan Scarab, the national director of SAFETYS, the Society for Animal Freedom and Ethical Treatment Standards." Pearl unloaded the Marlin and let it rest in the crook of her arm. She snorted her indignation. "At the lab, we used to call George the UnSAFETY. I don't think Logan even speaks to him anymore. The SAFETYS have done some good work, but this brotherhood-of-the-brainless that George formed is using their name and going on these kind of nonsense missions."

I continued to watch the group through my scope as they milled around in front of my driveway. "So you've dealt with them before," I said.

"Oh, God yeah. It seemed like they were protesting in front of the building where I worked every couple of weeks. Logan and I actually were on a television show together once to debate the use of animals in lab work. He's mainly a lobbyist—he's helped pass some of the toughest legislation against animal testing. And he's extremely civil and we agreed on most things. But after that, George's group started picketing at the university lab. Logan called me himself to apologize and explain about George."

"But how did they find me and what is this all about? I don't have any lab here," I said, gesturing toward the skunk coop with the scope.

"They're against animals being kept in captivity—at all. For any reason. And they've taken it to absurd lengths. They're even against people keeping pets. They get wind of any kind of story about people keeping wildlife cooped up," she nodded at the skunk coop, "and they go absolutely bananas. As far as how they heard about you..." She shrugged. "Maybe your buddy Robby knows something about it."

I looked back over at the group. They were talking in pairs or groups of three and most had laid their signs on the ground or were using them as canes while they chatted. A few people walked off down the road toward Robby's place. I heard a siren far down the dirt road before the police car pulled up, parting the crowd, and then a white van with the name of a television station on its side pulled up and parked next to the school bus. "Oh shit," Pearl said. George appeared at the front of the group suddenly with a stepstool and a bull horn. The other SAFETYS folks picked up their signs and gathered around him as he began speaking.

"Friends!" he said, his voice made nasaly by the horn, but perfectly audible even from where we were standing. "Friends of the earth, friends of the earth's creatures, we've gathered here to be heard."

"Actually, you've herded here simply to be gathered," Pearl said.

A couple of people got out of the TV van with a camera, microphones, and trails of wire, and began moving through the group of SAFETYS. "And we're going to hear from everyone who wants to be heard, who wants to speak out against the horrible atrocity to which we are witnesses today. Anyone who believes concentration camps are immoral for any species."

"What in the world could he be talking about?" I asked Pearl.

"Damien," Pearl said, "he's talking about your skunks."

The tall man who'd held open my door had the bullhorn now. He didn't need the stool. "It's terrible to think we live in a world where people confine and torture animals whether it be under the guise of scientific research, or for their own sadistic pleasure."

"But isn't all this more than a little absurd?" I asked Pearl. "I don't torture animals. My skunks enjoy being milked of their musk. I don't keep them here. They've elected to stay."

Pearl shook her head. "You don't understand. I never did any animal testing either. But these people don't give a shit. George and his followers are fanatics. They're opposed to anything they can classify as captivity. One of them even said in an interview that she's opposed to people keeping any animals as pets."

"This kind of thing goes on even in a country where we're supposedly civilized," the tall man was saying. "Well, tell me this: Is it civilized when people in labs play God with animals, subjecting them to horrible diseases?"

The crowd, as if on cue, all shouted, "NO!" in unison.

"And is it civilized when some madman incarcerates his fellow mammals, locks them up as if he were their jailer?"

"NO!" they all shouted. A second bus pulled up and another twenty or thirty people with signs streamed out and began shouting and carrying on.

George took the bullhorn again. "Now I want you all to hear from the man who brought this violator of animal rights to our awareness. This is a new member, the first I believe, of the new SAFETYS chapter in this state—Mr. Matt Baxter."

I could hardly believe my ears or eyes as Matt stepped from the crowd, clad in a blue-and-black flannel shirt and, as usual, the dirty blue baseball cap. He took the bullhorn from George Frehse and climbed onto the stool. "That lousy bastard," I said. I remembered the voice that had said "That's him," when I'd opened the door to my cabin that morning.

"Well, truth be told, I actually don't give a flyin' shit what he does," Matt said. "I just plain don't like the motherfucker." The tall man who'd spoken before grabbed Matt's arm and pulled him down to whisper something in his ear. Matt straightened back up and said, "And I had a feelin' he was doin' somethin' perverted like maybe molestin' critters out here. And I just can't stand by while one a God's creatures is bein' abused."

"For the love of Jesus!" I said, lowering the scope. I couldn't bear to look at the lying monster. Something behind me smelled like stale smoke. "Father would be doing somersaults in his grave if he could get an earful of this malarkey."

"Dude, this is wild," I heard behind me. I turned around. Robby and Fiona were standing there as if they'd just dropped out of the sky.

"Now, where in the world did you come from?" I asked.

"The path, man," Robby said, jerking his thumb over his shoulder. Although it was the most direct route between the hunting lodge and my cabin, I didn't remember ever having shown Robby my path to the stream. There was another smell about them, besides stale smoke, that I couldn't place. Perhaps it was a new flavor of patchouli oil. I held up the scope to look at them and, adjusting the focus for the shorter distance, I recognized the heavy-lidded look of the stoned.

"Dude man, put that thing away man, it makes me paranoid. You were doin' that all night at the party, too. I think it freaked out poor old Peg."

"Wow," Fiona said, craning her head forward and tucking her shiny hair back behind her ears. "What are they all doing?" I wondered how Fiona could keep her hair looking so clean while living in such a sty.

"It seems our friend Matt Baxter has become an animal rights advocate," I said.

As soon as Fiona touched her hair, Robby, reminded of his own hair-fondling habits, pulled off the elastic band that held his ponytail together, tipped his head back and shook out his hair as if he were in the shower, only to pull it back into a ponytail again. He spoke during this pointless exercise. "Dude, when I heard those sirens, man I hit the freakin' roof, didn't I, Fee?" Fiona nodded solemnly as she recalled the momentous occasion. "I said shit, man, like, this is *it*, we're fuckin' busted! Like, I was shovin' shit under my mattress, into my socks and shoes, it was totally hectic. Felt like I was in a freakin' mob movie. But then Beazly was standing by the window the whole time we were running around tryin' to hide everything and he said they must've stopped at your place because they weren't comin' any more. So what's goin' on here anyway?" Robby hadn't paid any attention to what I'd said when his girlfriend had asked the same question. The crowd had taken up a chant, parading around in circle for the television crew, waving their signs.

"Stop-thee-in-san-i-ty, set-them-free," they sang, lingering joyfully on the Es.

"Have you met Pearl?" I asked.

"Oh, yeah, at the party, right?" Robby said, inclining his chin in her direction as he pulled his cigarettes from his t-shirt. Pearl glanced at him askance, then looked back at the SAFETYS crowd.

"When are you due?" Fiona asked.

"About three weeks," Pearl said.

"Hey, you know I'm trained in child care," Fiona said. "When it's born, if you ever need a sitter or anything..." she trailed off as if the words were a certain amount of moisture that had evaporated from her tongue mid-sentence.

"Thank you," Pearl said, turning to Fiona, "that's very generous of you."

Constance came up and rubbed against my leg. I bent down to pet her. Robby had lit his cigarette and now he waved it in the direction of the circus taking place on Fisher Lane. "Really, man, what is all this?"

It was at that moment that I remembered the magazine article Robby had written. I turned to face him squarely. "They say they've been reading about me," I said, my voice turning into a sneer. "They're subsistence farming fans, here to cheer me on in my Goddamned 'one-man revolution.'"

Red carnations bloomed in Robby's nearly hairless cheeks. He glanced from me to Pearl, and gestured at the Marlin resting across her stomach. "So what are you gonna do? Shoot 'em all?"

I couldn't believe he was trying to bluff his way through this. "Robby, why in the dickens didn't you ask me if you could interview me for a magazine article?"

"What? I thought you knew, I guess. Didn't we talk about it? I thought we talked about it. We did, we talked about it and you said it was okay."

"No, we certainly did not," I said, taking a step toward him. "I would never have agreed to anything like that and you know it."

Fiona looked at Robby as if he'd begun turning into a garter snake in front of her. "You didn't have his permission for that?" she asked, her voice stretched even thinner by bewilderment. "I told you I didn't think he'd like it, but you said it was cool with him."

Robby held out his hands as if to say "search me." With the scope to my eye, I did so: I looked down at his forearms, and saw that there were, as Pearl had said, little bruises near the elbow joint. "Hey man I thought it was alright," he said. "Sorry, okay? It was just a little magazine article. I thought it would be alright. What's the big deal? Why's everybody all bent about this? It's only the second thing I ever got published, after that poem in college. I was just tryin' to do something good, something with a purpose, okay? *Excuse* me."

In spite of myself, I began to feel sorry for him. His bruised arms were so thin, the bony shoulders so pitiful, and the wound left by his father's abandoning of him still so raw. I glanced at Pearl. She made a little snort, rolled her good eye and looked back at the crowd by the driveway. They'd stopped chanting and now someone else was on the stepstool making a speech. I heard something about whales being slaughtered by the Japanese, and owls' habitats being destroyed in the Northwest.

"Lemme see that thing a minute," Robby said, extending a hand for the scope. He dropped his cigarette in the dirt and brought the scope to his eye. "It's SAFETYS," he said. "They're a pretty cool organization, man. What're they doing here?"

"Protesting against my personal life, into which they've seen fit to stick their little snouts," I said.

"Oh," Robby said, still looking through the scope. "I wonder if anyone's got the scoop on this for the *Herald*." After a moment he said, "Hey is that George Frehse?"

"You know him too?" I said. "I didn't realize the little pest was such a celebrity."

"Dude, this guy is a total rebel. I've gotta meet him. Come on, Fee." To my consternation, the two of them walked off to join the protesters.

"There he goes," Pearl said, "the man of letters. What a guy, Damien. With friends like that..."

"What do we do now?" I asked. "When will they go away?"

"When they can't make the next mortgage payment, I guess."

"No, no. I mean the other potato beetles. The righteous animal rights people." Constance was still sniffing around us, so I picked her up, held her in the crook of my arm and stroked her.

"The SAFETYS? Oh they'll leave soon enough. Once the television crew gets enough footage for the news they'll leave, and the protesters usually don't stay around for long after that. What good would it do out here, anyway?" Pearl waved the barrel of the Marlin at the surrounding forest. "No audience for them."

We went into the cabin and Pearl got out a few cans of sardines to snack on while she cooked a fillet. I was too upset to eat anything at all. I sat at the table and sipped at a triple shot of musk, listening to the nonsense out on the edge of my property. They took up the chant again for a while. "Stop-thee-in-san-i-ty, set-them-free." The sheer idiocy of it made me grind my teeth. As the musk began to work its magic, however, the chanting bothered me less. I didn't hear the words after a while. I began to tap my foot to the rhythm of the voices.

"We're going to need a crib," Pearl said, after lunch. She got up from the table to toss her sardine cans on the pile.

The way Pearl could polish off cans of sardines, tuna, and clams was truly astonishing. A can of tuna was merely a snack she could devour in less time than Robby could eat a handful of sunflower seeds. In fact, she ate a can of tuna too quickly to even be seen doing it. Sometimes, if I were sitting reading, and I heard the crack of a can of tuna opening, by the time I'd turned around and picked up my scope, Pearl was already licking the fork clean and tossing the empty can over her shoulder. There was a towering heap of empty cans in the corner behind the door, and she'd only been living in the cabin a few days. Flies rose from this heap into a buzzing cloud every time I disturbed them by opening the door.

Another thing was getting on my nerves. Pearl never washed the frying pan when she was through with it. She left it sitting atop the stove, filled with grease that became a wading pool for the flies, and then, when she wanted to use it again, simply re-stoked the fire and plopped another fillet into the old grease.

I took another sip of my musk. I'd build a crib. That was something I didn't mind doing. I'd developed a love for carpentry while putting in the floor, building the outhouse, the bookshelf and bedside table.

"I guess I'll go into town and buy that and the other stuff we'll need for when the baby comes, so we don't have to worry about it later," Pearl said.

"No, I'll build a crib. I've got plenty of extra wood. I don't have much money and I don't like to spend it on frivolities."

"Well, I don't know if this qualifies as a frivolity, but don't worry about it. I've got money. I sold my house."

"But I would *like* to build the crib," I said.

Pearl dumped her fillet onto her plate, sat back down and smiled at me. She reached over and squeezed my hand. "You're so cute," she said. She took a bite of her fillet. "You remember when you followed me home that day?" Of course I remembered. "And I came up and knocked on your window?" Looking down at her plate, she started to chuckle. "You sat there like a little boy caught with his hand in the cookie jar and pretended you couldn't see me." She put her fork down and laughed so hard tears rolled out of the corners of her eyes. It was infectious. I took another sip of musk and chuckled.

Pearl was a surprisingly diligent worker despite being pregnant. That afternoon, while the circus continued in front of my driveway, she went up and closed the dam herself. This was not easy. My lever was very primitive, and I struggled with it every time I opened or closed the dam. When she joined me in the field, she moved quickly, picking ripe tomatoes, digging up potatoes, filling baskets with them and carrying them to the root cellar, managing to get twice as much done as I did.

As Pearl had predicted, the insanity in front of the driveway came to a stop soon after the television crew left in the afternoon. The air cooled significantly and by dusk, accompanied by some impressive rolls of thunder, the first large drop of rain tapped my shoulder like a taciturn acquaintance. Another drop hit the brim of my straw hat. Pearl and I put our tools in the chicken coop and washed off our hands in the basin outside the cabin. As if in reply to the threatening grumble of the thunder, the engine of the school bus came rumbling to life and carried the SAFETYS safely away. In the cabin, we lit the fish oil candles and got into bed. The pattering of rain on the roof sounded like a few pairs of hands clapping as Pearl slipped off her bikini. As she climbed on top of me, more rain, more pairs of hands joined in clapping until it sounded like a room full people. Pearl sat straddling me, pressing her hands against my stomach, and began moving her pelvis rhythmically. The applause grew steadily until it was a wild ovation of hundreds, then thousands, spilling out of an amphitheater across the field. The deluge flooded the field and the forest beyond it. We slipped beneath the surface, dove down together until the sounds above us dissolved and we drowned in each other.

20

She said she wanted to surprise me with the giant veggies when they were ready to harvest. Pearl tended that area of the farm where they grew and I did not visit it. I went about my chores as usual during the week. At my request, Pearl had limited the experiment to just a few rows of vegetables. But I didn't think about them—I was preoccupied with other matters. I watched her mix the chemicals at night and she dumped them in the water during the day after I'd dammed the stream.

Maybe I should drink some myself," Pearl said, one night while preparing a bottle of the growth potion. "Do you want a really big baby?"

I nearly choked on a mouthful of after-dinner musk. "Good God, Pearl, no! You don't know what could—" I stopped.

Pearl was chuckling. "Just kidding, just kidding," she said.

I wasn't so sure I always appreciated Pearl's sense of humor and the crass attitude that seemed to give rise to it. She had just interfered with my after-dinner musk, a quiet time I usually spent dreaming, restoring myself mentally and physically in anticipation of the next day's work—not gagging. My daily level of irritation rose steadily with the mounting pile of empty fish product cans behind the door and the increasing number of houseflies buzzing about the cabin. I diluted my irritation by drinking more musk. After drinking a few shots the whole cabin dissolved away—the heaps of empty cans, the tickle of flies landing on my ears or nose, and Pearl herself faded into the beatific blur of my musk dream. Of course musk is helpful as a lubricant for any situation of heightened friction, but after a while the musk itself became a source of irritation, because despite the fact that I squeezed each of the skunks regularly each morning, I did not seem able, for some reason, to keep enough in the jars. It was as if they all had slow leaks. I did not see how I could have let the levels slip down so low and I resolved each time not to let it happen again.

But other things were on my mind. Though we continued to have plenty of delicious sex, I found myself afterwards begrudging Pearl her half of the bed which, as the night went on, became three quarters of the bed, then eight tenths, and so on, until I woke in the morning to find myself pressed flat against the wall of the cabin. I would then look over at Pearl and see that she was comfortably on her back, her legs and arms flung out as if she had leapt from an airplane and was falling through the sky, snoring loudly as the great white dome of her belly rose and fell. Also, not only did she eat too quickly, the woman ate greater quantities than one would have believed possible. She was perpetually snacking on cans of tuna, smoked clams and sardines. The subject she most enjoyed discussing was her next meal. It began to sicken me; I found myself eating less and less. I sat despondently at the dinner table, sipping a glass of musk while she wolfed down platefuls of trout she'd caught that day, pausing only to ask me if I were going to finish mine, then plopping my plate down on top of hers and eating what was left of my portion.

One morning I awoke with an irritated stomach. I ate nothing for breakfast, and when we went out to begin working, I was suddenly overcome by the sinking sensation and slackness of facial muscles that heralds a bodily upheaval.

"What's the matter?" Pearl asked. "You look a little pale."

"Nothing. I just think I might vomit."

Pearl walked over, pressed her belly against mine, took my face in both her hands and kissed me on the lips. "You're so adorable," she said.

"You find nausea endearing?"

"It's sympathetic pregnancy. I've heard it happens to guys sometimes. I think it's cute. It shows how concerned you are." Terrific, I thought. Not only has she made a mess of my cabin, she's passed her morning sickness on to me as well.

One afternoon, Pearl said it was time for her to show me what she'd done. She blindfolded me and led me stumbling across the field until we were in her part of the farm.

"OK, are you ready?" she asked.

"As I'll ever be," I replied, and she untied my blindfold. I simply stood there in a state of shock. Having seen the SeaLawn, I knew what Pearl was capable of. Yet somehow the vegetables seemed to happen overnight. I'd known that they'd be big, of course—that was the idea. But big, when considered in the abstract, is not quite as big as big is when one is confronted with actual, physical bigness. I'd seen other things that were larger than they were supposed to be. For example, one of the few times I ever ate in a restaurant I ordered jumbo shrimp, and that was quite something. But one simply is not prepared to see a thing blown up to several times its normal size. The only experience to which I could compare the experience of Pearl's vegetables is the experience of seeing the Liberty Bell. In my first year at Rigby, my house parents took us on a field trip to Philadelphia. For some reason, I was expecting the Liberty Bell to be about the size of a dinner bell, something preserved under a small glass bell jar. I thought the Liberty Bell was what Paul Revere had waved in one hand as he rode through the streets of Boston, shouting that the Redcoats were coming. Perhaps, more than anything else, this example illustrates the quality of education at Rigby; but one can imagine my astonishment when I laid eyes on the actual Liberty Bell, about three times the size of the desk in my room back at Rigby, the huge crack running down the side of it, the thick metal rubbed smooth by the admiring hands of thousands of other children who'd visited it on similar field trips.

Such was the nature of my astonishment the first time I beheld one of Pearl's tomatoes, which was the size of a melon and must have weighed in the neighborhood of eight pounds. "So, what do you think?" Pearl asked. But I could scarcely think, because I was experiencing a novel sensation—that of feeling truly threatened by a vegetable. I looked at Pearl, unable to utter a word.

"Wait, come over here," she said, pulling me by the hand. "Wait until you see the radish." Apparently, she'd dug it up earlier in the day and washed it off to present it to me. And there it sat: a big red radish the size of a grapefruit sitting next to the substantial hole from which it had been dug. Then Pearl showed me a carrot that could have been used as a club.

"It's quite a marvel, Pearl," I said. I didn't say much else. I was too busy examining the giant carrot. Just as the large crack on the Liberty Bell had fascinated me, I was amazed by the huge rings and fissures in the obscenely large carrot. I found myself unable to summon the excitement for the giant vegetables that I'd genuinely felt for the SeaLawn.

That night over dinner Pearl talked about the giant corn she was planning to make the next week while we munched carrot sticks the size of baguettes and stuffed tomatoes as big as bowls. When she was almost finished with her meal, Pearl put down her fork. "My God, I could go for some fish sticks," she said.

I sighed. "Haven't you gotten your fill of fish over the last few days?" I said, through a cloud of flies buzzing over the fish oil candles on the table. I'd almost eaten one of the flies, not noticing that it was on my forkful of stuffed tomato until it was inches from my open mouth. This was not my style at all. Perhaps I was better off living alone.

Pearl picked up her fork and stabbed at her tomato. "I'm almost out of cans—only five more. And I think I've practically fished out that stream." She put the fork back down again and spoke with her mouth full. "But what I really want is fish sticks, anyway." She swallowed. "Some nice, breaded, deep-fried, crispy fish sticks, a few dozen of them and a big basket of fries."

The greasy image thus conjured was almost enough to ruin my appetite for the meal before me. Somehow, I managed to dismiss it from my mind, though Pearl and I did not speak very much for the rest of the evening and kept to our own sides of the bed once we'd gotten into it. In the middle of the night, Pearl shook my shoulder to wake me up and I thought she was going to tell me she was going out for fish sticks.

"Did you hear that?" she whispered.

"Mmhhmm," I said. I thought she meant the words she'd just whispered.

"I think it's some of George's people. It sounded like it was coming from the coop." She threw back the covers, pulled on her robe and grabbed the flashlight. "They're probably trying to set the skunks free," she said.

But the skunks were already free, and at this time of night they'd be out foraging for food anyway. There was nothing the renegade gang of SAFETYS could do, unless they snuck past us during the day and managed to kidnap all the skunks, which certainly wouldn't be easy. I sat up and rubbed my eyes. Pearl was already grabbing the pistols from the wall. She shoved one in the pocket of her bathrobe and held the other one in front of her the same way she held the flashlight. I put on my glasses and followed her outside. The beam of her flashlight cut through the darkness to reveal what could have been two figures streaking from the chicken coop towards the woods, in the direction of the path to the stream. It happened so quickly I wasn't sure whether I'd seen the figures or imagined them. It could have been a mist as far as I was concerned.

"Hey!" Pearl yelled. "Hey, what the hell're you doing!" She raised the pistol and fired a shot at the stars. I vaguely recalled doing something similar myself on another occasion. Or had I dreamed it? I couldn't exactly say. Pearl went into the chicken coop and looked around. "All the tools are here," she said. "They didn't steal anything. I wonder what the hell they were doing in here."

"Who?" I asked. "Are you sure there was someone here?"

Pearl turned and flashed the light into my face. "You didn't see them?" I shook my head. "Your eyes really have gotten a lot worse," she said. She put the flashlight under her chin so it illuminated her face, making her cheekbones even more prominent and turning her eye sockets into black holes. "It was Robby," she said. "Robby and that other creepy one."

The next morning, after popping the last sardine from her last can into her mouth and tossing it into an open trash bag full of empty cans, Pearl licked her fingertips and belched loudly. "God, I can't wait to get some fish sticks." She glanced at the three bulging trash bags full of empty cans. "We have to go to the dump anyway," she said.

"Maybe you can just go on your own," I said. "Perhaps I should stay here and safeguard my skunks while you go gorge yourself on saturated fats and so on." I was only slightly concerned about Robby trespassing on my property. Mainly, I was thinking it would be nice to have the farm to myself for a while, have some peace and quiet, even if only for a couple hours.

Pearl shrugged. "Alright, suit yourself," she said.

"Speaking of suiting oneself, you might stop by Jud's and get yourself one of these," I said, tugging on the strap of my overalls. "If you're going to work on this farm, you might as well be dressed for it. A bathrobe is hardly the sort of thing one wears for this kind of labor."

"Yes, sir. Anything else? Should I drink a pint of skunk musk before I go there, too? You know what? You should come into town with me and get your eyes checked." She pointed at my glass of musk. "That shit's making you blind." Pearl hoisted the black trash bags bulging with cans over her shoulders and went rattling out to the car. I slowly followed her outside like a forlorn and cranky child. She was sitting in the driver's seat of the Eldorado with the engine running, the trash bags stuffed into in the back seat. "Why are you taking my car?" I asked.

"It's got more trunk space. I'm gonna need it."

"You might've asked first."

Pearl puffed her cheeks and blew out a long stream of air, temporarily raising a ringlet out of her face. She began to back the car up. "You're sure you don't want to come?" she asked.

I said I was sure. I didn't need anything in town, was terrified of running into Margaret, and had work to do on the farm anyway. And at last I would have peace and solitude on the farm. But as I watched through my scope as Pearl disappeared down Fisher Lane in the Eldorado, I was overcome by loneliness. I started out into the field to work, and then, on second thought, went back to the coop, woke Constance up, put her on a twine leash and took her with me out into the field. I tied her leash to the wheelbarrow so I could have her with me while I harvested corn.

I stopped to examine one of the gigantic tomatoes, which had already begun to rot. What ambled to mind was Robby's probable reaction to such freaks of nature. He'd likely lump the inflated veggies into the same category with hybrid seeds and pesticides. And I had to admit there was something monstrous about this whole giant vegetable business. I did not want to see the giant ear of corn Pearl was planning to grow. I wanted to fill my root cellar with the normal-sized vegetables I'd worked all spring and summer to produce. I wanted to eat the fruits of my labor, not the fruits of genetic engineering, regardless of whether it saved me hours, even days, of work. For what would I do with all my days if I did not have to work for my food? In the shadow of these monolithic vegetables I was insignificant, my farming practices rendered absurd as I struggled alongside a beach-ball-sized tomato to harvest a little bitty potato I had labored over for so long. Pearl comes along one day and—presto!—it turns out I've been wasting months of time and gallons of sweat. And to Pearl it was all a game. She thought she could just materialize here and turn my whole world upside down. Then, once she was bored, she could go play pick-up-fish-sticks or whatever happened to be the next source of amusement. Well, I was just going to have to stand up to her. That wasn't the lifestyle advocated here on the Youngquist farm. Genius or not, if she wanted to live on my farm, by golly, she was going to live by my rules.

Such was my resolve as I finished the day's chores, including, grudgingly—as if the act itself were an admission of Pearl's victory—pouring the fish emulsion into the pipe when I closed the dam. After lunch I had several shots of skunk musk and drifted through the afternoon sitting in front of the cabin, listening to the birds singing, occasionally nodding off to sleep. After a time, there was a furtive scratching at my leg. It was Stripe, picking at a Japanese beetle that was climbing up my pants. "Hello old sport," I said, pulling myself out of a doze, "glad to see you're still fighting the good fight." It was dusk. Pearl had been gone the entire day. There was not that much to do in Highbridge, and I started worrying about what might have happened to her. Maybe she'd just decided not to come back. Who was to say she hadn't decided to skip town with my car, since hers was less likely to make it across the country? It was twilight now. She'd probably gotten some fish and chips to go and headed for San Francisco. I chastised myself for arguing with her before she left. What was it we'd been bickering about anyway? I realized I probably should have gone with her. Highbridge was full of savages and Pearl didn't have the experience in handling them that I had. Instead of protecting her from a real menace, I'd decided to protect my skunks from a nonexistent one.

But what Pearl really needed protection from, I realized, was me. I was ruining her life. I'd always avoided relationships with people because I did not want them to give me more pain. But now I was encumbered with a new emotion, the tremendous guilt and self-hatred that went along with suffocating someone else, stunting another's growth. I was the source of all Pearl's problems. I'd senselessly impregnated her and now she was a captive here on this dull farm, more captive than the skunks. She could have had a fulfilling life, highlighted by more scientific discoveries and interesting new friends on the West Coast. Perhaps all this had occurred to her while she'd been in the Highbridge grocery store and she'd simply gotten back in the car and headed west. Pearl was gone forever. But wasn't that what I'd wanted all along? To be rid of her—to be alone? Wasn't that the real reason I objected to the giant vegetables? Wasn't Pearl hogging my bed, filling my reading hours with her ceaseless chatter? Wasn't she constantly disrupting my day with her stupendous appetite and erratic mood swings? The only problem was this: how in the world would I get over her this time? I should have sent her away when I saw her there at Robby's, while I was still drunk and could have dismissed the whole incident later on as a bad dream, another storm.

This whole predicament in which I now found myself was a result of another of my catastrophic lapses into folly. These lapses had always kept me from the path of practicality that I'd tried to follow by being self-sufficient and solitary. They had resulted in the now imminent arrival upon this planet of another being with my genes, a catastrophe that could easily have been prevented. I hadn't had the time over the past two weeks to examine what was actually happening in my life, and the horror of it came rushing to the surface of my consciousness now. I knew I could only spawn another weak, worthless, unlovable creature that would be forced to suffer the pain inflicted upon it by others of its species as punishment for the crime of inferiority. The only purpose it could serve might be to play the role of scapegoat, a role with which I was all too familiar. The obviousness of the ugly pattern—which I'd not been left alone long enough to consider since Pearl had moved onto the farm—disgusted me and my disgust quickly boiled over into rage.

"Miserable idiot!" I shrieked. I pounded my head against the wall of the cabin. "Miserable, worthless bastard!" I yelled between the increasingly rapid poundings. "Bastard! bastard! bastard!" I yelled. The pounding became so fast and violent I could not speak. It became dark. I saw nothing.

At some point in the night a vision of Pearl appeared which I could not identify as part of a dream or reality. She was leaning over me, the long, wild mane of ringlets framing her face in the light of one of my kerosene lamps. I fell away from this vision back down into oblivion like someone slipping over the edge of a boat at night, plunging straight down into the darkness.

"Jud was asking about you," Pearl said, at breakfast the next morning. We sat there, in matching overalls and boots, like twins our mother had decided to dress in farmer costumes. Pearl must have carried me into the cabin the night before because I'd woken up in bed and watched from across the room as she sliced up the fire-hydrant-sized zucchini, fried it and put plates of it, with fish sticks, on the table. It wasn't exactly my idea of breakfast, but I didn't want to cause a fuss. "He wanted to make sure you'd started canning vegetables. He's all worried about you making it through the winter." She shoved an entire fish stick in her mouth, chewed it once and swallowed. "Boy, this sure hits the spot, doesn't it? I ate a few boxes of these last night after you fell asleep. Did you know there is absolutely no place to get fresh fish in this town unless you catch it yourself?"

I would have preferred dry toast, but I didn't say anything. I still wanted to voice my objection to the gargantuan vegetables, but after the previous night's tomfoolery I wasn't sure how to broach the subject. Pearl was so much stronger than I, it seemed almost as if the farm were hers now and I was just a helping hand. Pearl had found my glasses and had put iodine and fish oil on the bloody bump on my head, which now felt (and looked, I later discovered) like a small volcano erupting from my temple as it throbbed with a persistent, dull ache. "What else did you learn from Jud?" I asked. "He appears to be the consciousness of Highbridge."

Pearl sighed. "Well, school's started, and there seem to be a lot of drugs going around Highbridge High." She gulped down two more fish sticks. "Serious drugs too, not just pot. And it's a big deal I guess, because they don't usually see this kind of thing out here in the boonies. Jud was kind of hinting that he thought the drugs might be coming from the Krauthammer hideout." She waved her fork, with a fish stick stuck on its tines, in the direction of the hippiefied hunting lodge, then popped the fish stick in her mouth and shrugged.

"Do you think that's the case?" I asked.

"Could be. Where else are they getting the money to pay for that place, and to feed however many mouths they've got living there?"

"Robby *did* often complain about money when they first moved onto that land," I mused. I stopped trying to eat the fish sticks and took a sip of my morning musk. I shook my head. "He said they were farming—but I've seen what they're farming, and I've never heard of people living exclusively on cannabis salads."

"And they didn't raise enough to live off of selling the stuff," Pearl said. "I went up there to check it out. So maybe they are selling harder drugs. We know that they're using 'em anyway. And you don't have a problem paying your mortgage and then all of a sudden buy a new van."

"Who's got a new van?" I asked.

"Robby does. Brand spanking new, shiny green VW. He sure as hell couldn't've gotten much on a trade-in either."

I realized I hadn't heard the familiar chirping of Robby's faded, peace-and-leaf-painted microbus in quite some time. I'd thought the blue van I'd seen go by might belong to Beazly, who supposedly had independent means.

"Wasn't there some kid from California at that party?" Pearl said. "Maybe that's where they're getting stuff from. Oh well." She tossed back another fish stick. "Oh yeah, and I ran into your buddy Matt Baxter."

I almost coughed an entire fluid ounce of musk up through my nose and my pulse immediately quickened. "Where did you see him?" I asked.

"At Jud's," Pearl said casually, as if she were talking not about a dangerous threat to the wellbeing of all mammals, but some gossipy little old lady at the local beauty salon. With her usual reckless disregard of etiquette, Pearl licked her fingers, pushed her plate away, leaned back in her chair, belched and patted her belly. I knew that unless I washed it, the plate would sit on the table all day long, while flies used the puddle of grease in the middle of it as a swimming facility or an egg-laying landing pad. "God, what a creepy, low-life son of a bitch he is," Pearl said.

"What did he say?"

"Nothing worth repeating," she said.

I was so distracted by all this news that I stood up abruptly, intending to do I don't know what, but darkness rushed in at me from the walls of the cabin and narrowed my field of vision until it seemed I was looking through the wrong end of a telescope. I plopped back down in my chair.

"You better take it slow today," Pearl said.

"There's nothing wrong with me," I whined. "If he said anything deprecating about you, I'll, well, I think I'll—"

"Oh, he didn't say anything he wouldn't take back—after a good swift kick in the nuts."

"You kicked him?" I exclaimed.

"Twice," Pearl said. "Once for what he said to me, and then again when I found out he was responsible for getting the SAFETYS over here."

"But Pearl, he could have done something terrible. And besides, you're pregnant, you shouldn't be running around kicking men in the groin."

"Everybody else in Jud's thought I should have. They seemed to think it was about the funniest thing they'd seen in a long time. Especially the fat one."

That would have been Doug, the lummox. Now I felt even more helpless. Matt had punched me, roughed me up, run over my fence, killed one of my skunks, and still I hadn't had the nerve to strike him. Pearl came along and knocked him down as if he were a warped bowling pin. How was I going to ask a woman who went into town and defended my honor, who picked me up and put me to bed like an enfeebled old man, who out-worked me on my own farm—how could I ask this woman not to grow my vegetables too large? And when she pressed for a reason, I would be forced to confess that it was because her vegetables crippled my ego. She'd laugh at you Damien, I thought, certainly she'd laugh. But, maybe, you can tell her in the middle of a musk dream. A little liquid courage is all you need. Rising slowly, I went to the chicken coop to get more musk. I thought Inconstance's musk would suit the mood. But her jar was almost completely empty. Strange, I thought, very strange. Rousing Constance, I put her on the leash I'd used the day before and brought her with me. I filled my glass with Tripper's musk and headed back to the cabin. I stood outside for a moment, sipping. It was time to lay down the law. Yes, precisely. I would have to raise the issue in a tactful way, perhaps put it in Pearl's own mind, somehow, that it would be a good idea not to continue growing the offensive vegetables. I would say, "By the way, about those vegetables..." I would pause here, and often throughout my speech, to give Pearl an opportunity to offer to stop growing them, as I pointed out the various practical problems posed by such unwieldy vegetables. "When it comes to canning," I'd say, "I'm not sure such large specimens lend themselves to the process." I took a deep breath and pushed open the door. I walked in and sat back down at the table across from Pearl. Constance curled up under my chair. I noticed Pearl had cleared all the dishes from the table. This was unusual.

"By the way," I said. "About those cannings..." That didn't sound quite right. I noticed there was a big, bluish prune sitting in the middle of the table. "About those vegetables," I began again, then added, "*your* vegetables..." Pearl was silent. I took out my scope and looked at her through it. Her face revealed nothing. She sat tipped back on the hind legs of her chair, staring down at the table. Lowering my scope, I saw that it was not a prune, but a crumpled box sitting on the table between us. I put my scope down and opened the box. "Good God," I said. "Where did you find this?"

"I cleaned out your car this morning. It was under the seat." She rocked to and fro on the rear legs of her chair with her hands clasped on top of her stomach. "Anything you wanna tell me about?"

I examined the fish shapes on the gold ring and remembered how the Morecods had circled around and around in Pearl's SeaLawn tank. I began stammering hopelessly. "I... well, the vegetables, you know, have gotten so large now—"

Pearl cut me off. "I mean, I think we're getting along great one day, and the next thing I know you've sold your house and left town. When I find you, you're getting drunk at a party with some widowed librarian—I know, I know, you explained all that—and then we start living together. Things are going along fine again, I think I know you inside and out, and then I find a wedding band under the seat of your car. Damien, are you married?"

"Married?" I said. It was preposterous. "You mean to someone else?"

"You couldn't very well be married to yourself, could you?" Pearl said.

It had occurred to me before that Pearl and I should be married so that at least I would not be responsible for bringing another bastard into the world. I pictured a boy alone in his room, a tiny dried stream of snot beneath his nose as he gazed out a dorm window at the

Rigby School. This was not something I wanted to be responsible for. But the way we'd left things up in the air, Pearl could very well leave the farm any day and give our child to some orphanage. If she agreed to marry me, on the other hand, presumably she would stay around. But what sort of life did I have to offer a woman? How could I even ask her? "Darling, would you prefer to spend the rest of your days in a one-room hovel, grubbing a living from the ground in the middle of a nutty nowhere, or live a life of prestige and glamour with your sophisticated colleagues in a metropolitan setting, to which you were en route a few weeks ago?" No, that wouldn't do at all.

Another question was whether marriage was what I truly wanted. I'd taken such pains to be alone. On the other hand, I'd found that many things in life—sex among them—are not nearly as much fun on one's own. But regarding an actual marriage proposal, there were so many items to take into consideration: the possibility of Pearl laughing in my face when I popped the question; the size of the cabin in which three people would be living; the horribly long winter months I would face alone if Pearl left for San Francisco; the utter destruction of my solitary lifestyle if she said yes; the necessity of sending our child to school; the consequent nightmare of parent-teacher conferences. What I really needed was a sheet of paper divided down the middle, where I could list the pros and cons of asking Pearl to marry me in two columns. Then I would need about three months or so to measure the lengths of the columns and the individual weights of each pro and each con while I devised a formula by which the sums of the lengths and weights of both columns could be compared so that I could make the correct decision.

"Well," Pearl said. "Are you?"

"Am I?" I'd drifted completely away.

Pearl sighed heavily, then repeated her question. "Are... you... married?"

The response I wanted to give was, "I would like to be. I want to marry you, and that is why I bought that ring a long time ago. It looks more like a wedding band, but I have no experience in these matters, and I meant it as an engagement ring. Pearl, will you kindly agree to be my wife?" That was not what I said, however. Clever idiot that I am, I said, "These big vegetables, Pearl, I don't know what to make of them."

"Damien, yes or no?"

"No," I said, my temper flaring as a result of my frustration with myself. "And I've been meaning to talk to you about something. These gosh-darned vegetables are too big. I'm sorry, but I don't know how else to put it. I don't like them. I came here because I wanted to provide for myself. I wanted to be self-sufficient. I don't want to rely on this perversion of nature, which was none of my doing to begin with." I was aware that I'd gone too far even before I'd finished what I was saying.

Pearl's mouth hung open. I held up my scope and examined her tonsils. "Well, would you look who's talking," she said. Then she clamped her mouth shut and studied me for a moment. "Damien, put the scope down for a minute."

Aware that I'd struck a nerve, I did as I was told. Pearl was a brilliant scientist, and here I was babbling about the perversion of nature. I sat and looked down at the scope and the ring next to it on the table. Why couldn't I just say it? Four simple words: Will you marry me?

"Damien, look at me." I looked at her, but her voice was flat, and without the scope, I couldn't tell whether she was angry, conciliatory, or what. "How many fingers am I holding up?" she asked.

My heart began pounding. I looked down at my lap. I remembered the embarrassment to which I was subjected whenever my glasses were stolen at Rigby. The other boys would taunt me, put thumbtacks on my chair or move my chair just before I sat down so that I landed on the floor, throw things at my head that I couldn't see until it was too late, and so on. I remember one particular occasion when a teacher, a long, gangly old horse named Mrs. Tucker, gave me an upbraiding for my inability to see the blackboard. We were having some sort of a test, for which she was writing the questions on the board. Not knowing that I normally wore glasses, she'd demanded, "What are you, blind?" to the snickers of the rest of the class, which knew that I was as good as such without the glasses they'd stolen from me earlier that day. Mrs. Tucker told me to get out of my seat. She dragged my desk to the front of the room and planted it within three feet of the blackboard. "There," she said, and I had to take my test sitting there in front of everyone. Behind me, I heard the titters of my classmates and felt the occasional spitball land in my hair.

"Damien, how many fingers am I holding up?" Pearl repeated. There's no such thing as déjà vu. Life does in fact repeat itself over and over. I looked up, and could see that Pearl's hand was held up to the level of her shoulder, but the hand was just a flesh-colored blur, even with my glasses on.

"Three," I guessed.

Pearl lowered her hand. "Damien, when I was in town yesterday, I stopped by the library." Oh wonderful, I thought, now she's going to abuse me on account of my flirtation with Margaret. "I read up a little about skunk musk."

I interrupted her. "My prescription's probably changed over the years," I said. "I realize my eyes have gotten a little worse, I just haven't gotten around to getting new glasses—haven't had a chance to go to the eye doctor. I used to go regularly."

"Damien," Pearl said, her voice falling like footsteps on ice that one suspects is rather thin. "One of the ways a skunk's musk deters enemies is not only the smell, but the temporary blinding it causes."

For a distraction, I picked up the ring box and began fiddling with it. "Mhm," I said, as if only mildly interested in what Pearl was saying. I opened and closed the ring box. When it opened, it made a sound like someone with very small fingers snapping.

"Damien, did you already know this?" Pearl asked.

I continued to open and close the ring box. When it closed, it clapped shut with a sound like a small foot stamping on a hardwood floor. Open, close, open, close: snap, stomp, snap, stomp. It sounded like a little girl doing a soft-shoe routine.

"Damien?" Pearl asked.

"Well!" burst out of my mouth. I hadn't meant to shout. "Well," I repeated, at a lower volume, "I suppose maybe I did."

She picked up my glass of musk. "Damien, I think this stuff is making you blind."

"I haven't had a chance to get to the eye doctor. I realize my prescription may have altered a bit."

Pearl blew out a breath, as if she'd been swimming under water for the past few minutes. "Not this much, Damien. Look, how about we make a deal. I won't grow any more of those oversized veggies if you promise to cut down on the musk." Her voice suddenly changed to a higher pitch. I looked up; her face was red, but I couldn't see her expression without my scope. "It's only because I'm worried. I'm worried about you. I'm worried about this baby, I'm worried about how— her voice dissolved and she broke off into a sob. I held up the scope and looked at her. She was hastily wiping away the tears with both hands. This certainly was unexpected. A few seconds ago she'd been reprimanding me; now she was going to pieces. I'd never seen Pearl show weakness—this outburst seemed to contradict the very laws of nature. I couldn't have been more shocked if she'd suddenly turned into a bowl of gelatin. An excess of saliva built up in my mouth and I had to swallow. I wanted to go to her and put my arms around her, but I couldn't. It was one of those moments in which it seems too late to do anything, but in retrospect, one knows it was precisely the time to take action. At the time, I told myself this: no one wants the comfort of a weakling. So, as the moment slipped away, I sat there stupidly, watching the love of my life through a rifle scope, as she dug into her overalls for a tissue and blew her nose.

"Sorry," she said, sniffling and balling up the tissue in her hand. "I just get so emotional these days. I know it's just because I'm going to have a baby soon, and," the pitch of her voice rose wildly again, "and, it's wonderful, but I don't know how to care for it," she sniffled again, obviously trying to hold back more tears, "I mean I know, it's common sense, it happens naturally, and I was looking at all those baby books in the library yesterday, but I just," she made a slurping noise, "oh I just don't know," she said, and burst into another round of sobs, this time not even bothering to wipe the tears that flowed down her face, or the drool that dribbled from her lip down her chin. I hadn't thought it possible for someone to lose so much fluid all at once without dehydrating, and it was slightly disgusting to watch. I put the scope down in my lap. Pearl sat there wailing. "Oh, I just feel so lost," she said between sobs. "I feel like I'm alone. I don't know what I'm doing, oh." And then she abandoned herself to further effluence and put her forehead down on the table.

I stood up. I wanted to go to her but for some reason my body still refused. This was all very unsettling, to say the least, and I felt I had to do something—it hardly mattered what—or else I might catch this crying infection with which Pearl had been so suddenly and inexplicably stricken. "I'll go get you a glass of water," I said, and went outside to the tank on the side of the cabin. When I came back in, Pearl was still crying at the table, whimpering like a child whose candy has been taken by a bigger child, only she'd sat back up, and was in the process of pulling back the lid from a can of sardines. "Here's some water," I said, placing the glass on the table next to her.

"Thank you," she gargled through the phlegm and tears, without looking up from the can. She sniffled, then began picking the sardines out of the can, two or three at a time, and dropping them down her throat like a trained seal, hardly chewing them at all. She finished the can in seconds and tossed it into a bag behind the door. She got a can of tuna from the towering stacks she'd piled up behind the stove, sat back at the table and began working at it with a can opener. Pearl jabbed a fork into the can and took a mouthful of tuna.

"Oh, and don't skunks mate for life?" she said with her mouth full.

All at once I needed something to do with my hands. I picked up a can of tuna to open for Pearl.

"Skunks are quite solitary creatures," I said.

Pearl shrugged, sniffled, tossed the emptied can into a bag in the corner and took the can I'd opened for her. "Yeah, but still," she said, "do they or not? I thought they did."

"No, I don't believe they do," I said. "Their mating is best described as, um, seasonal."

"Well," Pearl said. The suggestion of a smile raised one corner of her mouth, though her cheeks were still damp with tears. "I guess, though, if a unique couple of skunks wanted to, they could. I mean, it's not inconceivable. Is it?"

"I suppose not, I suppose not," I said, trying not to sound too rattled. "It's quite possible."

21

"Well, I'm going to go start getting some of that corn in," I said. Pearl nodded at me as she shoveled tuna into her mouth. "Come along, Constance," I said, giving her leash a little tug to rouse her from her nap beneath my chair. She traipsed along behind me out the door. After about an hour, Pearl came out into the field and began working silently alongside Constance and myself. "You don't have to do this, you know," I said. "You might just want to rest." Pearl ignored me and we didn't speak again until that night.

At dinner Pearl ate approximately one trawler-load of fish. Then she belched and rubbed the sides of her belly. "Just promise me you'll think about the things I said this afternoon," Pearl said.

"I'll think about them," I said.

There was a faint rapping at the door of the cabin. For a second I envisioned another army of SAFETYS with their signs and slogans, waiting to pounce. "I wonder who the hell that could be," Pearl said, getting up to open the door.

I couldn't see the visitor, but the instant she whispered "Hello," in that faint voice, I knew it was Fiona. She drifted into the cabin as if blown in by a gentle breeze and stood trembling before us until I got up and offered her my chair. I examined her with my scope. Bony shoulders jutted from Fiona's sleeveless cotton blouse. With a scrawny claw, she pulled the hair back from her face. Her arms were so pale one would have thought it was the middle of February and that the little urchin lived in a city apartment with no windows. I noticed the marks on her arm. She glanced up at me and cringed, then put her elbows on the table and her fingertips to her temples.

"Damien, put that away," Pearl said. "It's rude." Then she sat down opposite Fiona. "How are you?" Pearl asked, though it was obvious Fiona was in a state of disaster.

"Okay," Fiona murmured in the tone of a dying baby bird. "How're you? It must be exciting to be so close to your due date," she said.

"Well, yes," Pearl said.

"It's wonderful," Fiona said, her voice growing ever more tremulous, "really, I'm so happy for you, that's a wonderful, wonderful thing, I wish I could... I wish..." she broke off in a sob.

Pearl came around the table and softly massaged Fiona's shoulders. "Now, now," Pearl said.

Well, goodness gracious, I thought. It must be a national day of mourning. Either that or the harvest moon is causing every woman in Highbridge to feel the effects of the tides, even though we're over a thousand miles from the ocean.

"I don't know what to do anymore," Fiona said, between sobs. "I don't know who to talk to."

"Damien, why don't you make some tea for us all?" Pearl said.

So, I thought, it's boss-Damien-around-day, as well—I hadn't known. Two women, both of whom I'd only met by chance, were having me play servant in my own abode. It was no time for an argument however, so I went out to the tank and filled the kettle with water. When I came back in, Fiona had started talking. I got out the mugs and the tea while she poured out her story.

"I didn't think there was any harm in it," Fiona said. "I mean, everybody was doing it, and Robby said Damien turned him on to it." I stopped what I was doing and turned to face Fiona. Pearl was sitting across from her. Deprived of my scope, I couldn't see their faces. "That day we were here, when those people were over there," Fiona waved in the direction of the driveway, "and I found out he lied about the article, I started wondering about other stuff." Fiona's flushed face turned toward me now. "So that night I confronted him and he said you hadn't actually given it to him, that he'd been 'borrowing' your skunk musk." Fiona looked down at the table and put her fingertips to her temples again. "Oh God, oh God."

Pearl glanced up at me, then leaned forward and patted Fiona's arm. "It's okay, honey, you go ahead. Tell us the whole story."

"Well," Fiona whispered, "by that time it seemed too late. I mean Jocko was already setting up in California, and Sam and Eric were already doing the Dead thing—"

"Alright, slow down a little," Pearl said. "You're going to have to explain to us who and what you're talking about."

Fiona sniffled and rubbed her nose. "Jocko is a friend of Robby's from when they were in college. He was at that party you guys were at? Well, he's been selling the stuff in California."

"The skunk musk," Pearl clarified.

"Yeah, well we call it SS. That's the marketing name."

"Schutzstaffel?" I said.

"God bless," Fiona said. "Of course we all know it stands for Skunk Smack. But to throw people off the scent we've said it stands for all kinds of things. You hear kids talking about the 'Secret Sauce' or 'Secret Service,' you know what they're talking about. And it went under the radar anyway because people are used to smoking skunk weed. I mean, I don't think many people have any idea what they're shooting up, they just think it's some new kind of heroin or something."

I could hardly believe my ears. People were selling and injecting Constance's musk? It couldn't be true. "But you couldn't be selling what you stole from me," I said. "I barely have enough for myself."

"Oh, Robby's got gallons of it that he's taken from your chicken coop," Fiona said. "And you only need a drop of the stuff. We mix a droplet of SS with something else for the one-fluid-ounce syringes we sell. I should know, I spent most of the summer in the lodge making thousands of those damn things. And we don't sell 'em too cheap."

"You inject the musk?" I said in disbelief. The tea kettle began a low whistle. "But you must not even know how it tastes. They must all be the same to you."

Fiona scrunched up her face. "Who wants to taste the stuff? And it's called SS, not musk."

What gall! Not only was the little hussy into my musk, she was telling me to use this misnomer made up by her thieving boyfriend. "But I've gotta say," she sniffled and perked up a bit, "it's the most awesome high there is."

The tea kettle was screaming. I jerked it from the stove, poured the lousy tea and plopped mugs on the table in front of Pearl and Fiona. "The only thing is," Fiona said, lifting her mug with both hands and blowing on her tea, "it's changing everything. Robby's different now. First we were just selling it to friends and stuff, and it helped us make the mortgage payments, then Sam and Eric started selling it at Dead shows—I mean, Grateful Dead concerts—and now they travel all over the country doing that. And there's Jocko selling it in California—he sells a lot of it, and he can get a lot more money for it. See, that's the thing—it's all money now. When we first moved here I thought it would be great; we were talking about growing our own vegetables, growing our own pot, and maybe selling some to make a little money and living in a state of peace and harmony with nature. But now we've got tons of money and I'm totally not at peace at all. I'm paranoid all the time. There's this guy Ralph who's been staying at the lodge off and on. He was at the party you guys were at. I mean, like, a lotta people stay at the lodge off and on, we're just real open like that, but this guy," Fiona shook her head, "there's something strange about him, like you don't trust him."

Fiona stopped talking, took a sip of her tea, and looked at me, then Pearl. Pearl, I imagined, was torn between wanting to put a motherly arm around Fiona and wanting to slap her upside the head. I myself was torn between two impulses with equal appeal: one was to slam my own head against the Franklin stove until the pain eclipsed everything, and the other was to go up to the lodge, rip Robby's head from his womanly shoulders and drop-kick it across the county. I began pacing around the cabin.

"I'm just so scared now," Fiona said. "And I know I should have told you before, but, well. I don't know, it's gotten so crazy—I had to tell somebody."

Pearl hadn't touched her tea. She leaned across the table now and grasped one of Fiona's hands with her own. "Fiona, we're glad you told us this now, really. And I want you to know that you're welcome to come stay with us any time you want to get away from there, okay?"

"Now wait just a min—" I began, but Pearl talked over me as if I weren't in the cabin at all.

"Any time you want, okay?" she said. "You can just leave the lodge, come here and stay as long as you want, and never go back there." Fiona nodded solemnly. "But tell me this," Pearl said. "Does Robby or anyone else know you came here or that you were going to tell us this?"

Fiona shook her head vigorously. "No. They wouldn't have let me tell, especially you guys. Robby, Trent and Ralph said they had to go meet some people somewhere tonight. He wouldn't even tell me who, or when he would be back or—"

"Okay, well then listen," Pearl said. "We'll just keep this among us three, okay? And as far as Damien and I are concerned, you never came over here and told us about this, alright? We still don't know anything about what you've told us."

Fiona nodded.

"Okay?" Pearl said, squeezing Fiona's hand.

"Okay," Fiona said.

The next day, Pearl went into town and came back with a copy of a national newspaper and dropped it on my lap while I was sitting in front of the cabin with Constance, lost in a musk dream I'd begun the moment Pearl left the farm. The newspaper was folded open to page three. At the top of the page a headline read, "Authorities, Specialists, Still Puzzled Over Appearance of New Youth-Culture Drug." I got out my scope and skipped further down the article. "The origin of SS, a new drug popular among young people, is still unknown. The ubiquitous drug has in recent months become almost as widely used as marijuana among people in their teens and twenties." I skipped down to the subheading, "A Generation of Guinea Pigs," and read, "'SS has yet to be tested,' says one narcotics specialist. 'We have yet to discover whether there are any serious side effects. This drug has not been approved by the FDA, and I would not recommend that anyone use it under any circumstances.' Though the specialist said it was not known for certain whether the drug is physically addictive, he said it seems 'at the very least to be habit-forming, and the fact that it is taken intravenously is a very bad sign.'" I skipped down the article to another quote. "'It's great, man,'" said one fifteen-year-old user at a Grateful Dead concert in Springfield Illinois. "'I've smoked pot for years, I've done coke, acid, X, but this is the best, man. It blows all that other [expletive] away.'"

I dropped the newspaper and went to the coop to get another shot of musk and came back out slightly more under control. "What should we do about this?" I asked Pearl.

"I don't think there's much we *can* do. Just don't put much in those jars anymore so Robby can't steal the stuff from you. If he figures out how to squeeze the musk out of them on his own, well," she shrugged, "then that's that. It's out of our hands, so to speak."

As Pearl had requested I do, I thought about what we'd talked about—the musk damaging my sight and whatnot. I thought and thought, while Pearl and I filled Mason jars with vegetables, pickled beets and cucumbers, made cornmeal and stored potatoes in sacks. The root cellar began to fill up. One afternoon, coming outside after taking a siesta, I noticed that Pearl had removed the rotting giant tomato and put it in the compost heap. She'd done the same with the remains of the giant cucumber and the giant potato.

Sometimes, at the end of the day, I sat down in the cool air of the root cellar, stroking Constance in my lap, admiring how quickly the root cellar was filling up with my fortifications against the coming winter. I felt safe sitting down there where it was dark, cool and quiet. Mason jars filled with peas, beans, pickles, and leeks stood in reassuring towers. Sacks of cornmeal and potatoes were piled like sandbags around the walls. It might have seemed they had appeared there by magic if I wasn't able to recall how I'd sweated over every seed.

I still carried the scope around in my hip pocket and kept Constance with me at all times. I let her sleep at the foot of the bed.

Though it took her a while to get accustomed to a diurnal schedule, Constance got to know my routine and soon led me outside each morning to do my calisthenics and helped keep me on the path when I went down to the outhouse. At the end of the day, she led me to the coop where she joined the other skunks who'd gathered to wait to be milked of their musk.

Because it seemed to upset Pearl so much, I tried to cut down on my musk intake, which had gotten up to about a quart per day, but my vision failed to improve. In fact, now that Pearl had made me more aware of it, I could tell that it was getting worse. I'd always been able to see the squiggly white line on my forearm while I worked—the scar from the time I'd wrestled with the tiller—and one day I realized I couldn't tell it was there unless I held my forearm within a few inches of my face.

I tried waiting until later in the day to have my first shot, but if I waited until lunch time, I was usually so crazed for the stuff I gulped down twice as much as I normally did, then sat in a stupor for the better part of an hour. I tried substituting my evening rests in the root cellar for the sunset musk cocktails I usually enjoyed in front of the cabin. Sometimes, while I sat down there, I would tell myself, well, perhaps if I just go into the coop, uncap one of the jars and sniff a little musk, without actually taking any, it will satisfy my craving. Once I got to that stage though, the craving became overwhelming and I decided just a shot or two might be acceptable. I had to wean myself off slowly, didn't I? Couldn't just go cold skunky—it might be devastating, to the skunks as well as myself, since they'd gotten accustomed to being milked each evening when they awoke. Because of the alteration of my musk intake, my temper was sometimes aggravated. I was plagued by frequent headaches and sometimes, sitting in the root cellar, trying to pretend I didn't need any musk, my hands trembled so much I had trouble climbing the ladder back out. In all, during this prohibitive period, I might have decreased my daily intake by only two or three shots.

Just to feel what it would be like, I began going about the farm with my eyes closed and Constance tied to my wrist by her twine leash. I went down to the stream to wash and use the outhouse, went up to the dam, found the lever and opened or closed the dam as need be, and squeezed the vegetables to see if I could feel whether they were ripe. I did not really need to see. My feet knew the paths from cabin to stream, from squash to corn. By smell I could tell how close I was to the compost heap, how far away Pearl was, which skunks were nearby. By sound I knew how far I was from the stream, and how full the jars of musk were when I squirted more in. I memorized the number of steps from the cabin to the stream, from the coop to the cabin.

If I'd had to choose a sense that I would lose it probably would have been sight. I'd never minded darkness, even when I was little, because most of the horrible things that happened to me happened in broad daylight. Scents, flavors, sounds, textures all meant more to me than sights. Going blind was not really so bad. Most of the people I'd met in my life I hoped never to see again anyway. I would never again be forced to look upon the likes of Matt Baxter. I would never again have to see the disgust registering on people's faces once they got wind of me. However, I wouldn't have to deal much with people again. Except Pearl, of course, and our child. There was little reason for me to leave the farm ever again, except perhaps to get something at Jud's, which Pearl could easily do.

It seemed that the harder I'd worked to carve out my own little corner in the world, the more the world closed in around me. In retrospect, I had been left much more to myself when I'd worked at Grund & Greene. Aside from Mrs. Endicott's mostly innocuous gossip, I'd been able to keep a lower profile as a deathly bored but functioning member of society, and had not found evidence of my activities blooming in various print media.

For Pearl's sake, I tried to hide the fact that I couldn't give up skunk musk. After dinner I'd announce to Pearl that I had to go down to the outhouse, which I often did, but I crept into the skunk coop first and took one of the jars with me so I could sit by the stream and sip from it. It was the first time I'd ever done anything behind Pearl's back and if she noticed she said nothing about it. I felt particularly guilty when I returned after half an hour or so of sipping musk and saw that she'd cleaned the dishes. She'd started doing them when I'd started my after-dinner musk cocktails, and I wondered if she only did them to compound my guilt because she knew exactly what I did during my outhouse excursions. I could never mention that I noticed she'd done the dishes—that would have created an opening for an oblique accusation about what I'd been doing in the meantime. Pearl rocked slowly in her chair and did not look up from her book when I came in after these debauches. I made extra noise around the cabin, fussing about while I fixed myself a cup of tea, mumbling to myself about the amount of potatoes we'd harvested, hoping all the while Pearl might speak up. Her silence made me nervous and lonely and there is no loneliness as gruesome as the loneliness of a man who deceives a loved one. Eventually, I'd work up the nerve to ask Pearl if she would like to join me in a cup of tea, which she would decline. I continued to putter around until my tea was ready, then, embarrassed, I sat on the bed with the wick of the lamp on the bedside table turned up very high, took out my scope and read a book.

One night, while we both sat there reading, Pearl said, "How are you going to hunt deer if you need that scope to read a book?"

I was more worried about how I was going to be able to keep reading. I wondered if the Highbridge library had Braille books, but I'd been afraid to raise the question with Pearl, or to go down to the library myself to investigate. It would have been an admission of defeat, a blatant admission to Pearl of my lack of willpower. "I should do fine," I said. "One uses the other senses as much or more for things like hunting." I imagined I'd be able to hear and smell the deer well enough to shoot him from a deer stand. The only problem was that I would not know until afterwards whether I'd killed a doe or a buck.

I looked through the scope at Pearl rocking slowly in her chair. She was blurry. I could distinguish her features, but could not tell what expression she wore. This was frightening because all at once I realized that this was the one thing I would miss. Without sight I would never again be able to look into Pearl's aqua eyes, see the magnificent, unruly mane of hair, the curve of her hips and the thick white thighs I loved so much, the strong shoulders, the light down of white hair on the back of her neck, the high cheekbones. I would never again see her cheeks grow red with anger, or the dewy perspiration that appeared on her face when she exerted her formidable strength. I'd never watch her open another can of tuna or see her round bottom in a bikini, would never see her dive into the water, would never see her reeling in her fishing line, never see her sitting here in her overalls, rocking gently in the lamplight, a few flies buzzing around her head, reading a book before turning in for the night. But worst of all I'd never see that smile again—the warm, generous smile that broke across her face like dawn.

"What're you looking at?" Pearl asked.

I put down the scope. "Nothing."

Pearl yawned; another thing which soon I'd never see again. "Is Constance going to be sleeping with us again?" Pearl asked.

"Does it bother you? She doesn't have to."

"No, it's just—" Pearl yawned again, clasped her hands together and stretched her arms above her head. I watched through the scope, memorizing how she did it, so in the future, when I heard her stretching, I'd be able to picture her. I quickly put the scope back down when she'd finished stretching. "I've been meaning to ask you what you're doing with her on that leash all the time," she said.

I don't think it had occurred to me what I'd been doing until I answered this question. I thought back to the day we'd met, when she stood looking in the open window of my car, sniffed with her rabbity nose—another feature I'd never see again—and asked if I had a skunk fetish. Now, in the cabin, I told Pearl what I was doing. "I'm training Constance to be a seeing-eye skunk," I said, then, after a moment, "probably the world's first."

Pearl smiled weakly. "Damien, I wanted to apologize for how I went to pieces on you that afternoon, the day Fiona came over." Her voice began to tremble as if the memory of crying were enough to elicit tears. "I only." She paused. "I feel like you're shutting me out, and it's not fair—" she stopped herself and coughed, then continued. "I just want to be part of your life, and I worry about you." She paused again. "I mean, don't you want to see your child when it's born?"

22

That morning, like all other mornings, the only sounds were the scrape of a knife as Pearl spread caviar over her cornbread toast and the slurping sound I made as I sipped my tea. The only difference, which didn't register right away, was that it was a little quieter than usual. No birds were chirping. If I'd been a more astute observer perhaps I would have noticed this and been more prepared for what was about to occur. I recall I'd slightly overfilled my mug, and when the metallic voice ripped like machinegun fire through the quiet of the morning, I splashed tea over the side of it, burned my fingers and dampened my toast.

"Damien Youngquist," the inhuman voice crackled over the bullhorn.

At least, I thought, they got the name right this time. With a bit more than a dollop of trepidation, I opened the door a crack and peered out. No one was there. My name was called again, so I stepped outside and looked around for the source of the voice. It was then that I noticed the black forms, human-sized crows, all over the field. Pearl and I had harvested most of the vegetables already. We'd knocked the stalks and vines down, leaving them to fertilize the ground, and we'd turned the soil over, so I was not too worried about things getting trampled. But I was alarmed by how many of the large, shadowy forms there were. They were standing, crouching and lying all over the place—indistinct lumps of blackness with no business swarming my property. When I came out of the cabin, a few got up and ran around to different positions, while some stood stock still. It was an eerily quiet moment that seemed to go on for a long time, though it could only have lasted a few seconds. Perhaps this is a trick of memory, because immediately after that silence things began to happen so quickly I felt as if someone had removed my head from my body and stuck it in a washing machine. I was to be caught in the crushing, inexorable tank treads of human society that had taken my mother and my favorite skunks. I was to be plucked up only to be quickly squashed down into the dirt.

"Damien Youngquist," the bullhorn voice said again. The sound of this voice was like someone taking a cheese grater to my eardrums. I couldn't see where it came from. My heart began pounding heavily. "Put your hands on your head and turn and face the wall of the building."

"I will do no such thing!" I called. In comparison to the bullhorn voice, my own was a squeak at the bottom of a well. Pearl came out of the cabin and looked around. She still had on her bathrobe. "Oh my God," she said, and that utterance frightened me more than anything had yet because it was the first time I'd ever heard real fear in Pearl's voice. I still could not see where the bullhorn voice was coming from. It had to be one of the big crows in the field. I reached into the pocket of my overalls for the scope.

"Stop!" the voice shrieked over the bullhorn. "Take your hand out of your pocket and put your hands on your head. Both of you!"

But I'd be gosh darned if I was going to stand in front of my cabin and be ordered around by someone I could not even identify. The scope was stuck in my pants at an awkward angle. I was trying to wriggle it out of my pocket when Pearl screamed. I never did manage to get the scope out. Something hard cracked the back of my head.

When I came to, a firm hand kept my face pressed to the ground. My wrists were cuffed and I was dragged to my feet. Unfriendly hands held me by the hair and both arms. Pearl told me later that one of them had jumped from the roof of the cabin. "No! No!" Pearl was screaming. My glasses had been knocked off, the scope was still in my pocket, and all I could see of Pearl was a writhing blue bathrobe being restrained by two of the huge crows.

"You fuckin' scum bag," one of the crows grunted in my ear as he jerked me toward the paddy wagon that was pulling up next to the cabin. His breath smelled of coffee and his bulky vest felt like a wrestling mat pressed against my shoulder. He was so close, his mustache brushed my ear and he spoke in a whisper strained with rage, as if confessing his darkest sins. "I shoulda taken you out right then, you homicidal fuckin' drug freak."

"God you people stink," another voice behind me said.

"Where they're goin' it won't matter—everybody stinks," said another.

"They'll stink even worse if they decide to fry 'em," yelled the one who'd been talking in my ear. "And I hope they do. I hope they give 'em the fuckin' chair. This one smells like skunk. Hey Bill, you ever smelled fried skunk?"

"This bitch smells like fish," one of the crows behind me yelled. "I bet she hasn't cleaned her pussy in years." The others laughed. We were shoved into the back of the truck. "Haven't you ever heard of a douche, you stupid bitch?" the voice said. They'd put us on opposite bench seats in the wagon, and the man insulting Pearl and another one were in the truck with us, while the others stood outside.

"Fuck you, needle dick!" Pearl yelled at him. I heard her spit. Though I could not see what was happening, I knew her saliva probably hit him in the face because the crows outside stopped jeering for a second, as if they'd been watching a parade and one of the clowns had been shot off his float by someone on the sidewalk. I saw the swift, black movement of an arm and heard the smack of the man's open palm meeting Pearl's face.

"You fucking coward!" Pearl screamed at him. Again I saw the movement and heard another smack. I knew that I was the coward. If I had any courage at all I would have at least lunged at Pearl's assailant and tried to bite him. But I didn't have much time to think about it.

"I'd love to kick the shit outta you, you stinky bitch," the man said. "But you know what? You're knocked up, and I'm a gentleman. So instead I'll do this." He whipped around and sunk his fist into my stomach so quickly I was gasping for air before I knew what had happened. "Maybe I'll do a little of this, too," he said. He grabbed my neck, slammed my head back against the wall of the truck and punched me in the face. The salty taste of blood filled my mouth and it tickled the skin beneath my nose as it ran from one of my nostrils.

"Stop!" Pearl screamed.

"Oh? Why should I?" the man said. "I was just starting to enjoy myself."

"Stop hurting him," she said. I could tell by the sound of her voice she was trying not to cry.

"You wanna take back what you said about me?" he asked.

"Fuck you," she sobbed.

"Okay, fine," he said. His fist hit my chin and the back of my head knocked against the wall of the truck. More blood filled my mouth. This time I'd bitten into my tongue.

"Alright, I take it back," Pearl said. She was shrieking hysterically. "But I'm gonna sue the hell out of you. All of you!"

"No," the big crow said. "Now that's where you're wrong. It's your word against mine. You guys saw this prick resisting, didn't you? He even tried to pull out a weapon back there when I told him to put his hands up." He was answered by a few affirmative grunts. "Now repeat after me, you little bitch: I take back everything I said, and I want to suck your big dick right now."

"Fuck you," Pearl said, but her voice was tired, defeated. I felt the fist in my stomach and was gasping for air again. I leaned forward over my knees and watched the blood and mucous drip in strings from my mouth to form a blurry puddle between my feet. Pearl's voice was like a robot's: "OK, I take back everything I said, and I want to suck your big dick."

"Yeah, you wish, you little fuckin' whore," he said. Laughing, he stepped down from of the back of the truck and the other crow followed him. The door slammed shut and there was only a little gray light coming in from a window at the top of the door. I heard Pearl shuffling around. The truck started up and began to lurch down Fisher Lane. Pearl dropped awkwardly onto the seat beside me. "I'm so sorry," she said. "Damien, I'm sorry." She too had her hands cuffed behind her back. She rubbed her cheek on my shoulder. I wanted to tell her it was fine, that I was sorry too, but my lip was beginning to swell and my tongue hurt when I tried to talk. "Ith alwaigh," I said.

"Shh," she whispered in my ear. She gently planted kisses on my cheek, my nose and my numb, bleeding lips.

❧

There were other people in the cell, but I couldn't see them. I could distinguish the shapes of humans and the smell in the unventilated room was a mixture of body odor, urine, vomit, feces and cigarette smoke.

"Well don't yew look purty," a voice said.

"Looks like someone stuck 'is 'ed in a meat grinder, don't it Gus?" another voice said.

"And man, does he reek," the first voice added.

My glasses had been left somewhere in front of the cabin, probably trampled beyond repair and the scope had been taken from me, so there was no way to examine my new environment and the creatures inhabiting it. I did not step further into the cell, but turned and pressed my face against the cold steel bars.

"Antisocial sonofabitch too," the second voice said.

"Hey!" the first man said, raising his voice as if I might be hard of hearing. "What're yew in for?" His voice labored as if with the strain of an attempt to push a weight off his chest—an inflection common among the obese.

"I honethtly haf no idea," I said. Speech was painful.

"Heh, yeah, that's a good one," he said, jovially enough, "same here."

The second voice laughed. "Yeah, me neither. None a us got no idea whut we're in here for. Guess they just decided to start lockin' up innocent bystanders. Hey, Matt, yew got any idea whut yur in here for?"

From the heaviness of the step, I guessed it was the bigger man approaching me. He must have been wearing boots with hard heels—cowboy or biker boots—which scraped the grit on the concrete floor. I turned from the bars to face the inside of the dank cell, and the tall, dark form separated from the rest of the shapes as it moved toward me. There was another movement in the back of the cell. The second, thinner man's voice came from the direction of this disturbance. "Hey, Matt, wake up man, I'm talkin' ta yew."

The heavy form towered over me. I looked up toward where I imagined the head was. "Maybe they brought yew in jest fer stinkin' so bad." He paused. "Well, I'll be dipped in shit. Yur blind as a bat, ain'tcha?"

It would have been pleasant at this juncture, I thought, to assume the consistency of hot wax and melt through the bars my back was pressed against and thus to escape the great reach of this behemoth. The blood on my lip had coagulated and I had no desire to taste it or feel it trickling down my throat again. Heaven knew when I'd be allowed to see a doctor, and I was afraid my wounds might become infected. "They knocked off my glatheth you thee," I began to explain, despite the pain it caused me. It was like trying to speak with a rubber ball stuck in a mouth coated with canker sores. "And I can hardly thee a thing without them. And then, before they threw me in here, they confithcated my thcope."

The big man burst into raucous laughter. His tremendous, dark form shook. Behind him, an argument had started. "Whut the hell you wakin' me up for?" said a voice that sent a shiver down my spine.

"Newcomer, man. Said he don't know why he's in here. We're gonna have some fun with 'im."

"Hey Jess, listen to this," the big man said. He must have turned his head toward the others because his voice seemed further away. "He said they took his Scope." The man turned back to me. "Is that why you reek so bad? They took yur mouthwash?" He and the thin man burst out laughing.

"God *damn*—let's just pray he don't *belch*," the thin man said.

"Or fart," said the hefty one.

"Shit, 'magine if that happens?" the thin one said. "I mean, I don't think I deserve the death penalty for knockin' over a convenience store."

Well, at least they're laughing, I thought. They're far less likely to pummel me to death while in the throes of mirth. I wondered where Pearl was, and if women were just as cruel to each other in holding cells. Surely they wouldn't pick on a pregnant woman, would they? But then again, Pearl was far tougher than I and could probably handle herself well in such situations.

"An' look et this," the big man said, "he's blind as a freakin' bat." He stuck out his right arm and waved it around—that much I could see. Then, suddenly, from out of nowhere, his large left hand slapped me across the face. He and the thin man guffawed like a silly audience at a Punch and Judy show.

"I know this sonofabitch," the third, gravelly voice said. He must have gotten up, and was now standing in front of me, a smaller, darker splotch next to the big man. 'E can't see cause 'e don't 'ave 'is glasses on." Of course it was Matt Baxter.

"I know, 'e just told us that," the big man said. "His voice is funny too cause they busted his lip." Like the other man, he raised his voice when he addressed me, as if deafness inevitably accompanied blindness. "Hey, say somthin' for us, Mr. Ray Charles."

"Wha would you like me to thay?" I said.

The big man burst out laughing again. "Whut wuz that? Could yuh repeat that," he said.

"I thaid, wha would you like me to thay?" A fist struck my jaw. Here it comes, I thought. I braced myself, leaning stiffly back against the bars, and hoped I would be knocked unconscious quickly so I wouldn't have to feel too much of the beating.

"Hey, whut'd yuh do that for?" the big man said. I heard his boots grinding on the floor as he turned, and, I think, shoved Matt, because the smaller form moved suddenly away toward the side wall.

"That fuckin' pervert," Matt said. "Yew know why he smells like that? He's a fuckin' skunk-fucker."

"Pervert, huh? Jess, yew hear that? If this ain't a case of the pot callin' the kettle black, I don't know whut the hell is."

"No shit," said Jess, "How kin yew go sayin' shit like that when yew fucked your own cousin, Matt. Not even old enough to get her period."

"I never did that. Nobody never proved nothin'," Matt protested. Then, in an attempt to keep them from changing the subject he said, "Because a this jerk-off's old lady it hurt me to piss for a Goddamn week."

"What, she give you the clap?" Jess said.

"No, she kicked me," Matt said, then added, "the uncivil whore," raising his voice and practically shouting his words in my direction. "And all I did was try and make conversation with the fat bitch when she come intu Jud's, and goosed her once to be friendly."

"You—you louthy weathel," I spat. "You thould never haf accothted a pregnant woman in the firtht plathe."

"Now, lemme git this straight," the big man said. "You just decked this blind little fella because his wife kicked you in the balls?" The thin man, Jess, snickered. "And you goosed his pregnant wife?"

"No, no, it ain't like that." Matt's voice had become a desperate whine.

"Man, yew just don't learn, do ya."

I heard a thump that must have been Matt's body hitting the cinderblock wall. "No, c'mon! He's the fuckin' weirdo." But that was the last intelligible remark Mr. Baxter was able to make; for the next few minutes he was unable to manage anything beyond a series of grunts and yelps. I heard his body drop to the hard floor and the repeated scrape of the big man's boots, as, I imagine, he kicked Matt decisively out of the realm of consciousness. It was quiet for a long while after that.

Though I was lucky to have Matt Baxter there as a substitute for the pain I might have experienced at the hands of the others in the holding cell, there was pain I knew waited only hours away, and for which I would have no surrogate. Crouched in a corner of the cell, I tried to get some sleep, since there was little else I could do. However, the floor was so hard and I was continually shifting my aching buttocks. I tried alternately slouching down and straightening up so that a different portion of my back rested against the cinderblock wall, which seemed to grind my spine either way. I tried not to think about squeezing a fresh shot from Constance, tried not to think about the case of jars in the skunk coop, the shot glass waiting beside them. I would have given my right hand for a single shot, a finger for a single droplet. Rhythmically grinding my teeth, I thought: just don't think about it, don't. Think about anything else, anything. But everything came back to that craving. My body needed musk more than it needed water or food.

Though I had no way of telling the time, it was probably late in the evening when the shakes started. I first noticed my hands were trembling when I raised them to wipe the sweat from my forehead. It felt as if someone had turned the thermostat of the holding cell to "broil." I wondered how the others could stand it. They talked about police, women, drugs, guns, dogs and television. They swore, spat, smoked. But they failed to comment on the heat. My head began to ache with a dull, throbbing pain and simultaneously a horrible nausea began to finger its way into my stomach. I shifted about restlessly on the floor. Every time someone lit a cigarette, my stomach became more sensitive. The smells of urine and body odor seemed to be getting stronger. The sources of my discomfort were no longer the hard walls and floor of the cell, but the walls and floor of my stomach, head and bowels. I thought urinating would help relieve me. "Ith there a toilet in here?" I asked.

"Yeah, over there," a voice said.

"Where?"

"C'mon," the voice said. Someone led me by the elbow. "Here," he said. I leaned down and felt the toilet with my hand. It had no seat. I began to urinate but soon realized I needed to sit down. The watery stream of diarrhea burned like a flame flickering up my anus. The stench of my own feces made my nausea overwhelming. I groped the wall, but there was no toilet paper holder to locate. I spun around, fell to my knees, vomited into the toilet. I flushed the toilet and vomited again.

"Aw man," said a voice a couple yards away, "that fuckin' *reeks.*"

I hardly noticed. This was a thousand times worse than the hangover I'd had after Robby's party. It was far worse than the comparatively minor withdrawal I'd experienced in New Essex. I gagged, heaved, and clutched the slimy sides of the toilet bowl as bile burned my throat and hung in strings from my face into the putrid water. Diarrhea trickled down the inside of my thigh. Too weak to move far, I lay down on the clammy, urine-stinking concrete next to the toilet as my stomach convulsed, waiting for the next wave of dry heaves. Two or three of the others had started banging on the bars. "Hey!" they yelled, trying to get someone's attention. "Ain't s'posed to put junkies in here with us!" one of them yelled. "He's kicking in here!" yelled another.

I was, in fact, kicking. My legs had begun to jerk around on the floor involuntarily, as if someone were running an electric current through them. "Junky! Gotta junky here!" they yelled, rattling and banging the bars. I heard some swearing, a latch clank, the high-pitched scream of unoiled hinges. I was vaguely aware of hands on both my arms as I floated up from the floor, my overalls around my ankles, my feet bouncing and scraping along the floor as I made an absurd, unnecessary attempt to walk. My bones were sore; the very marrow within them ached. My arms felt they were going to be torn from their sockets by the invisible tormentors who carried me; they were Satan's helpers apparently—I could hear their hooves echoing as they clomped down the hall, dragging me down to hell. My head felt as if someone had jammed a chisel into my ear and begun pounding it with a sledgehammer, each blow splitting my head further apart. I was dropped to the concrete and then heard the slam and rattle of a door.

My arm shot out from my body and hit something. It was a toilet. Maybe they hadn't moved me at all. I'd imagined it. I was still in the same cell, only the yelling had stopped. Or maybe I'd imagined that too. I dragged my chin up over the edge of the toilet and dry heaved, wondering when I'd finally see the lining of my stomach come up. My head was ripped further open by the hammer and chisel. Maybe the yelling was still going on, only I couldn't hear it because of the banging hammer.

I woke up sweating, but shivering, too, because now it was freezing cold in the cell. On my hands and knees, I felt my way around. Yes, I was in a much smaller cell now. There was a toilet, a sink and a metal bunk protruding from the wall. I climbed up onto the bunk and lay down.

I awoke again and Pearl was there, standing in front of the open door of the cell. I was lying on my back on a hard surface. I must have fallen off the bunk. Pearl was wearing the tan bathrobe she'd always worn in New Essex; it was untied and she had nothing on beneath it. I couldn't help noticing that from the waist down she was a fish and stood somehow balanced on the tip of her tail. She held a carafe filled with skunk musk. "Here Damien, I brought you some musk," she said. "Your favorite." She took a step forward and poured the musk on my stomach. It burned like a corrosive acid.

"Hey!" I shouted. I looked up from my scalded stomach, but Pearl's face had begun to change. The skin on her chest too was turning into scales. Her mouth grew wide like a fish's. "Pearl, you're changing," I said. The scales were green and, looking down, I saw she no longer had a tail, but heavily muscled dinosaur legs and a reptilian tail that came to a point where it ended in a half coil on the floor. I looked back at Pearl's eyes, which were several times their usual size. Her whole head had changed shape and she had the prognathous jaw of a lizard. The nails of the scaly hand holding the carafe had become thick, yellowed talons.

"Enjoy," she said. She poured the acid in my eyes while I screamed. I covered my face with my hands, but the burning acid seeped through the cracks between my fingers.

I awoke again later because of the heat. My entire body was bathed in sweat and I noticed my stomach was bloated to the size of a watermelon, but it was lumpy and the lumps began to move. A whole litter of blind, naked, blood-drenched skunks squirmed and writhed around inside me, trying to get out. I yanked my shirt open, popping all the buttons from it, and scratched at my bare stomach. They were gnawing at my insides. Though they were still unformed fetuses, they had large, sharp teeth, and they were trying to gnaw their way out of my stomach. They crawled up into my shoulders and down my arms into my hands trying to find a way out. They burrowed down into my legs. Trying to get them out, I scratched and tore at my sweat-slick flesh with my fingernails, gouging red claw marks into my stomach and chest, but still they gnawed incessantly at my innards. "Let them out!" I screamed aloud. "Let them out, please! This is not a sympathetic pregnancy, this is real! Please let them out!" I screamed, cried and tore at my skin and still the little skunks plucked at my veins and sunk their sharp teeth into my muscles. Just when it seemed it might never stop, it stopped.

Then I saw that there were potato beetles crawling all over my body, feasting on my flesh with their little pincers. Whenever I brushed them off they came right back out of nowhere.

Sometimes I felt as if I were in a sauna, sometimes as if I were in a freezer. Once I awoke and saw Piper sitting on the sink comfortably as if he were sitting on the edge of his desk, one foot on the floor and one dangling just above it. His arms were folded across his chest and his immaculate white hair glistened in the fluorescent overhead light. Homer and Louisa were each sitting on one of his shoulders like pet parakeets. Piper's ruddy jowls were gradually raised by a smile. He seemed to have been sitting there for a long time waiting for me to wake up. "Damien," he said, grandly. He hopped off the sink, grabbed one of my hands between both of his, and began shaking it energetically as he pulled me into a sitting position on the bed. "I'm glad to see you're back. There've been a few changes since you left. This is your new supervisor." He put an arm around Richard, Pearl's ex, who I now saw was standing next to him, slapping a tennis racket in his palm as if it were a billy club. "My wife and I thought this would be the best arrangement," Piper said, putting his other arm around Mrs. Endicott, who now stood beside him in her floral housecoat. Just beneath her chin, the head of a skunk I didn't recognize peeked up over her collar, the rest of him presumably crammed down in her withered cleavage.

"We've always wanted the best for you, Damien," Mrs. Endicott said. She and Piper turned to leave, their arms around each other. "Oh, and by the way," Piper said over his shoulder, "you're fired." He and Mrs. Endicott took turns stepping carefully down into the toilet, each reaching up to the handle to flush themselves before they disappeared.

Richard stepped toward me. "So," he said, smiling, still slapping the tennis racket in his open palm, "skunk lover, huh?" In a quick burst of motion, he raised the tennis racket over his head with both hands and brought it down on my head. It was dark again.

A man was asking me questions. His voice was an authoritative one, so, assuming he worked in the jail, I thought I should let him know what was going on inside it. I told him about Piper and Mrs. Endicott disappearing down the toilet. My mouth was dry. "I think you should get them out," I said. "I don't know what they were doing here in the first place, but they'll certainly clog the plumbing, and though I don't care for them particularly, I don't really want to urinate on them."

"Are you Tom Sawyer?" he asked me.

"Why do you say that?" I asked.

"You'll be better off."

The cell was gray and someone was sitting before me. A dark gray shape. "All my life, other people have told me what they want me to do," I said. "Telling me how I'll be better off. Piper was like that. Did he send you? Mrs. Endicott was like that, too."

The person sighed. "See, it's been like this," the man's voice said in the tone of an aside, presumably to another person who was in the cell. "He won't shut up, but he won't give a single straight answer no matter what you ask." He addressed me again. "Yes or no—do you want a lawyer?"

"Certainly not. A plumber, a plumber is the man for this sort of job."

"Okay, fine, have it your way," he said. "We got our answer," he said to the other and I heard the door whine open then shut with a heavy clang.

Since these latest visitors seemed the most plausible, it occurred to me that they might be able to get me a shot of musk. "Pardon me," I called. My tongue was like a dried sponge. "Do you think you, or whoever is in charge of such requests, could arrange for a shot of skunk musk for me?"

"What?" the voice asked in a tone of disbelief.

At least he hadn't ignored me and gone away. "Please," I said turning my head in the gray light toward the source of the voice, "I'm only asking for one shot. I require the musk of—"

"Yeah, sure pal," the voice said. "We'll have someone come by and give you a shot." Two pairs of footsteps began echoing down the hall.

"Thank you," I called after them. The only sound now was the steady, constant dripping of water from a faucet that I fixated on and which soon became a sort of Chinese water torture to my ears. My overalls were down around my waist and the buttons were gone from my shirt, exposing my chest. I pulled up my overalls. One of the straps was torn, but the other buttoned into place. Getting up off the bunk, I stepped slowly forward with my hands in front of me until I touched the sink, where I bent over, turned the faucet and slurped water from my hands. I heard three or four pairs of footsteps in the hall. They stopped in front of my cell. I turned around and detected some movement in the gray fog. I tried to give the impression that I was looking at them, whoever they were.

"We're here to give you a shot," a voice said, as the latch clicked and the door whined open.

The problem with blindness, I was quickly learning, was that it made one perpetually vulnerable. I pretended to watch them as they entered the cell. "Sit on the bunk," the voice said. "It'll be easier."

"I would prefer if you just handed it to me," I said, in the direction of the voice. "I'd like to take it at my leisure." I noticed a vaguely antiseptic smell in the air. Had I asked specifically for a shot of skunk musk, when the other men were in the cell? I couldn't recollect now, though it had only been, I thought, a few minutes before. I hoped they hadn't just sent along a shot of vodka, or any old shot. "It *is* skunk musk you brought isn't it? Not something else?"

Hands roughly grabbed both my arms and held me firmly. Before I even had a chance to struggle, there was a sharp piercing of my shoulder and I realized what kind of shot it was to which I was being treated. Immediately the muscles of my body relaxed, and even had I so desired, I could not have struggled. Whoever they were kept their hold on my arms and walked me over to the bunk and sat me down. I was suddenly very tired. "Oh," I said, lying down on my side, "it's that kind of—" and suddenly realized it didn't matter if I finished my sentence. The effort of moving my mouth was too much and anyway unnecessary. They knew what I meant. By the time the door clanged shut, it sounded like something far in the distance.

"Dude man, I did like you said." Robby was standing in the cell in front of me now. "I got one a those tillers," he said. He held out his arms to show me the deep, bloody furrows that stretched from the underside of his forearms halfway up his biceps. "It's fuckin' great man. I've never felt so good." His cheeks were hollow, his eye sockets dark holes in his face.

"Robby, you've got to stop this," I said. "That's not what I meant for you to do."

The flesh was falling away from his bones in clumps. "I think everybody should do it. Right Fee?" Fiona was standing next to him, bouncing a baby bundled in filthy rags in her arms. Fiona had no eyes either, just dark holes in her head. I looked closer at the baby and saw that its eyes were missing too. It was gray and stiff, and though Fiona bounced it up and down and cooed to it, something told me that it was dead. "This is the greatest day of my life," Robby said. I looked back at him. Most of the skin had fallen from his face, and the bare jaw bones chattered at me. "And it's all thanks to you, Damien. I love you man." He stepped toward me. "I never listened to them. I knew you'd come back." He raised his skeletal arms to embrace me. All the flesh had fallen from them. He wrapped the bones around me, pulled me close so that I pressed up against his hard, empty ribcage. "I always knew you'd come back," Robby said into my ear, "Dad."

I was running around the coop chasing skunks. They all seemed able to elude me. They ran at a much quicker speed than I thought a skunk capable of running. Sometimes I would get my hands on one, but before I could squeeze a shot from him, he slithered away, seeming to run through my fingers like sand. Even Constance proved untenable. She would rub against my leg, as she always had, and I would think, ah, yes, here we go, back to normal. I picked her up. She looked into my eyes, wagging her tail, as if eager to give me some musk. I lifted her over my head, and then, poof, she was gone. I held nothing at all in my hands.

"Here, let me have the pillow," a voice said. Someone was tugging—I could feel the strain in my shoulders. I squeezed tighter. "Let go of the pillow," the voice said, more determined this time. "Could you give me a hand here?" the same voice said, sounding irritated. Fingers began prying at mine, while someone else tugged at the pillow. I let them take the pillow away. They'd taken everything else from me, why not let them have a pillow, too? My fingers ached the way they had after I'd driven to Highbridge the first time, in a fit of rage and despair, gripping the wheel too tightly the whole way.

I was handcuffed and led out of the cell, down a corridor and out of the building. It was autumn, the air was cool, leaves burned somewhere far off. By the angle of the sun on my face I knew it was either morning or late afternoon. But the air felt more like morning air and a certain stiffness in the gait of the people gripping my arms suggested that it was early in the day. I wondered what had become of Pearl. It must have been months since I'd seen her. And I would never see her again, unless this was another dream, for in reality I could see almost nothing at all. Vague shadows moved in the murk around me. I stumbled down some steps. Arms supported and guided me. The most salient aspect of my incarceration was that it didn't seem to matter any more whether I could walk, or even stand, on my own two feet anymore. So much for self-reliance. I was put in a car redolent of coffee and cheap confections, driven somewhere, and taken into another building.

The air was tepid and stale here. It was the kind of air that induces yawning, and in which yawning is more contagious than usual. It was darker than it had been outside. One side of the room seemed to glow and I guessed there were large windows there, facing east. The room was rather empty for how large—judging by the echoes of footsteps and voices—I estimated it to be. The acoustics of the place were such that it was virtually impossible to ascertain from which part of the room a particular voice was being projected. They all seemed to come more or less straight down from the ceiling. I was put in a seat, then asked to rise. There was the bang of a gavel and from what was said I surmised that this was my arraignment.

Nothing to worry about, I thought. Of course I had no need of a lawyer. I was guilty of nothing. And after all, I'd written ads for law books; I thought I must have gleaned enough to defend myself (whatever the false allegations might be) or at least to garb my defense in a thick cloak of legal jargon.

"The State Supreme Court charges Damien Youngquist with the production and illegal sale of a substance as yet not tested or approved by the FDA," a litigious-sounding voice announced. "This is in violation of federal law and the offender is subject to up to twenty years in maximum security prison, and up to $300,000 in fines. In light of the facts peculiar to this case, including the deaths that have been a direct result of the defendant's activities, the DA recommends that the court extend the prison sentence, and Mr. Youngquist be sentenced to life imprisonment."

I could understand how they had gotten the wrong man. They'd simply come to the wrong address—an easy mistake, since we lived near each other. What I could not understand was how they'd gotten our names mixed up.

"How do you plead?" a voice asked. I could not tell where the voice was coming from. I turned around. "Mr. Youngquist, how do you plead?" the voice asked again. A pair of hands came down on my shoulders and turned me in the appropriate direction.

"I'm sorry to have to be the one to inform you, sir," I said, "I realize it must be rather an embarrassment, but you have the wrong man. I know of the matter to which you refer, but I'm not about to go pointing fingers at the people I suspect—"

"Mr. Youngquist," the voice broke in gruffly. I could easily picture a stern, heavy-set man with large, fleshy face glaring at me over a pair of reading glasses. I was glad not to have to see him. "How do you plead? Guilty or not guilty?"

"Not guilty," I said, and my words were punctuated with the crack of a gavel. A trial date was set for a time that was either in the recent past or several months in the future—I couldn't tell since the gruff voice did not give a year.

Back in my cell, I sat on the edge of my bunk and thought about skunk musk. The physical withdrawal was over, but now there seemed to be nothing to which I could look forward. An extremely bland meal was brought to me. I could not see it and could not tell what it was by taste either, though it had the consistency of mashed potatoes. I'd only been back in my cell a couple of hours when the lock clicked, the door swung open, and I was taken back out. Now what? I wondered. Perhaps they'd decided to go right to trial after lunch.

I was brought to what I believed was the front of the building, into a room through which I'd been led that morning. I could smell a draft of cool autumn air leaking in from somewhere, and there were voices jabbering and telephones ringing. I began to get an erection. It was the scent of fish. "Here, sign this," a voice said. A pen was put in my hand and then guided to a piece of paper on a desk. I signed it. The smell of fish was quite strong. An arm looped itself around mine and I felt a slippery hand touch my face. "Pearl?" I said.

"Yes," she said, in a hoarse whisper as she began leading me along. "Come on." She was wearing her overalls and I could tell by her posture that she was holding something in the crook of her left arm.

23

"What are you doing he—"

"Shh," she said, and patted my arm. She trembled slightly as she led me along, pushed open a door and helped me down the stairs. I heard the groan of the passenger-side door of her Tempest and I climbed in. Before getting in on the other side, Pearl pushed the driver's seat forward and placed whatever she'd been carrying in the back seat. I imagined a grocery bag filled with fish. She slid into the front seat and put her arms around me, still shaking like a leaf. I hugged her and patted her back. There was something different.

"I'm sorry I couldn't get you out earlier. They wouldn't let me post bail till after the arraignment. I was so scared for you."

I put my hand up to feel her face and discovered tears streaming down over her proud cheekbones. "What's the matter?" I said, fear suddenly leaping up like a frog in my stomach.

"Nothing, I'm sorry," she said, sniffling. "It's just when they led you out of there I realized, I mean, oh I don't know." She forced a laugh. "Let's just say you don't look so hot right now."

Of course I had no idea how I looked. "Pearl, what were you carrying?" I asked.

"Homer," she said. She sniffled and rubbed her nose.

"Oh, right," I said. It took me a moment to comprehend this, but once I did, I threw my arms around her again and squeezed her tight. Her bulging stomach was missing—that was what had been different. Pearl laughed through her tears. "But when, I mean, how, or why didn't I—" there didn't seem to be any logical place to begin all the questions I had. "Let me see him," I said.

"Well, I don't think that's possible," Pearl said.

"I mean hold him," I said.

Pearl reached across the seat and delivered the little tyke into my arms. "He's been very good. He's been sleeping for the last hour." I was surprised by how light he was. I felt the tiny little body, the frail bones of his arms and legs. He was like a plucked chicken in a custom-fit fleece sack. I felt his ridiculously small, soft hands, which grasped my fingers as if they were handlebars. "I wish you could see him," Pearl said. He looks and acts so much like you already. Almost the same birthday, too."

That was correct. I'd forgotten my birthday—an occasion I'd often thought of as cause for mortification—was the day after we'd been driven from the farm in the paddy wagon. I'd probably spent it thrashing about on the putrid cement floor of my cell. I felt Homer's face. A lump was forming in my throat. I ran my rough fingertips gently over the round, satin cheeks, the flaring, rabbit nostrils and the eyelashes that felt like miniature paint brushes. "He's not at all like me," I said. "He's beautiful. He looks just like you." I put my hands around his tiny rib cage and lifted him close to my face. Homer must have drooled in his sleep because I felt some moisture run down my cheek.

"Careful Damien. He's not a skunk, you know," Pearl said.

My voice was an alien-sounding gargle when I spoke. "Well, he's about the size of one." I lowered him down to my lap. "Homer, is it?" I said to the baby, as if he could answer for himself. A bit of his drool or something dripped from my face.

"Damien," Pearl said. I felt her hand on my cheek. "Oh, Damien, you're crying."

"I certainly am not," I blubbered.

Homer woke up and started crying too. His lungs were so tiny that his attempt to yell was quite patently absurd. Pearl rescued him from my trembling lap and held one of us in each arm. Homer's little voice was so silly I started to laugh, but I do not think the sound came out as the hearty expression of amusement I intended it to be. "Now, now," Pearl said to us both. She was joggling Homer in one arm, stroking my hair with the other. "Now, now," she said.

Once this perplexing little riot of emotion was under control, Homer was restored to his seat in the back, and Pearl was driving us to the office of the lawyer she'd hired, I learned about the birth.

"They let me go almost immediately," Pearl said. "It was just you they wanted, and they were already worried about the lawsuit they're going to get for arresting a pregnant woman against whom there were absolutely no charges."

"You're going to sue them? Who?"

"Damn right I'm gonna sue. Fuckin' FBI. Especially that bastard who beat you up in the paddy wagon."

"The FBI? Good lord. All I've done is to round up some skunks that were on land I own."

"Oh, there's a little more to it than that. You saw that newspaper, Damien. You heard what Fiona told us."

"But I had nothing to do with whatever Robby's been up to," I protested.

"It doesn't matter. Well, we'll talk about this with Frank. Anyway, the next morning my water broke. Luckily Fiona was there. She'd been outside when they showed up to bust everybody at the hunting lodge, and so she was able to get away and she came over to our cabin. But by then they'd already taken us away, so she stayed there. And she was still there when I got back that night—looking like a terrorized kitten. So when my water broke, we went up to the dam. Actually, Fiona pushed me most of the way up there in the wheelbarrow. She was an absolute angel. I was a wreck. I screamed like a banshee the whole time. But I was much more comfortable in the water, I think, than I would've been in the cabin, or in a Goddamn hospital for that matter. Jesus, I hate hospitals."

"Wait. Do you mean to say Homer was born under water?"

I felt Pearl's hand on my knee. "Yes. It's not that uncommon, Damien, don't look so appalled. When I was at the women's shelter a lot of women said that was how they wanted to do it. Could you picture me giving birth any other way?"

Homer woke and began crying, which, as I soon learned, was his custom. "Do you hear that?" I said. "He's still upset about it."

Pearl laughed. "He probably needs to burp. I just fed him not too long ago. Pick him up and bounce him for a little while, will you? But be careful."

I leaned over the seat, picked Homer up, held him against my chest and bounced him lightly. He stopped crying. "Well," I confided to him in a lowered voice, "we know you're not a sinker. I suppose you must take after your mother then. Lucky for you."

"He likes you," Pearl said. "Oh, you should see his eyes." My shoulder felt suddenly warm. "Oh shit," Pearl laughed. "Sorry, I should have told you to put something there. Homer just had his first spit-up on his dad. I brought you a change of clothes anyway though. We're going to Frank's hotel before we go home."

"Who's this Frank?"

"Your lawyer. He's great. I had him flown in from New York where he's based now. I used to use him all the time. He can get you out of anything."

"Pearl, I chose not to seek council. I'm perfectly capable of defending myself, you know. I used to work for a law-book publisher."

"Oh Damien, come off it will you? This is serious."

But I was serious.

"Look, just meet him, okay? Then decide."

Frank Worthing was a brisk, energetic man who smelled of breath mints, and whose manner of locution seemed to imply that he could analyze and solve virtually any earthly problem in a New York minute. In his presence it seemed that there were no problems, really—it was simply that certain other individuals failed to present the facts in a way that meshed with his inevitable web of truth.

"I've spoken with Robby's lawyer," Frank said, sitting across from me in his hotel suite. "Basically, Robby's cutting a deal in exchange for a lesser sentence. Part of that deal was pointing a finger at you."

Blindness made me feel more self-conscious than I ever had before. I could not see Frank, and I did not want to be staring in the wrong direction, so I kept my head lowered and my eyes almost closed. Pearl was beside me on the overstuffed couch, with Homer in her arms. I inadvertently kicked the coffee table in front of me. "I've done nothing illegal," I said, as if I were already on the stand.

"I know that," Frank said. "We just have to convince the rest of the world of that before the ruling that outlaws SS."

"What? First of all, I sip skunk musk. SS is Robby's invention. Second of all, what do you mean by outlawing?"

"I guess you haven't heard," Frank said, "but three people have overdosed and died from SS injections. Two of them were minors, high school kids."

"But how can skunks be legislated? Do they intend to outlaw an animal?"

"Yep. Exactly. Not too surprising, really. They've done just that with several plants."

I didn't say anything for a moment. Homer managed a gurgle and some wet smacking sounds.

"Well, I haven't been peddling musk, anyway," I said. "It was Robby. What do they want with me?"

"Damien, I'll level with you," Frank said. "I've spoken with the judge. They want a quick ruling on this case for two reasons. One, it's a high profile case. SS is the biggest thing since LSD in the sixties. And in the same way, it's become, on the one hand, a symbol of youth culture, opposition to authority, et cetera, and on the other hand, a target for these groups that rally together against those very same things. The parent of one of the kids who died is the leader of PAUSS."

I assumed Frank was being ironic by pausing after this nonsensical announcement. "That was meant to give me?" I said.

"What?" said Frank.

"Pause?" I said.

"Parents Against the Use of SS," he said matter-of-factly. "Now, the quicker the trial is over, the less time for the media circus that's already gotten underway. They don't want a rerun of the Benson trial."

"Pardon?"

"The Benson trial."

"What was the Benson trial?" I asked.

"You're kidding," Frank told me.

"Damien hasn't seen a newspaper or television for quite a while," Pearl said.

"Really," Frank said. "Wow. Well, whatever. There's not as much hype about your trial yet, since they only picked you up a few days ago."

"Just a few days ago?" I said. I thought I'd been in jail for a month at the very least.

"Yeah," Frank said, hesitantly, as if one more exhibit of ignorance might lead him to the verdict that I was indisputably guilty of being an idiot. "The second thing is," he continued, "the quicker this case is over, the sooner they can legislate SS. The feds have been all over this thing like a cheap suit. There's going to be a Supreme Court ruling before you can say habeas corpus. The FDA is going to set up a whole department just to deal with skunks. I know, it sounds crazy—there's the government for you. With the media doing what it's doing, a lot of people are in a tough spot. I guess you wouldn't have heard, but the President even had to hold a press conference about all this." Frank paused and made a short but loud exhalation, as if he were in the middle of a set of sit-ups. "The ugly truth is this: everybody's looking for a scapegoat. That's the bottom line. My job is to make sure it's not you. So, what I need to know is everything about this musk. How you get it, how you use it, what it does."

As briefly as possible, I described the history of my use of skunk musk, beginning with the day I discovered how to milk Homer's musk (I called him Homer One, so as not to confuse him with my son), and ending with the jars in the skunk coop. I could hear Frank's pen scratching across a notepad while I spoke. He stopped me occasionally to clarify things.

"So you had no idea Robby was selling your musk?" Frank asked at one point.

"No," I said.

I heard the top of his pen snap shut. He gave another of his little gymnasium huffs. Homer began a siren-like wail that rose gradually in volume and pitch. "Tell you the truth, Damien," Frank said, "I'm pretty damn optimistic about this. The prosecution's case is based entirely on hearsay. Be happy you're not in Robby Krauthammer's shoes—that kid's going down, no question. No matter what kind of deals he makes. One thing the prosecution's sure to do to us though, is try to make you look evil. Who are some people we could get on the stand as character witnesses for you—friends, relatives, people you've worked with?"

I drew a great big blank. After a moment I said, "Well, Pearl, I suppose."

"I don't think the judge'll go for that," Pearl said.

"Yeah, me either," said Frank.

Then I thought of Jud. He was better than nothing. Frank said it was worth a try. "Well, see you the day after tomorrow," Frank said, as we were leaving.

"That soon?" I said.

"Yeah, they're really serious about getting the ball rolling here. Look at it this way: the sooner it's all over, the sooner you can get back to your," and then there was a hesitation in his voice that was so slight I mightn't have noticed it if I could have seen his face, "normal life."

My stomach was in knots for the next day and a half. Pearl did her best to keep both our spirits up. During one particularly low point in the day, I made the mistake of saying that she could have saved herself a lot of money by leaving me in jail until the trial. Did I not care about my son? she asked. Did I not think she'd been worried sick the whole time I'd been incarcerated? I beat a hasty retreat, apologizing, saying yes, yes, of course.

The night before our first day in court, I tried to eat the fried trout fillet Pearl had put before me, but I couldn't get down more than two bites. My mouth was dry, the food tasteless, and I kept wetting my lips with sips of musk.

"I really wish you wouldn't do that anymore," Pearl said.

I could tell by the sounds that she was breast-feeding Homer at the table. I was in complete darkness now. I couldn't even see shapes or movement, as I had days before when people were like ships drifting by in an evening fog. "Does it really matter now?" I asked.

"Yes." She was trying not to cry. Homer stopped feeding and did it for her. "Shh," she said. Her voice undulated with the rhythm of her body as she shifted him and began bouncing him on her shoulder. "Sh-sh-sh-sh-sh-sh." Once he'd quieted down again, Pearl said, "You don't know what it's like to have to see—" she stopped herself for a moment, then continued in a hoarse whisper, "to see what's happening to you."

"Pearl, I think it's too late," I said. I wasn't sure we were talking about the blindness anymore. We'd been talking about everything in general terms for the past twenty-four hours, terms whose significance applied to the past and future as well as the present. "It's already happened," I said.

24

The sound of the prosecutor's voice was enough for me to identify him as one of those short men who spent most of his young adulthood lifting weights—hoping, by the increase of his width, to compensate for his lack of height—and who is always more than willing to pick a fight with someone taller than himself. His name was Anthony Corelli, and his opening remarks were completely mystifying.

"Ladies and gentlemen of the jury," he said, in a tone that was at once boastful, unctuous and condescending. "I am here to prove to you, and I will, that this man, Mr. Damien Youngquist, is a threat to society, a threat to our children and a threat to the American way of life. Not only is he a drug addict, a stockpiler of weapons, the boss of the infamous Krauthammer Compound, but he is also the mastermind behind the production and sale of what unfortunately and so quickly has become a household word—SS—a drug which has already killed three, and is destroying the lives of many others as we speak. The man before you today is more of a threat to the American dream than any foreign enemy ever was, because he is the enemy within, a modern-day Pied-Piper who is leading America's youth down a destructive, suicidal path."

As his oratory continued, the astonished butterflies in my stomach stopped fluttering while I tried to figure out what any of Corelli's remarks had to do with me. If he hadn't eventually used my name, I would have assumed Frank and I had walked into the wrong courtroom. When he was finally through, Frank got up from beside me and approached the jury box. "Folks," he said, in a conversational tone, "the man whose fate you are about to decide is no monster, no evil bogeyman out to get your children. In fact, he is only here today because of an egregious violation of the Fourth Amendment to the Constitution of the United States, under which he should have been protected in the first place." He paused. "Terrible things have happened because of the proliferation of a new drug. It makes us angry. When I read stories about kids getting addicted to this stuff, ruining their futures and sometimes even losing their lives to it, well I get so worked up sometimes I feel like I want to strangle someone. I want someone to be held accountable. It's only natural for our anger to seek an outlet and that's just what the media has given us. We all know it was the media that led the witchhunt that has brought us here. And now Damien, this

Everyman sitting before you, is at your mercy." Frank paused again for what I assumed were dramatic purposes, and I wondered if he was giving the jury a look calculated to inspire guilt or deep thought.

"People," he resumed, "my client, much like the skunks for which he developed such an affinity, is a solitary type. Think about it—if he wanted to oversee a large-scale drug cartel, would a guy leave a big city on the East Coast and move out into the middle of nowhere? It just doesn't make sense. The real story is that because Damien's neighbors disapproved of his keeping skunks in his yard in suburban New Essex, he moved to Highbridge, where he believed he would have no neighbors. At that time there was no such thing as SS. There was just a man with a farm and a few pet skunks—a situation that you or I might say really stinks, but nevertheless far from criminal. Damien liked the smell of skunks. He liked it so much in fact that he began to sip skunk musk the way someone who'd never encountered coffee before might sip some, and though it's a bitter drink, he might gradually acquire a taste for it. Just as I keep jars of salt and sugar in the house to add some spice to my life, Damien kept jars of skunk musk. It's a weird habit, I'll give you that, but I'd be willing to bet a lot of us here have habits that others would find as repulsive or as absurd as the customs in a foreign country. And you and I know, especially as citizens of a free country, but also simply as empathetic human beings, that an innocent individual, no matter what his personal tastes and preferences, should be given the same rights we have—and one of the most important of these is the right to be let alone."

From this starting point, Frank launched into a speech about our Forefathers, the Mayflower, the Declaration of Independence, abolitionists and whatnot. I was surprised to learn, by Frank's account, that the history of our country so closely resembled the events of my own brief sojourn within it. After a few minutes I began to feel offended that someone such as myself—who apparently exhibited all the sterling qualities Americans associate with Abraham Lincoln, Fredrick Douglass and Benjamin Franklin—was essentially being held hostage by a bloodthirsty band of unimaginative television executives.

The prosecution asked permission to summon a few character witnesses in order to assassinate said character. "Who's this guy?" Frank asked me in a whisper when Ken Conover was called to the stand. I had no idea. Then, when Corelli asked the man what he did for a living, Ken identified himself as the owner of Highbridge Guns & Ammo.

"Oh dear," I murmured.

"What?" Frank hissed. "You never mentioned this guy to me."

"How many guns did Mr. Youngquist purchase from your establishment that day?"

"Five or six," Ken said.

That was a lie. I'd bought four guns. Corelli asked him to describe the shotguns and pistols I'd bought, then asked, "And what did Mr. Youngquist say he intended to do with all these weapons?"

"Deer huntin," was the reply.

"In all your years of hunting and selling weapons, Mr. Conover, have you ever known anyone to hunt deer with a Heckler and Koch semi-automatic .45?"

"No, can't say I have. But I don't ask my customers a lotta questions neither."

"Good business policy," Corelli affirmed. "Good. But going back to this particular purchase... For the jury's understanding, what does one usually shoot with a Heckler and Koch semi-automatic pistol?"

"That's what we call—"

"Objection, your Honor," Frank said. "This information is irrelevant to the case."

"I hold that the purchase of numerous weapons by an individual culpable for murder *is* relevant," Corelli said, "and that the way he went about his purchase is in itself revealing."

"Overruled," the judge growled. Every utterance made by the judge for the entire length of the trial was delivered in a tone that suggested he suffered a permanent disgruntlement that was in constant danger of boiling over into rage.

"Mr. Conover," Corelli continued, "what is this type of gun most commonly used to shoot?"

"People," Ken said.

"But Mr. Youngquist claimed he was going to hunt deer with one of these pistols, is that correct?"

"That's what he said," Ken replied.

"Interesting. Ladies and gentlemen, as you'll soon see, there is very often a discrepancy between the actions and the stated intentions of Damien Youngquist. Oh, another thing, Mr. Conover. Did you notice anything else peculiar about Mr. Youngquist that day? Did he behave at all suspiciously?"

Ken said, "I think—" then stopped himself.

"I remind you that you're under oath," Corelli said.

"Well," Ken said, "he did almost blow my head off at one point." An impressed murmuring rippled through the courtroom.

"Oh God," I groaned through clenched teeth.

When asked to elaborate, Ken described the scene behind his shop when I'd discovered the magic of the scope.

"So first he comes into your shop and lies," Correlli said, "and then he points a deadly weapon at your head. Interesting. So, Mr. Conover, how would you characterize this individual?"

"Like I said, I don't ask customers nothin' about their business, but this guy did gimme the creeps."

In a brief conference before he cross-examined Ken, I explained to Frank what a revelation the scope had been, but somehow my side of the story didn't quite sound believable even as I sat there listening to Frank describe it to the jury, through Ken. But Frank did seem to undermine Corelli's case a bit when he asked, "So, do you keep guns in your house that would be used to shoot a person?"

"Well, of course," Ken snorted.

"For self-defense?" Frank asked. "In case, say, a violent intruder found his way into your home?"

"Zackly," Ken said. "Nobody's breakin' into my place and livin' to tell about it."

"I see," Frank said. I could hear his footsteps as he paced in front of the jury box. "And what percent of the people in Highbridge would you guess keep guns in their homes for the same reason."

"I reckon just about everybody does."

"Thank you, Mr. Conover. This has been a most illuminating glimpse into the environment in which this story takes place. You may step down."

I could hear the steps to the stand creaking with Ken's considerable girth as he descended. My spirits were buoyed whenever Frank Worthing got through cross-examining someone, but I felt myself sinking again when Corelli began interrogating a witness he'd located by what means it was impossible to guess. When he called someone named Jerome to the stand, and I heard the laborious speech of the trapper putting himself under oath, the awesome thoroughness of the prosecution's research into my past dawned on me with fresh horror. Then my stomach lurched with the nauseating memory of the method employed for the murder of Homer and the family.

"So he told you over the phone that he was from a magazine?" Corelli asked the trapper.

"Yeah," Jerry said. "I'd never heard of it."

"What was the name of the magazine?

"*Trapper's World*, I think he said."

"And then he came to your home," Corelli said. "And there he had yet another fiction for you, didn't he?"

"Well, I wasn't sure at first it was the same guy. We was thinking he was one of them SAFTEYS and that it might be some kinda trap."

Struck by the irony of Jerry's situation, which added another dimension to the disorientation of having one's life talked about in this professional and airless milieu, I was able to remain somewhat detached. Frank, on the other hand, was seething beside me. He kept making little huffs, tapping a pen on the table and moving back and forth in his chair. At one point he leaned over and said in a furious whisper, "Jesus Christ, Damien. How many of these Goddamn jack-in-the-boxes you got for me?"

"So, this man who is so concerned about his privacy," Corelli announced, "apparently feels no compunction when it comes to invading the privacy of others. He also gave you a false name when he arrived, didn't he?" Corelli said.

"Said his name was Joe," Jerry droned on in that way of his that made it seem everything that came out of his mouth was the continuation of a single line of thought and that no one had spoken since his last sentence. "He said he was interested in being a trapper."

Frank stood abruptly and the wooden legs of his chair made a short detonating sound on the floor as they moved backward. "Objection your Honor," he said. "We've been led off on an absurd tangent."

"Your Honor," Corelli said, "I'm simply illustrating the nature of the criminal mind that was at work behind the series of crimes for which the defendant stands trial."

"Overruled," the judge rumbled. "Proceed."

"Ladies and gentlemen," Corelli said. "As the record of his encounters with other people continues to demonstrate, this perverse individual, whose defense would like you to allow to walk scot-free, is in fact a compulsive liar who routinely endangers people's lives to get what he wants from them. What has brought him here is the death of his fellow men, an inevitable result of the game he plays, and which does not faze him at all. He will not stop himself. It is up to us to stop him."

Frank requested a brief recess, during which he grilled me about my trip to the Trappers' Workshop. I almost felt that I was on the stand when I spoke privately with Frank. In these meetings he seemed to distrust me as much as his courtroom opponent argued that people should, and I sensed his personal distain and his exasperation with my case. But these emotions were tempered by his respect for Pearl and, of course, the money she was paying him. In these conferences too I was able to maintain a detachment from my own situation, thanks partly to my blindness.

When cross-examining Jerry, Frank made a speech about my loving care of Homer, Louisa and the family, then painted Jerry's intrusion into our inter-species idyll much the way a SAFETY might. I doubted the effectiveness of this strategy because, as he had been when I fist met him, Jerry became increasingly taciturn and his articulations slowed to a crawl under his mounting suspicion that he was under attack. Then Frank suddenly shifted his line of questioning from an investigation of facts to an investigation of emotions.

"And how did Damien seem to you that day when he appeared at your door—what would you say was his state of mind?"

After a long pause, Jerry said, "Disturbed."

"Disturbed in what way?" Frank asked, quietly.

"Sad," Jerry said. Frank must have by now gotten the feel of the trapper's tempo, because he patiently waited for him to continue. "The way he acted," Jerry said, "reminded me of how my daughter acted right after her husband was killed."

One could feel the change of temper in the courtroom as distinctly as a change in temperature. Frank waited a moment before asking, "Do you know why he was acting that way?"

"I didn't understand at first," Jerry admitted in his trance-like monotone. "But after he wanted to see where them skunks was buried I knew they was to him like my dog is to me." Jerry paused again. "Only it was an even stronger feeling."

Frank said nothing in the moment of silence that followed, and I felt a lump rising in my throat for the family. "No further questions," Frank said.

The testimony of Robby Krauthammer struck me as the most surreal episode of the trial. After the usual rigmarole about how long he'd known me, etc., Robby related a version of reality that had been turned upsidedown and insideout, in a voice that was not his own. First of all, his speech was utterly devoid of the "dude-mans" with which it was usually littered. Then there was the fact that he kept referring to me as "Mr. Youngquist." His tone was that of an inebriated motorist who'd just been pulled over and was trying to talk his way out of a ticket. Each sentence was an announcement about some aspect of the alternate reality which, I gradually became certain, had been conjured in the offices of his attorney, rehearsed and perhaps even transcribed. While Corelli seemed to ventriloquize these stage statements from Robby's mouth, I kept leaning over to Frank and asking, "Is he reading something?" And Frank kept whispering back things like, "What do you mean reading?" and "No, he's on the stand for Chrissake." But even had I not been blind as justice itself and not been acquainted with Robby, I believe I would have heard the echo of untruth in his voice.

Robby described how I'd sought him out, as soon as I moved to Highbridge, because I wanted the benefit of his "expertise in organic farming." He said I then invited him to my farm and showed him the way I intended to make myself rich: with a chicken coop full of skunks. It took a while for me to stop making inadvertent gasping sounds and even a couple of loud "Good griefs," which popped out of me as the outrageousness raged on. But after a while I began to see the logic behind his lies.

"How many skunks did Damien keep in this coop?" Corelli asked.

"About forty," Robby said. It was one of the few statements he made that was merely a gross exaggeration.

"Forty. That's quite a number of skunks. Much more, I would think, than one man would keep if he simply wanted to provide his own supply of SS. That sounds closer to the number one would keep if he wanted to provide SS for thousands of people. So Robert, go on, tell us how you and Mr. Youngquist set up your business together."

"Well," Robby said, "since Mr. Youngquist was the only one who could get close enough to the skunks to squeeze the musk out, we had to play by his rules. He told us how much we'd be able to make off each syringe, but he sold the ingredients to us in bulk and he set the prices so that he'd get sixty percent of our profits. He said those were the conditions because it was his idea and he had to do the hardest part. Mr. Youngquist also made us work on his farm as a kind of advance payment." Robby's voice cracked and hit an unusual high note. "I had to install the whole irrigation system myself," he said.

"Sounds like something close to indentured servitude," Corelli mused. "I know this must be difficult for you, Robert, and that you've been through a terrible ordeal. I hate to see idealistic young people being bamboozled in this way and used by those who have more than organic farming on their minds. So it was after he put you to work on his property that he convinced you to quit your job and buy the adjoining property?"

"That's right," Robby said, as if he'd just remembered this piece of the puzzle. "That was when Mr. Yougquist told me I should buy the land next to his because the old hunting lodge would make a good SS lab. He said it would be more convenient for us both that way. I said why didn't we just make the stuff there on his property where the skunks were. But Mr. Youngquist was really clear on that. He said the chemical mixes had to be done at a different location from where he lived. 'Mum's the word,' he said."

"So he wanted to disassociate himself from the actual process of concocting and peddling this dangerous new substance," Corelli clarified.

"Yeah, he didn't want to even know who the distributors were that we used, even though I introduced him to a couple of them at a party we had. I could barely even get him to come to that. Damien wouldn't ever come over. The only other time I could get him to visit us was this once because there was a problem with the plants."

There was a pause more pregnant than a woman carrying septuplets. "You're describing the lab as an SS plant," Corelli said.

"Right," Robby said eagerly. "It was like a regular factory the way we worked it. Mr. Youngquist wanted everything to be real orderly. He kept comparing it to my job at the library."

"I see," Corelli said solemnly. "Perhaps trying to legitimize in your mind this illegal activity into which he'd coerced you. You and the other impressionable young people that were recruited into this destructive and, speaking plainly, evil enterprise."

At this juncture something in the air caused me to sneeze, and my sneezes were so loud that Tony and Robby had to stop their absurd parody of an attorney and a witness. The series of sneezes came to an end and Corelli said, "What is nothing to sneeze at, ladies and gentlemen, is the deforming of so many young lives by the diabolical designs of a hopped-up SS junkie who—" at which point a tickle in my throat caused me to burst into a coughing fit that after half a minute transformed itself into a uncontrollable case of the giggles, and I had to be escorted from the courtroom by a guard. I was allowed back in during the cross-examination, during which it seemed to me that Frank poked some enormous holes in Robby's story.

"And what did Damien do with all this money he was supposedly raking in?" Frank was asking as I was led to my seat.

"I dunno," Robby said. He sounded rattled. "Everything was cash, so he could have done anything with it. Damien—Mr. Youngquist—was digging this hole behind his cabin. I figure he might have put it in there."

"So you're asking sensible people here to give credence to your postulation that there is a drug overlord living in the woods in the middle of nowhere who buries his money in a root cellar behind his one-room hut where federal authorities found only legumes. Mr. Krauthammer, why don't you tell us the truth?" Frank went on to tell the truth and though I don't know for sure, I doubt Robby would have been able to maintain a very convincing poker face while the real, incriminating story was painted in front of him.

The trial went on for a few days that all blended together. People whose voices I'd never expected to hear again—including those of Mrs. Endicott and the strange duo I'd encountered at the Animal Control Center—were brought in to testify. There were times, such as when Jud was on the stand, that things seemed to be going in my favor. "Yeah, he's a bit odd, I'll say that," Jud said, when Corelli was cross-examining him. "But he ain't any queerer than most folks in Highbridge. Truth be told," Jud said to the prosecutor, "I'd be more suspicious of a character suchuz yerself."

One day, a scientist from the Food and Drug Administration was introduced and he proceeded to rattle off SS recipes so that everyone could go home and make some of their own. "At this stage of test results," he informed us, "we know that the concoction has a base of skunk musk, which is procured from a skunk. Sometimes it's simply diluted with water, but usually it's laced with other drugs, which vary depending upon where in the country you buy it. Some samples we've tested are three parts musk and one part amphetamine; in others, the musk has been mixed with a barbiturate." He went on happily listing possible combinations for a while until the judge grunted something to guide him to the negative aspects. "Overdose, as everyone knows, can prove fatal," he said. "There have been conjectures in the literature about the effects of SS use that include degeneration of the liver and lungs, the contraction of rabies, blindness and possible psychosis. But at this early stage of testing, we really can't say what the side effects of prolonged use might be."

The testimony of a woman named Mrs. Blake regarding the sudden death of her son, Billy, could not have failed to move even the most unemotional listener. Tears moistened my eyes as she described how Billy's friends brought him home from a concert during which he'd gone into convulsions. Afraid of having to answer to police if they took him to a hospital, his friends had instead brought him back to his parents' house, by which time he was catatonic. When he finally reached the emergency room he'd already been in a coma for forty-five minutes. Billy's pulse slowed steadily through the night while Mrs. Blake and her husband stood by. At four in the afternoon the next day, less than twenty-four hours after he'd shot up SS, Billy Blake, an obedient son, C+ student and beloved member of the punk rock band "Whacking the Muskrat," was dead. There was no denying that this was a terrible story, but I could not help feeling dismissive of it, which I recognized was a defensive reaction to being forced to listen to the sad tale as if I were responsible.

When I took the stand, Corelli asked me all kinds of embarrassing questions about my personal life, my habits and preferences. "So, you admit to being a SS addict?" was one of his first questions.

"I don't have anything to do with that nonsense," I said to the little homunculus. "I do partake of a fair amount of skunk musk and consider myself somewhat of a connoisseur. I object to your calling me an addict. Simply because you are a lawyer, I do not refer to you as a 'fact addict.'"

There were a few titters among the jury. Corelli went on, doing his best to present my decision to buy a large area of land and start a farm as a wildly irrational move for a copywriter. I tried to explain the circumstances, but he kept cutting me off. "You don't understand," I said, finally, raising my voice to be heard over his interruptions. "That life was over. I'd lost everything in the storm! That horrible, treacherous storm! They'd taken everything from me!"

"And did you not develop an alliance with a Robert Krauthammer, soon after relocating your SS lab to Highbridge?" Corelli asked.

"No, no. There was no alliance. SS is not—"

"Do you know Mr. Krauthammer or not?"

"Yes."

"And is it not true that you were in charge of the production of vast amounts of SS over the last several months which have been sold to thousands of young people across the country?"

"No! I mean yes, but no, I did not produce SS. As I said, I do drink skunk musk. I didn't know what Robby was doing with it."

"Ahh," Corelli said, as if I'd just enlightened him, "you didn't know what Robby was doing with it. Hmm. Yes, perfect. The left hand couldn't see what the right hand was doing. Isn't that convenient? You managed to remain ignorant of this nascent drug culture you essentially started up yourself, and about which there were reports by all the major television networks and articles in every newspaper and magazine in the country. That *is* quite a position, Mr. Youngquist, quite a daring, if ridiculous, position to take. I admire your audacity. However, I do not believe you. You are responsible for the deaths of the children of people in this very room and this is no time to prevaricate."

I fidgeted in my seat. It was obvious that Corelli felt he had me, and he seemed to be enjoying himself.

"Now. Let's see if you can answer this very straightforward, yes-or-no question without allusions to meteorological forces, shall we? Here goes. Did you, or did you not know that Robby was using the substance you produced?"

"Those lousy potato beetles! I never wanted anything to do with them or their silly hippie farm, I—"

"Mr. Youngquist! Yes or no, did you know Robby was using your substance?"

"I didn't—well—I had a hunch."

There was quite a commotion. People began talking in the audience as well as in the jury box, Mrs. Blake began weeping loudly, and Frank demanded a recess at the top of his lungs.

Frank led me through a crowd of people who jostled, bumped and yelled questions at us, and when he'd gotten me into an empty room and shut the door, closing out the voices of what I assumed were reporters, he said, "Just what the hell do you think you're doing?"

"Sitting down," I said.

"Sitting down," he said. "Great. Fine." I could tell from his voice that he was pacing the room in an effort to calm himself. "Fine, good, yes. Jesus fucking Christ, are you trying to indict yourself or what?" I said nothing. I heard his hand slap against a flat surface. "I look like a Goddamn fucking idiot out there. Good God!" He released one of his louder, work-out exhalations. "Why the hell did you lie to me?"

"I didn't lie to you," I said.

"You said you didn't know anything about the SS dealing."

"You asked me if I knew that Robby was selling it. I didn't know that. Corelli just asked me if I knew Robby was using it, and I told the truth—I had a hunch."

"You had a hunch. Fuckin' A, you had a hunch."

"The levels had gone down in the jars. There had been at least two midnight raids of some sort. I'd dismissed them as nightmares, but I started to think otherwise later on."

"Nightmare's right. This whole trial is a Goddamn nightmare."

"You were optimistic a few days ago."

"A few days ago you weren't raving about potato beetles and storms in front of a courtroom like some kinda luna—" he paused. "Wait a minute. I think I've got a bargaining chip there."

When we went back to the courtroom Corelli passed around to the jury photographs taken by federal agent Ralph Parson at an "SS orgy," held at the Krauthammer Commune. Apparently, I was leaning on Robby's shoulder in one of these photographs. In another, I was told, I was shaking hands with Jocko, the California SS distributor, and in yet another I was being carried out of the party by some of the other revelers, having passed out, presumably as a result of too much SS. Special agent Ralph Parson—I recalled the boy scout with the tucked-in tie-dye—testified to the fact that, like most of the people at the party, I'd been under the influence of SS. My dilated pupils, the distinct smell and frequent trips to the bathroom where the syringes were kept, were all evidence of this. He also testified to having been privy to the information, during the period he'd spent infiltrating the Krauthammer Commune, that I was the producer of the SS, for which I received payment from Mr. Krauthammer.

25

Frank Worthing fought valiantly. I have him to thank for the fact that I was sent to a psychiatric hospital, rather than the state prison. From the first, I was given my own room, which was a good thing because with a roommate I probably would have gone berserk. They ran a bunch of tests on me and after several days they told me my blindness was irreversible. As far as I was concerned, this was a blessing for the time being because it meant I would not have to see the collection of hopeless addicts with whom I had to meet every other day for what was termed "group therapy." This club of winos and heroin users sat around in a room for two hours, smoking so much I sometimes wondered if the room were on fire, most of them happily reminiscing about the good old days, which they had spent breaking into people's houses, getting into fist fights, getting fired from their jobs, retiring from bars to the homes of complete strangers for the night, tearing apart their families, wrecking automobiles and generally enjoying themselves while making a hash of things. Of course the majority of their anecdotes were delivered in very boastful gosh-how-could-I-have-been-so-horrible tones. Given the pervasive pointlessness of life in modern society, one couldn't help but sympathize with their destructive responses to everything that was keeping them imprisoned within it. There was one sniffling fellow for whom I felt especially sorry. He sounded quite young and delicate and he described his cocaine addiction with a quaver that sometimes gave way to quiet weeping through which he struggled to continue with his confessions. The group leader would occasionally prod me with questions and attempt to coax me into participating. Of course I was having none of it. I generally sat with my arms folded for the duration of the meeting and when asked a question I said I preferred not to say anything at the present time.

I don't think the staff was used to quite such antisocial behavior among their ranks of chummy derelicts, and it took them more than a month to decide to dismiss me from the cigarettes-and-storytelling room and schedule me to instead meet with a psychiatrist named Peter Clime three times per week. Dr. Clime had an odor that I can only describe as tweedy. During our first sessions, because of the nature of his inquiry and the busy sound of scribbling emanating from his corner of the room, I got the impression that he might be taking notes for an article or book he was writing. He wanted to know all about skunk musk, how it was extracted from the skunk, how it made me feel, and so forth. He also wanted to know all about how I grew up, beginning with my earliest childhood memory. So I furnished him with a colorful history that was actually an amalgamation of plot lines and characters borrowed from Victorian novels, updated and modified to fit in plausible locales. I found myself growing quite interested in this story as I spoke, and had been working steadily on my little invention for about twenty minutes before Peter interrupted me.

"Damien," he said. "That's good."

"Oh, I'm not finished," I said. "I thought you wanted me to continue right up to how I got here."

"That's good," he said again. "Good stuff. But maybe save it for when you're running scenarios by a film producer or something. Now, why don't you tell me the real story?"

Since we were the only ones in the room, it was a little more difficult to dodge Peter's requests, as opposed to those of the group leader. Also there was a strain of humorless authority in his voice that made one feel that it would be childish not to cooperate.

"Come on," he said. "Let's go back and start at the beginning."

So it was that this determined fellow inspired the feeling that it was incumbent upon me to tell my true story. It was surprising how closely he paid attention, which was indicated by the occasional clarifying questions he stopped me to ask. Otherwise he kept quiet, though the scratching of his pen seemed to follow my story like the needle of a polygraph machine. Even telling the tale in summary, it wasn't until the middle of the next session that I concluded it with my arrival at the building in which we were sitting.

"So you lost your job because of this stuff," Peter said. "And eventually had to leave town."

"Well, there were many factors involved in both decisions," I said.

"I'll venture a guess that you would still be working at Grund & Greene if you'd never taken skunk musk," Peter said.

"Perhaps," I said.

"Perhaps you'd also still be living in your house in New Essex if you'd never done skunk musk," he added.

I did not desire to reply to this, so I said nothing. But my back itched and I shifted about in my chair to try and scratch at it.

"Would you say that is also true?" Peter asked.

"Idle speculation," I said.

"Idle?" he asked.

"Speculation," I answered. A spot in the middle of my back that seemed impossible to reach now felt like it was being bored into by a mosquito and I rubbed more vigorously against the back of my chair.

"I'd like you to answer yes or no to that," Peter said.

It was growing intolerable, so I leaned forward, stuck my hand up under my shirt to scratch at the spot.

"Are you alright?" Peter asked.

I stood up, turned my back to Peter and lifted my shirt. "Is there something on there?" I asked. I heard him get up from his chair and step closer to examine my back. "Something biting me?"

"Nothing," he said, with that terrible, clinical tone. Here, then, is evidence of the man's single-minded lack of humor, for this was the obvious opening for him to say, "Just a monkey." Instead he said, "Why don't you sit back down." Again I felt like a fidgety child. After we'd both sat back down, he said, "OK, now please answer the question."

"Yes, fine, I suppose I would still have been living in New Essex," I conceded. "But that was no Garden of Eden."

"Do you want to live in a Garden of Eden?" Peter asked, all innocence.

"Of course not," I snapped. "I don't know why I said that. I mean it was time for me to make a big change in my life anyway."

"I see. Now that sounds like the truth," he said, as if he'd won a little victory of some kind. Then he told me the session was over. End of round one.

In the next session he asked me to give him detailed descriptions of how I'd spent my days before coming to the hospital, how I spent them in the hospital, and how I felt after each and every little thing I did or did not do until essentially he knew me like a book.

One day he told me I'd received a letter from Robby. Since I was unable to read it myself, Peter offered to read it aloud. It went like this: "Dear Damien, Dude I am so sorry about all the shit that went down at your trial. I never meant to hurt anybody, especially not you. The kids that OD'd on SS were trying to OD on anything they could, and did other drugs with it, so it's not like it was our fault for selling them something that helped them do something they were probably going to do anyway.

But dude, just be glad you're not at the state penitentiary like I am. I don't think you'd do so good here. I got beat up pretty bad on my second day but now I have some real tough friends I'm going to do business with when we get out. And I have to say, I really respect a lot of the people here. I mean they're way more revolutionary than anybody I ever met on the outside. Lots of leaders, like Malcom X, who I've been reading about, spent time in prison, so I don't feel like it's necessarily such a bad thing. It only makes sense that I would meet so many other people who are against the system. It's why they put us here.

Anyway, I hope you're doing OK. Fiona says she sees Pearl sometimes and that she's doing good. You didn't tell me you were going to be a dad—crazy, man. I know you probably hate me right now, but I hope we can still be friends when things settle down. Peace out, Robby."

When Peter asked me if I wanted to write a letter back, or perhaps dictate something to him, the only appropriate response to Robby's missive I could think of were the first words to pop into my head, which were, "Go stick your head in a bear trap, Mr. Mayonnaise Brains."

"I beg your pardon?" Peter said.

"That's my reply," I said. However—though it was comforting to imagine Robby opening an envelope and reading those words—after some thought I decided that the satisfaction of any response at all was more than I was willing to give.

In my first months at the hospital Pearl and Homer visited often. While a guard stood nearby, Homer sat in my lap and cried while Pearl gave me news of the outside world and told me how she and Homer were getting along. I spent a lot of time in those days thinking about how I could have done things differently. I should have sought Pearl out before fleeing New Essex in the midst of the storm, I thought. I should have dealt better with Robby, should have been more alert, should have seen what he was up to before it came to this. I thought about the forces that had conspired to deprive me of skunk musk and exiled me from my own farm. Of course all of the ruminating did nothing to liberate me from my room. The more I thought about things, the more often I banged my head against the wall until I was unconscious or they came in and stopped me. When they caught me banging my head they often put me in a straitjacket and took me down to solitary. I didn't mind solitary confinement at all. The walls and the floor were padded; it was quite like an oversized coffin. There, kneeling on the floor, I could quietly bang my head against the wall for hours and hours. I usually banged myself to sleep. I didn't understand why the other inmates object to solitary confinement. Solitude is quite natural. We enter this screaming world alone, and alone we must leave it.

It was while in solitary that I developed a new philosophy. Every time they took something from me, I simply walled off that area of my mind, so that in effect they had taken nothing. If they'd taken my freedom, well then I believed I was never free in the first place. So they'd grabbed for something that was not there and come up with their hands empty. They put me in a straitjacket to take away the use of my arms, well then my arms were useless anyway, so again they'd taken nothing. If I was not allowed to go to the visiting room to see Pearl and Homer while I was in solitary, well then Pearl and Homer had never existed. The more walls they used to keep me closed in tighter and tighter spaces, the more of my own walls I erected, narrowing the scope of my own existence until my mind was free. They would never invade the sanctuary of my mind. They only made more blatant demonstrations of their own insanity the more they treated me like a crazy person. Meanwhile, I found comfort in counting: counting the days; counting the hours, second by second, to my next meal; and counting the number of times I banged my head against the wall before I fell asleep.

I recognized that from another perspective my behavior would make it appear that I was acquiescing, that I'd accepted the fate prescribed for me. That, I reasoned, was precisely the genius of my resistance. My captors were imaginatively straitjacketed potato beetles and would fail to see how I'd thwarted them. After several months of putting me in solitary confinement for up to a week at a time, taking me out, then putting me back in again, they finally stopped taking me down there because I'd let my mind roam so freely that the physical behavior they saw when I was in my room was exactly the same as my behavior in solitary confinement. I had closed all the doors in my mind and thus any doors they used were superfluous. I'd given up my head-banging. Though I wore no straitjacket, I kept my arms folded. Though there was a chair in my room, I sat on the floor, sometimes rocking gently back and forth, counting the thousands of back-and-forths until I went into a trance or fell asleep. I stayed like this for months. I declined offers to be taken to the visiting room when I was informed that Pearl and Homer had come to see me. My behavior caused concern among the so-called doctors in that pitiful excuse for a hospital and they sent Peter to talk me into leaving my room. But I simply stared in a direction away from the sound of his voice so he would have to look at my profile while he tried to engage me in conversation. Peter began to visit my room every day, sit before me and talk, sometimes for almost an hour, often relaying news about Pearl and Homer. Blindness was handy in helping me see the institutional strategy behind Peter's efforts. I had beaten them at their own game. They had thought they were keeping me in, but now it was I who was keeping them out. Pearl and Homer had already been deleted from my mental files, so it was as if Peter were speaking to me of people I'd never met. Through rigorous concentration, I was able not to hear most of what he said for many months.

But the effects of time and Peter's wearying, practically incantatory style of locution eroded my willpower enough for some information to penetrate the cracks in my walls and infiltrate my consciousness. I learned that Frank Worthing was still engaged in negotiations on my behalf. Pearl had been determined to retain Frank's services after the trial, though I'd told her she should save her money for more pressing concerns, such as feeding and clothing Homer. The updates that traveled from Frank to Pearl to Peter to me suggested that the seesaw of opinion regarding my innocence continued much the way it seemed to while I was still on trial.

Then one day Peter said something that must have caused me to involuntarily alter my facial expression. "That's right," he added. "Your girlfriend is changing the world. She wants to tell you about it tomorrow." What piqued my interest was not what he said but the tone with which he said it. This was not another of his attempts to employ himself as my personal guide for a guilt trip into the dense jungle of thoughts and emotions around my abandonment of my mate and offspring. This was something very different. Peter's voice betrayed resignation tinged with jealousy.

So the next day, when I was told visitors had arrived to see me, I gave my consent for the attendant to lead me to the visiting room. When he released my arm, I walked in the direction of Homer's playful babbling sounds, which were occurring near a source of light that I'd always assumed was a large window on one side of the room. It must have been sunny outside because the area was brighter and warmer than on previous visits. It had been eight months or so since I'd last met with Pearl and the smell of fish was the first organic, non-institutional odor I'd experienced in quite a while. The processed food the hospital churned out smelled even worse than the general antiseptic odor that permeated the place. Pearl made a couple sniffles that let me know she was restraining tears as she held my face firmly in both her hands and kissed my cheeks and mouth. After a minute, she withdrew her hands and smacked the side of my head just above the ear. "Don't ever do that again," she said.

"What?"

"Retreat like that," she said. "You know better."

"Oo, oh ella," said Homer, who was apparently seated nearby.

I put my hands on Pearl's face to feel how she looked. I ran my fingertips over her features, tracing her jaw line, her mouth, ran a finger up the bridge of her nose, grazed her closed eyelids with the fingers of both hands and then let my hands rest on her cheeks. For a moment I stood there, feeling the nervous tension in her face, then let my hands drop to my sides.

"I'm sorry," I said.

Pearl guided me into a chair, sat down across from me, grasped my hands in hers and began kneading them as if they were two lumps of dough.

"You knead me," I said, and she stopped doing it.

"Of course I do," she said. She shook my hands vigorously. "*We* need you."

"Ee ee oo," Homer concurred.

"May I hold him?" I asked.

"He's in his car seat. Let me take him out of it." She moved from her chair and a moment later I felt Homer in my arms, a situation he rebelled against by announcing, "O, o, o, o, o."

"Sounds just like you," Pearl said.

I bounced him a little, but this only made him start crying. Homer had gotten heavier since the last time I'd held him and I wondered if he'd outgrown the bouncing stage. I doubt I would have been a natural at paternity, but spending the majority of my prime practice hours locked away in a mental institution hadn't helped matters.

"Here, he needs his bippy," Pearl said, and I felt the pressure of his head against my chest as she stuck something in his face. I gently moved my hand over his tiny features until I reached his mouth, which had been filled with a plastic stopper with a ring attached to it.

"So guess what," Pearl said. "We don't have to worry about money anymore."

"Well, it's not of much concern for me at the moment," I confessed, "there being so few opportunities for me to spend it in my cell—or, I suppose—room."

"You won't be in here for much longer," Pearl said, matter-of-factly.

"I think a decade was the rough estimate for how long it would take me to 'heal.'"

"I'm going to find a way to get you released. I feel like I can do anything. Listen, I did some more experimenting with the SeaLawn." That eureka tenor had now entered her voice. "Just a genetic modification that was actually pretty easy to achieve. You know what it can do now, in addition to feed the world?"

"Yes," I said. "Provide a fuel source."

Her seat cushion crunched as Pearl bounced forward in her chair and excitedly rapped my wrist a few times with her palm. "Not only that. It eats up petroleum." She left off there, as if I were to fill in the blank on my own.

"Ah," I said. "Another gas guzzler."

"Oil spills, Damien. It can absorb oil from the water and break it down, basically digest it. So SeaLawn is now a self-replicating oil-spill sponge that provides food and fuel. I had to apply for another patent on that aspect of it. I was thinking how wonderful it was, but when I thought about you in here, and how powerless that made me feel, I thought, why not finally make some money off this? So I sold the patent rights on SeaLawn to an oil company. Of course they don't care about feeding people, and they definitely don't care about global warming—in fact, the dinosaurs who run the company are still trying to convince people that burning fossil fuels isn't contributing to the greenhouse effect—but they *are* concerned about oil spills. It's a little more difficult for them to pretend oil spills don't exist. I talked to Frank about it. He thinks I could've gotten more for it if I'd let him negotiate, but he said it was still a good deal."

In my mind there immediately appeared a picture of Pearl, in her moment of triumph, throwing her arms around Frank, and Frank—suave, big-city, opportunistic attorney that he is—taking this chance to engage Pearl in a long, wet kiss that would be his opening statement prior to an interrogation conducted between satin sheets with a chilled bottle of champagne close at hand. It would only take a few days for Frank to persuade her to forget about the blind freak who'd knocked her up before being carted off to the loony bin.

"Why do you look like I just told you the world's going to end?" Pearl said. "This is good."

"Sorry to be pointing out a fly in the ointment," I said, "but might it be a bit dangerous to unleash that stuff in the open sea?"

"Oh, they have it all figured out," Pearl said. "They're going to do it way offshore where they'll be free of regulation and can contain it if anything goes wrong." She took Homer from my arms and put him back in his seat, then pulled her chair up so close to mine she was practically in my lap. Stray strands of frizzy hair tickled my cheeks. I allowed my hand to move forward and come to rest on her wonderful, round hip, which I took the liberty of giving a gentle squeeze. A part of me that I had all but forgotten existed sprang suddenly to life. Pearl put her arms around me and whispered into my ear, "Pretend you're kissing me. I don't want the guard or whatever he is to overhear." I did as I was told and kissed Pearl's fishy and familiar neck. She whispered, "Six million."

"Dollars?" I exclaimed, pulling away.

"No, potato chips, Damien," Pearl said, giggling. She cupped my chin in her hand, leaned forward and kissed me quickly on the mouth. "You know, I like you," she said.

"I see that. Not much else," I admitted, "but I do see that."

"Good," she said.

"SeaLawn. I never would've guessed the dollar value of Sea-Lawn."

With a slobbery popping sound, Homer ejected the pacifier from his mouth and said, "Ee aww, Ee aww."

"SeaLawn is his favorite word now," Pearl said.

"Well, in light of what you've just said, I think it's mine too."

"Alright, look," Pearl said. "I'm going to be busy for the next several days, but I want to visit next week. By then I should have a better idea of when we can get you home."

"To the farm?" I asked. "I mean, you're still living there?"

"Yeah, for the time being. I like it there, it's cozy. Kind of a nice refuge. I'm going to make some changes to the place, if you don't mind. I think we can stay there indefinitely. As long as you'll agree to take several seaside vacations with me every year. But let's not worry too much about all that at the moment. We're going to be busy with getting you out of here and for now I'm going to be traveling a lot, educating idiotic oil execs about SeaLawn. But listen, when I come next week, you're not going to hide in your room and not come out are you?"

"No," I promised.

Then, as I was being led back to my room, I began to reconsider this. Like the giant vegetables, the sale of the SeaLawn seemed at first blush to be another of Pearl's inventions that had the unfortunate side effect of emasculating me. And without even asking, she had presumed that we would continue living together. Seaside vacations? Good lord. It might be better, I thought, for me to put the walls back up and remain alone. But by the time I'd reached my room and sat down on my bed to think, I'd decided it might be wise to forsake this entrenched habit of behaving like such a goddamned fool all my life. There was even, I thought, the possibility that I might be able to sip skunk musk again after I was released. Of course, I would be sure to strictly limit this to holidays and other special occasions.

Extraordinarily vivid dreams began to disturb my sleep after Pearl's visit, so I had plenty with which to entertain Peter. When given the opportunity, he interjected questions into the little air-holes among the great cataracts of words that now came gushing forth from my lips, but I didn't give him many opportunities. At first he tried to steer me back toward a discussion of my musk habit, but perhaps he thought that for the nonce it was an auspicious sign that I was talking at all, or maybe he thought that what I was saying would shed some new light on things, because he eventually decided to let me get on with it.

My sight had almost always been restored in my dreams, and in one of them I dreamed of the first Homer, who seemed to be not so much a skunk as a young man in a furry tuxedo on his wedding day. I waited in the receiving line and when I shook his paw he gripped my hand fiercely, sprayed me in the face with skunk musk from a yellow carnation in his lapel, and then burst into a high chattering laughter that was quickly joined by the other skunks around us in the church. I wiped the musk from around my mouth and licked it from my hand until a glass tumbler appeared there. Then I was sipping musk, sitting on a crate outside the cabin. I could hear Pearl inside, cooing to our baby Homer, who babbled back to her. I knew I was neglecting them and that Pearl would be disappointed if she found me out here, happily falling off the wagon. I'd promised her, and myself, that I wouldn't. But the musk was so sweet and that delicious bliss was beginning to tickle my nerve endings. I examined the glass in my hand with a kind of awe—was I actually doing this? Why, yes. But there, on the threshold of euphoria, my glass was almost empty. I went into the coop where all the Mason jars were full and gleaming like gold canisters. I would go down the row of jars and pour myself a shot of each, I thought, downing one right after the other. I first reached for Father's jar, took it off the shelf, and found the lid was screwed on so tightly that I couldn't get it to budge. I tried Constance's jar, but it too refused to open. I tried a couple more—straining and swearing at the jars, growing increasingly frustrated—until finally I put one of them on the dirt floor of the coop, picked up an axe and was about to take a swing at it when I woke up sweating and blind again in my bed.

Then there was the SeaLawn dream. Though it had various permutations, it became so frequent for a while that I often recognized it as a dream even when I was in the midst of it. In the first one I had, Pearl, Homer and I were on the farm. The farm had somehow been transported to the coast, and instead of the stream, a stretch of shoreline was one of the property borders. Homer looked as if he might be about four years old and he had a wild tangle of curly hair like his mother's. Together on the beach, the three of us built a sandcastle. Once it was finished, we derived as much pleasure from knocking it down as we had from building it up.

"Let's go for a swim," Pearl said, and she grabbed hold of one of my hands and one of Homer's and led us into the water. But as we waded out into it, I gradually began to feel as if I were walking through a bog. When I looked down, I saw that the surface of the water was covered with SeaLawn, which had wrapped itself around my thighs. I heard a scream and when I looked over at Pearl I saw that a thick brownish blanket of the stuff had already climbed up to the middle of her chest. She was trying to wrestle Homer from a web of brown tentacles in which he was wrapped and that appeared to be dragging him down. It felt as if I were trying to walk with sandbags tied to my legs, but I was able to make my way over to them. I grasped the tentacles that were holding Homer. They were like slimy extension cords, and I was surprised to find that I could rip them apart. I freed Homer and the SeaLawn around us seemed to shrink away a bit. With my arm around Pearl, I began to trudge toward shore. I was trying to kick the SeaLawn away from us, and just as I was beginning to think that the proper tool for battling SeaLawn was a nice, sharp machete, Pearl said, "Oh, god, Damien. Look." I looked up and saw that the shore had retreated several yards. Then, with a wave of nausea, I saw the movement. The Sea-Lawn would look the way a vast, shaggy, foot-thick comforter might if it were sucking in its breath, puffing itself up, and then heaving forward. It was making its way up the beach. While we stood there staring, I could feel the SeaLawn around us renewing its effort, closing in and grasping my legs more firmly than before.

In one of the variations on this dream—one I still sometimes have—Pearl and I are swimming in the pool by the dam when I notice a dark green clump of what looks like algae on Pearl's shoulder.

"Wait, Pearl," I say. "What's that?"

"What's what?" she asks. As she speaks these words, I notice that what is on her shoulder is connected to a thick patch of SeaLawn floating on top of the water. It expands while I watch. I try to swim over to Pearl to swipe the stuff off her, but only manage to take half a stroke when my movements are arrested by what I realize are the spaghetti-like tentacles of the SeaLawn that have wrapped around my legs and arms. I turn my head and see that it is on my shoulders too. I feel it filling my armpits. Beneath the water it grips my thighs tighter while I watch the leafy vegetation on the surface of the pool close in around me. Soon I am like a man buried up to his neck in a field, across which I watch as Pearl suffers the same fate. I call out to her, but though her mouth is open and her face has taken on a pained expression, she's apparently unable to make a sound. The SeaLawn clenches me tighter and I have to stop shouting as it quickly becomes difficult to breathe. The tentacles seem to be invading my pores.

In yet another dream, I go out to the field one day and see that all my crops are draped with what looks like aquatic kudzu. It is SeaLawn, I soon realize; it has blanketed my squashes, hung dark green slipcovers over the tomato plant cages and bean poles, made shaggy swamp creatures of the scarecrows, and formed a thick shag carpet that covers the entire field, growing especially high in the trenches between rows. I trudge up to the north end of the farm and see that the Sea-Lawn is pumping itself through the pipes that feed water to the field.

It is my firm belief that dreams such as these are enough to drive any man to musk. I'm not sure I could be blamed, considering all the stress I've endured, for going back to a bit of musk sipping, even now that most of the main sources of stress have been eliminated. I wonder if other people's interests lead them into such quandaries. Then again, I was never convinced that my situation was comparable to other people's. How could it be? I have never quite been one of the other people. I still don't know if I've solved the problem for good. Sometimes I suppose I am more skunk than man, always have been and always will be, no matter what I do.

You know, Damien, I often said to myself—sitting there on the edge of a less than comfortable hospital bunk—there is no point in trying to change your skunky ways. I can't see one. But then, I would say, if you don't have a point, Damien, and don't know how to make yourself happy, why not make someone else happy? Someone like Pearl. Maybe that will benefit you if only by shifting the focus away from yourself, you nincompoop. Follow Pearl's plan, since you don't have one of your own, and be a decent husband and a responsible father.

But I wondered if this had to mean not another single musk dream for the rest of my life. I thought of sipping skunk musk as a fairly conservative, innocuous habit compared with others. There was, for example, Pearl's proclivity for treating all flora and fauna of the earth like a new chemistry set. Of course I did not want to ever have to repeat that awful withdrawal process; but it would be possible, this time, I thought, to keep my sipping within reasonable limits. After all, it was simply a superior pastime, not a need.

"I need to make a connection with a doctor on the hospital's board," Pearl said, the next time we met. "Someone who can make a case for releasing you early." She was sitting across from me while I held Homer, who, having recently been fed, seemed to be dozing off. Because I couldn't see Pearl, I slowly reached out toward her voice until my hand found her face, keeping Homer in the crook of my other arm. I stroked Pearl's soft cheek and ran my fingers over her mouth. She was biting her lip as she pondered the problem of my release. I kept my hand on the side of her face, gently cupping her cheek as she spoke. "They could describe how you went through withdrawal," she said. "And the behavior caused by your so-called disorder could be chalked up to the effects of the skunk musk. I'm sure the other doctors would buy it. They've seen you go through changes here. But you're going to have to do some more work over the next few months to convince them you've turned over a new leaf. And they'll probably have an interview of some sort with you to determine whether you're fit to be out in the world of normal lunatics, and to be sure you're not going to go back to drinking musk."

I removed my hand from her cheek. I pretended to need to adjust Homer.

"Damien," Pearl said. She lowered her voice so the attendant wouldn't hear. "Don't tell me you're thinking about doing that stuff again."

"Um," I said.

"After all that's happened because of it. Damien, it's the whole reason you're here in the first place. Do you like it here? Do you want to stay in here? Does that sound like a good life to you?"

26

This I considered. It was a fairly worry-free existence, what with the meals brought regularly and no chores to do—a sort of strictly regimented vacation. But naturally it would drive anyone crazy before too long. However, part of my reason for getting out would be to rustle up a skunk for some refreshment. So why, I wondered, must I comply with this request for abandonment of musk? Well, for the sake of my own health, I was forced to concede, but there was another reason: Due to Pearl's fishy windfall, and with her smelly fingers forever holding the purse strings, I'd be more or less beholden to her when I was released. And I could not be so spineless as to give up an activity that predated her appearance in my life simply because the woman had become my benefactor. Besides, what real reason was there for me to share the rest of my days with a fun, sexy, rich genius who'd demonstrated her love for me time and time again? Aside from the obvious ones. The fact that she's given birth to our son? That's the oldest trap in the manual, is it not?

"Don't clam up, Damien," Pearl warned.

"I just don't see what's the matter with skunk musk," I said. "The fact of an individual enjoying a natural substance available in his own back yard hardly seems a valid justification for outlawing an animal and locking people up."

"I'm not talking about that," Peal said. "I'm talking about you."

"Then I guess I don't see what's the matter with me having a skunk musk cocktail now and then either."

"Of course you don't see what's the matter with it," Pearl hissed angrily. "It's made you blind."

This gave me pause. Pearl shifted in her chair. I thought she might be recoiling a bit from the harshness of her own declaration. But I was wrong; she was only getting hotter. "Give him to me," she demanded, taking Homer from my arms. I heard her buckling the diminutive chap into the car seat that had been left on the table beside us. When she had finished, Pearl turned to me again and her voice was choked with anger. "You fucking *shit*," she said. "Don't you realize what I've gone through for you? You're going to ruin everything, aren't you? You're just going to sit there and ruin everything, you selfish bastard."

I don't know why it is, but just when one thinks one has gotten the whole business sorted out, has weighed this side and the other,

ruled out what one thought were the more extreme paths and found
a pleasing middle road on which one believes one could go trotting
off into the sunset, someone comes along and says, "Hey-ho—your
calculations were all off. Better bustle back to the old drawing board.
I recommend you use a pencil this time and keep an eraser handy."
I was so shook up by my brief interview with Pearl that I actually
brought it up in one of my sessions with the insufferable boob Peter.

"Do you think you're so disturbed by this," Peter asked, "because
you believe she has a point?"

"A point," I declared. "I should say so. She has so many points she's
like a porcupine, but twice as prickly, and I don't know what I'm supposed to do about it."

"I mean a valid point about your addiction," Peter said.

This popped me up off the couch and sent me so quickly toward
what I thought was the direction of the door that I banged my head on
a shelf protruding from the wall. "God damn it," I said. "What the hell
is that doing there?"

"Damien, please," Peter said, coming to my side and putting a
hand on my shoulder. "Let's talk about this."

I sat back down on the edge of the couch, and remained sitting
up. I didn't want to take his accusations lying down. "It is not an addiction," I said carefully, as Peter returned to his chair. "What I have
done is cultivated a taste for a wonderful, mind-expanding substance.
And frankly, I think that if more people did the same, instead of med-
dling in each other's affairs, the world might be a better place."

He was quiet for a moment, and I thought perhaps finally Peter
was beginning to see things in the proper light. "Let me ask you something," he said. "If I were to tell you I'd tailored my lifestyle to fit the
enjoyment of liquor, that the various fermenting processes and the
different vegetables and grains used gave each type a distinctive flavor, but you happened to know that I had been unemployed for years
and that I'd lost my last job because I kept showing up for work intoxicated, what would you say?"

"I *will* say, Peter, old boy, stop insulting my intelligence."

"How am I doing that?" he asked.

"By being utterly ridiculous while I'm attempting to discuss serious
matters affecting my life. You want to sit there and compare me to a
drunken bum? Perhaps you should think about how preposterous that
is. I beg your pardon, but I think I'll be getting back to my cell now."

But there was little to console me in my room. I simply sat around staring into the gray void of the daylight and the black emptiness of the night for a few days. They ought to assign you two or three shrinks when you're cooped up like this, I thought, because there is no one else to consult for a second opinion and you sit there reviewing—and gradually convincing yourself of the truth of—what has been said by the very few people with whom you've had contact. But I wasn't prepared to give in to Peter too easily and by the time of our next session I had worked up a full head of steam.

After chastising him for impudence earlier in the week, I said, "And besides, there is nothing criminal about anything I've done."

"But you've pointed out that the criminality of substance abuse—excuse me—use, is arbitrary," Peter said.

"Yes, but all I'm saying is I should therefore be left alone," I said.

"That's basically what's happened," he said. After a brief pause, he said, "Maybe it would be more useful to think of ways you've committed crimes against yourself."

"You're grasping at straws now, Peter," I said. "What do you think? That perhaps I robbed myself?"

"Well, it's possible that you've robbed yourself of the opportunity to explore fuller relationships with other people," he said.

"You mean Pearl," I said.

"That could be one, yes," he said.

This caused me, as Pearl might have phrased it, to clam up. The only reason I'm lying here listening to this malarkey, I thought, is because of Pearl. So they want to call it an addiction. Well. If allowing them to use that terminology made them feel so much better, I might be willing to go along with it. And I had to admit that Peter's alcohol analogy, though a gross oversimplification, was not entirely off the mark.

"When was the last time you spoke with Pearl?" Peter inquired.

"A few weeks ago. The time she referred to me as fecal matter."

"Have you thought of calling her?"

I hadn't, but of course once he put the idea in my head, I could think of nothing else. "Hi Pearl, it's me, the festering agglomeration of feces, phoning you from the hospital. How are things?" No, that wouldn't do at all. For the next few days, I thought of about a hundred different ways I might start a conversation with Pearl if I called her. Finally I mustered the courage to do the deed, summoned one of the attendants, and was led to the little, foul-smelling phone room. I took out the envelope on which Pearl had written a cell phone number on her first visit to the hospital, close to a year previous. I'd never used it before. The attendant dialed the number for me, then left and shut the door behind him.

"Hello?" Pearl said. Her voice was friendly but firm—as prepared to be happily surprised as angrily defensive. I felt the way I had the first time I'd ever called her, when I knew her only as a beautiful and mysterious woman who filled her shopping cart with cans of sardines.

"Pearl," I said.

"Damien," she said. "Is that you? Is everything OK?"

"Yes, well, not everything. But the main things, I suppose. I mean, I'm not calling because I'm currently bleeding to death or anything like that."

"Oh. It's good to hear your voice. I can't believe you called, actually. It's kind of a small miracle." There was warmth in her tone, but starchiness as well.

"Pearl, I just want you to know I'm thinking a lot about things you've said." That was how I'd decided to start off. But I couldn't recall the next sentence of the little speech I'd prepared, so, panicking a bit, I said, "I recognize now that it could be postulated that it might not have been possible for me to have made it to where I am today without skunk musk."

"Damien, I'm not going to joke around with you about this," Pearl said, annoyed. I heard Homer begin crying in the background.

"I'm sorry," I said. "I didn't mean that. I mean that my addiction has brought about the conditions under which, presently, I, um…"

She heaved an exasperated sigh. Homer's crying got quieter and I could tell from its cadence that Pearl had picked him up and was bouncing him.

"Are you at the cabin?" I asked.

"A hotel room," she said. "I had to meet with some people in New York about the SeaLawn deal."

It occurred to me that this was something she might not have been doing at all if not for me. As I had from the start of our relationship, I thought of how much better it would have been for her never to have gotten involved with me.

"Pearl, I owe you an apology," I said. "I'm so sorry. About everything."

She sighed again. "Well, you don't have to be sorry about everything," she said. "Everything's not your fault."

"What can I do to make it up?"

"You know, Damien, it's not really a matter of fixing anything. I think you have to make a decision about what you want to do. And I'm sorry to put it like this, but it's going to be me or the musk. You can't have both."

"OK, I think I can do it," I said.

"What?"

"Make a decision." Homer had stopped crying and now he was cooing very softly. "How's the little fellow?" I asked.

"Chip off the old block," Pearl said. "Complains about everything." Neither of us said anything for a few moments. Then Pearl said, "There is something you can do. I spoke with someone on the hospital's board and he's willing to help us out. One thing he said was that in the past, people whose situations were like yours have been released early and that one thing they did, which the board looks on very favorably, was to write a history of their addiction, how it caused the behavior that was the reason they were put in the hospital—whether it was criminal activity or something that seemed like evidence of psychosis, or whatever—and how they had overcome it."

"I see," I said.

Pearl sniffed. "Just something to think about," she said.

And think about it I did. After almost a month of that, I brought it up with Peter, whom I knew would find it a splendid idea. No doubt he'd been writing a similar history about me or had used episodes from our sessions in articles he submitted to those psychobabble journals that are passed around by the professionals. He immediately arranged for a computer to be installed in my room. It had a special keyboard with little warts all over it so I could find my way around. It also had speakers through which I could listen to an alarmingly digitized-sounding reading of what I typed into it. I didn't like the presence of this intruder in my room one bit, and I ignored it for two full weeks before turning it on for the first time. Once I'd done that, I thought of turning it right back off again and asking the attendant to take me to the phone room to call Pearl. But I had an idea of what she would say. So I thought I might as well take a stab at the writing assignment. Now where, I wondered, does one begin such a history? Was there really a beginning? The odyssey that resulted in my incarceration seemed to me to have been inevitable. I was the cause of my own undoing. I could not blame it on a skunk. So I faced the thing, the addiction, as such, and delved into some of the reasons for it. Essentially, I agreed with some of Peter's suggested reasons for my overuse of skunk musk and explored them a little more fully than I had in our sessions. Once I'd gotten started, I found myself tapping away at my keyboard, making the sound of a cane-wielding blind man going through a long tunnel. Two weeks and forty-five heavily revised pages later, I gave my mini-dissertation to Peter to see what he made of it. He said he would take it home with him, and in our following session he brought it up as soon as my back met with the couch leather.

"You say you thought of calling Pearl before you sat down to write this," Peter said.

"That's right. So what did you think?"

"Why do you think you thought of her?" he asked.

I was about to call Peter a potato beetle, then thought better of it. By this time in our relationship it had occurred to me that this was the first time in my life I could think of that another man had tried to help me in any meaningful way. The poor fellow did actually have my best interests at heart. I'd begun to think of Peter as a pest for the best.

"Perhaps I thought I could talk to her instead," I ventured. "That talking to her might be something I could do instead of writing about my difficulties. Or that she might tell me I didn't have to do it after all."

Peter was quiet for a moment and I found myself in a mild state of suspense. It was more than a little embarrassing to find myself reduced to a state in which I was hanging on the words of a two-bit witch doctor. But there I was.

"I don't imagine writing this was easy for you," he said at last. "You actually identify the causes of your addiction and seem to recognize your own rationalizations. You even seem to understand how serious all this is and that overcoming this problem is crucial to your wellbeing."

"Well," I said, "once on the road to recovery I decided not to look back for fear of crashing into something. It's a rutted old road, with lots of twists and turns and I have to keep swerving to avoid the forest creatures that pop out into the open, endangering their little lives."

"Does that help?" Peter asked.

"What?"

"Making light of what you're doing?"

I felt I'd been caught in a trap. "Fine Peter, you've got me there. So, what am I doing?"

Peter sighed almost inaudibly. "I think what you said about not wanting to do this is true, is part of the reason you called Pearl. But I think there's another reason. You didn't want to write this paper because you knew you'd have to confront yourself and that scares you. In frightening situations we tend to want to go somewhere we feel secure."

"Well, I felt pretty secure back at my cabin," I said. "If I could be allowed to go there, maybe it would help."

"That's the argument I'm going to make on your behalf next week," he replied.

"Next week?"

"A meeting has been arranged for you with Dr. Kurtin, a few of the senior doctors, and myself. They've already met separately with Pearl. The fact that you're a father is being taken into consideration."

Since his name was bandied about the ward quite a bit by the staff as well as the inmates, I knew that Dr. Edward Kurtin was the hospital's director. An audience with him was not something one was given very often.

"Does this mean I'm going to be released?" My stomach jumped a bit as I uttered the final word of the sentence.

"It very well could," Peter said.

"Splendid," I said.

But upon returning to my room I found that I did not feel so very splendid. In fact I felt a little queasy. I could see that Pearl was good for me and that skunk musk was not. Yet from hour to hour I changed my mind between wanting Pearl at the expense of the skunk musk, and vice versa. I had mentioned this phenomenon, much less directly—frankly, by talking around the issue for about an hour—to Peter, and he told me that such was the nature of my struggle. The vacillating would probably go on for some time to come. He said it might even be worse for a while after I was released from the hospital.

So it was an uncertain Damien Youngquist who was guided into a chair in the office of Dr. Edward Kertin, at what I suppose was a kind of exit interview.

"Have a seat, Damein," the man I assumed was Dr. Kertin said, in a welcoming tone, as Peter guided me into a seat opposite him. There was light coming from the same direction from which Dr. Kertin's voice was emanating and I imagined he must have been sitting at a desk with a large window behind him.

"I'm not sure how much Dr. Clime has told you but we've been meeting with him, we've met with Pearl a couple of times, and we've been reviewing your records." Peter, who'd taken a seat beside me, cleared his throat, but Dr. Kertin went on. "I have to compliment you on your taste in women, Damien. Pearl is an extraordinary woman. Charming, too."

This seemed inappropriate, perhaps more so because Dr. Kertin's voice had a trace of a Southern drawl, which to me made it sound as if by "charming" he was referring to the physical charms Pearl so obviously exhibits. My position as a virtual prisoner made his freedom to observe Pearl as a specimen even more enervating. "She is a genius," I stated flatly.

"Oh, no doubt, no doubt," he replied in a comfortable way that made me imagine him strolling slowly along the links, abstractly gazing down at the flopping tassels on his shoes and allowing the nine iron dangling from his hand to swing back and forth. "Dr. Clime has updated us on your progress. He tells us you demonstrate a high degree of self-awareness and have taken some strides toward change." It had been so long since I'd heard his last name, and I hardly thought of him as a doctor, so it took me a moment to realize Peter was the person he was talking about. Dr. Kertin paused, but I had no desire to back up Peter's claims, if that was what was expected, and so he continued. "We've also all read the paper you wrote and Dr. Fujigaki said he's quoting from it in a paper he's writing."

"If you don't mind," interjected a voice from somewhere to the left of Dr. Kertin.

"Not at all," I said.

"But this doesn't make you special," said a voice to the right.

"Sure it does," disagreed a voice to the right of that one.

When one goes into such a situation blind, and is assailed by authoritative voices from various locations in which their owners have positioned themselves around the room prior to one's arrival, one feels something like what the God-fearing fruitcakes who say that "God is all around you" must perpetually feel. For the men present did have control over my life, a phenomenon that gives rise to a discomfort I had not felt since being employed at Grund & Greene. But this was worse because at Grund & Greene my superiors did not have the power to have me put in a straitjacket, injected with drugs and confined to a padded cell.

"I don't think we'd all be sitting here with him like this if it wasn't a special case," another voice to the left chimed in. How many of the dastardly squabbling doctors have me surrounded? I wondered.

"Gentlemen," Dr. Kertin said, "maybe we should be getting down to the point of this meeting. Damien, how would you feel about leaving this facility?"

"Exultant," I said. There was a quick chuckle from the left and an indignant snort from the right.

"Would you feel comfortable walking out of here right now? Readjustment to the world outside can be frightening and can take some time. It's nothing to be ashamed of."

For some reason I was more conscious of Peter's presence beside me at that moment and I inadvertently shifted on my chair. "I believe I could manage," I said. Then found it necessary to clear my throat.

"Without the musk?" Dr. Kertin pursued.

"I think so," I said. "I know it's not going to be easy."

"That sounded rehearsed," a voice from the right interjected. It was the same voice that had warned me against feeling special. Words shot out of the man with such vehemence I pictured him gripping the arms of his chair to prevent himself from flying from his seat and knocking me out of mine. "It's one thing to be self-aware," he spat. "It's one thing to recognize certain tendencies in yourself. But it's another thing to do something about it."

"You lost me there," I said. "Which thing was which?" There was another chuckle from the left.

"Dr. Nelson," Peter said. "Damien tends to retreat into sarcasm when he feels he's being attacked."

"I'm not attacking anyone," Dr. Nelson growled. "Recidivism is bound to be the main issue here." To indicate that it was directed at me, he uttered his next sentence a couple decibels higher than the previous ones. "How can we be sure you won't relapse?"

"You can't be sure!" I declared, matching his volume level.

"You are a high-profile patient for us," he practically yelled back. "Do you realize the reputation of this hospital is at stake?"

"Irv, will you please lower your voice?" Dr. Kertin said. "I don't think we can expect patients to be interested in preserving the reputation of a psychiatric hospital from which they've just been released."

"I'm extremely surprised," Peter added, in a tone that conveyed his complete lack of surprise, "that Dr. Nelson would put matters of concern to the institution before concern for the wellbeing of one of our patients."

"Something you should understand, Damien," Dr. Kertin said calmly, "is that we look at this period you're entering as a kind of—

probationary might not be the right word—trial stage of your treatment. And we think you should see it this way too. Something to keep in mind is that if you feel you're having difficulties you could use some help with, you're welcome to return here for a time."

Oddly, though I had to stifle an urge to harrumph, the suggestion was comforting.

"Dr. Clime has found someone who lives in your area with whom you can meet on a weekly basis or more often, if you like."

"But he won't know me," I said.

"That's true. But Dr. Clime has briefed him pretty thoroughly. Remember, Dr. Clime didn't know you either when the two of you first started meeting."

"That was different," I said. I turned my face in Peter's direction. "You couldn't come out to visit once a week at the cabin?" I asked.

"I'm sorry, Damien. It would be a three-hour drive. I don't have that kind of flexibility here."

"Fine then. Fine. I can hardly stand you anyway," I said cheerfully.

I was only half joking, but Dr. Kertin chuckled. "Damien," he said, "I think you're going to be alright."

❦

After a quick reacquaintance with the powerful smell of fish that permeated the car, I realized there was another odor emerging from beneath this one. It was familiar, but I had to travel so far down memory lane it took a few minutes before I arrived at a childhood Christmas where I'd last experienced it. It was the smell of a freshly manufactured product made chiefly of plastic and rubber. "This is neither the Tempest nor the Eldorado," I asserted.

"That's right," Pearl said. "It's brand new. Homer said he wanted to ride in style."

"Is the quality meeting with your satisfaction thus far?" I asked, twisting around in my seat to put a hand on the little lad. But what I lowered my hand onto was cold and scaly, with none of the movable limbs or the tiny torso gently rising and falling with each breath that one associates with a baby boy who is approximately a year old. "My god," I said.

"Oh, Damien," Pearl said, "you're grabbing at lunch, I think. I put his seat right behind yours. Why don't you wait until we stop?"

About an hour later we pulled into a rest stop that had picnic tables with, Pearl informed me, grills that were mounted on posts. She retrieved a bag of charcoal from the trunk of the car and went about starting a fire and frying some fish, while I bounced Homer on my knee and listened to Pearl talk about SeaLawn's new life in the clumsy hands of an unwieldy corporate entity.

"They've started testing it off the coast of California," she said. "It works like a charm. You should have seen how skeptical all these people were. Most of the scientists, who were all men, wanted me to fail. You could smell the jealousy coming off them when we did the first open-sea test. But the SeaLawn did just what I'd told them it would do. It worked almost too well."

"That's what I'm afraid of."

"Oh, I was too Damien, believe me. But they're doing a good job of containing it. Anyway, you should see the checks I'm getting working as a consultant on this."

At this, I stopped bouncing Homer.

"Sorry. I mean they're big."

"All this money talk..." I said. Homer started crying and I began bouncing him again.

"Oh Damien, come on," Pearl said. "It's just going to make things easier for us. I'm not interested in buying a yacht or anything." She paused. "Actually, a yacht might be nice. But really, we don't have to change anything we don't want to. We do have to think about Homer's future." She left the fish sizzling in the pan for a minute to sit down next to me on the bench. I felt her thigh against mine and she cupped my face in her fishy hand. "Please, Damien. It's going to be alright." She kissed me, then got back up to tend to the fish.

"How do you know for certain that it's going to be alright?" I asked. "They're going to put a patch of SeaLawn out there, God knows where, and it's going to gobble up everything in the ocean. And sunlight can't penetrate it. It'll be like an enormous cloud. It would destroy coral reefs."

"Damien, I told you it's going to be alright. When they introduce it into the ocean they're going to have it circled with these huge nets hung between fishing trawlers."

"Oh, that's reassuring. What's going to keep it from simply growing right through the nets? You know that stuff can spread like wildfire."

"The nets aren't like the regular kind they use when they're gill-net fishing. These nets have a mesh that's so fine they don't really look like nets. And they're made with this new durable plastic they've just developed." Pearl sighed. I still wasn't convinced, but before I could think of something to say, she changed the subject.

"So how did that meeting with Dr. Kertin go yesterday?" she asked.

"OK, I guess. All I had to do was listen to a bunch of flapdoodle from a roomful of lunatics with medical degrees, which was a little annoying. I'm sorry, I don't mean to sound so ungrateful. I know you had to do a bit of work to get me to that meeting. Anyway, now I'm free."

"Not completely," Pearl said.

"Meaning what?"

"I think you still have a ways to go in completely kicking the musk habit."

I offered no response to this.

"Don't you?" she persisted.

"Well," I said.

"'Well'?"

"Well. Well, I suppose I do."

Peter had almost been correct—it was a three hour and fifteen minute drive back to the farm. When Pearl told me were turning down Fisher Lane, I prepared myself for the spine-spraining bounces I was accustomed to on that road, but none were forthcoming.

"The shock absorbers on these new vehicles really are something," I said. "This feels nothing like Fisher Lane."

"I had the road graded," Pearl said. "Um, I've made a lot of changes around the house, too."

"House?"

"I mean the cabin. Well, we might not be able to call it a cabin anymore. I had an addition put on that's about three times the size of the cabin."

"Great Scott!"

"Had it wired for electricity too. Oh, and we have running water. We don't have to go to the outhouse. And we can take showers instead of bathing in the stream."

"I— but—" I said. "Ah, I happen to like bathing in the stream."

"Oh, me too. We still can. Please don't be mad at me. I just wanted to make it nice."

"It *was* nice, in my opinion. In my opinion you've been taking liberties with my property."

"You could've just said thank you," Pearl said.

The car came to a stop in front of what must have looked ridiculous. I imagined a tiny log cabin that had given birth to a modern house.

"Damien, maybe for a bachelor it was nice," Pearl said. "I'm sorry I didn't ask you about it first."

"Any other surprises?" I asked, pushing open the door of the car.

"Door is open."

"What?"

"Door is open," repeated the gentle female voice that I now realized was not Pearl's.

"It's the car," Pearl said. I heard the jangling of keys as she took them out of the ignition. "Damien, I'm sorry. Please. I thought it would be better for when you got back."

"You thought so, did you? Well that's just fine. Now that I can't see, I suppose I need someone to do my thinking for me." With that, I slammed the passenger door of the car, making an extremely unsatisfying sound that was like someone fluffing pillows. I turned and marched quickly off, but had only taken five strides before a fishnet caught me at mid-thigh and I tumbled forward. I caught myself with my hands, an instant before planting my own face in the dirt.

Homer, who had slept for most of the second leg of the drive, was now awake and screaming bloody murder.

"Are you OK?" Pearl shouted to me over Homer's cries.

"Just dandy!" I called back. But the force of the fall had knocked the wind out of me and I remained sitting as I regained my breath. From the cadence of his subsiding wails, I gathered that Pearl was bouncing Homer up and down to calm him. They were coming toward me and I wanted to get up and away again, but I had nowhere to go, so I raised my knees, put my elbows on them, clasped my hands and sat there. There was a hint of skunk cabbage in the air, commingling with something fishy, something familiar that reminded me of New Essex. It was not the leftover odor of our afternoon fish fry. What it smelled like, I realized, was the lab Pearl used to have in her garage.

"I put up this chicken-wire fence," Pearl said. "The one around the perimeter wasn't keeping the rabbits out."

"You've done all the planting and harvesting for the season?" I asked.

"I thought you'd want me to. You weren't going to be out in time to do it." Pearl sat down beside me and put a hand on my raised knee. Homer coughed and made a little complaint.

"Here's your bottle," she said, which was followed by the sounds of sucking.

"I'm sorry," Pearl said again. "I should have known this would upset you."

I put my hand on the one she'd put on my knee and felt the dirt between my palm and the back of her hand. It was good to feel dirt on my hands again. I thought of all the time I'd wasted trying to keep things clean when I'd lived in the suburbs.

"That's alright," I said, to Pearl.

"You know, it's OK to let people do things for you. It doesn't make you weak or something. It's how people live with each other." "I just don't know what I'm going to do now," I said. "I can't imagine blind farming."

"I'll be here. I can help you."

As Pearl helped me up and led me into the house, a sensation I would have to describe as coziness began to overtake me. I was hesitant to surrender to it completely, but recognized that it blocked out the annoyance that naturally arises due to the presence of other human beings and the irritatingly tenuous nature of the control one has over the circumstances of his own existence. Now, when I look over the life I led before I went into the hospital, I see a blind person making spastic attempts to organize his life in a way that might fool an outsider, and might even fool himself.

The first thing I noticed upon setting foot in the house was a burbling sound that immediately caused a sensation of familiarity that I couldn't quite place. It also seemed a bit more humid than it had been outdoors. Also, I noticed what I thought of as Pearl's more domestic fish smells.

"Did you have a bunch of fish tanks installed in here?" I asked.

"Yes, is that alright with you?"

"Wouldn't have it any other way," I said. "I'm just sorry I can't see them."

Pearl planted a kiss on my cheek. She led me through the kitchen and out a new back door. As we walked down a short flagstone path to another building, the fishy odor I'd noticed earlier became stronger. When we pushed through the door of Pearl's new laboratory, which turned out to be about the size of a two-car garage, I was enveloped in the scent of her aquatic experiments. As in her other lab, a large tank full of fish and SeaLawn dominated the room.

Back in the house, Pearl had spaced the furniture so that I had clear paths from room to room. She led me around and put my hands on corners of tables and chairs that I could use as touchstones. This was considerate of her, but inevitably caused me to reflect that though such a strategy is fine for getting around in a house, it's no way to chart a path through the unexplored wilderness that is the rest of one's life. Unless one prefers not to explore, which is to live a death. I began even then to realize that the pre-hospital Damien was caught in a trap that, with astonishing ambition, he'd designed for himself. That Damien, more blind than I, was fussily arranging the furniture of his cage and memorizing the routes of his routine in a way that made it possible for him to pass through life as if he could see. I still have frequent altercations with that Damien—the lousy, juvenile bastard. He wants his musk dreams back and demands them the way a baby screams for his bottle. I sometimes imagine going out into the woods at dusk to an area north of the dam (where I once met a couple of my long-since-released friends) with a bit of bait and waiting for one of those furry foragers to come sniffing along so I can pick him up and squeeze myself some musk.

It was a slightly harrowing homecoming—being shown around a house that still smelled faintly of sawdust and fresh paint. It was as if my old life had been paved over. The cabin had been relegated to the status of adjoining workshop, awaiting whatever work I would decide to embark upon. Pearl told me she'd been approached by editors who wanted me to write "the story behind the headlines," a notion that upset my stomach, so I thought the cabin might serve better as a carpentry workshop than a writing studio. Pearl fielded most of the phone calls in the following weeks. There were curious reporters who wanted to write follow-up SS stories and scientists who needed to know this or that about SeaLawn. These interruptions made my settling-in occasionally unsettling. But I can't say I didn't enjoy that first, refreshing shower, or the long session of sex that followed in the king-size bed Pearl had bought. The next morning, as I awoke, I heard the light clang of silverware and plates coming from the kitchen.

"Pearl?" I said, sitting up.

She came in and kissed me, then sat on the edge of the bed. Homer was in her arms and I felt a tiny thumb catch on the inside of my nostril as he grabbed my nose, as if to make sure it was real, then withdrew his hand.

"Yo," he said.

"Good morning, young man," I said.

Pearl kissed me again, this time on the forehead. "Welcome home," she said.

"Elum oh," Homer said.

"I have to finish making breakfast," Pearl said, getting up.

"OK," I said, then listened to her steps as she went back to the kitchen. I had to use the bathroom, which would entail getting up and finding my way there, but for the moment I didn't want to move. A window was open in the bedroom and fresh air, of which I'd had so little in the hospital, was blowing through. The breeze carried on it the hundreds of familiar olfactory pleasures of my small farm—tilled earth, leafy plants, mulch, fish. And faintly, mingling with the rest, the scent of skunk.

Justin Courter lives in New York and works for the Wildlife Conservation Society. A collection of his prose poems, *The Death of the Poem and Other Paragraphs*, is forthcoming in 2007 from Main Street Rag Publishing. *Skunk* is his first novel.